heartless heathen

NORTHERN REJECTS - BOOK TWO

ANNA FURY

copyright

Editing - Mountains Wanted Editing

Cover - GetCovers & Anna Fury

Cover Model - George RJ

Cover Photo - James Critchley Photography

❀ Created with Vellum

To every woman who ever distracted a man with her tiddies. This book is for you...

content notice

Heartless Heathen is an omegaverse romance, and as such, deals with difficult topics like generalized violence, possessiveness, physical dominance, consent and more. This book in particular also references kidnapping of adults, drugs and human trafficking at a high level. It is intended for mature audiences due to the dark themes.

Still, this series is all about the alpharoll hero - my men are possessive, dominant, and kind. They've got hearts of gold and abs of steel.

Hit me up with questions! author@annafury.com

a quick note

In this book, you'll meet a deaf character named Julia. She's not the main character in this book, but she will be in book three, Pretty Little Sinner. Julia is smart, loving, sassy and one of my favorite characters I've ever written!

Because this is a made-up world, I took a few liberties with my storyline as it relates to Julia's hearing loss. For instance, nearly the whole pack learned sign language quickly. In real life, sign language fluency would take a long time to learn well.

While I did have two sensitivity readers read Julia's parts to give me suggestions, I'm aware it's not possible to encompass all deaf and hard of hearing peoples' experiences. My fervent hope is that I've created an amazing character who feels real.

Huge thanks to Brittany, Alexis and her partner for taking the time to help.

what came before

When the Awaken Virus hit humanity, men became ravenous, uncontrollable beasts. They wrought destruction across the globe, causing humans to live in fear.

But then billionaire Mitchell Bancroft's alpha pack broke the news that the Awakened weren't all they seemed. There's a softer side to alphas, a side the world should know about.

This series takes place immediately after the end of The Alpha Compound Series. While there's no need to read that series to enjoy this one, it's got all the same vibes and it's hella sexy.

You can find it on Amazon.

get the freebies

WANT SPICY AUDIO AND EBOOK EPILOGUES?

Sign up for my newsletter at www.annafury.com to access the FREE bonus epilogues to every book I write.

A GENTLEMAN IS SIMPLY A PATIENT WOLF

lana turner

CHAPTER ONE

titan

IT'S SO peaceful in my bar this early. Bottles clink together as I refill them, prepping for opening. It's my favorite time of day, when I get all my thinking done.

A quiet knock at the front door has me turning from behind the bar with a grin. When I look up, a delicate head peeks through the doorway, the pretty omega smiling at me tentatively.

"Come on in, Isabel," I murmur, keeping my voice low and hopefully comforting as I come around the end of the bar, throwing my towel over my shoulder. As my pack's enforcer, I have the gift of reading auras, and Izzy's is a cautious pale yellow this morning.

She opens the door all the way and steps through, footsteps tentative as she tucks a lock of hair behind her ear. One hand goes to her big round belly.

"How are you feeling? You've got what, three weeks or so until she's due?"

"That's right," she says proudly, her happy expression growing wider before the look falls away.

"What's wrong?" The omegas from Declan's pack come to

1

me because my bar has always been a neutral place for them. I am Switzerland in a valley with three wildly different alpha packs. At least I was until I fought Declan and his packmates twice alongside my best friend, Stone. We did it to save lives, but I'm worried it'll jeopardize the bar as a safe place for Declan's omegas.

Isabel shrugs as her blue eyes lock onto mine, full of unshed tears.

I don't bother to ask why she stays. None of the omegas in that shitty pack have ever had a choice. If they left, Declan would find them and haul them back. He's done it before.

It doesn't matter how many times I remind them they can come to Stone's pack now that I've picked a side in this battle for our town, Ayas. The girls are running scared, and they've never been willing to risk their safety trying to escape Declan and his thugs. I can only hope and pray that'll change.

"I'm here for whatever you need, even now," I remind her. A deep alpha purr rumbles out of my chest, and it's easy to see the moment Isabel slumps into the noise, comforted by the dominance of my nature.

If she weren't thirty-seven weeks pregnant, Isabel would be my type—tall and fit with gorgeous long hair. Being pregnant looks good on her, even though I know she must feel miserable. Smiling again, I tell her to hang on and head back into my storeroom to grab the small wooden crib I built for her.

Returning up front, I follow as she opens the door for me to sail through, crib in hand.

"Declan would shit a brick if he knew I came here," she mutters as she watches me deposit the crib in the bed of her truck.

Putting my finger under her chin, I tilt her face up toward mine. "That's why you're not going to say shit to him, right? Just let me keep helping you and the other girls, anything I

2

can do. That's not changing now that I'm officially part of a pack. Better yet, come to Bent Fork with me right now. Don't go back to Declan…"

Isabel sighs. "And what? Have the other girls try to explain where I disappeared to? I can't, Titan. I can't leave anyone behind like that," she whispers mournfully.

Isabel rubs the back of my hand with hers, sensing my frustration for her. She's close to six feet, but I still tower over her. Shit, I towered over everyone in high school, but when the Awaken virus got its claws in me three years ago, I became practically monstrous. Of course, I wasn't the only male around Ayas to transition. My best friend Stone and a majority of the guys we went to high school with became alphas too.

Most of those assholes are gone now, and good riddance, but I'll never leave this tiny town on the western slopes of the Canadian Rockies. My other best friend Erin is the mayor, and Stone is the alpha of the best fucking pack there is. I'm not going anywhere.

"How's Cassian?" she asks tenderly. "We miss him like crazy."

I growl when I think about her pack's strategist. He's been at our lodge since he helped us rescue Rogue, Erin and her best friend, Luna, from Declan a week or so ago.

"He's fully recovered. Wants to leave but hasn't yet." I don't know how much to tell Isabel about Cassian's involvement in the fight between our valley's packs.

She sighs. "Declan would never let him back. They fight too much, and Cassian isn't submissive enough for Declan to allow him around. But with him gone, it's so much more miserable living in our neighborhood.

"Things are changing in our pack," she continues. "A new guy just showed up, Gabriel. He's not an alpha, but he says he's a relative of Declan's somehow. All I know is that he's a fucking weirdo." She points to her turtleneck sweater. "He's super religious, and he's convinced Declan that it's immoral for women to show skin. So the omegas have to wear clothing like this all the time."

"Why does he have any say at all?" I question, disliking this tidbit of information.

Isabel shrugs. "Declan listens to him, almost as if he's an advisor or something. There are two of us pregnant girls, and he moved us into the house at the end of the block. Says we're unclean until the children are born."

"What the fuck?" I bark. Unclean?

I open my mouth to remind Isabel for the hundredth time that she could come to our ranch and stay there. We've got plenty of space. But she holds up a hand and shakes her head before pointing to her swollen belly. "I know it would cause a fight, and I don't want to do that, first off. But secondly, I don't want to risk Baby Girl here."

"You'd rather raise her around Declan and his pack leader-ship?" I don't mean to be a prying asshole with the question, but if I worry about the women in Declan's pack, I can't even fathom children.

Isabel's dark eyes fill with tears as I start purring again.

"I'm sorry, Izzy. I shouldn't have asked that. You're stuck between a rock and a hard place, I know that."

She rubs nervous circles around her stomach. "One day, Titan. One day I hope I'll figure out a way to get around this that doesn't put anyone at risk."

I nod, because what else is there to say? If I could rip Declan's head from his shoulders and drop him into a deep hole somewhere, I would. But there are a million and one reasons I can't do that. First and foremost being his secret familial connection with Canada's Deputy Prime Minister. What a clusterfuck.

Isabel thanks me and takes my hand as I help her back into

the truck. I watch her drive away and wonder anew if there's some way to help the omegas that I haven't thought of. Cassian's been off property a lot since he healed. I need to talk to him. He's got insider info on how Declan's pack works that I haven't bugged him for yet. He's still healing from the grievous injury he sustained helping us save Rogue, Erin and Luna.

Ire rises in my chest when I think about Erin's best friend, who came from California to visit, but still hasn't gone home.

Luna-Fucking-Brooks.

Hot Sauce.

I love the nickname James gave her after watching her douse scrambled eggs in ten gallons of the spicy liquid. It's fitting for her, to be honest. She'll burn you right to the ground with her verbal barbs and constant chatter.

I really dislike that woman.

She irritates me on purpose just because she can. Luna is a brat of the highest order, something I'm not into. I like my women submissive and quiet. That's what gets me off. She is the polar opposite.

Not that I want to get off with Luna, I just–

The sound of a big rig rumbling up the road breaks through my thoughts as I walk out into the street to look. That'll be my delivery. Sure enough, when the big red tractor trailer rounds the corner, my best friend Erin beams and waves at me.

And next to her in the goddamn passenger seat sits Luna with big aviator glasses on. She looks so damn out of place, popping a huge wad of bubblegum between pouty, pink lips.

Grumbling, I turn and stalk back into the bar, propping the front door open and moving the ancient, creaky tables out of the way.

I urge the angry hornet's nest in my chest to dissipate. The days when Luna comes with Erin for deliveries, she always snarks at me. And I snark back. And it's mentally exhausting. Erin and I have an easy friendship; we have for twenty years. She, Stone, and I are practically the three Musketeers. But when Luna came to visit and support Erin through a rough divorce, that dynamic changed.

Things were fucking fine until that woman arrived.

I wish I could pack her up in a shipping box and send her right back to California. She's nearly small enough to fit.

Erin pulls past the bar before backing the fifty-three-footer expertly into my parking lot, the back facing my front door. The back doors unlock, and I shove them wide. If I get moving fast enough, maybe Luna won't start talking for another minute or two.

"Hey, Titan." Erin's voice reaches me first as I grab a couple boxes and turn to her with a smile. She pulls herself up into the truck with ease, winking at me. "Brought some help today. You ordered a lot of shit, and we have a couple big deliveries to make."

"Oh, goodie," I murmur low as Luna comes around the side of the truck. She eyes the distance between the ground and the truck bed, scowling at Erin.

"Girl, you might be six feet of heaven, but my five-foot ass cannot get up into this truck. Do me a solid and lift a sister up, would ya?"

Erin snickers as I hop down with boxes in hand and reach under the truck, pulling on the ramp and dragging it out as Luna scoffs. I give Luna a pointed look before turning back to the bar.

I don't bother to respond when Luna grumbles at Erin, "Damn, I didn't even get a chance to accidentally insult him yet. What kind of bug is up his ass?"

You, I want to growl. *You, Luna.*

CHAPTER TWO

luna

YOU'D THINK Titan saving me, and me subsequently asking him to teach me how to fight, would have changed the dynamic between us a little bit. I mean, damn, he helped me haul Cassian out of the old mill when he got injured. I thought it might improve things between us. But I'm sure as shit not forcing the issue. I have plenty of friends, and Erin's pack is fucking amazing.

I don't need a salty-ass bartender getting on my case for no reason.

Well, not for *no* reason. I did tell him his drink was a waste of a swallow after he took one look at me and watered it down. I can't help that Titan met me and made a snap judgment about who I am, five whole feet of curves and sass. Men underestimate me a lot. I'm a big fan of using that to my advantage.

It just doesn't work with him.

To everybody else, he's a gigantic fucking teddy bear.

To me, he's a gigantic, grumbly pain in the ass.

Not that it stops me from messing with him. Honestly, it's kind of fun watching him get wrapped around the barrel when we're in the same room. Case in point. I wore a super-tight, low-cut shirt today. I've noticed when I do, I'll catch him staring at my tits, and it makes me feel victorious.

To be fair, they're really damn nice. They cost me an arm and a leg, but they are *so* worth it.

I grab the closest box and walk down the ramp, striding purposefully through the front door of Teddy's. Following Erin's direction, I set the box down and jog back to the truck.

"Nice moves, shorty," Erin chuckles when I grab a couple boxes and do the same thing all over again.

"Somebody told me to move a little bit faster," I grouse as I bump my best friend with my hip. I've learned a lot about her trucking business in the last two weeks, and I'm in total awe of what she's built. My pride for Erin knows absolutely no bounds.

Titan watches as I set a box down, then points behind the bar. "That one goes back here." A wave of dark hair falls over steely blue eyes as he glowers at me.

My brows furrow as I look at the label on the box, which matches the huge pile growing at the end of the bar. "But it's the same as this stuff."

Titan snarls, "Yeah, but one always goes behind the bar. That's how Erin does it."

Anger flares in my chest at his comment, as if the way I'm doing it isn't good enough even though I'm still learning. "There are literally four feet between where I was about to set it down and where you're saying it goes. You can't just like, reach over and grab it? You're fucking enormous, Titan."

He scowls when I say that and grabs the box out of my hands with a huff, depositing it behind the bar.

"Hey, Titan," I purr, making my voice syrupy sweet in a way I know he hates.

The moment he looks up at me, those bright blue eyes meeting mine, I hop up and down a couple of times, pointing at my boobs. They bounce like crazy, and his eyes are drawn to them immediately before he gnashes his teeth and looks away.

"Thought so," I bark out. "Fucking typical."

Erin comes back in then. *Stop teasing him,* she mouths at me with a smirk.

I will when he gets cooler, I mouth back.

Douche.

WE LEAVE Mr. Grumpy Pants behind so he can put away the metric assload of booze and French fries we just delivered. I power through our next two appointments, making small talk with the customers and helping Erin ensure the deliveries go off without a hitch.

It's hard to believe it was just two weeks ago that asshole alpha Declan hurt Erin and me trying to take her truck. Her ex-husband orchestrated that shit, and while Ray's out of the picture now, Declan's been a persistent, prickly thorn in our sides.

When we finish the last delivery, Erin turns to me in her seat. "Girl, I am beat. I'd say we should grab a drink at Teddy's, but I suspect you're not up for more Titan this afternoon. Am I right?"

Crossing my arms, I grumble, "I'll go if you want. I'm just a little frustrated with him. We connected after the fight, I thought. I felt comfortable enough to ask him to help me learn to fight, since my karate skills haven't been useful against alphas. He said he would, but every time I've brought it up since then, he gets weird and ducks out of the conversation. I just...I thought it might be a nice little olive branch after our awkward start. I mean, shit, I told him I thought he was really brave."

Erin's dark red lips tilt up into a smile, which makes me follow suit. She's so damn beautiful inside and out. Burnished skin, dark hair that fades to blond tips. She's tall and stunning and the nicest person on the planet. Plus she's a badass mayor, and everyone in Ayas loves her. Except Declan, of course.

Ugh, she's perfection, and I adore her so much.

"Give him a break, Hot Sauce," she snickers. "He's a Leo; he's very loyal. But if you piss him off, you're dead to him. Plus, you tease him a lot. It's going to take him a minute to come back around to the idea, but I promise you he's worth it."

"I'll believe it when I see it. Take me home," I demand. "I wanna see what Clay and the twins are getting into at the house. I didn't see them in town any of the times we passed through today."

Just then, the rumble of motorcycles has me freezing in my seat, my heart whomping in my chest as I hoist myself out of the open window and look back behind the truck. "It's Declan," I hiss as Erin grabs her shotgun from behind her truck seat. Not that it'll do much to slow down this pack of assholes. But it's something.

I flash back to when Declan kidnapped Erin, Rogue and me not long ago. Rogue would have died if Cassian hadn't shown up with backup and helped Stone, Ash and Titan kick Declan's ass.

She hands me a shotgun as I grimace. I'm a pretty okay shot, but I don't want to have to use this.

Erin frowns. "I really don't want to deal with this asshole today. Even if the Deputy Prime Minister sent a handler for him, I don't trust him to stay in line."

I nod, tense in my seat as the motorcycles rumble right by, the alphas not looking our way. I recognize JB, Declan's enforcer. He's a piece of fucking work. Bek and Mark go next.

So not all of Declan's leadership crew is here, not Declan either.

The last motorcycle stops next to our truck, but I don't recognize this man. He's short and slight, wiry almost, so he's not an alpha. He's unnervingly pale with nearly white hair slicked back away from a face that's too harsh, too angular. A jagged scar runs from his hairline down over one eye, all the way to his chin. He's...unnerving.

Pale blue eyes look up at Erin and me before he smiles. It's more of a smirk, really, as he says nothing.

Erin peers at the man. "You must be new to town. I'm Erin Grant, Ayas' mayor. Welcome."

He tips his head once. "An omega mayor? How unusual."

Erin beams at him, the grin of a shark about to bite a tiny fish in two. "Yes, well, the people spoke with their votes, so here I am."

"I'm Gabriel," he replies, not responding to her comment. "Like the angel chosen by God to herald His vision to Mary."

He says nothing else, just grins at us like a psychopath as Erin's friendly expression falls.

"I'll be direct," Erin croons. "If you're here to handle Declan then—"

"Not handle," Gabriel corrects, swiping his pointer finger side to side as if gesturing at a naughty child. "*Guide.* I am here to guide Mr. Knox."

"Guide him to what?" Erin presses.

"Mr. Knox has been on his own for a long time. Our mutual acquaintance believes Declan needs to hear God's voice. He selected me to come here and bring Mr. Knox to a better state of being," Gabriel explains in a placid tone.

"As long as that 'better state of being' means he's not attacking my townspeople or anyone else, then you and I won't have any issues, Gabriel."

"Naturally," he agrees, inclining his head with a wicked

grin. He reaches forward and puts the bike back in gear, beaming at us before following the rest of the guys up the road.

Erin breathes out a sigh of relief when he's gone as I fold myself into her lap with a big hug.

"What the shit was that?" I question into her hair. "He was so fucking creepy."

Erin nods and squeezes me tight before gesturing toward the passenger seat. "Let's get home and tell Stone and the others. That guy seems like bad fucking news."

I am in one thousand percent agreement with that.

THE MOMENT ERIN and I pull off the highway and under the big sign for Bent Fork Ranch, I breathe a sigh of relief. I've only been here a few weeks, but this place is starting to feel like home. I never knew much about alpha packs before I came here, just what Erin shared in the last few years. Being an alpha is still a crime everywhere because of those rage-filled early days when the transitioned men hurt so many people. The Awaken virus nearly ripped our world apart, but I've learned a lot about alpha packs since then.

I roll open the truck window, letting the early afternoon chill pinch my cheeks as Erin chuckles from the driver's seat. "I'm going to turn you into a Canadian once and for all."

"Nope," I chirp. "You haven't seen my new place in Santa Monica by the beach, E. God, it's so fucking beautiful. Waking up to the sounds of the ocean? Heaven on earth."

Erin shifts in her seat. "Speaking of which, I don't want you to feel any pressure about leaving because I'd rather keep you forever...but have you thought about going home? We haven't talked about it with all the dramatics of the last couple of weeks. Plus, Mario asked me," she finishes with another little snort.

Mario. My sometime hookup and Erin's kick-ass lawyer.

Sliding my aviators high up on my nose, I shake my head. "It's easy enough for me to work from here, and there's nothing important at home to return to."

"Not even Mario?" Erin presses. I get the distinct sense she's a little worried about me leaving.

"Definitely not," I laugh. "We're not serious; we just fuck sometimes."

"If you say so," my bestie retorts. "He asks about you every time I talk to him."

"I called him last night," I bluster. "Just to check in. He offered to do the paperwork for the Omegamatic project. I think we should let him. He's got a great eye for detail."

Erin agrees. "We've got to talk with Titan about that and make sure he's down..." Her voice trails off as she gets lost in thought.

The Omegamatic. Apparently Titan designed and built it for the alphas because they couldn't date in the early days of the virus, but the alpha sex drive is insanely high. The giant sex doll on a stand is freaking genius. Because I work in the adult toy industry as a designer, it would be so easy for me to draft plans, get patents, and do the million other things necessary to take the Omegamatic to market. It would make the pack so much money, they'd float around, wiping their asses with hundred-dollar bills.

The problem is Titan. It's his design, so if I'm going to tackle this project for the pack, I've got to work with him and, ugh, get his permission.

The words "permission" and "Titan" in the same sentence make me want to scratch my eyeballs out. If I have to ask that man one–

"Luna, you're snarling. What's up, girl?" Erin's barely holding back a laugh as she reaches over and swats my leg.

I'm saved from having to answer as we pull up in front of the gorgeous, expansive lodge that sits in the middle of our valley. It was a resort back in the day, but when the Awaken virus got out into the world, Stone became an alpha, so his mother Betty closed it off to the world to keep her son safe.

Speaking of the devil, the pack alpha himself stands at the top of the lodge's front steps, arms crossed. Good God, he's hot. It never fails to hit me when I see him. Plus he loves Erin so damn much, it makes my heart ache to watch them together. She deserves all the happiness in the world, and he lusted after her for two solid decades. They're perfect for each other.

I don't want what they have, to be tied down. Except that, deep in my heart of hearts, I can admit that having someone to partner with and care for me the way he does with Erin? It's a little bit appealing.

Stone hops up onto the ledge on Erin's side, leaning in to kiss her lips tenderly. His humongous arm reaches through the window as he strokes the side of her face, then grips her throat with a gentle touch. It's possessive and so damn alpha, but that's how all these guys are. The news has only been telling humans half the story for the last three years, ever since the Awaken virus transitioned so many men.

The flip side of the story, the side we never heard about? It's how after the violent wildling phase, alphas form packs and families, how they take and adore and protect their mates, how they exist right under everyone's noses, still trying to live normal lives.

Stone breaks the kiss and looks over at me. "Hey, Hot Sauce." He winks when I groan, looking from Erin back over to me. "So, you saw Declan's new handler?"

Huh? How does he know? My brows curl upward in

confusion as Erin laughs and rubs Stone's forearm. "Mate bond, remember? I told Stone all about the new guy we saw."

"The mate bond, right," I murmur skeptically before nodding at our pack alpha. "Yeah, he referred to himself as Gabriel, like the archangel. I'm not sure what's potentially worse—a rogue asshole alpha or a religious nutjob."

Stone lets out a beleaguered sigh and opens Erin's door. "Well, fuck."

CHAPTER THREE

titan

NOW THAT I'M part of a pack, organizing my schedule has gotten trickier. I used to work constantly at Teddy's. It's my place, and I fucking love it. But accepting the role of Stone's pack enforcer means I need to be around the pack enough to know everyone and to enforce, if it comes to that. So far, it's been a lot of me making sure the twins aren't hustling the wrong people at pool in my bar. That's how I met them, and bringing them into the pack has been the best thing for them. But they still have a tendency to get into trouble. So much so that Clay has taken to calling them "the hooligans."

As the pack grows, my role will become more and more important. I'm definitely the right alpha for the job; it's just getting in the way of my typically flexible timeline.

My best employee is manning Teddy's tonight, and I plan to spend the evening with my people. Still, I drag my feet prepping for dinner until my bar manager kicks me out. It's not that I don't want to see everyone; it's more that I owe Luna some answers about the Omegamatic. It's a conversation I'm not dying to have with her. I handcrafted the machine in the early days of the virus, and talking to her about the giant sex toy is awkward.

I imagine a production line of womanly figurines, and millions of alphas the world over using them, and feel... disconcerted. When I built the Omegamatic in the privacy of my woodworking shed, I never imagined it would be something the general public saw. Or that I'd have to answer so many questions from Luna about its innermost workings.

I drive to Bent Fork, sticking to the speed limit, but eventually I get there. When I pull up front, I groan. Clay, our pack strategist, is on the front steps with his arms crossed. Shit, something must have happened.

After parking my truck up front, I stalk slowly up the stairs with a frown. "Lemme guess, the twins? Or Asher?"

Clay's green eyes spark with mischief as he slides both hands into his pockets with a laugh. "Unbelievably, the twins behaved today. But River is still stockpiling shit from the general store in her room. Stone wants you to talk to her. Have her take it back to the store and remind her she's part of the pack. We asked the twins to stay, and they agreed. She doesn't have to plan for the damn apocalypse upstairs."

I scoff at that. I'm of the opinion that if she needs the ramen to feel safe and secure, she can have them. Seems my alpha wants to make a point though.

Clay's face falls a little bit as I go to pass him. "Sal's been asking about you a lot today. Can you drop by her room and see if she'll come to dinner with the rest of the pack?"

My gaze meets Clay's. He's worried for the little omega we rescued from Declan. It was total happenstance that she came to the bar, terrified and running, and we were able to secret her away. She's safe here. She's connecting well with the twins, but she's still running scared around everyone else. Because I was always Switzerland, she trusts me.

"Thank you, enforcer," Clay says kindly. "That's not all,

though. Luna and Erin met Declan's handler today. He gave them a distinctly weird vibe. Stone wants to debrief after dinner."

"Jesus," I grumble. "You got anything else to lay on me right now?'

"That's about it," Clay chirps with a big grin. He claps me on the shoulder as I pull the big double doors open, ignoring the hustle and bustle of the kitchen where most of my pack-mates are congregated. I head straight up the beautiful curved staircase until I hit the second floor. Hanging a left, I go to the end where the twins and Sal picked rooms.

As I lift my hand to knock on Sal's door, she swings it open.

I'm sure I look shocked, but then River bounds up to the door and gives me a high five. "Heard you coming." She blinks big blue eyes wide. "Sir," she adds sarcastically onto her statement.

"I'll get used to your crazy hearing one day, I hope." I lean into the doorway, crossing my arms.

River's happy expression fades. "I heard Clay. I guess I'm in trouble, huh?"

I shake my head no but glance into the room. Rogue is seated in a chair by the fireplace with a book in his hand. He and River may be twins, but they couldn't be more different. When our eyes meet, he smiles. "River's gonna have to return the ramen noodles, right? Guess I'll get my ass up and help."

"Me too," pipes up Sal as River huffs and whines.

"Okay, I know Clay said I don't *need* to plan for the apoca-lypse, but if I had been better prepared the first time we had an apocalypse, things would have been easier for me and Rogue."

I tilt her chin up to look her in the eyes. "Honey, if things go that far south here, ramen noodles aren't going to make a bit of a difference. Keep a pack or two, and we'll take the rest back, okay? The store is a mile up the road; it's not like you can't grab more if you want them."

"Fine," River gives in, tossing her curly brown hair as she shoves her way past me and heads for her room. "I'll grab them now."

"Don't forget the ones in your closet," Sal calls out helpfully, winking at me as River disappears into the room across the hall.

Rogue puts his book down and crosses the room, reaching out to rub Sal's back gently. "Sal, how about that dinner with the pack tonight? It's chicken parmesan, your fave."

Sal's expression is sad as she crosses her arms and rubs the back of one with her hand. "I don't think so, Rogue. I'm not up for everybody all at once. Luna will bring something up to me; she always does."

Surprise spreads through me. I didn't realize Luna was the one making sure Sal got fed every day, but I'm sure Stone or Erin told her to.

Rogue heads out the door, disappearing into the room next to his twin's.

"Hey, can I talk to you about something privately?" Sal's voice is tiny as I look behind her at River's door. Sal laughs and rolls her eyes. "Well, as privately as possible."

Nodding, I head into her room and wait for her to share.

"I don't know what's happening with Declan's omegas now that I'm here, but I can't stop thinking about the girls I left behind. I know we can't just march in there and, like, save them, but living in Declan's pack is awful. The ramen noodles reminded me..."

"I'm not following, honey," I admit. "What does ramen have to do with anything?" My thoughts wander to what Isabel shared this morning, dread forming a pit at the bottom of my stomach.

Sal frowns, lost in thought. "The omegas there don't

always have enough food. It was a pretty common problem for anyone who wasn't a mate of one of the leadership alphas. We just have so much here, and if Declan still lets the omegas come to the bar now and then, can we slip them some food?"

"Declan doesn't make sure they're fed?" I can't help the snappish way the question leaves my mouth. I crush my fists to my thighs and urge myself to be calm. Sal doesn't have anything to fear from me, and I'm already enormous, even for an alpha.

Thankfully, the little omega knows I'm a safe space. She reaches out and places one tiny hand on my chest. "I know, alpha. And I know how important it is to you to help where you can. That's why I'm telling you. I'd tell Stone because I know he wants to help too, but I just…I'm more comfortable talking to you."

"Thank you," I whisper, the wheels of my mind already spinning about how to get food to Declan's pack without the alpha himself figuring out what I'm doing. Shit, I could have given Isabel food this mo—

"You're so growly today," River quips, slapping me on the side as she appears in the doorway with two grocery bags of ramen in her hands. When I turn, Rogue is right behind her with another six bags in his hands.

Sal laughs and follows me out the door, grabbing a few bags from Rogue. I watch him hand them gently to her, giving her a soft look. The young alpha has settled in so naturally here.

"Let's go," I grouse as Sal and the twins follow me back toward the front of the lodge. Clay meets us at the front door, pulling it open wide as he bumps River with his hip.

"Tattletale," she gripes as he reaches out to tug one of her bouncy curls.

"Not me," he retorts. "Asher can probably hear you in there reorganizing your stash."

25

"He and I are gonna have a chat," River declares, but there's no acid in her bark. She's full of bluster and sarcasm.

"Hey, guys!" Luna's voice rings through the lobby as she appears in the bar doorway and waves at the twins. Her bright smile falters when she sees me, but she plasters it right back on and keeps coming.

I definitely don't watch the way her tits fill out her tight tee shirt. And I most definitely don't reminisce on the way she bounced them earlier, purposely riling me up because she can. She's a damn menace. But they're really fucking nice; I'll give her that.

She comes to a stop in front of the twins and Sal. "Why are you growling?"

"I'm doing nothing of the sort," I huff. I follow Clay out the front door and wait on the porch for Luna to finish whatever she came over to start.

I hear the concern in her voice. "Sal, honey. You wanna join us for dinner tonight? I asked Clay to make your fave."

Sal declines, but Luna remains positive. "I get it, I really do. We're here whenever you're ready. I just didn't want to stop inviting you in case that was all the encouragement you needed. I'll bring a plate up for you as soon as it's ready, okay?"

Moments later, I hear Luna's footsteps trail away as Sal and the twins come outside.

"Okay, hooligans," I laugh to brighten the mood, "let's return Stone's noodles before he goes pack alpha on you three. Then let's get back for grub."

The twins hoot and holler as Sal rolls her eyes. But we make quick work of returning River's stash back to the store on our property, meant for our pack and the occasional tourist passing through.

By the time we get back up to the main lodge, the entire first floor smells like Clay's grandma's chicken parm recipe, and the twins run off to find their places at the communal tables in the dining hall. Sal hugs me once but heads upstairs by herself. Her aura is peaceful and green, and I don't read a scared feeling from her. Still, it's clear she's not ready for prime time with our small but growing pack.

I watch her go, my mind spinning around what she shared regarding Declan's omegas. I'm lost in thought when I turn for the dining hall, passing the kitchen. Luna rounds the corner right as I do, running smack dab into me. She yips as the plate she's carrying tilts upright, chicken parm splattering across her neck and chest as she freezes like a bunny.

Blue eyes dart way up to mine as I bluster, "Why don't you look where you're going?"

"Alphas have way better senses than us measly humans," she bites back. "You didn't hear me coming?" She doesn't wait for an answer, just drops to the ground and starts picking up the noodles and bits of breaded chicken.

God, I'm an asshole—seeing Luna on her knees makes me hard. But with my luck, she'll notice my growing erection and point it out for the rest of my life.

Dropping to a knee in front of her, I take the plate. Sauce drips from her full breasts, hard nipples visible through the wet fabric. It's clinging to her, sauce traveling a path from her neckline down between her tits.

"You're staring," Luna deadpans. "Wanna lick it off me, alpha? You look fucking ravenous." Her voice is a deeply sensual purr, sending my dick leaping in my pants.

I hold back a groan as I imagine my cum dripping from her nipples instead, my big hands massaging it into her skin as she whines.

What the fuck am I doing?

Letting out a growl, I gesture to the plate in my hand and ignore her seductive comment. "I'll clean up. You grab another plate for Sal."

Luna narrows her eyes at me. "That's it, huh? No 'what the hell are you doing, Hot Sauce'? No other snark of any sort? Are you ill?"

I roll my eyes at that, not bothering to answer as I scoop noodles back onto the plate.

Luna mumbles about asshole alphas all the way back into the kitchen, but reappears with a fresh plate for Sal by the time I've picked up the last slippery, buttery noodle.

The salty omega gives me a wide-ass berth before disappearing up the stairs.

And I sigh. Despite the fact that Luna was supposed to head home to California any fucking day now, she's still here. And I'm still running into her–literally.

luna

I DELIVER Sal's dinner to her room and chat with her for a few minutes while she eats. It's not my job to bring the scared omega out of her shell, but I recognize a girl who needs a friend. I can be that for her as long as I'm here.

When she's all done and swears she doesn't want seconds, I insist on taking her plate back down with me. This girl has had a hard life with Declan's pack. I'm on a personal mission to make sure she knows this pack isn't like that.

Not even Titan, as much as we love to hate one another. He's got a kind streak a mile wide, and a big soft spot for helping people. I love that about him. It's the only thing I love about him, because everything else sucks.

Case in point? My shirt. It's practically see-through with how soaked in spaghetti sauce I am. I don't want to go downstairs looking like I got run over by a truck, so I head to my room and change into something comfy but still classy and cute: a long-sleeved black turtleneck. Taking a quick peek in the mirror, I run my fingers through my mid-length beach waves and wink at myself. "Lookin' hot, lady."

The mirror pep talk is something my dad taught me when

I had tough times in middle school. I scoffed then, because I don't know how many girls actually pep talk themselves in the mirror, but my dad was doing the best he could, raising me by himself. And he thought girls did mirror pep talks. So here we are many years later.

Heading back downstairs, I make myself a plate and slip into my usual seat next to Erin. She reaches over and squeezes my leg as Stone leans over her and pats the back of my hand. "Thanks, Hot Sauce. Does Sal need anything?"

I grin, because, from Stone, the nickname is endearing. When I look over at Titan, though, he's lost in thought, picking at the chicken on his plate.

To my right, Asher, the pack's seer and occasional crazy person, looks at Titan with an odd expression. There's a forkful of food poised halfway between Asher's mouth and the plate. "Titan, what are you doing?"

Titan looks up and composes his scowl into something more neutral. "Eating."

Asher puts the fork down and looks at me, then back at Titan. "You're saltier than usual. I want to know why."

"Did Luna do something?" James quips from his place next to his mate, Julia. He signs the barb with both hands as he delivers it, and Julia slaps him playfully on the back of the head.

I'd scoff except I'm a little curious to know if running into me, literally, is the source of Titan's bad mood today or not.

Stone is next to speak up. "What's going on, buddy? Everything alright?"

It's easy to see the effect his alpha-ness has on Titan. Titan sits back in his seat, rolling his shoulders so he's a little straighter. He meets Stone's gaze with his own, his eyes such a bracing shade of blue, I have to do a double take. I find myself wondering what it would be like to have those blue eyes that intent on me.

Weird, probably.

For a long beat, Titan says nothing, and I worry he won't share what Sal told us about Declan's omegas.

So, I speak up first. "I've got to talk to y'all about something—"

At the very same time, Titan says, "Actually there is–"

We both pause awkwardly before Titan glares at me and gestures for me to continue. "By all means, Hot Sauce. Spit it out."

I sit back and shake my head. "Go on."

Titan's nostrils flare, but he brings those blue eyes back to Stone and Erin with a frown.

"I'm worried about the omegas from Declan's pack." Titan's deep voice echoes across the table. And despite how quietly he said it, the whole pack goes silent and turns to look at him. He runs one hand through his dark waves and frowns. "Apparently Declan doesn't always provide enough food for the non-mated omegas. Sal wondered if we could figure out a way to help them, since we can't just go over and rescue them all."

The entire table is silent as a grave, but Erin and I turn to look at Stone at the same time. Fury at the women's treatment has me seeing red, and I splutter before I can even find the words to express my outrage for them. God, Declan is such a fucking asshole.

Erin beats me to the punch, though, rubbing the back of Stone's hand. "I sense your outrage, alpha. You're right to be mad. Knowing we can't just go over and take women from his pack, what are our options?"

"They still come to me for things they need, furniture and the like," Titan continues. "Isabel came in this morning for a crib. I could have given her food, had I known. She's never asked. None of them have ever asked, and I didn't realize."

"It's not your fault," I bite out before realizing I'm defending Titan. And I don't even *like* Titan.

Piercing blue eyes glance over at me as he narrows his gaze but says nothing. My whole body is tense and tight, my jaw locked as I try not to scream in rage at the situation we're in.

"There's more," he bites out. "Isabel says Declan's new handler calls the pregnant girls unclean. He's moved them to the far end of their neighborhood."

Erin and I sputter at the same time as I whip around to face her. "So there is some kind of religious bullshit going on with that guy."

"What?" Titan demands. "What are you talking about?"

Erin fills him in on our earlier meeting with Gabriel. It's clear to see what we share is unsettling to everyone. The table is quiet for a minute. Even Clay sits silently, stroking his chin. As the pack's strategist, I imagine he's thinking through the complexities of this bullshit.

"What are our options? How can we help?" I bite out the words, looking at Erin. "You're the mayor; are there actions we can take or systems or processes we can use?"

Erin frowns, brows furrowing as she looks from me to Titan and back again. "I'm not sure, to be honest. I mean there are food programs in the valley for sure, but getting the omegas access to those might be hard. I'll ask around at the next town council meeting. Maybe Rue Jenkins or one of the other folks will have an idea. We won't stop until we can help them, okay?"

Titan and I both sigh at the same time, his bright blue eyes looking in my direction again before he looks away with a scowl.

Looking over at Erin, I get an idea. "You've said they go to the hot springs sometimes. What if we built like, a food drop-off? I'm happy to help with this, whatever we decide to do."

Across from me, Asher sighs. "This is when it would be really fucking nice to have normal seer powers. I could just like...ponder it and tell everyone what to do."

If Cherry were here, I imagine she'd scoff at his proclamation. Shit, I've only been here a couple weeks, and I can tell they're meant to be together. But Asher has his own demons to deal with, and they hold him back from claiming her. She's started skipping pack dinner a few nights a week. Clearly she's avoiding him.

Stone scoffs as he looks at Asher. "I know I don't have to say what you know I'm thinking right now."

Asher rolls his eyes but looks at Titan and then over at me, intensely focused. "Don't want to talk about my mating bond; I can see the state of it just fine. Let's talk about the bond I see between these two instead. Sounds like more fun..."

My blood freezes as my heart takes off at NASCAR pace. I'm rarely struck mute by someone's words, but I can't summon a fucking thing to say as I gape at Asher, my mouth open like a fish.

Across from me, Titan scowls and tosses a piece of garlic bread right at Asher's face. Ash ducks and snorts out a laugh as Titan grabs a second piece off James's plate and chucks it at Asher.

I'm still too horrified by his words to absorb what's going on as Titan growls, even though Erin and Stone are chuckling next to me.

Titan's fangs peek out from his lips. "That's not funny, you ass. We couldn't be farther from one another's types."

Asher grabs a wayward piece of garlic bread and throws it toward the other end of the table, clobbering River right in the face with it as her twin roars with laughter. Ash looks over at Titan as Rogue sends the bread back up the table. "Oh, I've seen the Omegamatic, brother. You have absolutely got a fucking type."

My cheeks heat when the big alpha looks over at me with a wink. Oh, thank fuck, he's just kidding. Hopping to my feet, I lean across the table, dodging a piece of garlic bread as someone turns Asher's jest into an official food fight. The pack is starting to go wild when my eyes meet Titan's. He cocks his head to the side, glaring at me.

"Can we talk?" I bite my lower lip as he sits back in his chair, running both hands through his hair before nodding. Titan shoves his seat back, dodging when a plate full of noodles barely misses his big chest.

I stalk around the end of the table, glowering at the twins when they catch my eye with a fresh plate of spaghetti in hand. "Don't even fucking think about it, hooligans," I bark when River waggles her brows and holds her plate up in my direction. She whines but uses the chance to slap the noodles into her twin's face instead.

I pick up a jog as I exit the wild dining hall and plaster myself against the wall just outside the door. Titan shows up a moment later and puts both hands up in supplication. "Asher's just fucking around. He didn't mean anything by what he said." He looks just as horrified as I am, thankfully.

"It's not about that," I bluster, crossing my arms. "I asked you to teach me to fight after the big battle with Declan, and you said you would. It's clear to me we're not in any less danger now than we were. I want to learn to protect myself. Please help me."

Titan leans up against the dining hall door and shoves both hands into his pockets, looking down before meeting my eyes again. "Thought you were going home, Hot Sauce."

"I am for sure. But I don't know when. I told Erin I'd stay until it felt right to leave, and there's still the Omegamatic project. I need your help with that too, since it's your design." I'm babbling, I know that, and Titan looks skeptical as fuck. "If you're willing to help, that is."

"Seems like you need a lot of things from me, Hot Sauce," he purrs. "What am I getting out of this arrangement?"

I shoot daggers from my eyeballs as my foot starts to tap of its own accord. "How about a stable financial future for your pack? How about doing something kind?"

One of his perfect brows slides upward as he frowns at me. "That's it? That's your sales pitch?"

Ugh. "I promise to behave. No taunts, no snark or sarcasm. I'll just be…quiet."

One of Titan's dark brows curls upward skeptically.

"Quietish," I add. "We both know I can't be like, totally quiet. But I'll do my best to just listen." Pausing for a beat, I hiss in a breath. "There's something else," I barrel on, wanting to get it off my chest. "I want to help with whatever you plan for Declan's omegas. It crushes me to think of them not having what they should."

Titan looks at me again, and my earlier question about the intensity of his gaze is answered. Because, right now, every bit of his attention is on me as he assesses me somehow. For a long minute, he says nothing, those blue eyes so focused, I squirm under the immeasurable weight of his stare. I lift my chin and force myself not to look away first. I'm damn near to begging him for a clear answer.

Finally, he agrees. "You know what me teaching you means, I presume? I'll have to put my hands on you, correct you, tell you when you're fucking up."

"I get it," I murmur as he looks at me, but continues on.

"If you promise to behave and listen to me, I'll do it. We can start tomorrow."

My cheeks heat at his words. They're not inherently sexual, but my brain goes right to the idea of Titan's big hands on my body. I imagine him correcting my stance and leaning in close to my ear to call me a good girl, and wetness floods my panties.

Titan sucks in a breath and glances down at my body before zipping his lips and looking away. "Like I said, if you promise to keep it together, we can start tomorrow."

I jump up and down with excitement, but Titan's eyes go immediately to my boobs, which bounce like crazy.

"Goddamnit, you didn't last two seconds," he gripes as I cross my arms over my chest.

"Total accident," I shout. "That wasn't on purpose. Won't happen again."

Titan's only response is a disbelieving grunt as he turns and walks toward the bar.

Yessssss. I'm gonna learn to fight.

CHAPTER FIVE

titan

SEA SALT. Caramel. Cotton candy. Those scents filled my nose when Luna and I talked. And because I'm out of sorts about what Asher said, I made the fucking mistake of referencing putting my hands on her body. Her sugary sweet smell took on a smoky, burnt edge to it. Deeper, stronger, more enticing than usual. Between that and her bright aura, so vibrant and overwhelming, I'm disconcerted.

This day has been one rollercoaster turn after the next. First Sal's insider info about the omegas, and then Asher's joke about seeing a bond between Luna and me.

No. Not just no, but a hearty fuck no. No matter how delicious she smells.

Although watching her promise to behave when we both know she's incapable of it was a little fun. The mental image of her being forced to behave while tied up in my bedroom makes my dick jump. But the reality is that she doesn't have the right personality to be a good bedroom partner for me.

I can one thousand percent guarantee she's going to fight me before we finish our first lesson. I grab a bottle of Jack Daniels from the bar and head out the front door. My truck is still parked out front, so I hop in and take the long dirt road to the first of a dozen cabins that line the valley floor.

Stone gifted one of the cabins to me so I could ease myself into pack life. Shit, I may never move up to the main house, although being close would have its advantages as enforcer. For now, I'm happy with the little cabin that's finally starting to feel like home.

My walkie pings before I even get the truck parked. It's Stone. "T, the twins are cleaning up this damn mess. Are you planning to tackle your workshop tonight?"

I sigh as I depress the button to respond. "You know I am. Whatever you need to say, just spit it out."

Stone chuckles on the other end of the line. "I still wanna debrief. Plus, Clay and I have something to discuss with you. We'll head out there in a bit, okay?"

I don't bother to respond as I park in front of my cabin and haul my backpack inside, setting it down in the kitchen.

Pounding footsteps reach my ears a few minutes later. When I stalk out onto my small front porch, I see Clay and Stone racing one another up the road on foot, giggling like schoolgirls. My alpha pumps his arms hard, but I see the moment when Clay pulls ahead. I won't pick sides in this little race, but I do snort when Clay kicks out a foot and trips Stone. My alpha goes down hard as Clay sprints up the road, both arms raised above his head as he cheers for himself.

Green eyes spark with mischief as he looks over at me and winks. "He was getting distracted daydreaming about Erin. Hope he's not planning to be a sore loser."

Stone jogs up then, slapping Clay on the back of his head. "Asshat. I ate shit so hard back there."

Clay winks as both alphas turn to me. And then I'm under the microscope the way I often am when they're together. They're highly intuitive, both leaders in our pack. And Stone was crazy intuitive to begin with.

My pack alpha gives me a knowing look. "You're upset about what Ash said." It's not really a question.

I shrug. "He was joking. Har har."

"Was he?" Clay questions, the look on his face unusually serious.

"Fuck yes," I retort. "There's no way in hell. I agreed to help her learn to fight, but we're gonna irritate one another so much, she'll probably give up after a lesson or two. It's never happening. Don't look at me like that."

Stone grins but shrugs as he looks over at Clay. "I'm hearing a lot of 'can't' and 'won't' here tonight, strategist. What do you think?"

Clay looks amused, and I find myself disliking this new, stronger relationship between them. It was easier when Stone hated the former Task Force alpha. Now that they've gotten past that for the betterment of the pack, they're close as shit, and I dislike getting ganged up on.

"I still need you, T," Stone assures me, sensing the direction my thoughts have headed. "I don't want to lead a pack without you, and you know that."

I turn and head back into the house as both alphas follow me. "You wanted to debrief and chat through something? What's going on, apart from the handler bullshit?" In the kitchen, I grab three glasses and my Jack, pouring one for each of us as I lean over my island.

Stone downs his, but Clay sips like a goddamn gentleman as I watch them both. "Something's up," I mumble. "You're being weird."

Stone nods. "We can't get out of the Alpha Research Group shit we got signed up for. I still have no idea how we got registered for that, and we confirmed nobody on the town council did it. We're between a rock and a hard place."

Clay seems to be in agreement. "The government is sending a research team out here to stay on site and work with our pack as soon as next week. We want you to be our pack liaison."

Surprised, I step back. "Me? Why me? I'm not fucking friendly. Erin should do this."

Stone shrugs. "Erin will be part of it too. But you give people a lot of comfort, T. You help people all the damn time. You're a pillar of the fucking community. There are a million reasons you're the right alpha for this job. I trust you, and I want you to do this."

Shaking my head again, I cross my arms. "You want me to, or you're telling me to?"

Stone's gaze turns icy, and I know he's remembering our disagreement about addressing the Declan situation so directly. It forced me to pick a side, and that's been hard to come to terms with. While he's still my best friend, it's driven a slight wedge between us.

He sighs. "I'm not telling you to, Titan. I'm asking. If you say no, I'll find someone else. You are my first choice, for so many reasons."

Clay says nothing the entire time, clearly aware there's been tension on the topic of Stone alpha barking at me.

"Let me think it through tonight? I'd like to know more about what it involves, if you have any details on that."

Stone nods as I lift the Jack to my lips. "Erin's got a packet they sent us with a shitload of details. Come grab it whenever you have a minute, and you can look it over." He picks up his radio. "Shit, I bet I can get Luna to run it out he–"

"Fuck no," I shout, swallowing the Jack down the wrong way. It burns like shit as I cough and sputter, shaking my head at my pack alpha. "Don't call her."

Stone and Clay watch me in companionable silence as I choke until my face is red, finally looking up with a grimace. "Don't call her. It's bad enough I agreed to teach her to fight."

Clay snorts. "I don't know that I've ever seen you this out of sorts, brother."

Don't I fucking know it. Goddamn Luna and those fucking tits I just can't get off my mind.

———

STONE AND CLAY stay at the cabin a couple hours with me, chatting through their thoughts on Declan's new handler. They help me frame out an addition to the cabin that I can turn into a workshop. The physical labor is a good outlet for the frustration we all feel. I've been using the empty space behind the lodge, but it's too busy there. I crave peace and quiet. The last time I worked on a piece in the current workshop, Luna ruined it, and I had to start over.

The following morning, I wake and head to the main lodge early. I'm opening Teddy's this morning and working through the lunch shift. I jog upstairs and check in with Sal, but she's got plans to go into town with the twins and work with Stone's mother, Betty, to unpack their newest shipment of clothing from Paris. Betty's boyfriend, Arnaud, is still in town, and I think Sal and the twins are secretly infatuated with the verbose Frenchman. Betty is happy as shit, though, and that's all that matters. She was there for me when I was a younger man and needed a mother figure. I adore her with my entire heart.

When I hit the kitchen to grab some breakfast, Luna's already there putting a plate together for Sal, I assume.

"Hey, watch it, big guy," she jokes as she heads for the kitchen door.

When I frown in confusion, she gestures to the door and her shirt. "Remember yesterday when you ran into me, and shit went everywhere?" There's nothing but lyrical joking in her tone, but I grunt as she rolls her eyes and heads out of the kitchen, mumbling.

"Hey," I call out after her, willing myself not to stare at the sweet peach of her ass in tight designer jeans.

She turns with a bright, forced grin. "What's up, Titan?"

Okay, I see what's going on here. She's trying to catch more flies with honey by being nice. I'll take it, because it's a hell of a lot easier than fighting this woman tooth and nail.

"I'm working the lunch shift, but we can do your first lesson once I get back, if that works?"

Luna puts the plate down and rushes across the kitchen to me, a grin plastered on her delicate features. "Wait, are you serious? We can really start today?"

I nod as she crosses her arms and hops up and down in place. "See? I can behave," she chirps as she spins around and hops again, doing a little victory dance of sorts. When I shoot her a look, she stops and tucks a stray blond wave behind her tiny ear. "Do you mind if some of the other girls come? I know Julia and Cherry are interested too."

"Not a problem. The more the merrier." What the hell am I saying? I don't invite groups of people to interact with me except for at the bar. Because behind my bar, I am the king. I have the ultimate say, and nothing happens in the bar that I don't approve of.

Luna pats me on the chest with a wink. "You gonna threaten to put your hands on everybody during class, or just me? I'm fully prepared to get manhandled as I try to kick your ass." She waggles her brows at me as I press my lips firmly together. She fucking loves teasing me, and it's getting under my skin.

Those damn visions are at the forefront of my brain again, playing across my consciousness like a movie reel. Cum dripping off her big, soft tits. Them spilling out of both my hands togeth—

"Sheesh, chill out, dude," she mutters, rolling her sea-blue eyes. "I'm just messing around. If your supreme alpha domination turns me on, I've got a battery-operated boyfriend to take care of that itch. You don't have to worry about anything."

My eyes flick to hers, but I don't see the usual taunt there. She's looking at me like I'm a scientific specimen. We hold that for several long seconds as my need for dominance chokes me.

I take a step closer to her, waiting for her to look away. Lashes flutter against her cheeks as she blinks slowly, plump lips parting. Her tongue slips out as she licks her lower lip, eyes still locked onto mine.

I gaze down at that pouty mouth, desperately willing Asher's words from last night to leave my brain. When I do, Luna coughs and takes a step away from me, breaking the tension of the moment.

"See ya later, professor," she quips as she sails out of the kitchen without another look.

I am so screwed. Clay was abso-fucking-lutely right.

CHAPTER SIX

I SPEND NEARLY all morning sitting in Stone's office, working at my day job. Thank fuck the lodge gets great internet, and I can still do my work from here. Corporate isn't even aware I'm not home in sunny Santa Monica right now, and that suits me just fine. Mario's the only one who knows, and that's only because he works for my company's legal department when he's not moonlighting as a divorce lawyer.

Stone is also in his office all morning, working to manage the ranch's investment portfolio. Apparently he's a stock whiz, and he's been able to make sure the ranch has plenty of cash to keep going, even though it's no longer a tourist destination. He's at it for hours, poring over his computer screen with a scowl on his face.

Erin's in town meeting with the council to update them on the Alpha Research Group that's arriving next week. I'm dying to ask Stone about it, but I don't want to bug him when there's so much on his mind.

Also, I can't fucking wait until class with Titan. I'm so goddamn excited I can barely hold it in.

"Spit it out, Hot Sauce," Stone says after I squirm in my chair for the hundredth time.

"Spit what out?" I question with an innocent look on my face.

Stone smirks at me. "I don't know if you have questions about the researchers, or Declan's omegas, or maybe even Titan, but you've got questions, I can sense it."

"Why would I have questions about Titan?" I mutter, crossing my arms as I slump back in my chair.

One of Stone's perfect dark brows heads upward as he cocks his head and gives me a look. "Just a wild guess."

"I don't have questions about that big dummy."

"Okay. Let me hear it then," Stone retorts with a beleaguered sigh.

Pulling my knees up onto the chair seat, I hug them to my chest. "What's the scoop with the researchers? I know you didn't apply, but what exactly are they going to research? Aren't you like, worried at all?"

Stone cocks his head to the side. "Worried? What do you think there is to worry about?"

"I dunno. Them learning all about healers and spirits and pack designations. There are a million things that seem too private to be shared so publicly."

Stone sighs. "I've given this a lot of thought, and while I'm not excited to share omega powers and pack designations, I believe we'll have to. The American Task Force captured and experimented on alphas since the early days of the virus. They know a lot already. I think it's safe to assume that information will make its way into the public eventually. We can't keep it all a secret."

"You don't think having all this power puts a big target on your back?"

The big alpha nods again. "Yeah, I do. And I know Mitchell's pack is worried too since he's been so publicly involved in breaking his pack's story on the news. But the thing is, we had targets on our backs before. If we could get our rights back, things have a better chance of changing."

"You seem awfully positive about the whole thing," I grumble. "I'm less than confident in any government handling the news of what alphas and omegas can do very well."

Stone smiles again and powers his computer off without saying a word. When it's done, he leans back in his chair and steeples his fingertips in front of his chest. "Why'd you ask Titan to teach you to fight, Luna?"

I point at the faint line running down my cheek from the injury Declan gifted me. "Isn't it obvious, alpha."

"That's not what I meant, and you know it," Stone mutters, his voice deepening in intensity. I don't understand the desire it produces in me to roll over and answer whatever question he's asking. It's like my body recognizes he's in charge, and it wants to do whatever Stone needs me to do.

"Why'd you ask *Titan*, of all people. Why not Clay?"

Ah. I blanch a little, hugging my knees tighter. "Titan's the enforcer; it seems like it should be in his bag of tricks, right?"

"That all it is, little omega?" Stone's soft-spoken question catches me off-guard, but I roll my eyes.

"Don't know how many times I can tell you I'm not an omega. I don't know how you'd even know, to be honest. And even if I am, it doesn't matter because I'll go home once the Omegamatic project is good to go."

"Is that so?" Stone questions again, leaning forward in his chair.

Before I can answer, Erin sails through the door and flings herself into his arms, capturing his lips in a searing kiss. I should get the hell out of here before they start fucking right on his desk, but I can't help watching how beautiful they are together.

Stone slides both big hands up the back of Erin's shirt and

presses her as close as he can to his chest. "I missed you," he murmured. "It sucks when you're not here."

"Ouch," I complain as I flop back into my chair and cross my arms.

"You were busy anyway," Erin chirps back, kissing the tip of his nose. I watch Stone's eyes flutter closed as he lets her lavish love all over his nose and cheeks and forehead.

How awkward is it going to be when I stand u–

"Hey Lu," Erin's throaty voice rings through the office as I force my gaze back over to her and her mate. Stone is gazing at her with complete adoration as she looks at me. "I heard you talking about Titan. What's going on with that?"

"Absolutely nothing is going on with Titan," I snap. "Why does everybody insist on asking me about him? We are enemies to enemies, remember? Except for in a little bit when he's teaching me and the omegas to fight."

Erin smirks. "It's nice to see you two attempting to get along. He's the freaking best. If you could just get to know that teddy bear side, you'd love him like we do."

Sighing, I nod. "I get that, I do. He's so kind, and he cares so much for people. But we bring out the worst in each other. Maybe training and the Omegamatic project will change that though."

"Maybe," Erin agrees, her voice disbelieving.

Stone laughs a little as he pulls Erin into his chest and hugs her tight. "You remember how much trouble he got us into in high school?"

Erin laughs and winks at me. "It's amazing Rue Jenkins voted for me after the shit we pulled with his kids. Titan was our class valedictorian, crazy brilliant, just very quiet and reserved. He used to come up with the wildest plans, but we got out of it almost every time. I always said he could have been a criminal mastermind if he really wanted to."

"Valedictorian, huh?" I'm skeptical. Although it's true I

haven't had much of a conversation with him to gauge his intelligence. It's just been one barb after the next between us.

"I think he gets underestimated a lot by people who mistake him being quiet for not having anything to say. He's got plenty on his mind; he just shares it with a small group of people he's close to."

I listen intently as Erin talks about Titan. And I know some of this already, because she talked about him plenty over the years. I just never met him, and I was always a little jealous because he was another bestie out there somewhere. My heart pangs in my chest. "TBD on if it's going to go well or not," I pronounce sagely as Erin smirks.

"We'll see, Hot Sauce," Stone agrees with a wink.

Bastard.

AT 3:30 Cherry radios me while I'm changing for the lesson.

"Titan just got home; he wants us to meet him in the gym downstairs. You still cool if Julia and I come with you?"

I snort into my empty room and depress the button. "Of course. I'd prefer it if you two were there."

I hear sniggering on the other end as Cherry comes back on. "As you wish."

We both laugh at *The Princess Bride* reference as I clip my radio to my belt and look in the mirror to check my hair. I tuck a few baby hairs back, grumbling at how unruly they can be, and then I head downstairs to find Erin waiting for me at the bottom.

"You coming to learn to fight too?" I hop up and down before throwing myself in her arms.

"Oh no," she laughs. "I'm grabbing my popcorn and coming to watch the show."

"There's not gonna be any show!" I shout when she puts me down, but it sounds like an excuse even to my ears.

Erin wraps her arms around me, and we head down the hall along the back of the house toward the basement gym. When we get there, Cherry and Julia have arrived. Titan wraps them up in big hugs, blue eyes flicking to mine when I come in. Erin lets go of me and crosses the room to him, giving him a quick squeeze as his attention turns to her.

"Thought I'd come see what the fuss is about," she says. He nods once at her, a grin pulling the corners of his mouth upward.

I'm woman enough to admit Titan smiling is smoking hot, and I find myself wishing we weren't complete enemies, because those hugs look kinda nice. Erin hugs me all the time, and I adore her. But a man hug is entirely different. It's been weeks since I wrapped my arms around a good-looking man. Titan's so big. I bet his arms would go all the way around me. I bet when he hugs, he buries his face in the crook of your neck and sighs. I *bet* his five o'clock shadow would rub all over my—

Oh fuck. I'm staring. I'm staring right at him and licking my lips. Julia hides a smirk behind her hand, Cherry's brows are practically in her hairline, and Erin crosses her arms with a meaningful look.

Titan breaks the awkward silence, his low-pitched voice echoing in the dark basement gym. "Let's get started, shall we?"

We form a half circle around him as he rolls his sleeves up to his elbows. God fucking help me, his forearms are thick as fuck, every big muscle visible. Even his hands are manly, all rugged and rough-looking.

"Luna!" Titan's bark breaks me out of my reverie.

"What?" I snap back, surprised at the sudden noise.

He steps past the girls and stops in front of me, so close

he's all up in my fucking space. Leaning down toward my ear, his lips practically tickle my skin. Goosebumps travel down my arms as I hold back a full body shudder.

"Five minutes in and you're not fucking listening to me. Is this gonna be a problem?" He shoots me a skeptical look as I shake my head, begging my brain to focus. I wanted to learn this, so I shove my weird emotions down deep and look at Titan.

"As I was saying," he gives me another irritated look, turning from me to the head of the class, "if you get in a fight with an alpha, your primary focus should just be getting away, for now. Without years of specialized training, it would be hard to take down an alpha in a fight, so that shouldn't be your goal if you find yourself in a dicey situation."

His words bring me back to Declan fucking attacking us, and then kidnapping us and nearly killing Rogue. Steely determination takes over my brain. I felt helpless that day despite my karate background. I need an edge. Because what happened that day can never happen again.

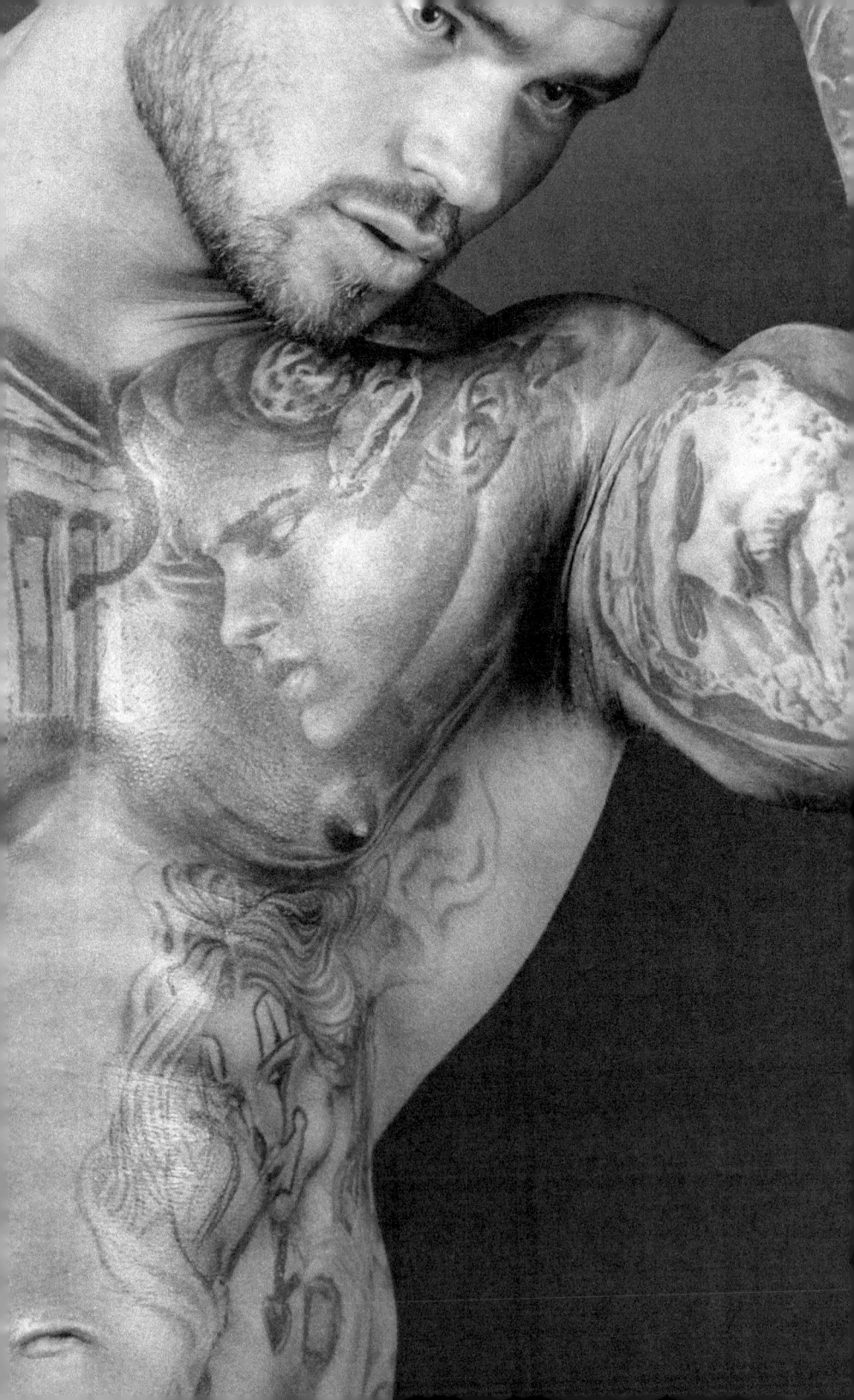

CHAPTER SEVEN

titan

LUNA SURPRISES me by going from distracted to determined in the span of ten seconds. Her gaze narrows as I instruct the omegas.

I can tell they dislike my mandate that their best bet is to take an alpha down fast and run. It's clear they'd all like to be able to simply kick ass, but that can't be learned in a day. We have to start small.

"What's the easiest way to take a man down?" I ask the small group, grinning when Julia raises her hand like a kid in school.

"Kick him in the nuts!" she signs, shooting me a devious grin.

"Bingo," I agree. "Even for an alpha, that's incredibly painful. So whatever you have to do, you want to go for that first. The eyes are another good target, because an alpha who can't see will have a harder time hurting you."

I show the girls a few quick self-defense moves and they practice as pairs with me alternating between them. I'm careful to keep my hands respectful when correcting their stances.

Luna's aura was a steely, focused gray when she came in, but threads of angry red begin to take over. She's already a black belt in karate, so this probably feels like child's play to her.

"Let's move on to breaking out of a hold on your throat," I suggest, grabbing Erin's hand and pulling her toward me. She's the closest in height, so it'll be easier to demonstrate. I wrap my hands around Erin's throat as she waggles her brows at me and starts gyrating her hips suggestively.

"E, get serious," I command as she starts the running man with my hands still wrapped around her. When I let go of her neck, she gives me a look.

"Aww, come on, T; I'm just playing."

"Declan wasn't when he attacked you," I remind her as her eyes narrow to slits. "Or when he attacked Luna. Or when he kidnapped you both and Rogue. That's why we're doing this, right?"

Erin and Luna frown at the same time, then Erin grabs my hands and puts them back at her throat. "Point taken. Let's fuck some alphas up."

I show the girls how to use their hands to break out of the grip, kicking the nuts at the same time. Erin does surprisingly well. I find myself wishing I had put on something to cover my dick, because if I get kicked today it's gonna really fucking hurt.

Cherry and Julia go next, and they're slower but equally focused.

"Great job, ladies," I praise them as Luna steps forward.

I'd swear the air between us heats, her aura bursting into a myriad of colors. Iron focus, red anger, black determination. I will my breath to stop coming faster while I reach up and collar her throat. Our gazes meet. She doesn't hesitate, shoving her arms up through mine, breaking the connection so fucking fast, I'm taken off guard.

She brings her knee right up to my goddamn nuts and almost makes it, but I block at the last second, pushing her ankle away from me. The move spins her fast. I use that momentum to grip her throat from behind, yanking her to my chest. She hits my body hard, a whoosh of air rushing out of her lungs as she struggles against my hard grip on her throat.

In her struggle, her body rubs all over the front of mine, and, goddamn, but it's making me hard. Hell no. I don't want that.

Leaning down, I bring my mouth to her ear. "Good, but not good enough, Luna." I drop her throat and push her gently away from me, painfully aware of the other omegas watching us, the room tense.

"Again. When I block, be prepared to spin and drop to a knee. Then use your elbow, if you're fast enough."

Luna's aura swirls bright red; she's fucking angry. But she grabs my hands, pulling them to her throat again.

A growl rumbles out of my chest, fangs elongating, because touching her like this...fighting...it's making me harder and harder. I'm thankful I'm wearing jeans and not sweatpants because my raging erection would be obvious. I need to rein it in.

Instead, I squeeze my hands tighter around her throat as her aura sputters angrily.

Luna breaks the hold, kicking at the same time. Her foot brushes across my cock. Not close enough to hurt, but she's really fucking fast.

I shove her away like before, but she drops fast to the floor, one elbow moving so quickly, I almost don't block in time. As it is, I throw my hands over my nuts, but her elbow forces me to essentially crunch my balls with my own hand. Anger rises in my system, but pride too, because that was really fucking good.

"Good," I snap as she rises from the floor. "Again."

My body's angry that this feisty omega is trying to hurt me. My mind is proud of her for focusing, and all I can think about is manhandling her without everyone watching us.

This time when I grip Luna's throat, I yank her straight to me instead of letting her break the hold. I'm curious with her karate background how much natural ability she'll have to improvise.

Immediately, Luna's knee comes up, connecting with my nuts as I bellow. Red anger flares in my chest when she shoves her arms up through my hold and breaks it. I sense the moment she's going in for the kill, bringing her knee up to fucking kick me again. I block it and roar in her face, shaking the walls of the gym as the other omegas squeak in surprise.

Stalking to Luna, I push my chest against hers so hard, she starts to fall. I catch her throat on the way down, landing her smoothly on her back as I straddle her on the ground.

"When you take an alpha down, Luna, make sure you take him all the way down," I command as I lean over her. Her blue eyes are wide as she scratches at my hand gripping the slim column of her throat. My forearms are brushing up against her huge tits, and I growl as her chest heaves, rubbing that softness all along my skin.

"If you don't make sure he's down, you'll find yourself in a situation like this," I snap. "You're totally fucked at this point. No goddamn options."

I'm suddenly aware of the presence of Erin, Cherry and Julia in the room. Turning to look at them, I find shock on their faces. Cherry coughs helpfully, barely concealing a knowing smile.

Underneath me, Luna bucks and squirms, but she's well and truly screwed. She's frustrated and angry. She wants to kick my ass in a day. But it doesn't happen like that.

I push myself upright and pull her up with me. She straightens her shoulders and glares at me. "Again," she commands. And that fucking command makes my dick leap, despite me being the one who usually does the commanding.

"That's enough for today." I look at the other girls.

"Fuck that," Luna spits. Without warning, she leaps up onto my back, wrapping her arms around my neck in a chokehold. Time slows for me, anger that Luna's pushing harder, wrapping me up until all I want to do is fucking dominate her, teach her a lesson. I knew she wouldn't goddamn behave. Not for a single second.

Reaching up, I grip the back of her neck and pull her hard, tossing her toward the wall. She hits it with a bang and slides down, blue eyes narrowed at me as she gets to her feet fast. Before she can sprint the short distance between us, I cross it, gripping both her shoulders and pressing her hard against the wall with my much larger frame.

"Goddamnit!" Luna shouts, struggling as I pull one of her hands up over her head, then the other.

Snarling, I lean into her, far enough in that she leans back, pressing her head to the wall. She can only go so far, and I press until my lips are almost touching hers.

And there it fucking is. Burnt, smoky caramel. Sticky sweet cotton candy. Depthless seas. Her scent and her aura bloom at the same time. She's mad, but she's aroused too.

"I told you this wasn't going to work," I state. "You're not fucking listening to me, Luna. This is why I didn't want to agree in the goddamn first place. Look at you now, tossed up against the wall like a rag doll and utterly at my mercy. You screwed up."

Luna's big blue eyes lock onto mine, and I'm surprised to see hurt there. Anger too, but mostly pained disappointment.

Dropping her arms, I back away from her. I'm too close. Much too close. Getting lost in those sea-blue eyes. Physically fighting her does things to me, things I don't want to shine a light too closely on. Because if I look too closely at what she brings out in me, I don't know what I'll find.

I'M an unfocused mess by the time I leave the gym. The girls stay to stretch, and all I can think about is Luna bent over in yoga pants, reaching for her ankles.

I've got to get my head screwed on straight. Stone, Erin and I have an introductory call with the Alpha Research Group team assigned to us. My only goal is to figure out who the fuck signed us up for this.

I head to Stone's office and find he and Erin there already. They log into the meeting link on Erin's laptop as I sit down next to her. It's just like high school, E right next to Stone, her arms threaded around his. Me right beside them, ready to stir up trouble as needed.

There's a ringing sound, and then a conference room pops up, an older man waving into the screen. "Alpha Stone and Mayor Grant? I'm Devraj Eller, pleased to meet you." I get a generally positive vibe from the pleasant look on his face, although I can't see his aura through the screen.

Erin grins big, the same small-town politician smirk she used to weasel her way right into the hearts of everyone in town. "Mr. Eller, it's wonderful to meet you. This is my mate, Stone, and our pack enforcer, Titan."

There's scrambling as Eller picks up a pile of papers and shoves his glasses farther up his nose. "Yes, let's see. I've got down that you have as well a pack strategist and seer, but no healer or spirit. Is that correct?"

"Question for you, Devraj," I butt in. I'd rather get to the point. "We didn't sign up for this, so I'd like to understand who submitted the application for our pack."

Eller's friendly expression falls as he nervously looks

through the file in his hands. "You didn't sign up? That makes no sense. All packs who were chosen had to apply and go through a preliminary screening process."

"We didn't," Stone confirms. "Suffice to say we were surprised to receive your note that we'd been accepted."

"Well, shit," Devraj says, throwing his hands up. "Apologies, this is most unusual. I'm not certain how to handle this. I intended to speak with you about your team today, but perhaps that's not our best course forward."

Stone catches Eller's eyes. "Whatever you can find out would be most appreciated."

Devraj frowns. "I believe the team is on their way to you tomorrow morning. I don't know that I'll find out the answer before they arrive."

"That's fine," Stone says as I lean over Erin.

"We'll be good hosts," I assure him. "We'd just like to understand what's going on."

"Noted," Devraj agrees hastily. "I will find out as quickly as possible."

He proceeds to tell us all about the team assigned to our pack. When we hang up with him, my eyes meet Stone's.

This has Declan written all over it.

CHAPTER EIGHT

luna

THE OMEGAS DIDN'T SAY shit after our first self defense lesson, but I felt the way they all looked at me. To be honest, I still need to process my feelings about Titan's proximity and the warmth that sent through my whole body.

The morning after that damn lesson, Erin pokes her head into my bedroom where I'm finalizing some design paperwork for the Omegamatic's patent application. "Luna, I've got to run into town for something with the council. Can you help Titan get the researchers settled? Workers dropped off their trailer an hour ago. The team is arriving in a few minutes."

Dread settles in my gut. "Uh, he and I aren't on great terms after yesterday's lesson. Can Cherry do it? She's so fucking friendly."

Erin winks. "Hey, you and Titan have to get past the angst. All of this over a couple initial misjudgments on both your parts?" She emphasizes the last half of her sentence as if I'm somehow to blame for Titan being a big hulking asshat. Not that I necessarily behaved well either, but still.

Sighing, I slam my computer closed and head to the

mirror, running my fingers through my waves. "I suppose I look presentable enough, but I'm not even staying here long-term. It should be someone who can be a good liaison."

"That's Titan," Erin deadpans. "He's literally the liaison. I just want you to be there as another friendly face for day one. You're perfect for that."

"Fine, fine!" I agree. "I'll just steer clear of that neanderthal, and it'll be fine, I'm sure."

"Yeah," Erin says with a sarcastic wiggle of her perfect brows. "What a neanderthal. Planning how to feed hapless omegas and teaching other omegas how to fight, and running a bar and giving people free fo–"

"I get it. No need to go on." I slap the side of Erin's tit hard as she yelps and leaps back into the hallway, snorting with laughter.

"I'll give you a ride, bestie. Come on." She grabs my hand and drags me up the hallway as I look around for a lifeline. Someone, anyone else who can do this job so I don't have to face Titan after my little blow up during our lesson.

Nobody comes to save me though, and five unfortunately quick minutes later, Erin drops me off in front of the researchers' trailer. She drives off with a backward glance in her mirror and a shitty little wink as I throw my middle finger up.

Titan pulls up at the same time and watches me before exiting the truck with a wry look on his face. "Guess eventually you behave with everyone the way you do with me, huh?" He doesn't bother to wait for a response as he steps up to the trailer door and raps on it twice.

The door opens, and a woman peeks out. Damn, she's freaking beautiful. Chocolate hair pulled back into a bun with icy blue eyes that remind me of Titan's. She's pale, but her nose and cheeks are covered in freckles, a nose ring glinting from the edge of one delicate nostril. The girl is put together.

Okay then.

She opens the door and steps out with a broad smile. "Hey! You must be William? I'm Bianca, the head researcher for this team."

Titan smirks and reaches out, shaking her hand vigorously as she beams at him. "Nobody calls me William; it's too formal. Titan is good. And this is Luna, but we call her Hot Sauce."

Bianca looks over at me, confused. I struggle to hold back the eye roll, stepping forward to shake her hand too. She chuckles when she takes it. "Hot Sauce implies quite a back story. I'd love to hear it sometime."

My cheeks heat. "It's not a long story, really, but I'll definitely share at some point. Erin got called into town to deal with urgent town council stuff, but we wanted to see if you have everything you need? Is there anything we can do to help your team get started?"

"Actually, yeah." Bianca waves us into the trailer. "I want to talk you through our current process and get any feedback you might have on areas we should be focusing on but aren't. My boss had an initial call with Stone and Erin yesterday, but now that we're here, I'd love to get eyes on our plan."

Titan stiffens in the doorway when she mentions the research, but Bianca doesn't miss a beat. She leans back against an island that runs down the middle of the trailer. "Hey, I know having a team of government researchers on your property, in your business asking you questions about your whole life sounds like total shit. Just know that all of us, everyone on this team, are dedicated to the truth about alphas and omegas."

Titan gives her a look. "I'm curious if Devraj shared with you how we didn't apply for this program?"

Bianca frowns at Titan's words, crossing her arms. "He did, yeah, but we were on our way here already. We left it that he'd look into it, but we should continue as planned for now. Does that still work for you?"

Titan gives a noncommittal grunt as I think back to what she previously said.

"I thought this was an impartial group," I comment as Bianca's brows rise.

"I don't believe it's possible for anyone to be truly impartial when it comes to alphas and omegas," she admits. "Each team is screened for where they stand opinions-wise so we have a mix before going into the field. My own sister transitioned in the early days. She's an alpha, and she ran at first. But once Mitchell Bancroft went public with the story about alpha packs, she came home."

"Female alpha?" Titan sounds skeptical as Bianca nods.

"I know, right? Incredibly uncommon, as far as we know. But where she spent the last three years, there were two female alphas in that pack. So that's where I stand on the topic. But there are others on our team who are skeptics through and through. You'll see that."

"Talk to me a little about the research itself," Titan commands. I swear his voice travels straight to my bones. The way he talks to Bianca is totally different from the sarcastic punch of our regular communication.

She smiles and tucks a stray wisp of hair behind her ear. "The rest of my team should be here shortly, and I'll introduce you to everyone then."

For half an hour she chats through the research, starting with simple things like how the pack is set up, what designations or roles everyone has, how everyone came to be at Bent Fork. There will be a medical element too. Titan questions her extensively about the information the researchers plan to gather.

It's clear he's concerned about privacy, but Bianca does a good job explaining how the government plans to keep each individual's information anonymous. She's incredibly organized, and the conversation is forthright.

Still, the way she pivots toward Titan when she speaks? I don't like it. She thinks he's hot.

I mean, he *is* hot, when he's not being a jerk. But I find myself scowling when I consider how her impression of him might affect her research. Still, my job here is done. The researchers are in good shape, and Bianca will be able to get started when the rest of her team arrives.

"Do you want to come up to the lodge for dinner tonight?"

Titan's question surprises me. I blurt out a "huh?" at the same time as Bianca chirps out "Soon, I promise!" We stare at one another awkwardly before I giggle and shrug, promising to see her later.

Titan follows me out of the trailer. I can already sense him scowling before I turn to look. "What is it?" I bite out as I cross my arms. I'm surprisingly fucking irritated at the way Bianca ogled him.

"What is *what?*" he growls back.

"You're scowling at me; it's like bugs marching down my spine. What gives?"

Titan scoffs. "You're being weird. Do you need a snack?"

I resist the urge to stomp my foot as I pray for something hard to throw at his head. "Do I need a *snack?* Are you kidding me right now? I'm just asking if—"

"I heard you, Hot Sauce," he sighs, running one big hand through his dark waves. "Come on, let's go back up to the lodge. I'll give you a ride."

Goosebumps pepper my skin at the deep timbre of his voice. But I don't want my body to notice how handsome he is after watching another woman practically salivate over him. I just...I don't want him, but this lady is gonna be an issue.

Hopping into Titan's truck, I zip my lips and tell myself to just be cool. I did the thing Erin asked me to do.

"Hey, do you want to do another lesson before dinner?"

I whip around in the seat, shocked. "You'd do that? Even though the last one was awful?"

Titan's lips tip into a hint of a smile, but he doesn't look away from the road as his old truck rumbles along the gravel. "You fought me, just like I knew you would. Think you learned from that experience, Hot Sauce?"

"Yes," I breathe out. "Hell yes. I'll find Julia too because I know she'll want in."

Titan nods once before peering out the windshield again. "It really bothers you that Declan was able to get one over on you, huh?"

My gaze travels out the window before I slump up against the seat and look over. "I just...being a black belt in karate always made me feel so safe. It's something my dad got me into after my mom died, and it bonded us. He was always so proud of me, and it gave me so much confidence to feel like I could take on anyone. But the day Declan slammed me down in the road, I felt fucking helpless. I hated that."

Titan says nothing until we get back to the lodge. He puts the ancient truck in park and turns in the seat to face me. "I can't imagine what it must be like to be helpless physically. I don't have a frame of reference, but if it bothers you this badly, I'll help you fix it. Alright?"

Fuck me, it's hot when he's kind. And this might be the nicest thing he's ever said to me. I don't want to examine it too closely, or how irritated I am knowing Bianca finds him good looking. The reality is that I'm still leaving at some point. So, yeah, I wanna learn to fight from him if I can in the meantime. But then I'm out of here for sure.

CHAPTER NINE

titan

HELPLESS. The word plays over and over in my mind. I hate it. Luna may be a pain in my ass, but there's a soft side to her that I've seen with Sal. On top of which, she's taken charge of developing a plan to get food to the omegas in Declan's pack. She's a woman on a mission, and I have to admire how dedicated she is to helping people.

To be frank, I wouldn't have thought it when I met her. I made assumptions about her, and she's probably made a few about me. But I'm man enough to know we should move past all that. I didn't expect her to share about her mother passing, though. And the way she talks about her father makes it sound like he's gone too.

Is this girl all alone in the world except for her friends? That thought sends a painful stab through my chest. I'm well aware of what it's like to experience loss on that scale.

Luna follows me up the stairs quietly, but the second I open the door for her, she bounds through with a big grin on her face, heading for the stairs.

Reaching for my walkie, I ping James. "James, is Julia with

you? I'm going to do a lesson with Luna, and I know Jules has been interested."

"Not…now," James gasps out. "Busy."

"Why'd you pick up the goddamn walkie, then?" I snap out as James chuckles, his voice ringing through the receiver.

"Could have been an enforcing emergency. Since it's not, I need to get back to my woman."

I click off without responding, then make my way down to the gym.

Luna shows up a few minutes later, her face flushed as she grimaces. "Julia's umm…not available. So I guess it's just you and me?"

I give her what I hope is a friendly look. "You ready, Hot Sauce?"

"Probably not, but I'm gonna give it my best." She looks frustrated already, her aura an angsty green, but I'm hopeful we can turn things around.

An hour later, Luna's getting faster, but she's still miffed at how quickly I block her. It's an improvement, although I sense her exasperation. She doesn't bitch about it today, just nods when I give her a few pointers and promises to work on it on her own.

"Hey, you're gonna get it, alright?" It feels weird to encourage her when we've been at such odds, but she slumps against the wall, blue eyes bright on mine. Sun-kissed skin is damp with sweat, and it runs in a trickle down her chest right into her shirt. I don't mean to look, and I sure as shit don't mean to lick my lips. But to my surprise, she says nothing when our eyes meet again.

If anything she looks…intrigued. And unsurprised.

Luna smells so goddamn good.

Without meaning to, I take a step closer to her, close enough that we're mere inches apart. I'm so tall she has to rest her head back against the wall to look up at me. "What are you doing, William?" She delivers my given name with a snarky smile, all bluster again.

"Not William," I purr. "Titan."

"Nobody calls you William?"

The urge to fuck her into silence hits me so hard I throw one arm up against the wall to steady myself. I want her, God help me. I don't want to, but after spending an hour correcting her stance and praising her, I'm hard for her. Again.

"Nobody calls me William outside the bedroom," I correct, my voice husky.

Luna gasps and leans in with an over-exaggerated glance around, as if she's about to tell me a secret. "You mean your lovers call you William? How very...formal."

If only she knew, I think to myself as I take a step back to put distance between us. This right here, this snark? It's one of many reasons we wouldn't be a good fit. I don't like snark. I prefer quiet obedience, two adjectives that could never describe her.

Luna grins at me as she crosses her arms, lifting her huge tits up as she does.

It takes a herculean effort for me not to stare down at them, but I force myself to meet her gaze instead. She's snarky, but she's not unaffected by my closeness. Her chest heaves slightly, but it's not due to exertion. Goosebumps travel down both of her arms and the side of her neck. Even now, a vein throbs there. I can hear the pounding of her heart in her chest. Every signal she's giving off is prey-like, and I am made to chase.

I shouldn't, but I want to taste her there. To press my lips to that vein and feel it throb between my teeth. I want to–

"Titan? Luna? Are you down there?" Stone's voice echoes down the stairs. Luna slips sideways along the wall and trots out the door, responding for the both of us.

Fuck me, I almost bit her. I slap myself once across the cheek to encourage some sense into my brain, and then I head out the door after her. I almost lost control, and it can't fucking happen.

I manage to avoid direct contact with Luna for most of dinner. Stone and Erin sit on one side of me, Julia on the other. Her hand is on James's thigh the whole time, and I get the distinct sense she's feeling him up under the table. I don't begrudge any alpha their happiness, but goddamn, I'd love a moment *not* surrounded by so much alpha pheromone.

Erin grins over at me. "T, how'd it go with the research team?"

"The head lady's gonna be trouble," Luna chirps as I open my mouth to respond.

"Trouble. What do you mean, trouble?" James questions Luna with his fork halfway to his mouth. "What should we prepare for?"

Luna shakes her head emphatically. "Nothing crazy, her sister is a female alpha, so I believe she's on our side actually. I just..." She looks up at me, and I don't miss the blush that pinkens her cheeks before she looks back at James. "She thinks Titan's hot, and that could get weird."

The table falls silent as everyone turns to look at me.

Glaring over at her, I shake my head. "It won't be an issue. I'm sure Bianca will have no problem remaining professional. And neither will I."

"Bianca, huh?" Erin teases. "First name basis on day one?"

"Not a big deal, E," I retort as James laughs.

"Is she hot?" He signs his question to me, and Julia turns in her seat with a big grin.

"Yeah, T. Is she super hot? Tell us everything," she signs back.

Well, this is fucking awkward.

"She's, umm...she's very nice."

Luna helpfully pipes up, "She's gorgeous, you guys. Tall, long wavy brown hair and these gorgeous blue eyes. Yeah, she's hot."

James snorts as he translates for Julia since Luna still doesn't know sign language.

Stone smiles over at me with a wink. "Sounds like she's exactly your type, T. This should be interesting."

"How about we all focus on something other than the hot researcher, shall we?"

The moment I say that, Luna gets up out of her chair, looking over at Erin. "I've got some things to do so I'm just, umm, gonna head to my room for a bit. Catch you later." Without another word, she grabs her plate and leaves.

I watch her go, and the whole pack *watches* me watch her go. When she disappears around the corner, I turn to Stone with a scowl. "Do not question me about either one of them. You're the one who asked me to be the liaison. So here's me, liaising."

"Oh, yeah," James mutters. "You liaised Luna right outta here. Well done, big guy."

Well, shit.

Growling, I get up to leave, wondering if Luna's alright or if I should check on her.

No. Fuck no. What am I doing? Asher's words have settled uncomfortably in the pit of my stomach.

There's a fuckload of unresolved sexual tension in my life right now, so what I need is release, and I'm gonna take care of that right now.

I leave the lodge, jogging down the stairs and up the road toward my cabin. My mind wanders to Luna, assuming she's in her room. I find myself wondering if she feels hot and achy like I do after our lessons. If she's in her room doing what I'm about to do in mine.

Goddamn, I need to come. I throw my cabin door open

and sail through it, straight to my bedroom. I yank my clothes off and flop down onto my bed, pulling up a saved video of an old sub on my phone. I press play, watching myself in my condo as I tie her up to the hooks in my bedroom wall. In this video, I tease her for a while, so I set it on the bedside table and reach into the drawer, grabbing my handheld cocksucker. It's a newer model, and it's still too loud, but it's pretty damn good. It's not lost on me that Luna designs toys like this for a living. I can just imagine those blue eyes peering inside the machine, pondering how to design it to fit a man's cock perfectly.

Groaning, I coat my already hard cock with lube and shove it deep inside the machine. When I turn it on, an intense sucking sensation pulls a whine from my throat.

My eyes roll back in my head as I force myself to be still, to focus on the sloppy sensations of the machine on my dick. I do nothing but hold it in place, the machine sucking slow and light, a simple tease to get me hot.

A thin sheen of sweat coats my forehead as pleasure builds in my stomach. Turning my head to the right, I watch myself drop to the floor and bury my mouth in my sub's pussy. I feast on her as pressure grows between my thighs, my balls tightening up as the toy begins to suck a little harder and faster. I watch myself on video, the way she almost comes on my tongue before I pull away. My sub bites her lip but says nothing.

And that's the moment I know I'm fucked. Because I imagine what Luna might say to me if I did that to her. How I'm a thousand percent certain she'd demand for me to finish her, or pull herself out of the restraints and tackle me to the floor.

I don't want that. I want control. I want power.

Grinding my teeth, I slap my cell down on its face and throw one arm over my head, my eyes closing. So what if I jack off to thoughts of that cotton candy smell and the way it strengthens when we fight? There's nobody here to know my sinful secret. Against my better judgment, I want Luna.

I gasp as lightning streaks down my thighs, the machine building into a faster, harder rhythm.

Imagining Luna's big breasts in my hands, I picture what I suspect are rosy dark nipples. And I bet she shaves. She's so perfectly manicured all the time. My mind helpfully supplies an image of Luna beneath me in front of a fire, its light casting shadows across her buttery soft skin.

In my daydream, I bite my way from one hard nipple to the other before sliding inside her. "Luna," I growl out. Her name feels so fucking good to say.

Nobody has to know, I remind myself. Nobody has to know you're fantasizing over her like an idiot.

Her name falls off my lips louder and louder as the machine sucks my cock hard, until I explode, curling in half at the strength of a powerful orgasm. Pleasure blooms outward from my core as I scream her name into my cabin, gasping as I spurt into the toy. Sloppy, wet sounds ring as my bellowing becomes desperate breathing, trying to wrap my mind around how I came so fucking hard.

And then I remember goddamn Asher and River have such incredible hearing they probably heard that entire thing. I lay in my bed, staring at the ceiling as irritation swirls in my chest.

Fuck me.

THE NEXT MORNING, I walkie the twins and Sal from my cabin. They've all offered to help me with building something to hide food in for Declan's omegas. It was Luna's idea, and I agree it's solid.

When I see River, I'm definitely going to assume she didn't hear me jack off and scream Luna's name last night. And if Riv is feeling generous, she won't fucking mention it.

Growling at the anxiety this produces in me, I dress and grab a coffee to go, calling my bar manager before he goes in to open for the lunch shift. I've done a damn good job hiring. I don't need to check in on him, but I can't help it. I like things to be done a certain way in all areas of my life.

Not that I have control everywhere, which is why, when I get up to the lodge and Luna stands there with the twins, I hold back a frown. God, if River heard me last night and says something, I'll lose my mind.

Forcing a smile to my face, I wave at the small group as they head down the stairs. Luna hovers behind the twins and Sal as they pile into the back seat of my truck. Blue eyes land on mine, pink lips parting as if she's about to say something.

River pipes up first, giving me a suggestive look. "Luna's being weird, but she wants to come with us to help. That's cool, right? Rogue is gonna be like Charlie and the angels." Rogue snorts out a laugh, and even Luna smirks a little bit as she looks back up at me.

"Not a problem," I murmur as I open the passenger door for her. She hops in, giving me a soft look.

The twins chatter about utter nonsense nearly the entire car ride, Sal laughing every now and again in agreement with them. It's nice to see her being comfortable with the exuberant teenagers. I don't miss the way Rogue's big arm is around Sal's shoulder, his hand resting on her upper arm possessively.

My enforcer nature pings a little bit. Rogue is young, and Sal's dealt with years of bullshit from Declan's pack. I'm not one to stop people who want to consensually play together, but I may need to have a talk with him depending on how far they've taken things.

We pull off the main road onto the pothole-filled dirt road leading to the hot springs. Luna grips the door handle as the twins start joking about how horrible the road is.

"Bet you're regretting getting those boobs right now," River snarks out as Luna bounces in the front seat next to me.

Luna claps one arm over her chest and turns to the twins and Sal with a laugh. "This is literally the only thing that sucks about big boobs. Bouncy roads and running are not my friend."

My face heats as my dick hardens in my jeans. Glancing over, I see Luna's boobs spilling over her forearm. We hit a pothole, and they bounce like everything else. I barely hold back a needy whine. They look so soft, and it's easy to imagine how they'd look with her bouncing on my di—

"Earth to Titan," Luna laughs. "Want me to move my arm so you can ogle me unhindered?"

I open my mouth to shout no, but Luna waves both arms up in the air. I hit another pothole, and I swear time slows. Luna's breasts sway from side to side, rubbing against one another before jiggling upward as the truck dips.

And that's when I'm truly fucked, because I'm so intent on Luna's goddamn tits that I've driven right off the road. The truck hits a small fallen log as I shout, and everyone in the car goes flying. Including Luna, who yips and sails across the front seat, landing face down in my lap.

Slamming on the brakes, I look down in horror. My hard dick is literally poking her in the face. If she hasn't noticed yet, she's sure to in a moment.

Luna grips the wheel and turns to me with a devilish glint in her eye. "I'm inclined to believe you did that shit on purpose."

Her blond hair brushes against my thighs as I struggle to form words at the sight of her hovering over my legs. She's so damn close, her scent intoxicating like this. One of Luna's hands is on each of my thighs, and she pushes up, gripping my muscle as she moves a hand to the steering wheel to pull herself out of my lap.

River cackles in the back seat. "This is so deliciously awkward. Oh my gawd, I love it!"

Rogue and Sal join her in laughter. I'm so out of sorts, with visions of Luna face down in my lap, that I can't even laugh it off. I run a hand through my hair instead. Studiously ignoring Luna, I pull the truck carefully back onto the road and avoid all the major potholes, driving more slowly up the gravel road.

Luna's sugary sweet scent fills the car, amplifying how much I notice her. When I risk a glance in the rearview mirror, Rogue is giving me a shit-eating grin. He can smell her arousal too. God, I'm never gonna hear the end of this from the twins.

We round a corner, nearly to the parking lot, when River leans forward. "Cassian's at the hot springs; I can hear him." Her incredible hearing still shocks me; it's even more than what a seer might have. Still, it's handy. I'm thankful to have something else to focus on.

"What's he doing?" I grunt, glancing over at Luna, who winks at me.

"What do most people do in the hot springs?" Luna snarks.

I nearly blurt out that most people fuck in the hot springs, but the last time she and I were in there together, she stared at my ass when I got out. I spent the whole truck ride home wondering how she felt about what she saw.

"Mmm, sounds like he's grumbling about something," River pipes up. "He's alone."

We pull into the parking lot, and sure enough, Cassian's motorcycle is there.

"This could be good though, right?" Luna looks up at me. "I've been wanting to ask him if he has any details on

Declan's omegas, but he hasn't been around the lodge much."

"Much to Julia's chagrin," River mutters as I turn around with a questioning look. "What? Everybody knows she has the hots for him. I mean, God, who wouldn't?"

Luna laughs next to me, a bright, cheery sound that used to grate on my last nerve. Somehow today it doesn't. "Hell yes, Riv. Cassian's got daddy vibes all day long."

I don't even realize I'm snarling until the twins and Sal run off into the high meadow. Luna looks up at me with both hands on her hips. "You're all growly, why? Because I said Cassian has daddy vibes?"

I'm painfully aware that we're alone. My sexy imaginings from last night come back to me. Luna on her back before me, tan thighs spread wide. Not to mention hovering over my lap in my truck.

The rumble in my chest stops abruptly as Luna takes a step closer, putting her hand on my chest. Through my flannel I can feel the warmth of her tiny palm as she rubs one of my pecs in small circles. Her next question surprises me. "You're a teddy bear softie with everyone else. Why don't I see that side of you?"

Her touch has my desire to dominate on overdrive, and I'm still horny from what just happened and my fantasies last night. Alpha sex drive is high as hell, and a pocket pussy has nothing on the real thing. Even so, talking to Luna is like moving chess pieces across a board.

Some days I'd like to pick her up and just toss her off the chessboard entirely.

"What are you doing, Hot Sauce?" I bite out, taking a step closer so the front of her body is pressed to mine.

She shrugs, her aura going from a sensual cherry red to midnight black in the span of a second. Her knee comes up fast, nearly connecting with my groin, startling me. I manage to grab it and yank it out to the side, my other hand going immediately to her ass.

Spinning us, I slam her against the truck as she yelps angrily. Snapping my teeth in her face, I snarl as she pushes against my chest, her cheeks blushing pink.

"Goddamnit, you caveman, I was just trying to put the moves into pra—"

I clamp my hand over her mouth to shut her up. My control is hanging on by a fucking thread as my muscles quiver in anticipation of dominating her.

Closing my eyes, I will myself to be calm. I'm simultaneously shocked and proud. She's fast as hell, and that would have hurt like shit.

But there's a deeper part of me that wants to fight her for real. To toss her around and take what I want. And I shove that way the fuck down. I tower over her. I might lose control in a fight, and I've worked hard for twenty years to develop perfect control at all times.

"Whatcha gonna do now, Hot Sauce?" I question with a chuckle. "Seems to me like you're well and truly fucked."

She mutters under her breath as I tip her chin up.

"What was that?" I question, trying not to laugh at her.

"I said you're right," she agrees finally. "Put me down, Titan."

I pin her harder to the truck. She's so pretty caught like this. Fisting one hand through her blond waves, I tug her head back and bring my nose to her neck. I just need one hit, one quick breath of that sugary sweetness. And then I'll put her down and not look back.

I breathe in over a throbbing pulse at the base of her throat, Luna freezing in my arms.

"What are you doing?" she hisses, but she stops pushing against me.

Reality crashes in on me. I've got a much smaller omega

pinned to the goddamn truck with my hips, her hair wrapped around my hand while I smell her like an animal.

And this is precisely why she's not right for me, no matter what Asher suggested. Because she pushes me out of my comfort zone, and I could hurt her so fucking easily.

Stepping back, I lower Luna to the ground, not missing the way her aura bursts with triumphant shades of purple and gold.

"I'm sorry," I tell her, running my hands through my hair. "I took that too far."

"I'm sorry too," she whispers. "Kicking somebody in the nuts sucks. I just wanted to see if I could follow your instructions in the moment."

I sigh, glancing up the trail toward the hot springs. "Let's start over, Luna. Okay? For the good of everyone and our joint sanity."

"I'll keep the nut kicking to the classroom," she agrees, grinning at me. Then she turns to go, and God help me, I stare at that sweet peach of her ass as she hikes up the rocky trail toward the open meadow.

luna

I DON'T KNOW what got into me, testing Titan like that. All night I thought about our sessions and wondered how he was feeling about them.

He grabs a toolbox and some wood, stalking quietly behind me as we hike to Sal and the twins in the meadow. Selfishly I'm planning to head right to the hot springs to see Cassian, because if anyone knows whether or not our food-drop plan will work, it'll be him.

When I crest the hill at the top of the trail, the gorgeous meadow opens in front of us. There's a faint dusting of snow up here, and it almost smells like snow in the air still.

"We'll get a storm in a few days," Titan muses as he stops next to me, setting everything down.

Looking up, I frown. "That an alpha thing too?"

"No," he laughs, "I've got an old injury that acts up before it rains or snows. My foot hurts, so it's going to snow." He shrugs and heads down into the meadow as I jog to catch up.

A minute later we're at the hot spring. The twins are already in the water, dunking Sal and acting like kids. It warms my heart to see. My skin pebbles when I sense the intense gaze of an alpha male. Turning toward the far left-hand side of the large hot spring, I find Cassian sitting along the edge. Stormcloud eyes are focused on Titan and me, his huge arms spread along the bank.

Poor guy is just up here relaxing, and I'm about to grill him within an inch of his life.

"Spit it out, omega," he says in that low-pitched baritone so common with alphas.

I'm not even surprised he can tell I want to talk to him. All alphas are intuitive, but pack alphas more so than any. Stone has already told me Cassian could easily have his own pack, so it makes sense that he's reading me in the same easy way Stone does.

I shuck my coat off and reach for my shirt just as Titan's big hand clamps down on my wrist. "What are you doing Hot Sa–Luna?" When I turn to face him, he looks concerned as fuck.

"Getting naked to go in the hot spring? Isn't that the thing you do around here?"

"Shit, yeah, we do but..." Titan looks over at Cassian, who's now smirking, and then back at me. His dark brows form a dramatic vee over those shocking eyes. "But usually there are a ton of us. This'll just be you and Cassian, naked and in close proximity. It's too much."

"I'll show you too much." I laugh, waggling my brows.

Titan growls, "We just agreed to start over, Luna. For fuck's sake." He looks away as I take a step back and smile, pulling his attention to me.

"I'm gonna enjoy this hot ass water for like twenty minutes, and then I'll come help you with the box, okay? I just want to talk to him. I promise to be quick."

"This whole thing was your damn plan," he grumbles, but he turns from me to get started.

"Come in, Luna!" shrieks Sal from the middle of the pool.

Shrugging, I strip my shirt and bra off and chuck them at Titan's head. He catches the delicate lace and sexy flannel and snarls at me, fangs fully descended.

"Oh, come on." I laugh, sliding my jeans down next. "It's not like I threw these at you." Stepping out of my panties, I swing them around my finger before aiming them at him, closing one eye as I prepare to fire them straight at his face.

"Don't you fucking dare," he yells, both fists balled as I prepare to let the panties go. But then I remember we just said we'd start over, and I'm already taunting him. Hard to get around my natural personality, I suppose. I drop the panties to the ground and stand naked in front of him instead. "As you wish."

Titan makes a good show of not staring at my naked form, but his chest heaves as he maintains steady, delicious eye contact. Grinning, I turn from him, knowing he'll watch me go.

I step into the hot spring and stride across the large pool to sit close to Cassian. Cassian's gray eyes follow movement behind me, which I'm sure is Titan grabbing his stuff to start building the box we've envisioned for the food drop-off.

"How's it going, Cass?" I keep it friendly at first, even though the enormous alpha is intimidating.

With a sly smirk, he turns toward me in the pool. "I'm just fine, Luna. How can I help you?"

Gesturing to his side, I grimace. "How's your injury? I know Brady from Mitchell's pack has been by to heal it a few times. It looked so fucking awful at first."

Cassian's gaze goes cloudy as he remembers the fight where he nearly killed Declan, but had to make the choice between doing that or saving Rogue's life. He picked Rogue, and he's been stuck at our lodge ever since. Not that he's there very much.

"It's healing slower than I'd like, but my guts were spilling out, so I guess it takes time."

I nod. "I haven't seen Brady at the lodge, though. Are you spending time at their new compound?"

Cassian looks suddenly wary, as if my next question is a lure right into some kind of verbal trap.

"Can I ask you a nosy question?" I'm so fucking curious about a few things regarding the big alpha.

"I get the sense you're going to no matter what I say." Cassian chuckles. "Am I right?"

My cheeks go pink as I laugh along with him. "Touché. I'm curious why you don't spend much time with us, even though Stone is alright with it."

Cassian sucks in a breath and lets it out as a big sigh, glancing over at the kids in the pool behind me. "Stone says it's alright, but we're both strong alphas, pack alphas. Me being around will get in the way. He's building his pack. Shit, he's got teenagers all of a sudden. I'm not...I'd just get in the way. Two alphas in a pack doesn't work well. Trust me, I am painfully aware of that fact."

"What about Julia?" I probe.

Cassian's gray eyes narrow as he cocks his head to the side. "What *about* Julia?"

"She's..." Shit, now that I opened my big mouth, I'm not even sure what to say. I'm not the pack matchmaker.

"She's *mated*. *Happily* mated," he presses in a bitter, frustrated tone.

"Healers and spirits mate in a throuple," I point out. "How do you feel about James?" I don't know why the hell I just got so forward and personal, but there's something about Cassian I want to unravel and figure out.

"I don't know him well," Cass hedges. "But they seem happy."

"That's not really an answer." I laugh as I play with the

water, letting it drip between my fingertips. "That's not why I came in here, though." Glancing to the side of the pool, I see Titan setting up two sawhorses and getting right to work.

Cassian follows my gaze. "What are you up here for? What's he building?"

"That's what I wanted to talk to you about," I press on, meeting Cassian's steely gaze. "Sal told us Declan doesn't always provide enough food for his omegas. She asked if there was any way we could help them without Declan knowing."

Cassian's chest rumbles with the vibrations of a growl as he looks over at Sal. "It's true," he shares. "I helped as much as I could when I was still there. That's one of many reasons Declan and I were on the outs before that final fight."

"We had the idea of creating a drop box out here, since the omegas use the hot spring sometimes. We thought if we could leave food here from the general store, they might be able to pick it up. Thoughts?"

Cassian watches Titan for a moment, the sounds of a handsaw blaring across the pool. "I want to help," he pronounces. "This isn't foolproof, but most of Declan's leadership crew stays close to the neighborhood and Ray's bike shop. They don't come out here as much. I used to bring the omegas out here, and Declan thought I was being soft on them. But I convinced him it was good for them to get away sometimes."

Fine lines between his dark brows grow pronounced as his look morphs into a scowl. "What a fucking asshole. Yes. There's a solid chance this plan can work, and I want to help. Right now."

Cassian is a natural leader; I can sense it in the way he maintains incredible eye contact, and the way he's such an active listener. Everything about him is utterly commanding, from the relaxed set of his strong shoulders to the way he's completely and totally focused on me and this project.

When I look over at Titan, he's standing at the edge of the pool. I assume he heard the majority of that conversation, because he's grinning at Cassian. "Ready to get off your ass and help me, brother?"

The big alpha nods and glances at me before looking back up at Titan. "Hell yes. Anything we can do for those girls, I want in."

The tension between us has a somber, solemn edge to it. And when I look up at Titan, he's gazing at me with something like honest-to-God fondness in his eyes. It's new and different. And it makes my fucking nipples hard because he's not scowling.

No, no, no, I mentally chide myself. *We are not attracted to him.* I mean he's hot, but everything else is wrong.

Next to me, Cassian cocks his head to the side and inhales before winking at me. "Seems like you might have a secret or two yourself, Luna."

"Not hardly," I snigger back as I splash water in his direction. Anything to take that alpha focus off my body's reaction to a polite version of Titan.

It takes us the better part of four hours, but between the three alphas and Sal, River and myself, we get the box built. It's hidden right between a bunch of downed trees, barely visible to the naked eye. Titan included a latch so bears can't get into it, although he swears they won't be around until spring anyhow.

Shit, I hope we've figured out a way to rescue the omegas from Declan by then, but at least this is something in the meantime.

titan

SINCE CASS AGREED to come to dinner, I head directly to the lodge and drop everyone off. Returning to my cabin, I shower quickly and then go back up to the lodge. It's Stone's night to cook, which means Clay will be doing it instead. Stone is the fucking worst in the kitchen, the absolute worst.

When I get to the lodge, I'm surprised to find Julia and Cassian having a heated conversation on the front steps. She's in his face, signing ferociously as her pale eyes focus on him.

Since I took the enforcer job, that second sense of knowing when I should get involved has ramped up. And it's telling me to get involved now.

"Hey, you two," I purr, careful not to bark too hard at the powerful alpha with my pack's most delicate omega within claw's reach. Not that I think he'd ever hurt her.

Cass whips around and takes two steps away from Julia as she turns to me and scowls. "Tell Cass we need him to stick around," she demands.

"He's a grown man, honey; he can decide for himself if he wants to stick around." It's a gentle reminder that, while we took Cass in and helped to heal him, he's not part of our pack. Not technically.

She sighs at me before turning back to him. "Please. Please stay, for me. I want you to; I need you here."

Cass responds, although he screws up a couple of words. She and I still get the gist. "You and James, you're together. Please don't ask me to stay."

Julia shakes her head, running one hand through her strawberry blond hair before she looks back up at him. Cassian's pale eyes are locked onto her, a look of pure longing on his face.

"We're safer with you here," she presses him. "I'm safer with you here. Tell me you'll consider it, at least."

Cassian runs both hands through his manicured hair. "You're goddamn persistent."

I've always been surprised that he was the only alpha from Declan's pack to learn ASL after Julia's accident, but it endeared him to me because he fucking tried.

"I am," Julia confirms. When they seem at an impasse, she gives him a disappointed look and turns to head into the house. He watches her go before looking at me, schooling his features back to neutral.

"I can't stay here and cause trouble," he mutters. "This is the fifth time she's cornered me like this. I don't know how much more I can take."

Cassian's aura is a sickly green, confirming what he's sharing with me. But I'm curious.

"Is she coming on to you? Or just asking you to stick around..." Julia and James seem really fucking happy, and I can't imagine she'd put their bond in jeopardy.

"She's just...there's a lot of attraction there," he admits. "I want her, God help me. But I'm a pack alpha, and she's already mated. There's no room for two of us in her life."

Smiling, I clap him hard on the shoulder and gesture for him to follow Julia into the lodge. "Cassian, why haven't you ever left Declan, or us, for that matter, to start your own pack?"

Steel gray eyes flick to mine, his aura turning an angry gunmetal gray. "Three packs in this valley are plenty."

"You're lying." I laugh. "Your aura's all fucked up and angry. How about sharing the truth?"

"You sound far too much like the pack alpha right now," he grumbles, sailing through the door when I hold it open with a smile. "Maybe it's from your nights bartending and giving drunks advice?"

I laugh, because that's exactly what it is. I've given advice on nearly every topic one can imagine over the years.

Cassian's eyes crinkle in the corners as he hisses out an unhappy breath. "I could have started a pack many times. There are guys in Declan's who'd leave if they had an alpha to stand with. But I stayed there for the omegas. And I stay here because the thought of leaving makes me fucking sick."

"Because of Julia?" I confirm.

Cassian looks over at me. "You ever heard of a pack alpha mating a healer or spirit in any other pack?"

I shake my head to confirm that I've not heard that, and the look on Cass's is unsurprised.

"Right. If I thought that was a thing, I'd knock their door down right now. But serving a pack in a role I wasn't meant for hasn't worked out well in the past. If I thought it could, I'd explore what she wants."

"How do you know it's just her who wants it?" I question. It's something I've been curious about. I'm sure I'm not the only one who notices the way James's eyes follow Cass when we're all together.

Cass licks his lips, pale eyes locking onto mine again. "You're suggesting James and I…"

"Not suggesting anything, friend," I confirm. "I just mean maybe Julia isn't the only one who wants you to stay here."

Cassian nods thoughtfully as we arrive in the dining hall. The room goes quiet, but Stone stands up to welcome Cass to dinner. They shake hands, but I read my alpha well, and Stone is genuine when he tells Cass he's glad he stayed.

Glancing over at Julia, I watch James peck her shoulder with a knowing look before he looks up at Cassian. While his desire isn't as blatantly obvious as Jules', his dark eyes are intensely focused on the big alpha.

Cassian sits at the far end of the table with the twins, Luna and Sal. Dinner's loud and intense, but it's fucking funny watching the twins and Sal pick on each other back and forth. Luna meshes seamlessly with the pack. It's so fucking easy for her, being the center of attention, being loved by everybody. She's more at home here than I am, and I've known some of these people for decades.

Another food fight nearly starts until Cass commands River to put down her plate, before looking at Stone apologetically.

My pack alpha simply smiles and raises his glass in a mock salute. "Welcome to teenage parenting, brother."

THE NEXT MORNING, I'm scheduled to accompany James and Julia out to the research trailer to meet Bianca. They've agreed to be our first guinea pigs, and it makes me nervous. But I'm also proud they were willing to bite the bullet. I'm surprised when Cassian walks up the road from the lodge with them, James correcting some of his signs with an encouraging look.

Julia beams from her place between them, giving me a surreptitious wink as I struggle to hold back a laugh. She may be our pack's sweetest omega, but she's got a backbone of steel. Julia gets what she wants, and she loves our pack so damn hard.

"You got wrangled into joining us, huh?" I question, reaching out to shake Cass's hand once the trio joins me. He nods, and I hold back a laugh as his expression morphs from intent on Julia to carefully guarded. He distances himself a little when the trailer door opens and Bianca steps out with a big smile on her face.

"Hey, Titan! It's good to see you again. I'm looking forward to meeting your people today." She beams at me, her eyes traveling down to my mouth.

Luna's fucking right. This woman is attracted to me. I can't do that, not as our pack's official liaison. Dating me isn't going out for cheese fries on a Friday night at the bar or hitting up a movie at the theater. Dating me means submitting in my bedroom, and it takes a certain type of personality to be into that.

My brain flashes helpfully to Luna gagged and bound in my bed. I clear my throat as James, Julia and Cassian come up behind me. Julia's the first to reach her hand out and shake Bianca's vigorously.

James goes next. "Hey, I'm James, and this is my mate, Julia. She's deaf, but I will happily translate for her and vice versa."

Bianca looks at the group. "That's so great, James; thank you both for being the first to agree to come out here." Turning back to Julia, she smiles and speaks aloud, "I know a couple words in American Sign Language, but I'll do my best to pick it up fast so I can make this process as easy as possible for you."

I don't miss the way Cassian shifts so he's slightly closer to Julia, or the way her lashes flutter when his forearm touches hers. He looks over at the researcher. "I'm Cassian; I'm not technically part of this pack, but I'm staying here for a little while. I'd like to be part of today's session to gain an understanding of how you plan to use your research to help packs."

Bianca agrees. "Sure, and it's nice to meet you too. But I do want to clarify one point. The Alpha Research Group was formed to find the truth about packs, not simply to help packs. I can't promise you what's going to come of our research. We're not just here to learn the amazing things about packs, we're here to learn what possible threat they represent too."

Cassian's fangs descend as he takes a step in front of Julia and James. "Threat? Are you telling me there's a chance, depending on your research, things could get worse for our nonexistent rights?"

Bianca straightens her shoulders and grits her teeth. "I don't truthfully know the answer to that, alpha, and I'm sorry I don't. My sister is a female alpha. I'd love nothing more than to make sure you all have rights and my sister can remain home without worry. But we have to understand packs to decide that. One of the ideas the government has thrown around is creating sanctuaries states specific to alphas and omegas. There are a lot of ways this can go, but it can't go anywhere at all without us understanding more about you."

"Governments have tried segregating people like that in the past," Cassian retorts. "It's never worked out well."

Bianca blanches. "I get it; I really do. So please help me understand all the amazing things I can share with the government so we can help them make an informed decision, okay?"

Cassian snarls again, glowering at me, but his scowl falls when Julia puts her tiny hand on his forearm, rubbing it before signing to him, "We should do this, alpha. You are amazing. This pack is amazing. Mitchell's pack is amazing.

We have a responsibility to show the world the good side of what we are. I'm proud to be here doing this."

James rubs her back, his dark eyes on Cassian. I watch the exchange as Cassian looks between the two of them. James translates what Julia just shared as Bianca claps her hands together.

"That's awesome, Julia, thank you. And if you ever change your mind about sharing, you're under no obligation to; I want to remind you of that."

She gestures us into the research trailer, and I nod when Bianca introduces us to the other two members of her team. Sam, the tall lanky anthropologist is a surly fuck, but Zee, the physician, is friendly and kind when she says hello to everyone.

For the next half hour, Zee takes measurements from both James and Julia while Bianca walks me through their process. They'll take measurements several times over the course of their research, and they're looking for differences between alphas and omegas and regular non-transitioned humans. Apparently that's the formal term now. Those who contracted the Awaken virus are Transitioned humans. Non-transitioned are everyone else.

Zee hunches over her workstation after she's gotten her data, and we move on to Sam.

Julia sits herself down with a bright look at Sam, who doesn't return it. James and Cassian hover just next to her as I lean back against the work station with Bianca to watch.

Sam looks up from his computer with a frown. "Please tell me a little bit about your medical history."

James translates for Julia as she looks at Sam again. She answers in a flurry. "There's not much to report as far as medical history. I was always a healthy child and a healthy adult, even once the Awaken virus made an appearance."

Sam scoffs. "Healthy except for your hearing, you mean."

It's not a question; it's a rude-ass statement. James, Cassian and I all growl but Julia smiles even bigger, signing again and gesturing for James to translate.

His voice is tight and angry. "Jules says lack of hearing isn't a disability; it's simply a different way of being. She was born hearing, but lost it in an accident two and a half years ago when a truck hit her while she was riding her bike."

Sam blanches, and Bianca is tense next to me, but she allows the interaction to continue.

Next to Julia, Cassian is stiff as a board watching everything. It's clear he hates that Julia and James even have to explain this. He shoots me an angry look. "I'm in the way here; I'm going to go. You've got this handled, right?"

I agree as James turns to look at the older alpha questioningly. "You're going? You don't want to stay for this?"

"I really don't," Cass snaps, turning and stalking out the door.

Julia's face is carefully neutral as she turns to Sam and gestures for him to continue.

Julia and James give up two hours of their time in the research trailer, answering dozens of questions about their life and health before the virus and since, how they found one another, what it means to be mated, what they'd like people to know about alpha packs.

Julia's demeanor only changes when Sam asks about the type of threat alphas could present to regular humans.

"Anyone is dangerous with a gun," she signs. "Anyone is dangerous with negative intent. Alphas are the same. Humanity is already its own greatest threat."

Sam groans and rolls his eyes, but she shrugs and winks at me.

It's clear her answer frustrates the research team, but they don't press her.

Once James and Julia leave, I turn to Bianca. "I need to be

here for every one of these interviews until I'm more comfortable with your team. Is that understood?"

She agrees, but I sense uncertainty from her team at my command. Sam looks up at me, so I speak frankly.

"I'm not comfortable with the insensitive way you addressed Julia. Please keep future commentary like that to yourself. We're willing to partner with you, but only as long as this is mutually beneficial."

"Of course," Bianca agrees, giving Sam a shitty look as he purses his lips but agrees.

We may not have asked for the researchers to come here, but I won't let my pack suffer at their hands.

CHAPTER TWELVE

luna

I SPEND all morning out at the Omegamatic, compiling a list of questions I have about certain parts of the design. It's impeccably designed, and the alphas all rave about how well it works. It's pretty loud, though. I've got a few ideas for how to tone that down in the final products: one alpha-sized and one for regular dudes.

Titan is with James, Julia and the researchers all morning, so I hold off bugging him until lunchtime. Finally, though, I can't make any more progress without his help.

Picking up my walkie, I ping his channel. "Titan, are you around to chat through some Omegamatic details with me?" I purposefully keep my tone pleasant and polite since we've "started over."

"Be there in five," he responds, clicking off before I can say anything.

So much for the pleasantries. I shove down frustration, because I don't know how his morning went. Maybe it was awful with the research team.

A few minutes later, I hear an ATV coming up the path from the main house. The rumble of its engine sends butterflies rocketing around my chest. That never happened until Titan got in my space twice in the gym and then again at the hot spring. He was so big and warm and intense. I was so certain he was going to kiss me, bite me, or something very alpha.

He didn't, but I'd be a damned liar if I said I hadn't thought about that moment since. We haven't scheduled another lesson, and I haven't asked, either.

I head for the door, computer in hand as Titan comes around the corner on the ATV and parks out front. He swings one big thigh over the seat, and God help me, I stare at his ass the whole time. He's just fucking huge. Big and thick and stacked, and then those intense blue eyes find mine with an almost disapproving glare.

"You okay?" I'm dying to ask what's got his knot in a twist, but this is me, being nice.

"Had better mornings," he grunts, and that's all. Titan looks behind me through the open door where the Omegamatic is currently on, the loud suction noises of the fake pussy sounding absolutely obscene.

That's awkward. Turning, I hustle to the machine and cut it off, and when I turn back around, Titan is leaning in the doorway, watching me. The weight of his stare is so heavy, my nipples pebble. I clench my thighs together because he's so fucking handsome, albeit grumpy.

"You needed something?" His voice sends hot shards through my core. I resist the urge to make a joke about all women having *needs*. That's not the kind of joke I can make with him, no matter how attractive he is.

Titan cocks his head to the side, sucks in a ragged breath and grits his jaw. "I want a drink. Come on." Without waiting for me, he leaves the cabin the Omegamatic is housed in and gets back on his ATV.

I shove my computer back in my bag. A drink does sound

pretty nice. It's five o'clock somewhere, they say. Pulling the door to the tiny cabin shut, I give him a skeptical look. "You want me to ride with you?"

"You'd rather walk?" he questions, giving me a tense smile.

Throwing my leg over the seat, I squish my laptop bag between us so it doesn't bounce off. Titan throws the ATV into gear, and I have to fling my arms around his thick waist when we take off. His abs are obvious even through the rough fabric of his flannel shirt. My fingers want to explore all the dips and valleys between them. He's so damn big.

But then he rockets the ATV back up the path, bouncing me around like a coffee bean in a grinder.

Oh he's mad. He's mad as hell about something; that much is clear. My only saving grace is that I haven't been around him all day, so it's probably not me.

I cling to Titan like a spider monkey until he stops in front of his cabin and climbs off before I do. He seems to think better of our entire interaction because he reaches out a hand to help me off, although I debate taking it.

I swore to start over and be pleasant, but my ability to hold my tongue is about to snap. Instead of taking his hand, I hand him my computer bag and hop off the back of the ATV, stepping past him and letting myself in the front door of his cabin.

I've never been inside, and I'm honestly curious. Knowing how much he loves woodworking, I half expect his entire cabin to be coated in fine dust. It's not, although there are tools all over the place in the main area, and a couple half-finished projects in the living room.

Titan comes in behind me, setting my bag gently on the kitchen counter. He moves purposefully, grabbing two glasses and pouring whiskey in them. Shoving one across the island toward me, he leans up against it and blows out a breath.

"I can't possibly have pissed you off yet today," I tease

lightly, trying to dissipate the tension. "Is everything okay with the researchers?"

Titan looks at me, leaning over the counter to rest his elbows on it, the crystal glass still in his hands. Like this, he's at eye level with me. I seat myself on one of his bar stools, maintaining eye contact as he watches me.

"Sam, the anthropologist, was fucking rude about Julia's hearing."

"The fuck?" I bark. "What did that asshole say?" I cross my arms and scowl as Titan takes a sip of his whiskey.

"Something to the effect of 'healthy except for your hearing,'" Titan murmurs, pale eyes still on mine.

"You must be shitting me," I blurt in anger at the researcher's callous words.

Titan shakes his head. "Then it turns out they're here to find out the truth about packs, not necessarily to help." I can't help the noise that comes out of me then, and Titan nods, reaching for the Jack to pour us another drink. "Apparently the government is considering creating alpha states where we can all go live happily ever after if we're deemed too dangerous for normal society."

"You're not dangerous," I counter. "I mean you could be, obviously. You've gotta weigh three hundred pounds. But you don't choose to be."

One side of Titan's mouth curls up. "Anybody ever tell you you talk a lot, Luna?"

I grin, the whiskey warming my belly and chest as I lean over the bar toward him. Giving him a devious look, I swirl the Jack in my glass. "Best way to shut me up is to put something in my mouth."

The second the words are out, his nostrils flare, eyes dropping to my lips. And then I realize what I fucking said. I have zero goddamn filters sober, and the whiskey is loosening my lips.

"Is that right?" he questions, a rumble echoing out of his chest as he leans across the island, close enough our hands nearly touch.

If I had to catalog one moment in our relationship where I knew I was well and truly fucked, it's this one. Because looking at his soft lips, listening to that rumbly vibration, it's giving me ideas. Ideas like leaping across this island and taking that pouty mouth.

"Luna," he growls, using my real name, which he does so rarely. The purr increases in intensity as I clamp my legs together and let out a little whine.

But that noise seems to snap him out of the delicious reverie he's in, and his purr stops quickly. He shifts away from me, pouring another glass of Jack before passing the bottle to me.

"You had questions about the Omegamatic?"

Clearing my throat, I grab my bag and pull out my notebook. "I've completed the external designs, but obviously I don't wanna take it apart since, errr, dudes are probably still using it."

A pink blush spreads above Titan's five o'clock shadow, but he tilts his head in agreement.

"I've got questions about the mechanics inside. I can't finalize interior designs, and I need to in order to have legal finalize the patent paperwork."

"Hit me," Titan nods. For half an hour he answers every question in extreme detail. I'm in awe of his brilliance. When I share my ideas for making it quieter, he laughs.

"I wasn't going for quiet when I built it, Hot Sauce."

My own cheeks heat at the saucy look he's giving me. "Going for realistic sex noises then, huh?" I deadpan as he laughs again. And his laugh is so beautiful. It's deep and hearty and joyous, and I rest my chin in my hand listening to it.

"What are you doing?" he questions, giving me a pointed look.

"Admiring your nice laugh," I admit.

He grins again. "What else, Hot Sauce? You all done with the questions?"

"Oh, I've got a nosy personal one."

"'Course you do."

Titan's always been so quiet, I assumed he never dated much. Our own interactions have been awkward at best. But the look on his face now, focused and intense, and the way he's leaning back over the bar with both big arms on top of it? His demeanor tells another story, and I'm fucking fascinated. I want to know everything.

"How many women have you dated?"

CHAPTER THIRTEEN

titan

THAT'S A LOADED FUCKING QUESTION. The answer is technically zero. I don't date.

"What are you really asking me, Luna?" I question her, leaning farther over the bar as her pupils begin to overtake the blue of her iris.

"I—" she starts, the words falling off as her eyes drop to my mouth.

And I'm screwed, because watching her get off-kilter and go quiet makes me hard. I want to drag her on top of this bar and kiss her. I want to see that rosy red aura burst with passionate purples and fiery maroons. I want to know what color she radiates when she shatters on my knot.

"I've dated zero women," I answer as she gasps and looks up.

"You've never dated? Then how—"

"I said I never dated, Luna, not that I'm celibate."

"Oh Christ," she mutters. "So you're a big ole manwhore. You've fucked every available woman in Ayas. Is that what you're saying?"

I laugh at that. I could hardly be described as such, but it's humorous that's the first place her mind goes.

"Not really."

Her brows pull together into a vee. I know I'm being vague, but watching her get flustered is so fucking fun. Especially considering the multiple times I've been caught off guard by her since we met. It's usually her flustering *me*, and having the upper hand feels fucking good.

Leaning farther over the bar, I grip her chin and force her gaze up to mine, close enough that my lips hover just inches from hers. I let my gaze wander to those plump lips, sighing. Just looking at her is a pleasure.

"Wh—what are you doing?" she whispers, even though she leans in closer, her mouth nearly touching mine.

"Would it make you jealous if I said I *had* fucked every available woman in Ayas?"

Luna sputters indignantly, but I grip her chin harder, bringing my mouth closer. The tip of my nose touches hers, and her lips part. She's waiting to be kissed, her aura swirling with bright splashes of color. It's goddamn beautiful, so beautiful, I'm rubbing my dick against the counter for some friction.

"Answer me," I command.

"No," she lies immediately, shards of black streaking through the colors that surround her. If I wasn't already losing my cool about this girl, I am now. Because watching her lie about feeling jealous makes me all kinds of possessive.

"Lies. I can see them," I share as she shudders, the command in my voice telling her body to submit to me.

"See them?"

"Yes." I bring my lips to brush against hers as she gasps. "As the pack's enforcer, I see everyone's aura. It changes based on their emotions. When you lie, yours is black."

Luna rips her chin out of my hand and sits back on top of the barstool, chest heaving.

"Bullshit," she declares. "Nobody's ever said anything about that."

I stand upright and shrug. "There probably wasn't a reason to. Yours is an angry red now. Why?"

She sputters again. "You've been able to do this since we met?"

"Since I transitioned," I correct.

"Fuck me," she hisses, sliding off the barstool. Clearly what I shared makes her wildly uncomfortable. She straightens the hem of her shirt and looks up at me, building walls up fast in the carefully wary way she looks at me.

"I've got everything I need for the plans. Thanks. I'll finalize the drawings and have legal do the paperwork. Then we can talk through what's next."

"Luna."

"What."

"It's no different than Stone sensing emotion."

"It is," she hisses. "Because you can literally read me like a damn book. It's highly disconcerting. I've gotta go."

Sighing, I round the island and open the front door for her. She passes through it quickly, giving me a wide berth before thanking me once more. I stand in my doorway and watch as she walks quickly up the road toward the main house.

Angsty green, uncomfortable yellow. Those are the colors that surround her as she leaves me.

Damnit.

luna

THREE DAYS. It's been three days since I've seen Titan. I know he's been at the lodge, because Cherry and Julia mentioned seeing him at breakfast yesterday. Cherry and Asher spent time with the research team, and he was around for that.

He's giving me space. That much is clear. Not surprising after he dropped that bomb on me and I freaked out.

Reading auras? I questioned Erin to death after he told me. Somehow the topic of him reading people that way just "never came up." The idea that he's able to see my emotions this entire time? It's unwelcome.

Even though the aura thing made me feel incredibly spied on, not seeing Titan is depressing. I try not to examine why that might be too closely. I'm going home once the Omega-matic project is done, and I've made great progress on it. There are only a few steps left for me to do.

But tonight is the Valentine ball at Mitchell's, and I want to know if Titan's going. I know Stone invited the researchers, but they declined. So now I'm stuck not being sure if Titan will come or not. Despite everything going on in our world, we're still going to the dance.

Declan and Gabriel haven't made any appearances at the bar or anywhere else. Titan was able to mention our plan to one of the omegas at the bar a couple days ago. The food we dropped off to the high meadow got picked up, so we're helping at least a little bit.

A knock rings out through my room, interrupting my rousing rendition of "Man, I Feel Like A Woman." I holler at whoever's at my door, "I'm curling my hair, come on in!"

When the door swings open, Julia and James come in, and she looks fucking gorgeous. James winks at me and then takes Jules' hand, spinning her around so I can see the front and back of her gorgeous pale pink gown. Thin straps accentuate her delicate figure, the fabric hugging her thin chest and gripping her hips where they flare out. It suits her complexion so perfectly, and she beams from ear to ear as she does a little dance and then grabs James's big thigh, pretending to hump him.

"Get it, girl" He laughs as he signs. She stands upright, giggling when she looks over and I'm still in just my bra and panties.

I snort at James with both hands still on my hair and curling iron. "Please remind Julia I have zero fucks to give."

He relays my comment as she smacks my ass and flops herself down into my fireside chair. James grips her waist and hauls her bodily up out of the chair. It's a powerful but gentle move as he sits and pulls her onto his lap, her bare back to his chest.

"Better," he signs as she runs her hands up his strong forearms.

I'm dying to ask if Cassian is coming, but he's been MIA the last few days except for the one time we went to refill the food drop.

Julia and James keep me company as I fix my updo and step into the slinky hot pink silk dress Betty ordered for me. Julia hops out of James's lap to zip up the back of it, and then I hoist my tits up high in the front. I do a sexy spin as Julia pretends to fan her face and wink suggestively at me.

"I love you," I sign at her, hauling her in for a hug. Julia is so damn easy to fall for. Ferociously kind, endlessly thoughtful. She's amazing, and I'm thrilled Erin has someone like this in her pack.

"You two are so damn beautiful," James offers, smiling at me and then his mate. "Luna, I'd be honored if you'd attend this evening alongside Julia and me?" When he smiles, beautiful white teeth show from his perfect lips. I'm certain he's about to add something snarky to his sweet request, but he holds out a hand to both of us.

Julia spins into his arms immediately, but I cross my arms and give them a faux scowl. "What about Cassian? He's not going with you tonight?"

Julia rolls her eyes and signs so fast I can't hope to get any of what she says.

James's grin broadens. "Jules did her best to convince him, but he says it's best if he sits this one out. Still, we're going to head to his room and let him get a peek at the dress before we give up."

"Okay, okay." I laugh, throwing my hands up in the air. "Please tell me what's going on between the three of you, because I'm nosy as shit and dying to know. Dyingggg!"

James laughs. "Nothing's going on, Luna. *Yet*," he finishes with a dark look at Julia, who beams from ear to ear and throws herself up into his big arms for a scorching kiss.

A minute later, they leave me to go tease Cassian. I head downstairs to Stone and Erin's room. After knocking on the door, I stride right in and regret it immediately. Stone sits on the edge of the bed with Erin's foot pressed to the center of his chest. She beams at me as I enter, but Stone doesn't bother to look up. He kisses her instep tenderly, sliding a beautiful black heel on her foot, fastening the strap without taking his eyes from her.

I should leave, I know I should, but they're so damn beautiful together. In step, in tune, totally perfect. With a sudden ferocity that surprises the shit out of me, I realize how badly I want that. I want what they have.

And the first person I think of when I realize how badly I want it is the one person I shouldn't want it with. I hold back a remark as Stone grips Erin's ankle and sets it gently back onto the ground, kissing his way up her thigh before standing and pecking her on the lips. "You're stunning in this dress."

"You don't look so bad yourself, mate," she murmurs. She's right. He's dressed in an inky black tux, blond hair slicked back. He looks like he stepped right off the concert stage, complete with high-shine wingtip shoes.

"Get a load of Luna, though," Erin jokes with her mate. "She's going to give Titan a heart attack."

Stone laughs when he turns, holding one hand out for me. I place my tiny palm in his huge one as he gives me a spin with a wolf whistle. "You look fantastic, Hot Sauce. E's right. Titan's going to have a hard time not staring."

"Pfft," I bluster. "I didn't do this for him. But I am super excited for tonight."

"Okay." Stone agrees, struggling to keep the corners of his lips from turning into a huge smile. "If you say so. Let's go, ladies. I can't wait to see what kind of a party Bancroft puts on."

FORTY-FIVE MINUTES LATER, we pull up in front of a gorgeous mansion in the next valley over. I don't mean to look around for Titan's truck, but I do anyhow.

Asher's in the seat next to me, and he thunks my nose. "He's almost always late for stuff like this, Hot Sauce, but he'll show."

I roll my eyes as Cherry looks back from the front seat with a knowing grin. Guess I'm not as surreptitious as I'd like to believe.

All thoughts of Titan flee my brain when the front door opens and Mitchell Bancroft steps out with his mate, Alice, on his arm. His strategist, Griz, follows with his mate, Jude, the researcher who's doing so much amazing work related to the Awaken virus. Their pack was on the run from the American Task Force for years, and they've been at the forefront of efforts to show the world that alpha packs can be good.

I have so much admiration for them.

Alice wears a skintight navy silk dress that accentuates her tan skin, with a slit up to her hip on the side. Mitchell's navy tux matches her dress, and he's got the top three or four buttons undone. Griz and Jude wear matching black formalwear. God, they look beautiful.

It's easy to tell Mitchell and Alice are the leaders of this pack. There's a natural dominance that rolls off Mitchell as he pulls Alice close and reaches out to shake Stone's hand. Alice pulls Erin in for a hug, and then we're all hugging and oohing and aahing until it's time to go inside.

Some members of our pack have been here before, but I never have. Honestly, I can't wait to see the house. Erin already told me Mitchell built it as a backup location when they were running from the American Task Force. Calling it a house doesn't feel right; that word isn't grandiose enough. This place is a mansion of epic proportions.

Cherry and Julia each grab one of my arms as we skip

through the front doors to another round of hugs with Mitchell's pack, and then down a long hallway that opens to a beautiful library. Shelves soar up multiple levels, with walkways all the way around and sliding ladders. It's like something out of *Beauty and the Beast*, and it's so damn gorgeous, I tear up looking at it.

Lights are strung all along the ceiling, creating the appearance of the underside of a tent. Their gentle glow highlights every beautiful corner of this incredible room. Music plays softly as I make my way around the room, mingling with the members of Mitchell's pack I haven't met yet.

"Lot of unmated dudes here," Cherry whispers in my ear, bumping her hip with mine. "We might could get you hooked up with someone if you want."

I look over, sniggering. "How would that work, exactly? Poor human woman with a big old alpha male. I'm not built the way you two are."

Cherry points at Julia's delicate frame, signing as she does. "If Julia can handle James's big ole D, you can too. Plus, we all know you're an omega. I don't know why you won't admit it to yourself."

She brings up a good point—one I don't examine too deeply. Because being an omega means things, and I'm not ready for that.

"Hey, friend," I suggest instead. "Why don't we be the first on the dance floor, and we can drive your mate crazy by dry humping each other like chihuahuas?"

Cherry throws her head back and laughs, and it's so loud and beautiful as she translates my words for Julia, who slaps me on the arm and drags me toward the dance floor. Nobody's on it yet, but that doesn't stop us.

James comes to join us, tapping out a beat on Julia's back so she can easily sway along with it. Cherry and I dance together, not giving a fuck who's watching until a strange heat blooms in my chest so hot and fast, I suck in a breath and put my hand on my chest.

"What's wrong?" Cherry questions, going into nurse mode immediately.

"I just… My heart just dropped, maybe too much dancing before food," I hedge.

Cherry's eyes travel over my shoulder. "Could be that Titan just walked in, and he's watching you? Damn, girl, he looks really fucking good."

Oh God, oh God, what is my damn aura telling him? Does it look hot and achy? Angsty and unsure? I fucking hate knowing he can read me so much more easily than I thought.

I'm dying to whip around, but I don't, instead meeting her knowing gaze. "Walk me over to get a drink, okay?"

"I gotchu," Cherry whispers into my ear, slinging her arm around my waist as we laugh and head for a drink table set up in a corner. A handsome alpha hands me a glass of wine with a wink, and when I turn around, Titan is headed toward me.

Oh fuuuuck. If I thought he was fine in tight-ass jeans and a flannel long-sleeve, it has nothing on Titan in a suit. It's huge, because everything about him is huge, but it accentuates his enormous broad shoulders and trim waist. The pants are tight around his muscular thighs, tapering down to shiny black shoes in size ten million.

When I look back up, those ice-blue eyes are intent on me, and so easy to see without his dark waves falling over them. He starts to cross the room as Cherry skitters away from me, leaving me all the fuck alone, watching the big alpha come for me.

CHAPTER FIFTEEN

titan

I ALMOST DIDN'T COME TONIGHT. The bar was busy as hell, but my bar manager kicked me out the same way he's done multiple times in the last few weeks. He knows I've avoided Luna for the better part of three days. I shocked her with the aura info, so I've given her space since.

I usually hate events like this. There's too much socializing, too much talking. I'm always so conspicuous because I'm so big. But the good news about a pack party is that all the men here are comparable in size. I'm not as out of place as I would normally be.

But then I see Luna in a hot pink, curve-hugging dress. My body is drawn toward her, remembering the way she felt so close to my chest. Her gown, if you could call it that, is nothing more than two flimsy spaghetti straps and a cinched waist that highlights her enormous tits. A piece of fabric crosses her lower stomach and then flares out long to the ground. A slit up the side reveals firm, tan legs. The shoes she picked are a brilliant sapphire blue. They tie around her ankle, and, goddamn, I want to unlace them with my teeth.

Luna looks up from the drink table, eyes on me, her aura

twisting anxiously. I can't have it. Somewhere, somehow, I've gone from disliking her presence to craving it. Like now. Crossing the room to her, I smile.

"Hello, Hot Sauce." My voice is so damn low for her, my body thrilled when her nipples pebble under the tight satin.

Luna gives me a confident look and does a little spin. "What do you think, Titan? Like the dress?" There's a devious sparkle in her blue eyes as she looks up at me. Her aura fades to a hopeful blue.

"Looks good." I hold back the urge to stare down the front of the barely-there silk; I'm tall enough to do it. She's not wearing any perfume, but her natural scent wafts off her, all sunshine and salt and caramel. Luna smells like a trip to the beach, and that urge to bury my teeth in her neck and cover myself in that scent hits me hard.

Luna scowls up at me, slapping me on the chest with one tiny hand. "I'm waxed and plucked within an inch of my life. It took me two hours to get ready, and all I get is a 'looks good'?" She scoffs as she looks at the alpha bartender, who's clearly holding back a laugh but shakes his head instead. "Give me your best white please."

He pours Luna a glass of wine, and I don't miss the way he brushes his fingertips across hers when she takes the glass. Or the way his dark eyes rove her hungrily as he leans slightly forward over the table. Or the way his aura morphs to pitch-black need.

I shoot him a death glare so hard he staggers back and composes himself, straightening his tie and walking down to the other end of the table.

"What did you just do?" barks Luna. "To make him walk away like that? Some magic alpha shit? "

James comes up with a helpful clap on my back, Julia clinging to his arm. "Oh that? That's just a little alpha dominance, plus T's our enforcer, so that 'in charge' attitude hits the rest of us hard. Isn't that right, T?"

I don't know how to answer that; he's right. But what Luna's going to ask next is why I did it. I'm not ready to examine that closely. So instead, I tip my head to everyone, grab a beer from the drink table and look around the room for Mitchell. As the liaison with the researchers, I want to talk to him about how it's been going.

Glancing around the room, I count my pack, making sure we're all here. Sal even opted to come, which surprised the shit out of me since she hasn't come to dinner. But I suspect Rogue and River coerced her somehow. I get my answer when she shows up next to me the moment I find Mitchell to speak to him.

"Hey Titan, congratulations on your new role," Mitchell purrs, reaching out to shake my hand. The dominance of a pack alpha slaps me, so different from Stone's. Probably because this alpha isn't mine, so it rankles in a way Stone's power doesn't. Mitchell smiles, knowing it's like this for me, and looks over at Sal. "You must be Sal; Stone has told me all about you. I'm so sorry for everything you've gone through."

Sal straightens her back a little as River joins her and grips her hand. I know Sal's not unaffected by Mitchell's power, and the only alphas she's known are Declan and Stone. She's so goddamn brave to come here and stand in front of Bancroft like it's no big deal.

Riv and Sal share a look before River speaks up. "I'm sure Stone has shared with you the situation for Declan's omegas?"

Sal quivers slightly as River talks. Clearly they orchestrated this ahead of time.

Reaching out, I place my palm on Sal's upper back, willing it to soothe her. She sinks into that heat as River continues, "We came tonight hoping that, between you and Stone, we can find a plan to help the rest of the girls. We're doing food drops, but it's not enough. We've got to get them out."

Mitchell cocks his head to the side, looking at me and then back at the girls. "We can't just go over and take his omegas. You must know that."

Sal shakes her head. "We can't go over and kidnap them; that's true. There might be some girls who don't want to leave, but most do. What if we can figure out who wants to go, and set up a time to help just them."

Luna walks up then, seeing my hand on Sal's back. "Sal, honey. Is everything okay?"

Sal points at Mitchell. "We were talking with Mr. Bancroft about a plan to help the omegas who remain in Declan's pack."

Luna's blue eyes narrow as she looks at Mitchell. "I am definitely of the opinion that we need to get the girls out who want out. They might be ready, but too terrified of Declan to leave."

Clay walks up to our group then with a quick nod my direction. "I heard you talking about the omegas. Titan and I were just tossing around an idea last night. What if we used the bar as a sort of meeting point? And the omegas who are interested in leaving can let us know when they come in. Once we know everybody who wants to go, we'll figure out when and where to help them."

"It'll be a fight; you know that, I presume?" Mitchell's voice has gone full steel, and it's easy to understand how he runs a multi-billion dollar corporation.

Luna wraps her arm around Sal's waist, meaning it brushes along my hand as she looks Mitchell right in the eye. "We're here tonight to have a great time with you, and we're thankful for that, *so* thankful for your partnership and friendship. But there are easily a dozen or more girls who don't get to experience pack life like this simply because they landed in Declan's pack. Some of the girls are pregnant, Mitchell."

He blanches at her statement as he swirls a glass of whiskey. "I won't take omegas from a pack who don't want to go, but if we want to devise a plan to figure out the women who want to leave, I'll help with that." Looking over at me, he frowns. "Enforcer, there's a solid chance this will cause further issues with Declan's pack, which could affect the researchers. You and your alpha and strategist will have to weigh out how to handle that."

He's fucking right.

"Aww, we're not worried about that," Luna quips. "The head researcher has a huge crush on Titan, so he can just sweet talk his way right out of any mess we get ourselves in, I'm sure."

I grit my teeth as Mitchell laughs and raises a glass to me. "You might want to use that to your advantage, Titan. Hey, maybe she'll turn out to be your omega, and it'll all work out in the end."

Luna stiffens as he says that, clutching Sal more tightly to her. She said I could sweet talk my way out of a mess, but we both know Bianca's attraction to me bothers her.

"Think about it; let me know how I can help," Mitchell says before nodding at Sal and heading away from us.

The omegas head for the dance floor, and I spend the next half hour with Clay and Asher, catching up with the other pack and spending time with mine. Eventually we sit at a table, watching James, Julia, Cherry and Luna dancing together without a care in the world. Members of Mitchell's pack join in as the party really gets going, and it's not lost on me that Luna's now surrounded by a dozen single young alphas.

Watching Luna dance is like sipping the finest bourbon. It's smooth and then goes down, sending heat blooming through my chest. She's got incredible rhythm, and even manages to drag Sal onto the dance floor for a while. The twins join in, even though they were highly skeptical about even coming to this shindig. Luna manages to get Rogue moving, and he's clunky and awkward, much like I was as a teen.

Stone flops down into the chair next to mine, clapping me on the back. "Having fun, buddy? Or is this your personal nightmare?"

"Definitely prefer the bar," I mutter as I glance around. The room is nearly full now with Mitchell's pack of nearly thirty people and our much smaller one. "Lot of dudes," I grunt, scowling over at Stone.

Stone laughs but shifts in his seat, straightening his junk. I swear I hear a metal clink.

"What in the fu–" I blurt out.

He sighs. "Cock cage. Erin thought it would be hilarious to try it out here, knowing how hot I'll be for her in that goddamn dress. I can't get hard, or it hurts, and it's making me crazy imagining taking this thing off and ravaging her."

Well, that was a shitload more information than I needed.

Clay snorts from across the table, "When you undo that thing, your dick's gonna pop out like a snake from one of those practical joke cans."

I scrunch my eyes and nose up at that fucking visual, but none of us can help but laugh as Stone winces and adjusts himself again.

"Wonder how long I have to stay before I can rip this thing off." He's grumbling, but he's flushed and tense watching his mate. It's easy to see whatever shit they're into turns him on. I'm happy for him, because having sexual freedom and finding a partner who's into what you're into, that is perfection.

"Luna's sure getting a lot of attention," Clay murmurs, glancing over to the dance floor.

Sure as shit, the alpha bartender from before is behind her, one big arm around her trim waist as he grinds into her from behind. She holds onto his forearm and sways with the music, but parts from him when the next song comes on, dancing with River and then Rogue.

My pack leadership starts chatting again. I miss every fucking word because I can't stop watching the way that goddamn bartender follows Luna around the dance floor like a dog searching for a scrap of bone.

When he reaches out and grabs her hand, pulling her away from Sal, I shove my seat back and pull to a stand. Stone and Clay bark my name at the same time as I cross the room toward her.

The alpha's eyes meet mine just as Luna's do. His widen in fear as hers widen in relief. Her lips part slightly when I take her fingers from his hand and pull them onto my chest, inside my jacket. I shoot the kid a daggered look. "Get the fuck out of here." He scampers off without a backward glance as Luna gazes up at me with a relieved expression.

"Thanks, he was a little insistent. I guess I shouldn't be surprised when there are so many more alphas than omegas in this pack." Her fingertips trace tiny circles on my pec. I don't know that she's even aware she's doing it, but I keep one hand over hers above my heart. The other I slip around her waist and pull her tightly to me as I lean into her ear.

"Now that he sees you with me, he won't bother coming back. None of them will." My voice goes low-pitched as that vein in her neck throbs, goosebumps traveling down her delicate shoulders.

"So you're cock blocking me for the night. Gee, thanks?" She's poking fun at me, but she doesn't sound serious. I want to push her, though.

I press my lips harder to the curved shell of her ear. "Did you come here hoping to get fucked by an alpha, Luna?"

She mumbles under her breath as the hand on my chest

tightens into a fist. "I didn't come here for that; I'm just kidding."

"Do you know how easy it would be to take you with the slit up the side of this dress?" I growl it into her ear as I resist the urge to drag my lips down her neck. "It would be so simple to slide my hand underneath this fabric and touch you."

Blue eyes shine up at me, full of anger and frustration. "I can't do this with you, Titan. This back and forth. One minute you're ignoring me, then you're saving me on the dance floor and whispering dirty shit in my ear. Pick a fucking side, bro." She presses away from my chest and slips off the dance floor.

Bro. She called me bro.

Fuck. That.

Rage and dominance crash their way through my system, taking over my thoughts until it's all I can do not to rip my shirt open like a caveman and throw her over my shoulder. I don't *do* this. I don't lose control.

She's driving me to the fucking precipice of sanity, and I'm about to dive over and lose myself completely.

Stalking after her, I grip her hand in mine like a vise just as she reaches the table with the rest of our pack. I don't bother to look at anyone's faces as she squeaks. I turn from everyone, dragging her out of the enormous library and through long hallways until I find an empty room. I pull hard, yanking her through the door and up against the nearest wall.

Her chest heaves as she takes on the stance I taught her in our last session. She's tense and tight.

She needs a good fucking.

Shoving my way up into her space, I push and push until she backs into the wall, hitting it hard. The breath leaves her lips in a huff as I slip both hands through the slit in her skirt and split it wide. My fingers go to the back of her toned thighs as I haul her up into my arms, wrapping tan legs around my waist. She barely fits around me, pressed against the wall, unsure what to do next.

Her aura is an explosive mix of dark desire and crimson anger and cherry red lust.

That fucking vein in her neck throbs again, and her blood calls to me. I can't resist, and I don't want to. She brings out every wild, animalistic tendency I have. Those deep dark wants I shove down because they're uncontrolled, and I'm too fucking big to be uncontrolled with women.

I've missed her the last three days. I want to do anything but cherish the woman in my arms right now. Gripping her beautiful updo, I yank two bobby pins out and wrap the fingers of one hand through it, tugging her head back.

Luna presses against my chest. "Titan, what are you–" her words die off the moment I bring my mouth to her neck and suck at the skin over that pounding vein. Her soft groan urges me on as I close my teeth around it and bite my way down to her shoulder. Like a goddamn animal, I rub my cheek along her collarbone before biting again, until pinpricks of blood well up along her skin.

More. I need more. I lick my way back up along the surface wounds, the taste of her blood coating my tongue. Sunshine. Pure fucking sunshine.

Luna grinds her hips against my stomach, her head still back against the wall, hair still wrapped around my fist.

I'm nothing more than feral energy as I release her hair and slick my mouth over hers, our first kiss a clash of fangs and tongues and her blunt teeth. I devour her as my body screams for me to take more. Luna opens for me, her scent blooming, that sea salt perfume growing stronger and stronger as slick wets my hands.

She's fucking soaked for me. With one hand, I reach down and free my aching cock from the confines of my formal suit.

Luna whines when I slide myself between her thighs, wetting my length with all that beautiful slick.

"You smell so fucking good," I groan as I bring my lips to her shoulder and nibble. She pants, her head lolling to the side as she presents her neck to me.

Seeing that submission sends a victorious thrill shooting through my stomach as I hump her into the wall steadily, teasing her pussy with my fat cock.

Luna pants, pushing those obscene tits right up into my face. Reaching up with both hands, I drag the front of her dress down, hearing the fabric rip. But I don't give a shit; all I want right now is to be inside this omega who drives me crazy in every possible way.

Luna yips as the fabric tears, and when our eyes meet, she looks guarded, streaks of yellow claiming her bright aura. The heat from a moment ago chills, and reality comes crashing down on my head. What the hell am I doing? I'm about to rip the dress off an omega and fuck her in another alpha's house. I'm not thinking clearly; I'm not in control.

I can't have that. I could hurt her if I let myself go.

My eyes meet hers, and what I see crushes me. She's hesitant. And if I hadn't paused for a moment, I'd be buried inside her right now. I didn't ask for her consent. We didn't have a conversation. I took what I wanted, because she makes me feel like a dam about to break. I'm losing the war for my mind.

Gently I place Luna back on the ground, tugging her dress back up over the tits I almost got to see. I tuck my dick back into my jeans and spin on my heel, practically running to get away from the mistake I just made.

Luna doesn't call for me to come back either, and that's how I know I'm making the right decision.

FORTY MINUTES LATER, I rip open the door to the Omegamatic shed and tear my clothes off in a frenzy. The entire truck ride home I could smell her in my car, on my fingers. I can still taste her blood in my mouth, the sweet kiss of her skin under my bite. I can't stop reliving that breathless moan when I hauled her up into my arms.

I don't even bother to coat my dick in lube, I'm leaking so much precum, I could drown someone in it. I kick the Omegamatic up to high and grip the big wooden breasts, punching my hips as I slide home.

Grunting, I press on the suction and gasp out when the machine pulls my dick farther in with even, sucking strokes. I'm going to come so damn fast like this.

And that's when I realize this entire place smells like her. She's been all over this goddamn machine. But there's nobody here to watch me unleash. Nobody to know my sinful secret.

I want her, God help me. I want her because I sense her in my chest. And that means something significant.

"Luna," I heave. "Goddamn." Her name falls off my lips over and over. So good. It feels so good to fantasize about her, to remember how it felt to have her for a moment.

I shove all that aside as the Omegamatic starts fluttering around me. My brain wanders to Luna's big tits in that gorgeous dress, to the way her back was bare for me to see all that smooth, tan skin.

Bucking into the machine, I come with a choked roar, stars taking over my vision as I imagine Luna falling apart around me. And then I do it over and over, until that need has faded to a dull roar.

CHAPTER SIXTEEN

luna

THERE ARE KISSES, and there are kisses. And the searing, soul-igniting thing Titan just did? That's another level entirely. I know we've got the whole enemies-starting-over vibe, but now I can imagine just how good a hate fuck with him would be.

When I hesitated, he dropped me like a hot potato and turned tail. But when I look deep inside, I have to ask myself why I didn't just encourage him. We both wanted it so bad.

The thing is, no matter how sexually charged our interactions are becoming, I'm still leaving. I'm not ready to catch feelings for someone when our relationship would be so fraught and wild. That's the first thing I thought of when he ripped my dress.

Because, if I know anything, it's that if I fuck Titan, there's no turning back. He'll destroy me for all other dick, and I can't have that. I'm going home soon. It doesn't make sense to start something here. Not that my body agrees with that in the slightest.

My dress is torn down the side, and there's not shit I can do about that. But I straighten the straps and hoist my tits back up, lift my head and go back into the library. Erin corners me almost immediately.

"Tell me everything. Don't leave out a single detail. Are you and Titan getting together?"

I scoff. "E, that man does not know what he wants, and I'm not here forever."

Erin quirks a brow at me. "So…nothing happened?"

I rub at the back of one arm. "Errr, I'm not saying that, but…"

Erin grabs my wrist and drags me into a corner by herself. I'm aware everyone can hear our conversation. Alpha hearing is really fucking good.

Mal and Pen come over, the mates of this pack's enforcer and spirit. I've met them a few times by now. Pen waggles her auburn brows at us. "OMG, alpha gossip, I can tell by the awkward way you're standing. Tell us everything!"

Mal rolls her eyes at Pen's exuberance. I let out a sigh, sharing the whole story while Pen nods sagely. Erin gasps for dramatic effect when I'm done.

"You know, I got the brilliant tortured one too, but it turned out alright in the end," Pen quips, pointing to Samson on the dance floor. Her mate is huge, so handsome dressed in a maroon tux. He holds his daughter's hands, dancing with her to the soft music. She's wearing a dress that matches his tux, a flower corsage on her tiny wrist.

"God, they're cute together," Pen sighs wistfully before turning back to me. "Not that you asked for my advice, but I'm giving it to you anyhow. Broken alphas run from confident omegas. They get wrapped up in their own bullshit. That's just what they do."

"Well, how the hell did you ever sort that out?" I question. "I'm not much for chasing a man."

Pen scoffs. "Oh, I smothered him with my love despite his best efforts, and then he had to chase me."

"There you go, bestie." Erin laughs. "Smother Titan with your boobs and then make him chase you. Easy does it."

We have a good laugh about it, but my mind is still spinning from that fucking kiss.

I make it through another hour of the party before pretending I need my beauty sleep. James and Julia are ready to head back, so we go together. I ask them to drop me at Titan's, but when I knock on his door, nobody comes out. Like a crazy person, I peek in the windows, but he's truly not home.

Well, shit.

I sleep terribly that night, despite three searing orgasms with my rose vibe while remembering a certain alpha's mouth on mine.

The next morning, I'm determined to talk with him, but it's a big day. Things are improving with the researchers, and nearly the whole pack has been out to visit the research trailer and share a bit about their experiences, even Sal. But today's the day we show them a wolf shift. Since Stone is the only formally mated alpha here, he'll be doing the honors.

I head out to the research trailer with him and Erin, squirming with anticipation as I wonder if Titan will be there. He should be; he's the liaison, and this is really important. Still, when we pull up, and he's standing in front of the trailer with Bianca, I have to rein in the urge to scratch my nails across her face. I don't want her to want him. And when I think about what might happen when I leave, how she might make a move, I feel ragey.

Stone gives me a hand out of the truck after he helps Erin, and I stalk around the side, smiling at Bianca. She returns the happy look. "We are so excited for today and can't wait to get started. Titan's already been kind enough to explain the mechanics of shifting to the team, but I'll admit, it still sounds very much like science fiction."

I look over at Titan, who studiously ignores me like a middle schooler ignoring his crush at a dance.

Stone smirks at Bianca. "There's a little bit of nudity involved in this process, Bianca, but I'm sure your team can overlook that."

She blushes a little but looks over at Titan and back at Stone. "We talked about filming this. Does that seem inappropriate to you? I don't want to make you uncomfortable, but it would be helpful for us to have this on video."

"Don't mind at all," Stone chirps. "Tell me when you're ready."

Bianca knocks on the door to the research trailer, and the rest of her team piles out with their cameras. There's a fair amount of apprehension from them, obvious in the anxious set of Sam's shoulders and the way he backs up against the door as if he can't wait to flee back inside.

"Please go on, Stone," Bianca encourages, glancing over to make sure the video camera is ready.

Stone smiles. "Any last questions before I shift? I won't be able to speak then, although anyone in my pack can answer."

Bianca looks around at her team as they shake their heads. "Not yet, thank you. I'm sure as soon as we see it, we'll have some."

Stone rips his shirt over his head, and then the pants come off next. I'm sure I'm not the only person staring at his giant partially hard dong, feeling super thrilled for my bestie that she gets to ride that beauty all the time. I can sense Titan scowling at me, but I refuse to look over at him. There's a sudden cracking sound, and the shift happens so fast, it's almost imperceptible. One moment, Stone's human form is there, and the next he's a humongous black wolf with steely gray eyes.

Bianca throws herself up against Titan with a gasp. "Holy shit. I...I knew what to expect, and I was not ready."

Titan presses a hand to her back, pushing her gently toward Stone's wolf, who now stands in the middle with nearly our entire pack surrounding him. "You can talk to him, and he'll understand you but won't be able to respond. If you ask him questions, Erin can translate for you since they're mated."

"Okay," Bianca bursts out, "I have a shitload of questions about that."

For the next hour, Stone calmly sits and stands and allows his wolf to be poked and prodded as the team peppers him with dozens of questions. Erin stays close by, answering for him, which prompts a new barrage of questions about the mate bond and what that means.

My bestie is so open and honest with her answers, and I'm so proud of her. I try my best not to stare at Titan, but twice I look up, and those blue eyes are leveled at me, plush lips formed into a scowl.

Eventually the researchers have their data. Titan heads back into the trailer with them to wrap up, and I head back, my arm linked between Erin and Stone's.

"You were awesome today," I tell Stone as I bump him with my hip.

"Plus you're so hot," Erin chirps, looking over my head at her mate.

He laughs and leans over me to kiss her as I laugh, wriggling out from between them.

"Shit!" Erin blurts out when they part. "We forgot to invite the researchers up for dinner. It would be helpful for them to see how we are outside an official interview. We do family dinner just like everybody else."

"I've got it. I'll run back and invite them."

"You sure?" Erin questions. "I can go with you."

I level her with my best stare. "I can liaise just as well as

Titan, thank you very much. I'll see you back at the lodge in a few."

Erin squeezes me into a tight hug. "Love you, Hot Sauce."

"Love you too, bestie," I grit out around the pressure of her arms. She sets me down, and I turn to jog back toward the researchers' trailer. The brisk air makes the roof of my mouth hurt, so I zip my lips and hunch over as I jog up the trailer's steps and swing the door wide.

What I see stops my goddamn heart.

Titan leans up against one of the computer consoles, Bianca pressed tight to his chest. His hands are on her fucking hips, although he removes them and steps away from her when I come in. She blanches as if they've been caught in the middle of something shady.

"Luna, hey! What's up?"

Get your goddamn hands off of Titan, for starters, I want to shout. But I remind myself I pushed him away last night, and I'm still going home after I wrap things up here. I shouldn't care if he's into someone else. Right?

So I grin like a crazy person, despite the flare in my nostrils. "Stone and Erin asked me to invite you and the team up to the lodge for dinner."

Titan takes another step away from her, blue eyes locked onto mine as if he's willing a fucking message into my brain. But his face is neutral and cool. He's not happy to see me.

"Dinner's at seven," I say finally, before leaving. I leap down the stairs and stride to the only remaining ATV, thankful someone left the keys in it. Turning it on, I put it in drive and fly back toward the lodge, willing tears not to stream down my cheeks.

I don't want him, I lie to myself. I was hesitant last night because we've always fought, and I'm still going home.

So why does seeing him close to someone else make me feel like shit?

CHAPTER SEVENTEEN

titan

"I'VE GOT TO—"

"Go," Bianca reassures me. "I totally get it, go."

Leaping out of the trailer, I grimace when I realize Luna took my damn ATV. She's already halfway to the house, but I take off at a sprint after her, calling her name. The air has chilled fast as the sun sets.

I watch her throw the ATV in park and dash up the front steps. Goddamnit. Pushing my muscles harder, I rush toward the house. When I finally get there, I fling the front door open, but she's nowhere to be seen. Scenting the air, I realize she's gone upstairs, so I follow her until I hear her inside one of the rooms.

Frustration wells in my chest as I pound on James' door. It swings open, and I'm confronted with not only James, but Cassian as well. Cassian steps in front of the other alpha, giving me a knowing look. "You will not get whatever you came here for, enforcer."

Anger erupts hot in my chest as I get into his space, pushing my larger frame against his. "We've had a misunderstanding, and we need to talk."

Cassian's brows travel up as he looks down at my chest, then back into my eyes. "You don't. If she wanted to speak with you at this moment, she would be at the door instead of me. Go cool your heels somewhere—you can catch up with Luna later."

It's a pack alpha's dismissal, but he's not my alpha, so I push harder against him. To my shock, James shoves his way through the door, one hand on Cassian's chest and one on mine. "Stop it, both of you." His dark eyes peer up at me. "Titan, now's not the time. I'll talk to Luna, but she can find you later, alright?"

A noise echoes up the hallway. Sal pops her head out of her door, and the twins emerge behind her. This is turning into a fucking scene. I'm happy to listen to others' drama from behind the safety of my bar, but I never ever want to *be* the drama.

I back away from both males, not bothering to look behind them for a glimpse of the woman I'm chasing and pushing away all at the same time.

Stone comes down the hall from the opposite direction. "T, a word?" It's the overwhelming alpha command of my pack leader. I'm helpless to decline.

I turn from James and Cassian and stalk past Stone, all the way downstairs and into the bar. Clay is already there. He gives me a soft smile, sliding a bottle of Jack Daniels across the bar to me before shoving both hands in his pockets and leaving toward the kitchen.

Stone settles down onto the stool next to me with a sigh. "I know you don't wanna talk about it, but maybe we should? Luna showed up looking pretty upset." My best friend scans me with that alpha intuition, and I can't help but spin on my chair and cross my arms.

"Not really. It's just a misunderstanding; she read the room wrong."

Stone leans onto the bar and takes a sip of his drink. "Seems like a lot of that between you and Luna these days. The tension between you is strong; everyone is aware of it. Asher especially."

He leaves that little tidbit as if he didn't just drop a bomb on my head. Goosebumps travel down my entire body as I scan Stone's face to see if he's serious. "Are you saying what I think you're saying? He wasn't fucking joking that day?"

Stone shrugs, a noncommittal look on his face. "Can't be certain; Asher's just getting glimpses here and there. He hasn't come into his power since he hasn't mated Cherry, but he believes he sees a golden bond between you and Luna."

"Doesn't this seem like something that's better to be certain about?" I snap. My brain is spinning a mile a minute. Mate? Hot Sauce? It explains a lot but, no, I can't, no matter how enticing she is. "She's not staying; she's not right for me." I'm blurting out a series of excuses it's clear Stone doesn't agree with.

"I'll tell you what, buddy, I'm going to give you some friendly advice and some space to wrap your mind around the concept of her. It's about to snow a ton. Head out to your cabin for a couple of days. I'm aware that you've been spending the majority of your time here, but you like your personal space. Reclaim that for a few days. We'll talk when you come back."

The moment he says it, I know he's right–I need space. I need to fucking think. "And the advice?"

Stone winks at me as he tips his glass toward mine. "Oh, that's a little easier. I was gonna say you never know until you try."

I groan as I down the Jack Daniels, shaking my head. "She brings out bad things in me, buddy. Wild, bad things."

"Wild sounds like a shitload of fun, to be honest." Stone

claps me on the back. "Go on, get outta here fast. By tomorrow afternoon, you're going to be buried under snow."

I grab the bottle of Jack and leave my best friend to pack for a few days of blissful silence. Maybe when I'm alone, I can figure out what the hell to do with this blinding desire I have for Luna Brooks. And with enough time and space, maybe I can rip her right out of my brain.

CHAPTER EIGHTEEN

luna

AFTER TITAN LEAVES, I sit with my friends for a long time. They're kind enough to talk about everything under the sun except for him. They take my mind off him, and Erin shows up after a while and hangs out too.

My brain is an evil bitch, constantly replaying that vision of fucking gorgeous Bianca with her fit thighs pressed to Titan's.

I was just wrapped around him myself, and the heat between us was freaking delicious. I'm not imagining there's something there, but I'm also not going to chase a man. I never have, and I never will. Although I was initially compelled to have a conversation with him, I'm done with that at this point. The moment I found his hands on someone else's hips, the desire to talk disappeared.

Why the hell am I even mad? My hesitation stopped him at the ball, and I still haven't sorted through those emotions. I didn't call for him when he left. I'm going home soon, and he's not mine.

Once dinner's ready, we head downstairs. Titan and the

researchers aren't there. I wonder if he's at the trailer with goddamn Bianca again.

Dinner is as rowdy as usual, and to support me, Sal shows up for the first time. Although I feel the need to help her integrate into the larger pack, she does it seamlessly. She's making progress by the day.

"Luna?" I look over as Sal's soft tones question me somewhat insistently. "Girl, I've been calling your name for a solid minute." She laughs, leaning over Rogue's lap to swat me on the forearm. "Guess you've got something on your mind."

"Titan," Rogue coughs under his breath as River snickers and takes a sip of her drink.

"Could you be more obvious?" I snap at the hooligans as Sal sits back up and grins.

"Hey, Stone is taking us out to the food drop after dinner. We're going to leave a bunch of canned goods for the omegas. Tony at the bar is going to let them know if anyone comes in. It's supposed to snow a shitload tomorrow. Want to come with us?"

"Hell yes," I assert, pushing my mac and cheese around my plate with the fork.

I sense Clay's eyes on me. His mac and cheese is my fucking favorite, but I'm not in the mood to rehash what happened with Titan again.

After dinner, Stone and Erin pile Sal, Clay, the twins and me into one truck. Erin breaks out a huge thermos of hot chocolate and a shitload of candy. The twins make a ruckus singing. Sal snort-laughs at their antics while Clay shouts at Stone to keep his eyes on the road when he joins in.

I can admit, they do take my mind off things to a degree. Especially when we pile out of the truck, hauling bags to refill the drop spot. When Erin unlocks and opens the top of the box, I'm a little sad that our last drop is still there.

"Don't worry, Luna," Erin reassures me. "We're doing what we can. Cassian is working on a plan with Titan, alright?"

I nod, but deep down I'm certain our days of helping Declan's omegas are coming to an end. Maybe he realizes we're doing it, or maybe–

"Lu, you wanna do a quick dip in the hot spring?" Erin rubs my back as she watches Stone and the twins cannonball into the steaming water.

Shaking my head, I follow her as we head for the hot spring. She laughs as the twins splash one another before dunking Clay, Sal attacking Stone. He pretends to go under, sputtering, and I love him for it. The fact that Sal is comfortable enough with him now to be playful, to understand he'd never hurt her–it's huge.

"I'm so happy you have this family," I whisper to my bestie, wrapping both arms around her trim waist.

"It could be your family too, honey."

"I don't know," I counter. "I bring too much tension to the pack. Cassian and James were kind enough to stand between us earlier, but I can't ask people to get involved in my drama. Shit, I don't even want to be involved. It's one thing to love hearing about other people's shit, but I don't want to be in the thick of it myself."

"I get that," Erin says, squeezing me tight. "Selfishly I just don't want you to go, because I love you so much, and you do fit here."

Something squeezes my heart tight in my chest, so tight I have to resist the urge to rub at my skin and loosen that terrible pressure. Because Erin's right. Somewhere in the last few weeks, this place started to feel like home. When I think about my sunny beachfront house I just purchased six months ago, I'm not eager to go back.

"You wanna talk about what happened?" Erin's voice is soft as she plays with my long hair.

Shrugging, I look off into the distance, hoping answers will miraculously appear for me. "There's chemistry, for sure," I admit. "Really damn good chemistry. But my plan is still to go home, E. Seeing him and Bianca together pissed me the fuck off, but it shouldn't. He doesn't owe me anything. Ya know?"

Erin opens her mouth, then bites her lip, seeming to think better of what she was going to say. Eventually she pinches my side playfully. "I'm solidly in the 'you should stay until you figure out what you want' camp, because I'm going to be so damn sad if you leave."

We laugh together at that, although there's a thread of sadness in my thoughts. Together we turn to watch Sal and Stone and the twins act a fool with Clay in the hot springs. It warms my chest, thawing that tightness I feel when I consider leaving them.

Still.

"Come on, bestie," I sigh. "Clay's making eyes at me. I suspect we won't be allowed home if we don't at least get naked in the hot springs once."

She laughs and bats her eyelashes playfully at me, stripping fast and leaping into the warm water as I follow.

THE NEXT MORNING, banging on my door wakes me up. Well, that's presuming I ever fell asleep in the first place. Which I didn't.

"God in fucking Heaven, what is it?" I bellow out into the empty room.

Erin flings my door open wide and Julia sails through it with a happy-go-lucky smile on her delicate features. "We want to take you somewhere today," Julia signs as Erin helps me out by repeating the words aloud. "You deserve resolution to this Titan issue."

"Agreed." Erin laughs. "So get dressed. Clay's making French toast, then we have a surprise for you."

I'm skeptical they can fix whatever's broken between the big enforcer and me, but I'm curious enough to bite. Dressing quickly, I curl the very tips of my hair as Julia beams and Erin rolls her eyes at me. "Not gonna need that where you're going, you hussy."

Turning on my heel, I scoff at my best friend. "There is literally nowhere on Earth where I don't need my hair to look nice."

An hour later, I'm proven absofuckinglutely wrong. Because I'm on the back of a snowcat, clutching tight to Asher while we follow Stone, Erin and Clay along a snow-covered path into the middle of nowhere. They're being cagey as shit about where we're going, but it's just me and them. Maybe a middle-of-nowhere heart-to-heart or mediation session? I don't know.

All Stone will say is "you'll see," and "It's gonna work out in the end, Luna." As if that's not the most cryptic thing he's said to me the entire time I've known him.

Honestly? I'm too fucking cold to even guess. I hoped resolution meant we were going shopping, but this is the farthest possible cry from that.

When we pull around a large lake, I'm hella thrilled to see a cabin on the other side. Smoke curls slowly out of the chimney, and all I can think of is warmth. Blissful fucking warmth please.

We pull up in front of the cabin and Asher hops off, lifting me gently.

"Okay, Hot Sauce," Stone laughs, "in you go."

"And what? You guys aren't coming with me? What is this place?"

Clay smirks. "Just go on in, Luna. We'll be here if you need anything, okay?"

This is feeling way too much like some kind of family mediation, but for the sake of the pack, I'm willing to do it. Pulling my coat tight around my body, I push through the growing piles of snow until I get to the front porch. I kick snow off my boots and knock on the door, but nobody answers.

"Go on in, Hot Sauce," Stone calls out helpfully. "See you in a couple days."

I whip around at his words. "See me in a—what in the actual fuck? Days??"

All three snowcats take off, Erin winking and waving goodbye as Clay and Asher follow their alpha. I holler and run off the porch, sprinting to follow the guys. And then I scream and shout every curse word I know as I demand for them to return. But they don't. The snow piles up around my boots until I'm so fucking cold, I'm worried I might actually get hypothermia. I stand in the snow, mad as hell, until I can't take it any longer.

"You have got to be fucking kidding me," I grouse as I stomp back toward the little cabin. When I open the door, a tiny waft of warm air hits me. It's not super warm inside, but a banked fire crackles slowly in the fireplace.

The cabin itself is one tiny room with a bed covered in pillows, a teeny kitchen and one big cushioned chair in front of the fireplace. It's cozy, if one wanted to be stuck in a tiny cabin in the middle of a goddamn snowstorm.

I brought nothing with me. No walkie, no cell phone. I have no way to call back the assholes who just dropped me here. But when I do get back, because I absolutely will, Stone and Erin are never going to hear the end of this from me.

Just then, the front door swings open, and all the air gets sucked out of the cabin.

"What in the hell are you doing here?" The alpha growl causes my nipples to pebble as I swing around with a scowl, glaring.

Titan.

CHAPTER NINETEEN

titan

A NIGHT at my remote cabin has done wonders for my mind. The crisp air and impending storm brought peace to my tumultuous thoughts. I thought I'd get to spend three beautiful days eating and drinking and not daydreaming about Luna.

Except that's a lie. I can't get that kiss at the ball off my fucking mind. I've never felt that depth of emotion and connection. It's unsettling, and she's leaving anyway. It makes no sense to get involved with a girl who isn't staying in Ayas.

Yet here she is, in the flesh, in my goddamn cabin, looking mad as hell.

It's an illusion; it must be. I'm seeing her everywhere because my body wants her, despite my mind being completely torn.

"Not gonna say anything about me showing up at this cabin in the middle of goddamn nowhere?" Her voice is tense and tight as she crosses her arms, tan cheeks flushed with pink. There are still snowflakes in her hair; she can't have been here long.

Snarling, I stomp out onto my front porch. There are snowcat tracks in the snow.

I'm going to murder Stone when I get back. Unfortunately I came up here in my old truck. There's no way to return Luna to the lodge.

We're snowed in. We're snowed in for *days*.

I sigh and let my head fall back, snowflakes landing with icy precision on my cheeks and forehead. Please, God, give me the strength not to kill or fuck this woman. Nearly every interaction we have ends in misunderstanding.

Luna doesn't appear in the doorway behind me, and when I turn and go back inside, she hasn't moved.

"This is Stone's doing, isn't it?" I know the answer before she even says it, but her confirmation makes me angry nonetheless.

Kicking my boots off, I stomp over to the fireplace and bank it higher, watching the flames lick at the wood as the fire grows. Luna doesn't move behind me, so I turn. "Look, here's how it's gonna go."

"Are you fucking kidding me right now?" she snaps. "Take me home. Take me home right now."

Home.

She called the lodge home.

Something about that sends a stabbing warmth through my chest, but I squash it down hard.

"I can't take you home, Luna. That's why they dropped you off the way they did. The only way anyone can get outta here before this monster snowstorm is a snowcat. I don't have one."

"Argh!" she yells as she balls both fists and screams. She stomps past me to the door and out onto the porch, where already the snow is falling steadily. I can no longer see past my truck, which is parked just off to the side of the cabin.

"Look," I say a little more gently. "Come back inside. We're stuck here. We'll stay out of each other's way. We can ju–"

"For days?" Her voice is pure angry acid. "For days in a space that can't be more than six hundred square feet? You've got to be kidding me."

"Okay," I agree. "You're not wrong. But I'll do my best to steer clear."

"Perfect, I'm sure that suits you just fine," she barks. "Steering clear of me."

I don't bother to respond, because if I do, it'll open up a whole can of worms I'm not ready to open. Instead, I push past her, looking down as she looks way up, until our eyes meet. "This sucks, but let's make the best of it, alright?"

She doesn't bother to nod, but instead sits at my dining room table, pulling her feet up under herself and laying her head down on her forearms.

Sighing, I turn to my small kitchen and start browning hamburger for chili. I didn't bring enough food for two people, but I won't let her go hungry. Grabbing my walkie, I check to see if there's a signal back to the lodge. There usually is, but with this much snow and cloud cover, the signal just doesn't make it.

Luna says nothing the entire time I cook, and even when I put a bowl of my mother's best chili down in front of her, she doesn't look up. In fact, she doesn't look up the entire time I eat, not until a horrible screech sounds from right outside our door.

She jumps up fast, eyes wide. "What the hell was that?"

"Something getting eaten, I expect," I respond. "This is the wild, Luna. That's what happens."

She throws my front door open, ignoring the cold as she runs off the front steps. Right out front, a fox chases something in the low wintry light. A bunny. It's already dragging a

ANNA FURY

leg, but the fox pauses when Luna barrels off the porch and starts screaming her head off.

The fox takes one look at the wounded rabbit, another quick look at Luna, and darts off into the shrubs that line one side of my cabin. I watch with something bordering on concern and amusement as she darts over to the bunny, who freezes at her approach. She lifts it up gently and jogs back up onto my porch, not stopping to kick the snow from her boots as she heads straight inside.

"Luna, you're dragging snow inside," I point out as she rolls her eyes.

"Get me a box, you heartless fucking heathen. Can't you see he's hurt?

"He's food, Luna. He should be that fox's dinner right now," I counter, one hand on my hip as she gasps and clutches the bunny tight to her chest.

"Well, I couldn't let that happen, Titan. Not right in front of me like that. Look how teeny he is!" She holds the bunny out, and she's right. Blood already covers one leg, although it looks to be intact. I don't know what she would do if she'd found him mangled already.

"Can you get me a box, or should I just hold him all night?" Her voice loses some of the anger, and a mournful, tender thread replaces it, reminding me that she has a big heart for everyone apart from me.

Grumbling, I head back into my closet and search for anything that might work as a resting place for the bunny, knowing full well that if he heals, he'll jump right out and make a mess in my goddamn cabin.

When I emerge from my closet with a shoebox, she's seated in front of the fire with the bunny clutched tightly to her chest. "There, there, Roger. Everything's gonna be okay, little friend. I'll get you fixed right up. Rest easy." She glances up with a renewed scowl when I drop to a knee and hand her the shoebox.

"Seriously? Put some towels or something squishy in there, Titan. What the hell, man? Do you know how to care for somebody else at all?"

I grind my teeth at that, because I do, of course I do. I'm a Dom. Caring for my subs and then the aftercare is something I pride myself on. Not only that, but I've always cared for the omegas from Declan's pack. She knows this. Well, some of it.

Standing up, I stomp to the bathroom and grab an extra hand towel, folding it so it trails up the sides of the box. "Can't believe this shit," I mutter to myself. "All for a fucking rabbit."

When I return to the living room, she crosses to me and sets the bunny gently in the shoebox, taking it from me. She sets him down on the dining table, shucks her coat and then returns with him to the fireplace.

I watch silently, because what can I say to this display of affection from her? It would be charming if it were anyone else. Her aura simmers with angry red tension. She's still mad about what she walked in on with Bianca, and I'm mad she never gave me a fucking chance to explain.

The bunny falls asleep, lulled by the warmth and probably half-dead from terror. Luna watches him in silence, and then comes back to the table, sitting herself in front of the chili. "Thank you," she whispers before tucking in. She says nothing else, but eats the whole bowl and then crosses to the sink to wash it.

When she leans over the sink, she flips her hair around her fingertips and then throws the whole blond swath over one shoulder. An intense desire to wrap my fist in those blond strands and yank her head back to bite her neck hits me.

"You can take the bed," I offer as she shakes her head, staring at the fire.

"I'm fine here." Her voice is steely and cold, her aura a dark angry gray as she studiously avoids me.

So be it.

I pace across the cabin, folding myself down onto the bed as it creaks. I remember I should bank the fire again, so I get out of bed and grab more firewood. She's there, though, seated in front of it, cooing softly to the baby bunny again.

She moves aside, gently pulling the bunny's shoebox away from me as I drop to both knees and throw firewood in. "Careful," she cautions. "You're going to wake him up."

That does it. Turning to her, I sneer, "You do realize he's probably in shock, and, even if he does heal, he'll be disadvantaged if he's injured. He's going to be someone's meal sooner or later, Luna."

Tears fill her eyes. "I know that, Titan. I'm well aware of how the world works. But I couldn't stand by and watch him get hurt. Can you understand that at all?"

God, I'm being an asshole. I turn away from her before I do any more harm to her mental state. When I get into bed, I hear soft sniffling from in front of the fireplace, and I fall asleep with images of her crying at the forefront of my mind.

CHAPTER TWENTY

luna

SLEEP ELUDES ME, even though I eventually drift off in the chair. Somewhere around dawn. Roger starts shuffling around in his box, squeaking as if he's in pain. I don't know what to do for him; I'm not a vet. But he probably needs food and water, so I head into the kitchen to look for both. Of course, there's nothing a bunny might eat, although I opt to try a cracker.

I place a cracker and a tiny bowl of water in his shoebox. He gulps the water down quickly. Reaching in, I rub the back of my fingertips along his snow-white back. He freezes but allows me to do it.

On the other side of the small room, Titan is sound asleep in his goddamn bed. He's a front sleeper, so the view I have is his bare feet and that round, muscular ass that leads into broad, muscled shoulders. It's a shame we aren't lovers, because he looks good enough to eat laid out in the bed like that. For someone. Not me. Because I can't take any more of the waffling with him.

I hate him. If I didn't before, I do now. He would have let Roger get eaten, and I just, I could never do that.

Almost as if I've willed it, Titan stirs, turning over in bed as he mumbles in his sleep. Oh God, the moment he does, it's clear he's got morning wood, and it's…Christ, it's huge. It tents the front of the jeans he fell asleep in, creating an enormous bulge that makes my mouth water. My mind helpfully supplies the memory of that gorgeous cock between my thighs at the ball, the way he coated himself in my wetness. God, we were so close to fucking. It's a good thing we didn't, because seeing him with Bianca would have crushed me for sure.

I slap myself mentally. I'm sure as shit not going to lust after him when I caught him groping another woman.

He grumbles again and sits up in bed, his dark waves mussed from sleep. Titan rubs both hands over his eyes and then shifts forward, bright blue eyes finding mine. I swear to God, if he asks if I slept okay, I'm going to lose my shit.

He instead gets up and heads into the bathroom. The sounds of a shower reach my ears, and he stays in there for a solid half hour before emerging again. When he comes across the cabin, I'm thankful the bulge in his pants is gone, but I can't meet his eyes. Not when I ogled him.

"We should talk, Luna." He drops to one knee and shoves wood into the fireplace, banking it again.

"About?" I'm not going to make this easy for him. I'm still mad.

He cocks his head to the side and scoffs. "You know what. Bianca. I figured you'd bring it up right away; I'm surprised you didn't."

I shake my head. "You're a grown man; you can do whatever the fuck you want to with Bianca."

"You didn't give me a chance to explain," he presses.

Oh hell no. We aren't diving into that. "Starting something with her is unprofessional," I hedge. "She's supposed to be researching you. She can't possibly be impartial if she's fucking you."

Titan's dark brows form into a vee as he smirks at me. "Ah, but we don't want her to be impartial, do we?" He says nothing else as my blood heats to a boil. He's basically just admitted to fucking her for the benefit of the pack.

Titan says nothing as he turns from Roger and me and heads for the kitchen, bringing a box of powdered eggs out of his cabinet. Fucking gross. God, I can't believe he's going to eat them.

But then he reaches into his small refrigerator and pulls out bacon, and I'm sold. Not that I'll tell him that.

Half an hour later, Titan's already eaten in silence and cleaned his plate. He piles a second plate high with bacon and eggs and leaves it on the counter.

"I'm going out today. I'll be back later," he growls, his voice booming in the small space.

"Fine," I bark back.

He grabs a coat and beanie from his closet and stalks out the front door without a backward look.

Great, just great. I don't even know what to do with myself for God knows how long.

OKAY, the reality is that I can't sit still. I know that about myself. After checking on Roger and changing his pee-soaked towel twice, I've come to the determination that I'm going to organize the cabin. It's not that I want to help Titan; I just can't sit here. He's been gone for hours, two, if not three or four. I don't know what an alpha might do outside in the crazy snowstorm, but he's out doing it.

Shit, maybe he hiked back to the lodge just to get away from me. Nothing would surprise me at this point.

Eventually he shows back up with an enormous fish. Without a word, he comes into the newly clean kitchen and sets the dirty, slimy fish on the clean countertop. Reaching into a drawer, he pulls out a knife and starts cutting the scales off in efficient, backward-sweeping motions.

It's on the tip of my tongue to yell about how I just got done cleaning, but all the energy disappears from me.

Titan glances over before reaching into a drawer and grabbing another knife, which he hands me. "Chop me an onion, would ya?"

Choking back any sarcasm that threatens to erupt, I grab an onion from the countertop and set it on a cutting board, slicing it as he works in silence on the fish. I'm about to lose my breakfast when he slices the fish's stomach and takes out all the insides, but I manage to keep it together.

Half an hour later, Titan plates the fish and some reheated rice and hands me my dinner. He sits on the floor in front of the fire, and I take his chair. We eat in near silence until he looks up, blue eyes dazzling me with the strength of their intensity.

"Why'd you run when you found me with Bianca?"

"It seemed like a private moment," I deadpan. "What with your hands on her hips and all."

"I called your name outside," he presses. "You didn't stop. Why?"

"Why'd you ever even kiss me?" I question instead. "Why do that if you were just going to fuck Bianca to get on her good side?"

"I didn't fuck Bianca," he retorts.

"But you said—"

"I said we wanted her on our good side; you assumed that meant I fucked her. Or that I even kissed her. Which I didn't."

I sigh as I cross both arms. "Seems like you and I do a lot of assuming about one another, Titan."

He nods. "Seems that way, Hot Sauce. There's crazy chemistry, but apart from that, we bring out the worst in each other."

His admission makes me sad because it's the truth.

He continues, "What if I don't want us both to assume so much? What if I'd like to really know you? Maybe we could appreciate each other like everyone else does."

"What do you have in mind?"

Titan grins, and it's dazzling to see him like this. "Tell me something I don't know about you, maybe something I've assumed and am wrong about."

Titan frowns and looks down at Roger as he snuffles around in the shoebox, munching a cracker. When his bright blue eyes find mine again, I struggle not to gasp in a breath at the surprisingly vivid color of them. "I'll go first. I assumed you were a lightweight when I met you. I'm told you're not."

"Not hardly," I laugh. "Erin and I used to drink frat boys under the table in college for money."

"That's one way to earn money," he growls, looking at the fire again.

"Well," I offer, sinking down into the fireplace chair, "between that and dancing, I managed to pay for college without asking my dad for the funds. He didn't have much, and he raised me by himself, so it felt like the least I could do."

Titan's blue eyes find mine again. "Your mom was gone?"

I frown. "Please don't make some scathing commentary about how that must have made me what I am today." I'm joking, but his scowl falls.

"I would never joke about losing a parent." His voice is soft, making me wonder what experience he has with parent loss. He doesn't say anything, even when I wait for him to expound on the topic.

"What have you assumed about me?" he asks finally, the hint of a smile tugging his full lips up at the corners.

"I assumed you never really dated, because you're so quiet. But you've proven that to be absolutely false." I remember the scorching tension between us when he kissed me.

"I've been around a few women," he agrees as heat pushes its way through my chest, traveling down to my core until I'm slick between my thighs. My body is well aware that he knows his way around a woman's body. Why the hell did I even bring this up?

Titan sucks in a breath and grins, and for the first time, it seems genuine. It's mischievous and playful, nothing like the forced looks I usually get from him.

"I'm not dating anyone now. Not even *Bianca*," he adds with a meaningful look. "But it's been a while since I took a partner."

Something about the way he says "took" and "partner" in the same sentence makes me want to pant with need. I can just imagine the way he'd be, taking someone in the bedroom.

"Why did you kiss me?" I ask the question, so faint I barely realize I've asked it aloud.

Titan crosses his forearms over both big thighs, steepling his fingertips together. When he looks back up at me, his bright eyes shine with intensity. "I wanted to," he murmurs. "I had to."

Had to? "I don't understand. You had to?"

He nods, licking his lips slowly, provocatively as he cocks his head to the side and assesses me. "I like you, Luna. Against my better judgment. Despite the fact that you don't plan to stay. You drive me crazy in all the possible ways. I wanted a taste of you. So I took it."

My body heats as I shift forward in the chair, realizing I'm soaking the seat with wetness as Titan sucks in a deep, ragged breath before focusing his gaze on me once more. "You're wet for me, omega." It's not a question; it's a simple statement. But it's so true.

I sink onto the floor on both knees, my legs straddling his outstretched ones as I look up into those surprising eyes. "Why'd you touch her?"

Titan's eyes cloud over as he runs both hands through his wild, dark waves. "I didn't touch her." The tension between us grows so tight, I might go mad. "She came on to me. When you came in, I was gently rebuffing her, reminding her we should remain professional."

A thrill zings through my core at his words as I lean in closer, close enough to rest my hands on Titan's big, broad chest. I look up at him with what I hope is an inviting smile. "Did you enjoy kissing me at the ball? Would you do it again?"

Titan leans forward into my touch, stroking his fingertips along the outside of my left arm. A shudder rocks through my entire frame when that hand snakes around my back, wrapping through my hair and tugging. My head falls back, my throat bared to the predatory male I'm straddling.

"You look good enough to eat like this," Titan growls as my thighs quiver with anticipation.

I want him to touch me. Scratch that. I need it like I need my next breath. Squirming, I rock my hips against his as he lets out a low chuckle.

"Do you rush headfirst into everything, Luna? Do you ever relax and savor the moment?"

I can't summon an appropriate response as I urge my body to calm itself, slumping against Titan's chest with my hair still wrapped in his fist.

"Close your eyes," he commands.

When I do it, he laughs again, a masculine sound that sends my hips rocking again. God, I crave more touch than this. I'm so frustrated, I might combust right here.

"You do things to me, Luna. My lack of control around you is deeply unsettling. But when you're close to me like this, I can't find it in me to give a shit."

I'm so busy thinking about his words that when Titan's teeth clamp gently down on my throat, I squeak and shoot upright, struggling against the sudden sharp prick of his fangs. The fangs, oh my fucking God, I forgot he had them.

The sudden remembrance that he's a predator, that he's built for speed and stealth, built for violence, sends me struggling against the bite at my throat. But then Titan wraps both big arms around me, letting go of my hair and holding me close to his chest as he relinquishes his hold on my skin. I could almost sob with a mixture of relief and disappointment, until those sharp teeth drag down the side of my neck and along my shoulder, a direct contrast to the soft, warm lips that accompany them.

Warring sensations swirl in my chest as Titan grips my neck with one hand, the other firmly planted in the middle of my back.

"More. God, Titan, I need more than this, please." I'm not above begging.

"Be precise, Luna," he demands, removing those talented lips from my skin and looking at me with an intense gaze. Most men aren't great at fucking you with their eyes, in my experience, but Titan has that skill down. His gaze never moves, never wavers as I struggle to maintain eye contact with him.

I lose the battle, diverting my eyes when I can't hold that connection any longer. Titan leans into my ear with a throaty laugh. "Good girl, Hot Sauce. I like it when you submit."

CHAPTER TWENTY-ONE

titan

I'M PUSHING LUNA, testing her for compatibility without even really meaning to. I know one thing for certain —I can't fuck her. If I fuck her, I won't let her go back to California. If I fuck her, something monumental is going to change inside of me. I've experienced profound loss in my life. I guard myself against situations like this for a reason.

But the longer I spend around Luna, the more I lose the ability to push her away. Between her beautiful aura and the stirrings of connection in my chest, I'm a goner. Plus she's responsive, so goddamn responsive.

I'm compelled to share what Stone mentioned about Asher seeing a bond between her and me, but hold back. Maybe it's knowing that, if I tell her, she'll hop up out of my lap and start demanding answers I can't give her.

Right now? Right now I'm enjoying this tease, despite the fact she'd clearly be a brat in the bedroom. I've never wanted that; it's not how I enjoy the women who sub for me.

Still, I can't deny the insistent tug I feel toward her now that she's in my arms. I'm barely holding back a purr watching her squirm under my praise.

"Have you got a praise kink, Hot Sauce?" I press a line of tender kisses along her jaw as she rocks her hips against me again.

"Doesn't everyone?" she questions, wrapping both arms around my neck.

"They do not," I confirm. "What other kinks do you enjoy?"

Dark blue eyes narrow on mine. "Why don't you find out for yourself, Titan?"

Something about the challenge in her voice causes my alpha dominance to build in my system until I have to do something. I prefer a long game though. I love the tease and the build-up. Most of my subs wait multiple sessions before we fuck. That's how I like it.

But this girl rips my steely resolve into tatters. She makes me want things I've never wanted before. She makes me lose control, and I can't have that. I can't take that risk.

Standing with Luna in my arms, I turn her in the chair on her knees. "Hands on the back of the chair, Hot Sauce." It's a simple command, but she obeys beautifully, and my dick twitches watching her small hands grip the aged fabric.

For me, being a Dom means appreciating all the fine details, the way her perfectly manicured hands clench the fabric, the slight tremble of her thighs visible even through her tight jeans.

I reach around her waist and unbutton the jeans, sliding them over round hips and a perfect peach of an ass. She's tan everywhere, which shouldn't surprise me. She's a Cali girl through and through. An image of her sunbathing nude slaps me then, tearing a low, appreciative growl from my throat.

Luna pants softly, leaning forward into the chair as I slide the jeans all the way off her ass and down her pretty thighs. She's wearing delicate red lace panties, an intricate design from a well-known luxury lingerie brand's winter line. Ah, Luna is into fancy frills.

That knowledge makes me harder still, because gorgeous lingerie is a personal pleasure of mine. I've occasionally gifted sets from this brand to previous subs, but seeing Luna wear it is special.

Because she's mine.

I'm on the knife's edge of completely losing my mind. My thoughts all revolve around the beautiful omega in my chair. I'm fucking falling for her. I can't. I shouldn't. But when I look at her like this, I know my heart and body have decided what they want, and are simply waiting for my mind to catch up.

I snarl the moment my brain goes to that line of thought. Dragging my nose up the back of one quivering thigh, then along the seam of her panties, I inhale a full breath as slick starts to drip down the backs of her legs. She says nothing, but she's breathing hard into the chair's back as I sit on my heels to observe.

I watch Luna for a long time, the way she shifts in the chair, desperate for touch. The way she arches her back to show me that beautiful lace-covered heat. She doesn't know how to get more from me, but she's aching for it.

My lips part as I take a ragged breath, growling as her flavor bursts across my senses. Her aura swirls dark purples and reds. She's so needy. And that ache calls to me. Because it's my job to slake her thirst.

My job.

Fuck me, she smells so good. Her arousal amps up that sea salt and caramel perfume. All women smell good, but Luna's scent is divine. I want to dip my tongue into it and enjoy her for days.

Shifting forward, I slide my fingers along the seam of her panties, tugging them aside for my first glimpse of her naked pussy. She waxes, so every inch of her is on clear display for me, slick dripping steadily from her. Luna gasps when I stroke my way from her back hole all the way down to her clit, pinching it gently between my fingers.

"Fuck, oh fuck," she grits out, her arms starting to quiver as she grips the back of my chair hard. Streaks of brilliant purple explode in her aura.

I'm certain she's going to ask me to stop teasing her, to demand I put my mouth on her, but she doesn't. She waits. And it makes me so goddamn hard.

I want to take her like this, waiting quietly in my chair. I want to pound into her from behind until she's falling apart at the seams. But I also want to taste her. She is a first for me in so many ways. My first and only omega partner. My first time in decades with someone who isn't a sub. My first time clinging to my desire for control like a life raft, despite watching the shore happily drift farther from me.

Leaning forward, I use my claws to rip the lingerie from her, ensuring the sharp points scratch her skin as she yelps indignantly. I bury my face between her thighs and lick a stripe from her ass all the way down to her clit, swirling my tongue around that hard nub.

Luna and I groan at the same time, her flavor bursting on my tongue. She's a delicacy I could never get enough of, so I taste her again. My usual control fades, my movements losing their purposeful cadence as I eat her roughly. I take and take as she rocks back to meet my mouth. When I'm certain she'll command me to finish her, she curses and grabs the back of the chair harder.

I bring her right to the edge, and then I sit back to watch. Slick squirts out of her, her body desperately preparing her for me. It coats my hands as I run them up the backs of her thighs. And then I shove her forward into the chair and start all over.

Thinking better of it, I yank her back to me and flip her

easily, throwing one tan thigh over the chair's arm, and the other up over my shoulder. And then I lock eyes with her as I bring my lips to her clit again and tug. She's sensitive, and so fucking close, her back arching. She's wearing far too many clothes still, and I'm losing my mind with the desire to see all of her gorgeous skin exposed.

Reaching up, I shred my way through her shirt and bra, yanking them aside as she sputters and scowls. "That's really fucking expens—"

"You're goddamn magnificent," I utter, drinking in the sight of her huge tits. I can't stop looking at how perfectly round and full they are. Where I thought her nipples would be a rosy dark pink, they're pale. Delicate and feminine and hard.

"I knew you were a boob man," she snarks, grinning at me from the chair. She runs her small hands up over both her breasts, tugging at her nipples as she hums.

A whine leaves my throat as I watch her touch herself, deviant shades of gray spiking through her aura.

"Maybe it's my turn to teas—"

I haul Luna into my arms and silence her taunt with my mouth on hers. There's a momentary pause before my lips crash down onto hers, tasting and devouring just like I did at Mitchell's house. I can't get enough of her. I want to destroy her, to tie her to my ceiling and watch her spin from the ropes. I want everything so very deeply.

"Need you naked," she demands, parting from that scorching kiss as she shucks her shredded bra off, tossing it aside.

"We aren't fucking, Luna." I laugh. "Good things come to those who wait." I nip along her jawline as she moans and reaches for the buttons of my flannel shirt.

"I hate that saying. I want what I want, when I want it."

"You usually get it, too, don't you?" I tease, kissing my way down her neck as she frantically unbuttons my shirt, shoving it down over my shoulders.

Blue eyes rove my upper body appreciatively as I toss the shirt aside. Luna reaches out and rubs her hands along my pecs, meeting in the middle and traveling down over my abs. I'm stacked; I always have been. Transitioning into an alpha just made me bigger, and it's clear Luna is very into it.

"Sit back," I command, holding back a smirk as she obeys, although the pout on her full pink lips is enough to bring me to my knees. Almost. "Stay where you are, Luna, and watch me."

Blue eyes dance in the firelight as she meets my gaze, nibbling apprehensively at her lower lip. I'd like nothing better than to bite and tug on it, but I'll save that pleasure for later. For now, I want to get off on her watching me.

Shifting onto my knees, I fully remove my shirt. Luna's eyes drink me in greedily, following my movements as I unbutton my jeans and slide them down. My dick is hard as a rock behind the uncomfortable fabric, and it pops free the moment I shift my briefs and pants down far enough.

Luna's eyes fly open wide when she takes in my size, and the slight movement of her shifting away from me makes me laugh.

"I've rendered you speechless, Luna?" It's a tease when she looks back up, dark eyelashes fluttering as she collects her thoughts.

"You're huge everywhere; I expected that. But I'm still just, I'm–"

"*Speechless*," I reiterate, reaching down to cup my balls with one hand, tugging on their heavy weight.

Luna shifts forward, reaching for my cock as I shake my head. "No." It's a one-word command that forces a scowl to her face. She sits back with a huff. "You can look, but no touching, omega."

Luna rolls her eyes and crosses her arms, those rosy nipples barely peeking out from behind her forearms. I laugh as I reach down again and stroke my length with even, purposeful strokes. Heat streaks along the back of my neck and down my spine as Luna's blue eyes drop to my hands. Precum leaks profusely from the head of my cock as a whine builds in her throat. Gathering as much of it as I can, I spread it along myself, coating my thickness with it.

Luna opens her mouth to say something, but thinks better of it when I give her a dark look. She's a natural brat, and she's resisting the urge to do something bratty just to see where it gets her. With anyone else, anyone else at all, I would hate that. But a mental image of me punishing her snarky mouth with my dick shoves all other thoughts aside.

Letting out a needy groan, I take both hands to my cock, starting to rock my hips up into them. I'm a creative masturbator; I've got dozens of toys at home. Some I bought, some I designed, but I love jacking off. I love the tease of it, edging for hours until I wrench a bone-shattering orgasm from myself.

But this? This is perfection. My movements grow faster and faster as a pink tinge travels from Luna's cheeks all the way down her neck and chest. She drops her crossed arms and slips one hand between her thighs to stroke alongside her clit.

"No," I demand. "Just watch."

She whines and sputters until I swipe precum from my cock and bring my fingertips to her mouth, smearing my essence along her lower lip. "Open your mouth and suck, Luna," I command as her pink tongue licks up the sticky substance.

She closes her eyes and moans as I shove two fingers into that tight, wet heat. Luna's silky soft tongue swirls around my fingertips before a hard, sucking pressure replaces the softer touch.

My other hand drags up and down my cock, squeezing hard enough that I'm nearly ready to come. I haven't come this fast in a long time. But Luna starts losing her mind on my fingers, licking and sucking until I can't take it anymore.

Heat clouds my vision, my focus narrowing to a single point–the omega seated in front of me. Snarling, I yank my fingers from her mouth and wrap them around her throat instead, squeezing hard as she gasps. I expect her to throw her head back and wait for me to do something, anything about this searing pleasure.

She shocks me to my core when she levels that blue gaze on me, predatory and steady. "Come for me, alpha."

The one-sentence command sends a dazzling, white-hot heat barreling through my core as I point my cock at her and explode all over her beautiful tits. Cum shoots out of me as I scream into the cabin, bellowing at the soul-deep fulfillment of doing this to her.

I can hear nothing, see nothing, one hand still wrapped around Luna's throat and the other around my pulsing cock. Release continues to batter me as my hips quake, the shattering, falling sensation of orgasm obliterating any conscious thought from my mind.

When bliss finally recedes, I shift back onto my heels, my eyes only opening when Luna chuckles. I snap my gaze to her, and she preens under the attention, smirking at the absolute mess coating her obscene tits. I fully expect a snarky comment, but she says nothing else. She just smiles.

CHAPTER TWENTY-TWO

luna

I'VE NEVER SEEN Titan so open, so unguarded. But right now he looks freshly fucked and totally sated. A girl could get used to him like this. Plush lips are parted as he sucks in rapid, even breaths. There's a slight pink tinge on his cheeks just above the five o'clock shadow.

Titan rolls onto his back, pulling me down with him. Both big hands go to my ass as he shoves me up his chest, pulling until he seats me on his face.

I haven't come yet. And I'd like to. Right now.

The first swipe of Titan's tongue has my back arching. He laps softly along the side of my clit, his lips taking a lazy circular tour over the top before sliding back down again. He uses his bruising grip on my ass to hold me wide open, controlling the movement. I can't even rock my hips, because I'm so caught.

Slick floods his face as he growls into my pussy, the tips of his fingers sliding between my ass cheeks as he plays back there too.

"Oh, God," I cry out, bringing my hands to my nipples to pinch lightly.

Titan's lips grow more insistent, tugging my clit before sucking it gently. The sounds of him eating me are the only thing I can focus on as heat builds between my thighs. And then my entire body contorts, and every one of my senses narrows to the big alpha's mouth. I wrap my hands through those dark waves and fuck his face as I scream his name over and over. Orgasm assaults me from every side. He's buried in my chest, his tongue in my pussy, his fingers in my ass.

And then he growls, rumbly and low into my thighs. I fucking come again. I come so long and hard that I swear I stop breathing. Afterward, I slide sideways off him and slump into the chair, gripping it as I try to figure out what the hell kind of sexual magic he's capable of.

Titan lets out a throaty laugh and shifts up onto his elbows as I catch my breath and give him a longing look.

"Don't give me that look." He laughs, and if I'm not mistaken, there's a hint of mischief in his tone. His expression falls into something more serious as he shifts forward, pressing his lips softly to mine. "Don't give me that look, because I'm dying to take everything from you, Luna. I'm barely holding back from fucking you. But if I fuck you, I'm keeping you. If I fuck you, and you try to leave, it will goddamn crush me."

I suck in a breath at his blatant admission. This is something more serious for him, something more than just a wild attraction.

"I don't want to crush you," I admit as he gives me a sad look.

"Then we're not having sex," he responds, rocking back onto his heels before standing. He holds one hand out for me.

I take it, trying to ignore the disappointment that settles in my belly when I think about *not* connecting more. Because I desperately want to watch him fall apart when he takes me. I want to know how it feels to have him buried deep in my body. I do want all that.

But I'm still going home. Right? I nibble my lower lip as I consider the fact that Titan is catching fucking feelings, and I am too.

Just then, Roger shuffles around in his box, hopping up so his teeny ears poke up over the edge. I drop Titan's hand and head for the fireplace, peering into his box. Roger is up and at 'em, drinking water and doing playful little hops.

"Time to put him out, Hot Sauce." Titan's breath is warm against the shell of my ear as I stand up with Roger and box in hand.

Turning, I force a smile to my face. "He does seem okay, right?"

Titan agrees, but his expression is wary and guarded again.

Better to just get it over with. I can't keep a wild bunny around forever. Crossing the cabin, I grab Titan's big coat and tuck it around my shoulders, then open the front door as he cusses up a blue storm behind me. "Damnit, woman, you're not even putting clothes on? It's fucking snowing still."

"I'll just be a second!" I chide him as I head outside, tucking my head to ward away the intense cold. After hopping down the front steps, I set the box on the bottom one and dump it carefully over on its side. Roger hops out and looks around, rising up onto both hind legs before he takes off into the shrubs on the side of the house.

"Same fucking shrubs the fox ran into, you dummy," I grouse as I turn back toward the house. When I step back up onto the top stair, a slick patch of ice causes me to tumble forward through the doorway. I go down hard on both knees, knocking into the pile of firewood by the door, shrieking as my coat flies open and the wood scratches all across my chest and stomach.

I fall in a heap off the pile of firewood, but Titan's already there, reaching both big arms underneath me and pulling me up to his chest, purring gently. He kicks the front door shut and heads back into the bathroom, the purr picking up resonance as I groan.

My fucking chest is on fire. "If I got splinters in these nice tits, I'ma be so mad."

"Long as you don't pop one, we'll be okay." Titan laughs as I swat his chest.

"It doesn't work that way; they're not balloons."

"Plus, you got the expensive ones," he deadpans. "Should hold up longer."

"Are you teasing me right now?" I grip his chin and turn his head to me, even as he sits down on the side of the tub with me still wrapped in both arms. He removes my hand and nods, reaching over to turn on the water in the ancient clawfoot tub.

I manage an incoherent response. This teasing, playful side of Titan is something he's shown everyone but me. And I like it. I like it a lot.

Titan says nothing else, but props me up on his lap, carefully removing his coat from my shoulders. He sucks in a breath as he stares at my naked figure. "I do believe you've got a splinter or two, Hot Sauce. Let's get those out, but a hot bath will do you a lot of good."

Looking down, I frown. Deep, red scratches cross both of my gorgeous breasts and the top of my stomach. What a dumb way to bust my ass and get splinter-tit.

Titan reaches behind me, rummaging through a small cabinet and emerging with a pair of tweezers. "Sit still for me, okay?"

"Yes, Daddy," I agree as he blanches, those aquamarine eyes locking on to mine with ferocious intensity. "What?" I hedge. "Just checking to see if that might be a kink you're into."

"Not my typical thing," he admits as I rock my hips on his lap, rubbing the hardness under the backs of my thighs.

"You sure?" I joke, rocking my hips a little bit harder. "Seems to me like you enjoyed it. You want me to be your sweet little baby girl?"

"Luna," he barks, snarling at me with fangs fully descended. "Enough. I'm about to toss you in this water without checking the temperature first. Settle down."

"Fine," I snap back, rubbing the tip of one of his fangs. "Put the vampire teeth away. I'll behave."

Titan shoots me a skeptical glance but takes the tweezers to my chest, removing a dozen tiny splinters as I attempt to sit still. When that's done, he checks the water and lowers me in gently. "I've got a couple things to do out here. Let me know when you're done, and I'll find you some clothing."

I'm dying to tease him about how he ripped mine to shreds like a wild animal, but I think I'll save that for later. Now that we're not in the thick of it, so to speak, he's cagey and on edge again.

Now that I've had a taste of him, though, I don't want it to be over.

HALF AN HOUR LATER, I emerge from the bathroom with a towel wrapped around my curvy frame. The scratches and slight punctures on my chest burn like shit, but I'll be fine.

Titan's stoking the fire as I cross the small space and flop down in his chair. Blue eyes land on my bare legs and travel up to my face. "Let's get some ointment on your scratches."

I grin as I unwrap myself like a present, baring my naked figure to his hungry eyes.

I expect him to say something snarky, to maybe ask me

what I'm doing. But he does none of those things. Instead, he shuffles his way across the floor and leans over me in the chair, bringing his nose to my stomach and sucking in a ragged breath. Rough lips press a kiss to a scratch just over my ribs. And then they make their way upward. First a luxurious, slow lick of his soft tongue along a scratch that travels over my left breast. Then a hard bite on my nipple as I arch up into his touch.

"I need more," I plead as Titan covers my stomach and chest in a combination of pleasurable licks and stinging bites.

"Not tonight," he confirms as I whine in frustration. I hate that something is holding him back just when we were starting to connect.

"Why?" I demand. "Not why about the sex, but why are you holding back from me? Talk to me, please."

Blue eyes cloud over as his dark brows slant to form the hint of a vee. "I can't take it farther with you, Luna. It would be unfair since your plan is to go back to California."

For one tense beat, I say nothing as I attempt to sort through what he just said. Pen's words at the ball ring in my mind, heat flooding my chest as I imagine Titan chasing me.

When I don't immediately respond, he hops upright and disappears into the bathroom, coming back with a small bag from which he extracts a tiny tube of Neosporin. I'm about to demand a response from him, but when he takes a blanket from the back of his chair and lays it down in front of the fireplace, I'm intrigued.

"Not what you think this is for, Luna," he barks, but there's no bite to the deep tone. "Come sit in front of me."

I'm skeptical as fuck, but I stand and then drop down in front of the big alpha when he crosses his legs and pats the blanket. I hear rustling behind me and then Titan's big hands come around front of me. He squirts a little Neosporin on his fingers and then rubs my tits with it, making sure he coats my scratches. But it feels so damn good as I lean back into his chest. He tugs at both of my nipples.

"I didn't get a splinter there," I grouse, playing with him.

"You tellin' me to stop?"

"I want more," I growl.

"No." That's all he says as I fall silent. Frustrated, horny, confused by the maelstrom of emotions in my chest after this evening of connection.

Titan plants a tender kiss on my shoulder. "Close your eyes, omega. Just relax."

"I don't claim that designation," I remind him.

"When you go home to Santa Monica," he says softly, "you'll still be an omega. And you'll still ache for an alpha. Human men will never suit you again, Luna. They'll never fulfill you like an alpha will."

Like I will, is what he's not saying. And we both know it.

I can barely think with his big, warm hands on me, but the thought of Santa Monica doesn't bring me joy. Titan rustles in the bag and picks up a comb, drawing it carefully through my tangled hair.

"This side of you is surprisingly tender."

I expect him to bristle behind me, but if anything, he scoots closer, his warmth bleeding onto my skin from proximity alone. He says nothing but works his way through the mess of my wet hair carefully, gently. This isn't his first time doing this, and I'm dying to pepper him with questions.

"Go on, Luna," Titan purrs from behind me. "You're dying to question me, so let's hear it."

I move to turn around as he redirects to face forward with a gentle grip on the top of my head. I'm prepared to ask him a million questions when he uses the comb to split my hair along the top of my scalp, combing down both sides in an even part. It feels so fucking good to have his hands in my hair that I forget the questions and sink into his heat instead.

The fire crackles in front of me, radiating warmth on my still naked front. Titan is a comforting, protective presence at my back.

He says nothing, waiting for me, but I find myself ready for a moment of quiet, to just enjoy, as he suggested. Titan combs his way through the entire length of my hair and then begins separating chunky strands along the front. When he starts a loose French braid along the side of my head

, I finally squirm.

"Okay, I was enjoying like you suggested, but a French braid? How do you know how to do that? Do you have sisters I don't know about?"

"Not hardly," Titan snorts, turning my head back to the front as he continues his steady braiding, big fingers tickling my scalp as I groan into the attention. "I used to have a girl-friend who loved to have her hair braided. She taught me this."

Girlfriend, ugh. I'm thankful he has the skill now, but the thought of him touching someone else's hair intimately like this? It sends a stabbing pang of jealousy through my body, so strong I grip my thighs tightly to avoid snapping about it.

"Easy, omega," Titan says, moving to the other side. "I can see your anger. That was a long time ago."

"I have no ground to stand on anyhow," I grumble. "You don't belong to me."

Titan gives no indication he's heard me other than a soft sigh as he continues braiding my hair. I've ruined the easy quiet between us with my jealousy, so I try hard to tamp it down. But the longer I ponder another woman touching him, the angrier I get. Finally, I cross my arms and bite the inside of my cheek to remind myself that twelve hours ago, he and I were still shouting at one another.

This version of Titan is so fucking intoxicating. I want to explore this connection and understand how it works. I want to know if it could be something. Something that might make me feel enough to change plans. Something that might make me stay.

"It stopped snowing while you were in the tub," he murmurs finally, knotting my braid at the end and tucking the whole thing back over my shoulder. Smooth lips plant a tender kiss at the base of my neck from behind before Titan's soft tongue travels along the back of my shoulder, a low groan rumbling from his big frame.

"I shouldn't want you, but I can't stop, Luna. I don't want to stop. Even though we'll probably fight about something stupid tomorrow."

I grunt my acknowledgment, because it's true. Still, I turn on my butt to face him. "I've always been mouthy, but I don't fight with everyone the way I fight with you." Looking up, I give him a hopeful look. "It doesn't have to be this way between us."

Titan's lips purse into a thin line as he nods placing the comb back in his travel bag. "We'll see how things shake out. For now, you need rest."

I don't want rest, but when he picks me up in his big arms and heads for the bed, I find myself dozing off, comforted by his heat.

CHAPTER TWENTY-THREE

titan

LUNA FALLS ASLEEP FAST in my arms, snuggled into my chest.

Mine. The simple word repeats in my brain as if it's my new mantra. I press my nose to her braided hair and breath deeply. Sea salt and caramel soak into my senses, wrapping around my chest and tugging. She's so peaceful like this, her aura a hazy, restful blue.

I recognize tonight for what it was—we have incredible chemistry. Off-the-charts, once-in-a-lifetime chemistry. But she didn't deny it when she said she was leaving. There are only a few more steps in the Omegamatic project. Her time at Bent Fork is drawing to a close.

Still, what's between us is significant to me. I've struggled with admitting to myself that when Asher saw a bond between us, I fucking knew he was right. And I told myself I didn't want that. But the reality is, I do.

This would be a meaningful conversation to have directly with her. But we were fighting yesterday. Then I ate her out, jacked myself off on her tits and braided her hair. We've done a full 360, but we've built next to no trust between us.

I fall asleep mulling over my approach, but I don't come to a solid conclusion before sleep takes me. I'm not anxious to put my heart on the line only for her to remind me she's going home, no matter what.

In the morning, I wake to Luna's ass pressing against me. She's dreaming, mumbling in her sleep, her hips thrusting against my morning wood. Goddamn, I want her. I want her with an intensity that buckles my knees as I stand and head for the bathroom to take care of business.

When I come out, she's waking slowly, blinking those gorgeous blue eyes. She looks to her left, smiling when she sees me come out of the bathroom.

I take a quick peek out my bedroom window. "Snow's melting, Luna. We should be able to make it back to the lodge today."

Her smile falls a little. "Are you ready to go back?" I know what she's asking. Do I not want to stay here and enjoy her a little more before we leave? I do. God knows I do. But I'm curious how this plays out when we're not isolated in a sexy cabin in front of a roaring fire. It's easy to fall into passion in a one-bed situation.

Not to mention I'm anxious to get back and see how the researchers are getting along, and if anything new has come up with Declan or Gabriel. As the pack's enforcer, I dislike being gone for long periods.

"I believe we should," I confirm.

She sits up in bed, hissing as her fingertips probe the still-red scratches on her chest.

"Lie back," I direct her, then grab the Neosporin. She obeys, sending an inconvenient zing right to my dick, which twitches at her submission. The mattress creaks under my weight as I shift onto it beside her prone figure.

Leaning over her, I rub the Neosporin onto each scratch,

holding back a stupid grin when she arches into my touch. Her pale nipples pebble as I stroke my way along her skin.

Luna clutches my sheets in both hands and gasps, "Do we have to go back right away?"

I laugh as I watch the sensual omega in my bed. I can't resist her like this. Sliding down so she's laid out in front of me, I bring both hands to the backs of her thighs and push them up to touch her stomach. She's spread open for me, wide enough for me to notice the slick dripping from her sweet pussy.

I lean in and inhale, rocked by the strength of my desire for her. My vision narrows again, focused on the beauty in my sheets, so desperate for my touch. I want to savor every inch of her, but I'm overwhelmed by the strength of my need that all I can do is groan as I lick my way up the back of one thigh, stopping to nibble every few inches.

"God. Fuuuuck. More, alpha. Please."

Her pleas send my lust sky-high as I turn my attention to her clit. I suck gently on it before slipping two fingers inside her and curling them. Rubbing in slow circles, I whine around her increasingly loud gasps. I'm desperate for her to come. Edging can happen later, if I get to taste her again. Right now I want this omega to flood my face with her sweet honey.

"Come for me, Luna," I demand, growling into her pussy as she shatters, hips rocking so my mouth slides along her clit as she comes. Slick spurts from her, covering my mouth and cheeks as I hump the bed ferociously, desperate for my own climax.

Luna cries out as I continue stroking inside her, her heat fluttering around me as orgasm prolongs, until she's screaming for mercy and trying desperately to rip her thighs from their position up against her chest. She wants control, but I crave it more.

I remove my fingers from inside her and shove her legs

back hard against her chest, licking along the side of her clit again.

"I can't. Titan, I can't come again. I never d—oh, God..." Her voice trails off into a deep groan as her thighs quake around my head. But I don't stop. Not until she comes twice more and falls into a limp, soaked mess, totally and completely exhausted.

AN HOUR LATER, I've packed up everything I brought with me, and Luna's dressed in her dirty jeans and one of my sweaters. A stab of pride shoots through me as I watch her fuss with her braids in the mirror, but she opts to leave them in.

"I'm ready," she whispers from the bathroom as our eyes meet in the mirror. It sounds like she's ready for far more than simply a trip back to the lodge, but I nod anyhow.

"Let's go, Hot Sauce." Unlike prior times, there's no snark to the nickname now. I like it for her; it suits her wild personality.

I grab her hand down the stairs as she snickers at me. "Not looking forward to patching me up a second night in a row?"

"Oh, I don't know," I purr back. "I enjoyed the hell out of it."

"Doting on me, you mean?" she snarks. "You're really fucking good at it."

"I know." I laugh, opening the truck door as she slides in with a throaty chuckle.

The ride back is full of chatter about our packmates and wondering what they'll say when we show up. We agree as a team to come up with some way to get back at Stone and Clay for forcing us into a situation that could have ended badly.

Luna's got a few ideas for retribution that are really, really appealing to me.

Stone is never going to know what hit him after we get our claws in him.

"We're gonna be a good team," she sniggers as we park in front of the lodge. Snow still covers the ground, but it's melting fast in the unseasonably warm weather. It's short-lived though. Already I can smell snow in the air. I ache to be holed up in my cabin with her again.

I round the truck, opening the door for her as she hops out, giving the lodge the side-eye before looking up at me. I'm so much taller, she has to tilt her head all the way back for our eyes to meet. "You know everybody is going to twenty questions us about the last few days, right?"

I nod. "And? What's our story?"

"What do you want it to be?" she asks, the question soft and unsure, so unlike her usual confidence.

"We don't owe them a single goddamn answer about anything," I respond finally. "But I'll take the lead if you want."

She reaches for my hand as we walk up the front stairs, her fingers trembling slightly in mine. I don't know this side of Luna, the side where she wants comfort and protection. We've been so consistently at one another's throats, there's been no time for this. In my chest, an ache takes up permanent residence. I want to learn this side of her. I need it.

I open the front door, smiling as she sails through, her scent drawing me to her like a magnet. To my surprise, there's nobody in the lobby, but Clay comes through from the kitchen at the same time as Erin. Erin grabs Luna's hand with eyes wide at the same time Clay opens his mouth to speak.

Before either of them get a chance, I hear a new voice, one I don't recognize.

"Luna! I'm so glad you made it back safely. I was so worried!" A very tan, very thin asshole crosses the lobby toward us, dragging Luna into his arms before planting a very sensual kiss on her lips. She stiffens in his arms and pulls back, but doesn't shove him away.

I watch with an increasing sense of dread as Erin forces a meaningful smile. "Titan, Luna. I didn't get a chance to share that Mario showed up yesterday to check on you and make sure you're handling all this Canadian cold alright."

Mario is too busy running his goddamn hands up and down Luna's body, and she's still fucking frozen in time, her body stiff as a board. Not that he notices.

When an angry noise rumbles out of my chest, Mario's dark eyes connect with mine. He takes a step back from Luna and blanches, glancing from her to me and back to her again. "Luna? Is that guy growling at me?"

Luna whips around, pleading for something with an anxious look that sets my teeth on edge. We should have gotten our fucking stories straight before we came in here, because I don't know how much she does or doesn't want to share. But she says nothing as anger rises in my chest.

When I don't respond to her look, she turns back around to Mario. "Hey, can we chat?"

Mario shakes his head as Luna grabs his hand and drags him toward the dining hall without a backward glance.

Erin rounds on me immediately. "I'm so fucking sorry, T. We tried to call and warn you, but there was no service."

"Warn me about what, Erin?" I snap as Clay takes a protective step closer to our pack omega. "Warn me that she has a boyfriend who came to our fucking home to see her?"

Erin purses her lips. "Not a boyfriend. They dated, but they're not together."

"She could tell me that herself, you know," I return as red takes over my vision. I want to rip the fucking lodge to the ground and bury Mario in a very deep hole. I want to punish the omega who didn't tell me there was a man in her life who cared so goddamn much, he flew out here to surprise her.

I turn from them both before I lose all control, something that hasn't happened to me since I was far younger and dealing with the grief of losing two parents. I hate this, this out-of-control feeling. And I wouldn't have it at all except for Luna-Fucking-Brooks and her not-boyfriend.

"Enforcer," Clay's voice is gentle but insistent. "There's more. We need you to chat with Rogue about Sal. They're connecting, but you're really the right person to talk through it with them both."

"Goddamn it," I snap, stalking up the stairs as I holler for Rogue. I hear his door whip open, and when he peeks his head out, his normal smile falters and falls. "We need to talk, alpha. Right now." I barge my way into his room.

CHAPTER TWENTY-FOUR

Luna

"OH MY FUCKING CHRIST, Mario. What the hell are you doing here?" I demand answers as I drag my sometime lover into the dining hall, shoving him toward one of the chairs as I sink into another.

I can practically feel Titan's fury from here. Anger that I didn't say "Hey, Mario, here's my new…not boyfriend. But the new guy I'm messing around with?" I don't even know what I should have said, but I'm off to find Titan the moment I get this straightened out.

Mario wears a confused expression on his handsome face. "I just…we haven't talked much since you came here, Luna. I missed you. I wanted to see you and make sure you were doing alright. All our friends are worried about you. It's like you dropped off the face of the earth. This place sucks," he whines, looking around as my blood heats to a boil.

"This place sucks? You mean this gorgeous lodge filled with really great people who are like the perfect family?"

"Geez," Mario blurts. "Didn't mean to insult your new friends. What's up with that? Who was that guy you came in with? Are you fucking him?"

My brows threaten to jump right up and off my face as I stare in shock at Mario. He's nothing I want at this point in my life. In fact, what I want has changed drastically in the last few weeks. He's too...put together. Too party boy. He's everything I loved about my old life and nothing like the people here at Bent Fork.

"Mario. Who I do and don't sleep with is none of your business. You and I hooked up occasionally, and that was great, but we were never exclusive. We're not together now. In fact, we won't be hooking up at all in the future. Are we clear on that?"

"Crystal," he says in a snappish tone.

I force my gaze to soften. He did come to check on me, which is...unexpected. "I appreciate that you came to see if I was okay. I truly do. But I'm great. Better than great. I love it and I'm staying for a while longer."

Mario's look of shock fades into a deep scowl as he leans back and crosses both tanned, toned arms. "It's because of that guy, isn't it?"

I shrug. "I don't know what's going on between us, not yet. But I want to know. He's...he's not what I thought he was."

"Sounds like a great start to a long relationship," Mario mutters before running both hands through his dark, wavy hair. He shifts forward, resting both forearms on his thighs. "Shit. This is awkward, I came out here, and you're...involved. Not your fault," he adds when he sees the scowl I send his direction. "I should have told you, or called like a normal person. I thought it would be a nice surprise. I'll stick around long enough to get the patent paperwork done, and then I'll get out of here."

I imagine Mario handing Titan patent paperwork and have to bite my lip. That's not gonna go well.

"What?" Mario questions before slapping his head. "That's

the fucking guy, isn't it? The guy who created the Omega-matic. Damnit, Luna, he's a fucking animal."

"Don't be an asshole," I retort. "I'll talk to him, that was just really awkward."

Mario gives me a disbelieving look, pursing his lips.

A knock at the door causes me to look up. Erin peeks in. "Can I come in?"

She joins us with a somber expression on her face. "I'm so sorry to you both," she says. "I wasn't entirely sure what we were getting into, but it was an uncomfortable situation."

"It's fine, Erin," Mario hedges. "I shouldn't have surprised Luna, but I'm still so happy to have delivered your finalized divorce papers in person. It was a pleasure working with you, and I'm grateful I got to meet Stone. He seems perfect for you."

"Mario's gonna stay a few days to finalize the patent paperwork with me," I share.

Erin looks over at Mario and smiles kindly before looking at me. "It'll be a full house at dinner then. The researchers agreed to come up for the first time, so that's awesome."

I know her well enough to sense the hesitation in her tone, but Mario beams. "Thanks again for your hospitality, Erin. I'm going to get some work done, but I'll see you both around." He turns to me with a baleful look. "Sorry again if I fucked anything up for you."

Ugh. Mario's trying to be nice.

He's so damn wrong for me. I look toward the front of the house, sensing Titan is up there right now. Mario looks at me, following my gaze as he laughs.

"Best of luck with...things." He gestures in the direction of the stairs before heading up them himself.

The moment he's gone, I whip around to Erin, placing both my hands on her shoulders to shake her.

"Duuuude, I needed a warning. Titan is freaking out."

Erin puts both hands over her face. "Duuuuude, we called you like a hundred times, but there's no signal. Was your cell even on on the way home?! You know what? It's neither here nor there."

I sigh. "I've got to talk to him pronto."

Erin strokes my hair as she pulls me in for a hug. "For sure, but give him a minute 'cause he's on enforcer duty right now."

"What happened?" My voice is urgent with worry. "What have we missed in the last few days?

"Nothing major," Erin continues. "Sal and Rogue are… connecting. We just wanted Titan to chat with Rogue about the alpha birds and bees, so to speak. Sal has a troubled past, but she trusts Titan."

My heart pangs with the desire to go to him, so I drag Erin into the lobby to wait with me. I need a girl chat ASAP.

"Tell me everything, literally everything," she demands as we flop onto one of the lobby's big sofas.

I glance upstairs, knowing River's probably snooping right this second. To be honest, I've come to terms with the plucky teenager hearing everything.

Turning to face my bestie, I pick at the fringe on a pillow. "He told me he likes me against his better judgment."

Erin laughs. "How romantic."

"And he…did things to me."

Erin rests her cheek in her palm, waggling her dark brows. "Now we're getting somewhere. How was it?"

I huff out a breath. "It was, holy shit, E. I don't even have words to describe it."

"Did you fuck him?" she whisper-hisses under her breath.

I shake my head, scrambling to figure out how to put into words what we talked about in the seclusion of Titan's cabin. "There's chemistry for sure. We're drawn together, but he said he didn't want to if I'm leaving. I'm still planning to leave eventually, so…" My voice trails off. I don't even know what else to say.

Erin reaches over and strokes my forearm. "You don't have to go anywhere, Luna. You can stay here forever. You know that, right?"

I nod turning to look up the stairs, pressure crushing my chest as I wonder how angry Titan must be.

CHAPTER TWENTY-FIVE

titan

I'M TRYING DESPERATELY to focus on this conversation with Rogue, but I can't stop thinking about Luna. I'm a messy jumble of emotions ranging from fury to terror to a strong desire to punish her for not mentioning Mario a single time in the last two days.

"Titan, you okay?" Rogue's voice breaks through my thoughts. "I mean, I know you came to talk to me, but you look freaked out." There's a horribly concerned look on his face, so I shove my own mess way down and look at him.

"I barged in here a little aggressively, but you're not in trouble, Rogue. Stone wanted me to chat with you about Sal, and your connection."

Rogue looks dubious. "Tell me you're not about to explain the birds and the bees to me. I don't know if I can take it."

River bursts through the door with a jubilant look. "Oh my gawddddd, you're getting the birds and the bees talk. I can't wait to hear this!" She flops down in a chair in front of Rogue's fireplace as he sighs and sits in the other one.

I'm left standing like a goddamn school teacher at the head of the class. My mind spins immediately to a daydream of me

223

teaching, with Luna sitting in the front row, a short schoolgirl skirt on and no panties, teasing me while I try to keep my cool.

The hold this fucking omega has over me is a powerful thing.

Clearing my throat, I look at both twins. "Are you clear on the basics of the birds and bees, or should we start there?"

River gives me a look that screams "Are you fucking serious?" Rogue snorts.

"Not that it's any of your business," he pauses as I glower, "sir," he adds at the last second. "But I've had sex before. I know the birds and bees."

"With Sal?" I confirm.

Rogue blushes and shakes his head. "We're taking it slow. She had a hard time with that other pack." I see how the tension in his body changes, his fists balling as his muscles begin to quiver. Whatever Sal has shared with him about Declan's pack obviously makes him protective.

"Sex between alphas and omegas is different from normal sex," I tell the twins, thinking humorously how this is the blind leading the blind. I've never fucked an omega either. But I've got a better sense after being holed up with Luna for two days.

"Alphas read emotion better than humans, so you'll experience things more strongly than you would if you bedded a non-transitioned human."

"Ohmygawd, you said 'bedded,'" River cackles, falling sideways in the chair as she covers her face with her hands. "This is so uncomfortable. Go on."

Grimacing, I look at Rogue. "How about I just answer questions you have instead of this?" My face heats. I've never had such an uncomfortable conversation with anyone.

River giggles as Rogue blurts out, "How's a knot work?"

His twin makes a horrifically exaggerated gagging noise, but they both look at me expectantly.

Fuck me. I don't know how many synonyms of the word "awkward" there are, but every single one of them could be used to describe this conversation. I'm a quiet person; I don't discuss the intricacies of sex with anyone beside my subs.

Running my hands through my hair, I blow out a breath. "A knot is a thicker section at the base of your penis, and it swells when you have sex. Not all the time, but sometimes."

"How do you make it not do that?" Rogue asks, his voice wavering slightly. I can't tell if he's about to burst out laughing or something else, but River is on the verge of a hysterical outburst, judging by the look on her face.

"It's connected to the strength of your emotion," I tell them. "It's a biological need to bind someone to you. Think of it as more serious than regular sex. Knotting an omega means something deeper. And when you knot her, you're stuck like that until it deflates. So you have to be careful."

"Wait one fucking minute," River yells. "It locks you together?"

This is a point to be very clear about, although if I know anything of Sal's past, it's that she, at least, unfortunately knows how this works.

"If you were to pull apart while knotted, it would tear your skin."

River crosses her legs and grimaces. "That's a bunch of bullshit."

Rogue looks up at me. "What about in here?" He places one big hand on his chest. "I sense her in here, Titan. What does that mean?"

"Gawd, we're about to get sappy," River proclaims, but even she looks curious about my answer.

My thoughts go to Luna again. To the way I can feel her in my goddamn chest right now. Distress, longing, worry. Those are the emotions I sense, even though we haven't tended to our bond or even fully admitted it to one another.

"Feeling her here, in a bond, might mean she's your mate," I continue, my voice barely audible in my own ears. "She's probably meant for you, no matter how unlikely it seems, or how surprising she is."

The twins are silent as they look at me. Finally, Rogue cocks his head to the side. "Are we still talking about me, enforcer?"

Shaking my head to encourage the pieces of my mind to fit themselves back together, I look down at the twins. "I don't fucking know, to be honest. Do you have any other questions for me?"

"Oh, we're pretty clear on things, aren't we, Rogue?" River turns to her brother, nudging him in the side as he looks up at me with a slight smile.

"*We* are, yeah." I don't miss the way he emphasizes "we," as if it's painfully obvious to them that I have zero clarity at all.

No shit, I want to shout. I don't know what to fucking do, other than go caveman on Luna and toss Mario into a lake somewhere. But I didn't come up here to ask for advice; I came to give it.

"Any other questions, come find me," I gruff out, heading across the hall for Sal's room. When I knock, there's no answer, so I listen and hear a shower. She's busy—we'll catch up another time.

That insistent pull in my chest yanks me physically, and I stride up the long hall toward the stairs. Luna comes up them, meeting me at the top. Blue eyes find mine, the tightening in my chest increasing as she takes one look at me, then grabs my hand. We head back down the hall to her room. All my focus narrows on her when she opens the door and pulls me through, closing it behind me.

I want to bite her. I want to fuck her. And I want to punish that ass when I consider Mario getting on a plane because he assumed she'd be thrilled to see him. She didn't tell me about him, and I'm beyond upset.

"That was a clusterfuck," she supplies helpfully. "And I'm so sorr—" I silence her with a look.

"Are you with him?" I'm about to rage around this room like a bull, I'm so goddamn angry when I think about him touching her.

"Oh, are we jealous?" she snarks, crossing her arms. "Now you have a sense of how it felt for me to see your hands on Bianca's hips."

I reach out and collar her throat, pulling her tight against my chest. "I've never fucked Bianca. I never will fuck Bianca. Answer my goddamn question."

"I'm not with him," she asserts, her aura swirling with intense focus. "But we were hooking up when I left LA. It was casual, so I was truly surprised to see him here."

I know right then that I'm lost to her. And I'm terrified to admit how deeply her claws have sunk into me, because I don't want my heart to get ripped to shreds when she leaves. But I feel her in my chest. Many of her emotions mirror my own.

Pulling her up into my arms, I brush my lips across hers. "I'm so fucking mad."

"I can see that," she murmurs. "I don't know what story we should have told when we got back, but right here, right now is the only place I want to be."

Desperation pulls my lips to hers as her scent blossoms all around us. My tongue slides alongside hers as I taste her. She strengthens our kiss, wrapping her arms around my neck as her lips become more insistent.

And that golden connection in my chest burns hot and hard with desire. Hers. Mine. When I think about her packing her suitcase and leaving sometime soon, that golden beauty turns to ash.

I open my mouth to tell her precisely how fucking terrified I am, to ask her if she feels that too, when my walkie beeps. Groaning, I set her down and listen in the receiver.

"Hey, buddy, the researchers are coming up for dinner. I need you here to liaise, please." Stone doesn't wait for a response before clicking off.

Luna glowers up at me. "I'm gonna be polite, but as we sit there, just know I want to scratch my claws across Bianca's stupid face for touching you." She flips her hair over her shoulder, pats me on the chest, and then opens the door to go.

Her possessiveness warms me from the inside out. Pride about what she feels for me bursts in my chest, heating the bond I've desperately tried to ignore but can't stop thinking about.

Reaching out, I grip the back of her jeans and pull her to my chest again, leaning down to bury my face in her hair. "Then know this, omega. If Mario so much as looks at you like he's daydreaming about you naked, I'll rip him limb from limb. You are not his."

You're mine are the words I'm not saying. The words we're both dancing around, because we're both running scared of this surprising, all-consuming connection.

Luna shudders and rubs her cheek against my mouth with a huff. "I wish we didn't come back here."

Ditto, I say to myself. Because I could be fucking her in front of a roaring fire right now. Instead, reality awaits us downstairs.

CHAPTER TWENTY-SIX

luna

TITAN HOLDS me for a long minute, his hand on the back of my jeans as he breathes evenly into my neck. We don't have the right words for what's between us, but the simple touch is everything.

Eventually, his lips travel to my ear, and he pulls on it once before nipping just below. "We're expected at dinner, Hot Sauce."

"So I heard," I grumble, walking into the hall as he closes my door behind us. When he takes my hand, threading his fingers through it, I preen. He stalks up the hallway silently, with me by his side. Titan never lets go when we appear in the doorway to the dining hall. I swear every goddamn head pops up to look at us, the room falling silent.

Every one of our packmates, plus all three of the researchers and Mario—even Betty and her boyfriend, Arnaud, are here tonight. Stone shoots me a victorious grin before I glare at him, hoping he can read how he's still on my shit list after dropping me in the middle of nowhere with Titan.

Despite how it turned out. That's neither here nor there. The point is, it was fucking rude.

The twins emerge from the kitchen, pushing a cart piled high with carne asada and tortillas. I almost feel a little bad for Clay stuck on dinner duty so much, but it must be Stone's night, technically, because our pack alpha hops up and helps place all the food on the table. He gives Clay a thankful grin before sitting back down and turning to the researchers.

"How's everything coming with your research?" Stone directs the question at Bianca, but Sam speaks up first, his face a mask of frustration.

"It'd be better if you all had been more forthcoming about the religious aspect of being an alpha. It was disheartening to learn that in town after meeting someone from another pack."

My blood chills, Titan freezing next to me.

"Explain." Titan's voice is a one-word command that nearly bowls the wiry researcher over.

He pushes his glasses up higher on his nose and turns to look at us. "I mean it would have been helpful if you'd been truthful about alpha religion," Sam states, glaring at us.

Titan opens his mouth to say something, but Erin speaks up first. "Excuse us if we look a little shell-shocked, Sam. There is no religion inherently tied to alphas. If someone was Christian or Muslim or Buddhist or atheist before they transitioned, they remain so afterward. Alphas don't have an alpha religion."

"That's not what we heard in town," Sam pushes back.

"From whom?" Stone questions, his voice low and even, although it's clear to see he's fucking angry. We all know the answer before Sam confirms it.

"Gabriel, from one of the other packs. He mentioned how alphas are God's chosen people and offered to let us come hear his sermon this weekend. We're going, obviously, because we need all the possible information."

Stone sits back in his chair with a sigh, eyes focused on Titan next to me.

Bianca puts both her hands up. "This came up for the first time today. I had planned to ask you about it over dinner, but not like this." She gives Sam a heated look, but he shrugs as if to say, "Better to get it over with."

Stone looks back at the researchers. "We have nothing to hide from you. We didn't tell you about this because it doesn't exist. If Gabriel believes alphas are God's chosen people, so be it. He's new in town. That pack never held that belief prior to his arrival."

"Still," Sam presses on. "We want to understand it."

"By all means," Stone continues. "But be careful around Gabriel and his pack alpha. They don't do things like we do."

"Meaning what?" Bianca questions, her tone worried.

It surprises me when Sal speaks up first, her voice silencing everyone else at the table. It's quiet and clear as a damn bell. "They mean Declan isn't a good person, alpha or not. Believe me. I used to live with him, so I know."

Next to her, Rogue shifts his chair closer and wraps an arm around her waist. She leans into his chest. Wordlessly he stands, gripping her hand as they leave the dining hall.

"Nice job," I snap at Sam, who grits his teeth as Titan leans over me, his giant forearm on the table.

When he speaks, I'm surprised at his warning tone as he glares at the lanky anthropologist. "Sam, this is the second time you've been rude to one of my packmates. We invited you into our home. We're baring all our secrets despite it being unbelievably uncomfortable. If this is the level of professionalism we can expect from you, I will request someone else be sent."

The whole research team blanches, but Bianca sits up straighter and looks at us both. I wonder if she's thinking of how she tried to kiss Titan, and how unprofessional that was too.

"We're grateful to your whole pack," she says instead, looking around to make eye contact with everyone. "Truly, we are. This whole experience is unchartered territory for everyone. Please know we want to help."

Sam grits his teeth as I debate whether I want to check on Sal or demand a word with Erin.

"Tell us more about precisely what Gabriel said," Titan demands.

For the next ten minutes, Bianca shares details of how Gabriel approached their team in town one night to invite them to his sermon.

We're all shell-shocked by the time the research team is done. Dinner's a disaster, and the research team begs off any post-dinner coffees pretty fast, returning to their trailer. The moment they're gone, Titan frowns at Stone.

"This is gonna be a fucking problem. We told the Deputy Prime Minister we'd expose his connection to Declan if he didn't send a handler. Instead, he sent a religious nut job? What's he playing at?" Titan turns to Clay. "I need options, strategist. None of this bodes well."

His cell phone beeps then, and he picks it up, frowning. "Damnit, I've got to get to the bar." There's pure steel in his voice as he looks at pack leadership. "We need a plan before this becomes an issue."

"Agreed," Stone says, his face thunderous. Erin looks over at me, her dark brows furrowed.

I don't know what this new angle with Gabriel really means for our relationship with Declan's pack or its omegas, but I know one thing for certain—I can't shake the horrible sense that this isn't going to turn out well.

CHAPTER TWENTY-SEVEN

titan

HALF AN HOUR LATER, I'm behind the bar at Teddy's, muttering as I sling strong drinks and engage in meaningless chatter. This religious angle with Gabriel is highly disconcerting. Declan is a stupid fucking asshole, which means he could be easily led by someone charismatic and smart. I can see an "alphas are God's chosen people" angle really appealing to him. Having a religious justification for moving drugs and kidnapping omegas is terrifying.

Realizing that none of Declan's pack is in the bar tonight brings me further discomfort. They're usually here on Fridays. I can't shake the feeling that trouble is coming.

By the time the bar closes, I'm pacing with nerves. Picking up my cell, I call Stone.

"Everything alright, buddy?"

"Dunno," I admit. "I can't stop thinking about Declan and the drugs and the omegas he was trafficking. And now this Gabriel bullshit. I don't know that he's dumb enough to continue what he was doing before, and not from the same place. But I have a pressing desire to check. Come with me?"

I hear grumbling and other voices before Stone comes back on. "You want anyone else coming with?"

I consider it for a moment. "Clay and Ash. There's something bigger going on here. I just know it."

"Meet you there," Stone agrees.

Hopping in my truck, I head for the old mill. By the time I turn off onto the overgrown road, memories assault me. The angry look on Luna's face as she attacked Declan. The relief that splashed across it when I barreled through the door to help. The terror we all felt when it looked like we wouldn't get Rogue untied from the railroad tracks in time.

Stone pulls up a minute or so after I do. I'm surprised to see Cassian in the car with him. They hop out, and Cass holds his hands up in supplication. "Hope it's okay I invited myself along. I might be helpful with anything to do with Declan."

"What's going on?" Stone prompts me as they come around the truck, looking from me to the old abandoned textile mill.

I grimace. "Declan's people don't come into the bar anymore. I confirmed with my bar manager. And I don't believe for a fucking second that they're finding Jesus. I think they're figuring out how to keep doing the shit off the grid. But on the off chance that Declan is still a fucking idiot, I wanted to start here. Maybe there's some clue for us..." My voice trails off when I can't think of anything else to say. "It's just an intuition."

Stone gives me an earnest look. "Then we need to pay attention to it," he agrees. "Your intuition is spot on. You've never led me astray."

I keep my eyes on the ground, looking for any sign of activity as we enter the mill. We head through the front entryway and out the double doors leading to the open back floor. A few blocks away, the railroad tracks are barely visible.

And next to the goddamn tracks are two shipping containers that weren't there before.

"You've got to be shitting me," Cassian growls. "How? Why? This means we have to assume Gabriel is aware of what Declan's doing, and either doesn't care or is party to it. And if that's the case, then the DPM also doesn't give a shit? That makes absolutely no sense. Why would the DPM allow Declan to continue this?'

"None of this fucking adds up," Clay muses, crossing the yard at a jog as we follow. We examine the containers, but they're unlocked and empty, and there's no trace of what may have been inside.

Clay turns to me. "James is a whiz with tech. I wonder if he could put some kind of surveillance in place to show us what's going on."

"Call him now," I direct. "Get him out here. Between this and the researchers attending fucking sermons, I see a million ways this could go south."

Clay agrees and jogs back to the truck for his cell.

Half an hour later, James pulls up, and we help him install microcameras all around the mill and tracks. It's gonna be a pain in the ass to monitor with the train coming through and setting off all the sensors, but we have to know what's going on.

Once it's done, we head back to the lodge. The omegas, Mario and Rogue are hanging out by the front fireplace. My heart leaps in my damn chest when Luna looks up at me, blue eyes sparking with mischief. I want to pull her close, to protect her, to make that beautiful aura spark and explode for me. I'm fucking thrilled when I see she's on the opposite end of the sofa from Mario.

Asshole.

After this evening's revelations, I'd love nothing more than to take her, break her and put her together again. I want to control something, because this situation with Declan is like a noose around my neck. She must sense it, because as Ash relays what happened to the group, her eyes don't leave mine. Once he's done, she gets up and takes my hand, pulling me toward the stairs.

But I don't want to be surrounded by a pack of people who can hear my every word. I pull her in the opposite direction, knowing Mario is watching.

Good. Fuck Mario. He'll never touch her again if I have anything to say about it.

Growling, I swing Luna up into my arms and head out the front door. I slide her into my truck and drive to my cabin, silent the whole way. When we get there, she follows me to my door. I put my hand on the knob, and she slides hers up my shirt to rest on my lower back. A second hand slides up to meet the first as I sigh.

"Your hands feel so damn good," I groan.

"I can do a lot more with these hands." She teases, a low throaty noise that has me reaching around to pull her to my chest.

I swing her up into my arms, her legs wrapping around my waist as our foreheads press together. "Why can't things ever just remain uncomplicated?" I sigh, my lips brushing hers. Her sigh matches my own as she presses her plump lips to mine.

I take her inside, fully intending to give her a deep massage and maybe a good tongue fucking. But instead she pulls me to my bedroom, dragging my head into her lap as she scratches my scalp with her long nails.

I fall asleep worrying about how fucking devastated I would be if something happened to her.

IN THE MORNING, I wake to find Luna in my arms, her face pressed up against my pecs. Stroking blond waves away from her face, I watch her snore. She's out.

The walkie she was wearing last night pings.

"Luna, you up? Let's get this paperwork done. I wanna get out of here. Canada is too fucking cold."

Grinning, I pick up her walkie and press the button. "Luna isn't available, but when she recovers, I'll bring her up to the lodge for our meeting."

There's silence on the other end of the line as I allow myself a victorious chuckle.

"Okay, great," Mario lies. "I'll be here."

I don't bother to answer, because I'd still like to pound Mario into dust, but Luna begins to stir at the noise.

When she blinks her eyes open and stretches tan arms over her head, I press my face to the center of her chest and suck in a breath. She hums happily as I brush my cheeks against her tits, reveling in the feel of their softness through her shirt.

"Mario needs us," I manage, glancing up with my chin on top of her boobs.

"Oh, does he?" she chirps. "I'll be glad to get this fucking paperwork behind us."

"So you can go home?" I question. Why the fuck did I just ask that out loud? I slap myself mentally as she shifts up onto her elbows.

"So I can file it and keep going with the project to make the pack a shitload of money. Because your invention is incredible. Plus, I'm not leaving until we figure this out." She gestures between us as hope blooms hard in my chest.

Rolling out of bed, I hand her her shoes, and she follows me out to my truck. We're quiet the ride back to the lodge, but when we get there, James comes out, grinning.

"Oh, Christ," I complain. "What now?"

"Not here with a security incident," he laughs, "but I knew you would come ask me again about the system we set up at the mill. There's been no activity, but I'll let you know if there is."

"Thank fuck." I clap him on the shoulder.

James gives me a wink. "Mario is in Stone's office working on the Omegamatic paperwork. Figured I'd let you know so you can go find him."

"Super!" I shout.

Luna scoffs at my uncharacteristic enthusiasm as we head back through the lobby and down a long hall to Stone's office. Mario, that smarmy asshole, sits at the head of Stone's small conference table, earbuds in his ears. His hair is perfectly coiffed, his hands smooth and manicured. Is this what Luna's into? This sort of man? I can't imagine someone more different than me.

She drops into a chair on Mario's left as he looks up from the earbuds and beams at her. It's easy to see it's the look of a lover, someone who knows your body so well they lean in and listen. It's impossible not to feel the heat.

I scowl as he looks up at me, his smile falling as he sits stiffly in his chair. Stalking around him, I take the chair opposite hers and next to Mario. I want him to see my damn ire for this whole meeting.

Luna looks at Mario and then me. "Okay, T, you and I have talked about this process a couple of times. I finalized the designs based on your assistance, and Mario will have a few questions so he can finish the patent paperwork. This step is critical to ensuring a recurring revenue stream on the Omegamatic."

Mario snorts at that, shaking his head.

"Something funny, Mario?" I question, my voice clipped.

He looks up and shrugs. "The name is fucking stupid. We considered renaming it but we thought regular men might like the idea of it seeming interesting and different, so Omegamatic it is."

There's so much blatant disregard in his statement, I have to remind myself he doesn't know shit about alphas. He looks at me, not seeming to realize how stiff I am in my seat, how irritated I am at the way he's approaching this meeting.

"Okay, so, William…"

"Not William," I remind him. "Titan."

"The paperwork says William," he offers, as if I don't know my own fucking name.

"I've never gone by that," I bite. "That's fine for legal paperwork, but my name is Titan." I make the mistake of looking over at Luna, but she waggles her eyebrows at me suggestively as she bites back a laugh. Well, I'm thrilled someone is enjoying this bullshit.

Mario makes an irritated noise and then looks at me again. "Okay, *Titan*. There's a section of the patent application for you to explain, in your own words, the purpose of the machine. I can take a stab at it, but how would you describe it?"

"Alphas fuck differently from you." I grin. "More, harder, longer. We need a toy to accommodate our…enthusiasm."

Mario visibly gulps as he looks at Luna. "Is this guy for real?"

CHAPTER TWENTY-EIGHT

luna

I KNOW the second Mario asks if Titan is for real that we're heading south fast. Titan is frozen like an angry statue in his chair. It's not lost on me that he's nearly twice Mario's size. Between that and his incredibly possessive nature, I can't imagine Mario wants to poke this bear.

"It's true," I confirm for Mario, who scoffs and sits back in his chair before shrugging.

"Damn, I am ready to get home." His voice is irritated, but it sounds like nails on my mental chalkboard.

I say nothing about that because, when Mario mentions home, Titan sits back, both elbows on the arms of his chair. He steeples his fingertips together and looks at me, a curious expression on his face.

Oh no. No, no. Something's going on in his head, and I can't ask about it in front of Mario.

Mario asks a few more innocuous questions, which Titan answers without turning away from me. When that's done, Mario prints out the paperwork and hands it to Titan. "I'll have you sign this, and then we can get it submitted."

Titan takes it and stands as Mario sputters.

When Titan turns with a bemused look, Mario points at the paperwork. "You're not gonna sign it right now?"

Titan crosses his arms, the paperwork still in his hands. "I'm sure you can understand as a lawyer that I'm compelled to read over this myself before putting my name on it."

Mario looks at me with his mouth open, then zips it shut before nodding at Titan. "Of course. Let me know if you have questions."

"I won't," Titan laughs, "but I'll get it back to you once I've had a chance to review it."

Now he's not looking at me, but he and Mario are having some sort of visual standoff that I want to head off at the pass.

There's a tense beat as I lean over the table to put my hand on Titan's forearm. When he looks down at me, he's carefully guarded. Shit, he's being distant. It's not hard to imagine what's bugging him. Having evidence of my life in California presented so neatly in front of him is a hard pill to swallow based on what he's shared with me in the last few days.

"I'm opening today. I've got to get to the bar. I'll return this soon."

Mario and I both watch as Titan leaves the office. The second he's gone, Mario slumps back in his chair, wiping his hand across his brow. "Shit, Luna, how can you stand to be here? It's like caveman central here. Jesus Christ. I'm outta here this afternoon if I can make it."

"Do what you need to." I nod. "I'll scan the paperwork back to you when he completes it. And he will," I assure Mario. "I've got some work to do, but I'll catch you later, okay?"

Mario gives me a disappointed look but agrees. I run to catch Titan, but he's already gone by the time I get up front.

I have plenty of shit to do today, and I know Titan's at work. But I don't like how we left things with Mario's commentary about me going home. The more I reflect on returning home to Cali, the more unsure I am that I ever will.

I'm definitely staying long enough to see what's between Titan and me. Considering leaving the pack makes me feel sick. Seeing Mario here cemented that for me.

By the time dinner rolls around, I know what I'm going to do.

"What's that look on your face?" Erin asks, squinting as she examines me from across the table.

"What look?" I ask innocently.

Cherry guffaws next to me. "Honey, if you think you're subtle at all, here's your kind reminder that you're not. You are clearly hatching a fucking scheme right now. Might as well spit it out."

Tucking my hair over my shoulder, I shrug. "It's a girl thing. Give me half an hour and then come find me. I could use some advice."

Cherry laughs again, bright and joyous as she yanks my seat away from the table. "Go on, Luna. I can't wait to hear this."

After I head to my room, I hop into my shower. I shave and sugar scrub my legs. By the time I get out, Cherry, Erin and Julia are all in my room, lying on the bed together on their bellies, staring at my bathroom door.

Julia holds a fucking bowl of popcorn in her hands, winking at me as I exit the bathroom without a stitch of clothing on.

"Okay, Hot Sauce," Erin starts. "Tell us everything."

I throw a robe on and quickly recap last night and today as the girls comment on how soap opera-esque my life is becoming. I can't even deny it.

"So Titan is falling for you, and you're staying for a bit to see what's up with that?" Erin translates Julia's question as I turn to them, my voice wavering for the first time.

"I don't know if it'll work out between Titan and me, but I want to try." It's an admission I haven't even fully told myself.

But it's completely true. "I want to give it a chance, at least. And if it doesn't work out, I can always go home later, right?"

"Duh," Erin reminds me. She points to my head as I do my hair in big curlers. "So, what's the plan for knocking his socks off?"

"Literally," Cherry jokes as she and Julia dissolve into fits of laughter.

Reaching into my drawer, I pull out the hot pink lingerie set I recently purchased. "This is what I was thinking." I chuckle, tossing the lingerie at the girls.

Julia catches it and gives me a skeptical look before signing something that I'm one hundred percent sure is snarky.

"She wants to know what you're going to do about the fact that it's twenty degrees outside." Cherry laughs.

I point to Titan's coat hanging on the back of my door. "Pretty sure that's all I need."

Erin sighs. "Damn, to be a fly on the wall for this..." She tosses the lingerie back, and I dash into the bathroom to put it on. When I emerge, Julia fans her face as Erin and Cherry grin at one another. I grab Titan's coat from my door and sling it around my shoulders, buttoning it up the front.

"You've got this, girl," Cherry says with a wink. "Now go get your man and then tell us everything when you come home."

There's a knock at the door, and Stone sails in, letting out a wolf whistle when he sees me. "E told me what you were up to, but try not to give my enforcer a heart attack, okay?" He tosses me the keys to his truck as I salute him with a middle finger up.

"I haven't forgotten how you dropped my ass off in the middle of nowhere. I'm mad at you," I snap.

Stone grins as he sits on the bed, pulling Erin into his arms. He looks at me over her shoulder. "Wasn't the middle of nowhere. I knew T would take good care of you."

I laugh as he flips me the bird too.

Erin smiles. "Get out of here, hussy. Surprise him and then come back and tell us all about it."

Laughing, I swing Stone's keys around my finger and head out the front door.

It takes me nearly an hour to head up the still-slick roads toward the bar. I'm careful the whole way, but nerves bundle in my stomach when I think about seeing Titan. For all I know, he might turn me down the second I strip his coat off. Having Mario here really upsets him. Still, I need to make my stance crystal clear.

When I pull up in front of Teddy's, I check my reflection in the rearview mirror. "You've got this, girl." I start in on my usual pep talk. "You are a princess. You are worthy. You are perfect." Flipping my blond waves over my shoulder, I hop out of the car, thankful his coat is so long it comes down to my knees.

I head into Teddy's and look for Titan. He's not behind the bar, but there's another guy there, a human. Shit, I have not thought this plan all the way through. Stepping up to the bar, I wave to catch his attention.

He looks up at me and waves. "Can I help you?"

"I'm looking for Titan; is he here?"

The bartender throws his bar rag over his shoulder and crosses his arms. I'd find him attractive if I never knew Titan. And that's when I know Titan's earlier comment was right— I'm a fucking omega because this fine-ass normal man does absolutely nothing for me.

"You must be Luna..." he murmurs, his gaze narrowing a bit.

"That I am," I agree. "So, Titan?"

He pauses for a second as if he's assessing me, before he jerks his thumb behind the bar. "He disappeared into the storeroom a few minutes ago. Perfect timing to, you know, do whatever it is you came here to do." He laughs a little when I give him a thumbs-up.

My heels click on the wood floor as I head down the short hallway to the back storage area. I enter quietly, spotting Titan immediately as he leaves the freezer with a case of burger meat in his arms. Blue eyes laser focus on mine as he drops the box of hamburger on a nearby table.

His gaze lowers from mine to his coat, all the way to my heels on the floor. He looks guarded, and I don't blame him. This is out of character, even for me.

"I'm surprised to see you here," he says when the air between us is so hot, I feel the need to fan my face.

"You neglected to give me something at the cabin, and I want it," I purr, unbuttoning Titan's big coat to reveal the hot pink lace set I picked for this conquest.

Titan sucks in a deep breath, his lips parting as he takes one step forward, then two. He crosses the room like a predator, eyes never leaving mine as his nostrils flare, his body tight and tense and completely centered on me.

My nipples pebble underneath the bra as Titan stops in front of me with a low, dark growl. "We shouldn't, Hot Sauce," he warns, reaching out to run his fingertips along the lace strap over my left shoulder.

"This is a 'Luna' conversation, Titan," I retort. "Not 'Hot Sauce.'"

"Noted," he whispers, sliding the strap off my shoulder and leaning down to kiss it tenderly, as if he can't help but touch me. He sighs as he drags his teeth along my shoulder, goosebumps following his attention. "You surprise me at every fucking turn."

"Oh, I'm about to surprise you even more." I laugh, shucking the coat entirely off. It lands on the floor with a thud as Titan sucks in a breath, blue eyes traveling down my body appreciatively. He bites his plump lower lip as his gaze moves back up, landing on mine.

"I want you," I say with all the confidence I have. "I want to know what it could be if we gave in, because when I think about leaving you behind and going to California, I feel sick. I—"

Titan silences me with a thumb pressed gently to my lips. "This could end in disaster; you know that. Right?"

I open my mouth, sliding my tongue along his thumb as he watches. I pull his thumb into my mouth and suck before letting it pop out of my lips. "I want to know," I encourage. "I will regret it the rest of my life if we don't try."

Titan tilts my chin up and presses his lips to mine. It's the most tender he's ever been, but there in my chest I sense heat. His kiss deepens for a moment before he pulls away.

"I might even be coming around to the whole idea of the aura reading," I grumble, pointing to my head as if I wear a halo. "What does mine say now?"

Titan smiles and looks at me. "Sultry red, a little bit of dark deviance. A thread here and there of a fairly apprehensive blue." He looks back down at me. "Talk to me, omega."

I suck in a breath at that term. "I am one," I whisper. "I know that now. And I want you to teach me, alpha. Teach me what I should know."

Titan whines at my words, his hands running up and down my arms as he looks around the storeroom. "Goddamn, Luna, I'm losing my mind. I don't want to do this here. Come on." He reaches down for my coat and pulls it over my shoulders.

"Where are we going?" I ask, my skin covered in goosebumps. Anticipation has me nearly panting, knowing we're finally going to take this farther.

Titan turns to me with a low growl. "My place. My bed.

There are things about me that you and I have never discussed. But if we do this, you need to know."

"Oh God," I bark out. "You're not super into foot cheese or something, are you? I can get down with a lot, but even I've got my limits."

He blanches at the word "limits" but shakes his head. "Foot cheese isn't really my jam."

I laugh so loud at his response. Witty men are the fucking best, and I'm dying to know just how dark and sarcastic he is when he's not holding his tongue around me.

Titan picks me up and throws me over his shoulder, stalking out of the storeroom. He stops for half a second behind the bar, but the bartender just shoots us a pleased look.

"Get out of here, T. I've got this." He winks at me when our eyes meet, and then I'm aware of an entire bar full of patrons staring at me, thrown over Titan's shoulder like a sack of potatoes.

We leave the bar, heading around back, and he deposits me carefully in the front seat of his ancient truck. It's fucking freezing in here so I rub my legs together. Titan gets into the driver's seat and pulls me close, sliding his warm hand between my thighs.

"I'm not far from here," he murmurs, kissing my forehead. "We'll get you warmed up fast."

"Bet you will." I laugh. "With your mouth, I hope."

Titan lets out a low-pitched rumble and steps on the gas, barreling up the street three blocks and parking fast. He swings himself out of the driver's seat and then hauls me into his arms. Reaching up under the coat, he lays a loud smack on my ass before heading through a coded entry door and up a flight of stairs.

I can't even whine about him going caveman on me because it's sexy as hell, so I take in the beautiful old details of his building. When he unlocks the first condo on the right, I gasp out in surprise. Titan sets me down and turns to shut the door behind us, watching in silence as I make my way around the stunning space.

A huge wall of windows on the right-hand side overlooks all of downtown Ayas. Off in the distance, I can see the highway leading to Teddy's just outside of town.

The apartment itself is furnished with big, chunky, over-sized furniture that fits him. The coffee table is littered with wood shavings and tiny carvings, but the rest of the space is immaculate. The back wall is a huge kitchen, and two doors set in the wall must be the bedroom and bathroom.

"It's beautiful, T," I whisper. "It suits you."

Titan looks at me with that same intensity he does everything. His absolute dominance is a tangible force, commanding me to cross the room to him, pressing my body to his as he looks down at me. The hint of a smile tugs at both sides of his mouth as he reaches out and unbuttons his coat.

When he stops, I pout and whine, reaching up to unbutton it myself.

"Remember, omega," he reminds me. "You wanted this."

CHAPTER TWENTY-NINE

titan

I HAVEN'T BEEN with a woman who wasn't a sub in years, almost fifteen years to be precise. Not until Luna in the cabin. I don't do one-night stands and hookups. I only meet and sleep with women already in the lifestyle. None of them have ever been omegas.

She came to the bar for me. She offered herself to me. And I want to take and take until the need I've been bottling up explodes and incinerates us both.

Collaring her throat with my hand, I shove her up against the nearest wall and take her mouth like I did at the ball, sucking at her lips and fisting her hair as she moans in my arms. Slick floods from her, coating my hands as she whines.

"Perfection," I murmur when we part and I set her down. "My bedroom. Come." Already I'm dipping into my Dominant side, ready to control my partner and push her however I want to, consensually, of course.

Luna follows quietly as I swing the door to my room open and observe her glancing around at the space. Everything in my bedroom is dark-toned; I prefer it that way since I transitioned. It's calming. On the outside, there's nothing truly shocking about my bedroom. Not until Luna notices the hooks in my headboard and then the varied hooks in the ceiling above my bed. She doesn't poke around in my cabinets, but I can sense she's dying to.

She turns to me with a question in her eyes, her aura swirling with confusion.

Giving her a heated, heavy look, I smirk. "I'm a Dom, Luna. Do you know what that means?"

Blue eyes widen before she grins. It's big and beautiful, and I want to choke her with my fat cock. "I thought you were hiding something surprising, Titan. But that? That makes sense to me."

Growling, I cross the room and grip her throat, my thumb running along her lower lip. "The part we should talk about is not me being a Dom, Luna. It's the fact that I always, without exception, take subs. I don't fuck brats."

Her face falls when she takes in what I mean. "You think I'm a brat?"

I take a step away from her and let go of her chin. "I don't mean in the general sense," I correct. "A brat is someone submissive in the bedroom who likes to taunt and tease their Dom in order to get punished."

"Sounds like fun," she laughs, "but...that's not what you want. That's what you're saying?"

"Right," I confirm. "I want obedience and full submission. Could you really see yourself doing that? Because if we do this, if we start something, that's one of the things I need."

Luna frowns, rubbing the back of her arm. When she looks up at me, she's wary and guarded. "I...I don't know. I've had dominant lovers but not anyone who truly considered themselves a Dom. I don't really know what that means, but the key to anything must be communication, right?"

I nod. "Communication, setting boundaries and limits,

having a safe word. Always being open to changing things depending on both partners' needs."

Luna's frown deepens. "Why didn't this come up when we were at the cabin?"

I look over at my bedroom window, watching as a few errant snowflakes fall from the sky. It's going to start snowing hard again. When I turn back to her, those dark blue eyes are focused on me. "It was unexpected and new. We've built no trust, Luna, and a Dom relationship is based *entirely* on trust between partners. I wanted to talk to you about it, but that assumed you and I were headed down the path to some sort of relationship. The cabin didn't seem like the appropriate time to have that discussion."

Luna sighs and crosses her arms before leveling a steady, confident gaze on me. "I'm not a submissive personality. You know this already. But I'm willing to try, to explore a side of myself I don't know well, if it's what you want."

I shake my head. "You don't just become submissive to please another person, Luna. It doesn't work like that." This is her last chance to run, her last possible out. Because if she doesn't run from me now, I'm going to take her as mine.

She kicks her heels off and pads quietly across my carpeted floor, running both small hands up my shirt. "What I'm saying is that maybe the right man could tame my wild side, Titan. If anyone could do that, it would be you. I want to try. If it doesn't work out, it doesn't work out. We can go back to being mortal enemies."

I huff out a laugh as I run both hands through our hair and bring my nose down to suck in a breath along her collarbone. "You smell like the sea," I murmur, licking her skin before I plant a line of kisses to her shoulder. I bite down hard enough that my fangs pierce her skin, and she shudders in my arms as she barks out a string of curse words that would make a sailor blush.

"This is your last chance to leave," I offer. "You can walk out that door right now." I move my focus to her face to gauge her reaction, but if anything, her expression morphs into steely determination.

"You don't scare me, Titan. Do your fucking worst," she whispers.

Anticipation has my skin tingling as I ponder the best way to ease her into what might be fun. I'm so hard and ready for her, I'm about to lose my mind.

Glancing around my room, I decide on a path forward and reach for Luna's hand, pulling her behind me toward my bedroom's back wall. There are all sorts of ties and hooks here for restraining my subs in different ways. "We'll start easy," I tell her. "Silicone cuffs and a blindfold. Are you okay with that?"

Luna bites her lip. "What are you going to do with me while I'm cuffed and unable to see?"

I push her gently to the wall and lean in, one arm on either side of her as I hover my lips over hers. "Whatever I want to, Luna. Since you've never done this, I'll keep it vanilla today. But if you like it, we'll talk about limits for future sessions."

She frowns at that, and in my chest I sense a mistrustful distress. "What is it?" I encourage her honesty as I tilt her head up to see me.

She's holding back a frown, already uncomfortable about what we're doing. Finally, she sighs. "Calling it a session makes me feel like one of hundreds of women you take to bed. It doesn't seem...special."

My heart aches when she says it, because all I want is for her to feel cherished right now. I press my lips tenderly to hers. "I've never done this with a sub, Luna. I've never taught anyone, never wanted to do that. This is far, far outside my comfort zone. We won't call it a session, but let's be up front about one thing—I would never do this with anyone else."

I hope the truth of my words reassures her, and it seems to, based on the way she relaxes, rocking her hips against me with a sigh.

Smiling, I lean over and drag my nose along her neck. She smells like our scents combined, and that heady perfume makes my dick twitch. I turn to hunt in my nightstand for a pair of simple silicone cuffs and a piece of silk. She can easily slip out of the cuffs if she's scared or uncomfortable.

Returning to where she is, I show her the cuffs. "We need a safe word if you aren't having fun, but these are easy to get out of if you need to. I'll never do anything to hurt you, unless we determine we both want that, but today is about simple."

"Foot cheese," Luna laughs, "that should stop things fast if I shout it."

I laugh when she holds her hands out for the cuffs. Where I was previously sensing a lingering concern from her, the minute I slip the cuffs over her tiny wrists, the scent of her slick nearly knocks me on my ass.

I groan as I tug her arms up above her head, hooking them onto a lower hook as she bites her lip. She says nothing as I pull a length of silk out of my back pocket to show her.

"Thoughts about the blindfold?"

A whine leaves her mouth, her desire slamming me in the chest so hard, I have to put one hand up on the wall to steady myself. "Do it," she commands.

Our eyes meet one last time, and she gives me a devious wink as I slip the black silk over her fluttering lashes and tie it behind her head.

"Now what?" Her voice is soft and subdued, but there's still a thread of the snarky brat underneath the question.

I lean in to growl in her ear, smiling when she gasps and arches her back. "Now you don't speak unless I ask you to, although if you can't hold back a moan or a scream, that's fine. I'll be back."

Luna rolls her hips against mine again as I place a gentle kiss in the hollow of her throat, letting my hands explore the soft tops of her breasts before teasing my way down the lines of her trim stomach. She cries out when my fingertips play with the top of her panties.

But when I stand and walk across my apartment, out of the bedroom, she lets out a soft, angry whine. I'm curious how long she'll make it in silence. I ache to find out.

I head into the kitchen and fill a glass with ice water and a straw. My favorite Jack Daniels goes in a second glass. I've got massage oil in my bedside table. We may not use that today, but we might in the future if this works out.

I drag a dining room chair back into my bedroom, almost panting with desire as she startles against the handcuffs and clamps her thighs together. I pull the chair in front of her and set the water and whiskey down next to it. Shucking my shirt off, I undo my jeans and sit in the chair.

"You're doing beautifully," I encourage, watching as she squeezes her thighs tightly together. "I want to look my fill of you for a while."

Luna lets out a desperate whine but then closes her mouth, every muscle trembling in anticipation of what she hopes is coming.

So I watch, quietly at first as she cocks her head from side to side, listening for any indication of what I might do. I give none, only reaching down for my cup and throwing the Jack back in one gulp. For ten minutes I watch as Luna's body betrays her. Her muscles tremble ever so slightly. Rosy nipples pebble through the bra as her breath starts coming at a more rapid cadence.

I let out a growl, and she yips and jumps, her chest heaving as I slide to my knees in front of her. Ten minutes and she's practically out of her skin.

"You running out of patience, Luna?" I press my lips gently to her stomach.

She opens her mouth to respond but then thinks better of it. I asked her a question, but she isn't sure if she can speak without clear direction.

God, that makes me hard. Because such clear obedience is what I love most in the bedroom.

"Good girl," I praise her when she doesn't answer without my allowing it.

Luna's breathing turns rapid and shallow, her gorgeous tits swaying softly as I watch her. I imagine they'd be heavy in my hands, big enough to spill out of my palms. So soft, so responsive to my lips and teeth. I could touch them right now if I wanted.

The fantasizing is killing me. I want to drag Luna to my bed by the hair and have my way with her for hours. I press my upper body against hers, sitting back onto my heels as I free my cock from the confines of my jeans. I double fist it and stroke hard, gasping at the red-hot pleasure that rockets through my system.

Luna strains against the cuffs, her lower lip trembling as she listens to me jack myself off at her feet. She opens her mouth, and I expect either our safe word or a command, but she closes those plush lips and lets her head fall back against the wall with a plaintive sound.

"My God," I purr. "You're so fucking beautiful like this. Submitting and waiting for me." Every moment I expect her to sass me and she doesn't is a personal victory. And to the victor go the spoils.

I cage her in with my arms and lean in, biting at the top of her panties. She jumps again as I drag them down with my teeth, my nose stroking her folds as I remove the beautiful pink lace. Luna hisses when I lick my way back up the inside of her thigh, opening her legs as she bucks her hips closer to my mouth.

Needy. So goddamn needy. She's been unsatisfied since the cabin. I've got to taste her, so I lean in and slip my tongue between her thighs, groaning when slick coats my face and neck. This is perfection, tongue-fucking a submissive omega in my bedroom.

Luna's cries grow louder and more insistent as I bring her right to the edge, but then back off. Over and over again I tease her, not letting her come, pushing her to see what she'll do. But to my infinite surprise, she says nothing at all. She never complains, not verbally at least. There are plenty of distressed noises, but other than that, she says not a word.

I've never been so hard and ready to fuck in my life. With my prior subs, I'd tease them for hours and hours until I couldn't take it anymore. But I've never dominated an omega, and this experience is wildly different. I want everything she has to give. Every single fucking thing. And I want it right now.

luna

HOLY FUCKING SHITBALLS. I'm losing my goddamn mind. Titan is everywhere and nowhere, all at once. I can't see shit, and I'm barely able to hear a thing, my big alpha is so quiet. Every time he touches me, it's a surprise, and the anticipation of what he'll do to me next has me leaking slick like my own personal oil spill.

Titan's incredible tongue returns to my clit, licking along both sides before sucking it into his mouth with gentle, pulsing pressure. I'm gasping for air, barely able to think straight when he stands, and I feel how hard he is for me. There's such a size difference between us that his dick is poking me right in the stomach. I want it. I've never been so desperate to get off in my entire twenty-eight years of life.

I open my mouth to demand something, anything from him. And then I remember I'm submitting. I didn't know if I could do it, honestly, and it's hard. But the goddamn payoff is going to blow my mind.

There's a rustling sound, and I feel Titan's jeans fall to the floor, landing on my feet. A slurpy noise tells me he's touching himself again, and that makes me unspeakably hot. When the noise stops, he reaches out and unclips my bra, yanking it off. I hear it hit the ground somewhere across the room, but then I'm naked in front of him.

Titan groans as both hands come to my breasts and stroke gently. I arch my back into the touch, desperate for more of everything when his mouth closes over one nipple. He sucks–hard–and I come out of my fucking skin. I'm on the edge of a blistering orgasm. I've never come from foreplay like this, but it's happening today if he keeps up this sweet torture.

"You taste so goddamn good," he growls, moving his mouth to my other breast, where he swirls his tongue around the needy bud before biting hard.

Orgasm begins to rise as my breath comes fast. Titan steps back. "Not yet, sweet girl. I'm not ready for you to come." He leans in and tucks my hair over one shoulder, his lips tickling the shell of my ear. "I'm going to fuck you, Luna. So when you come, I want it to be around my thick cock. How does that sound, omega?"

I don't know if I'm allowed to speak yet, so I rub my cheek against his face. Something, anything for more connection.

Titan reaches down and grips the back of both my thighs, stepping forward as he wraps my legs around his waist. Then, to my intense surprise, he removes the blindfold. Sea-blue eyes are focused only on me, scanning my face, checking in. "Are you ready to be fucked by a big goddamn alpha, Luna?"

I nod again, his mouth curving into a beautiful big smile that sends heat barreling through my core. "You can speak if you want to," he murmurs.

"Please," I gasp out, desperate to say words aloud. He just grins, that intense gaze not wavering from mine at all as the look on his face morphs into something dark and devious.

"When we're here like this, call me William."

"Please," it's all I can say. Rational thought is out the fucking window.

Titan laughs as he glances down, dragging his hard cock between my thighs, coating the entire incredible length with slick.

"I'm gonna fuck you so hard," he states, "you won't be able to tell where you start and I stop, Luna."

"Get to it already!" I shout as he lets out a possessive, toe-curling growl.

"Knew that sass would make an appearance."

Titan bucks his hips, sliding that entire incredible length inside me all at once, so hard and fast that my back slams into the wall, my breath leaving me at the force of his incredible hips.

"Oh, fuuuuuuck," I groan when he slips himself out of me with a roar and thrusts again, only partway, so I get the tip of his incredible cock but nothing further.

"I hope you like it rough, little omega." He fills me again as I scream his name.

I can't even focus around the mind-numbing pleasure of him. There's never been a dick this perfect in the history of dicks. I'm sure of it. I am ruined for all others after this. Because Titan's is a work of art.

He picks up a punishing, brutal pace as he fucks me against the wall. His lips hover above mine the entire time, those blue eyes boring a hole right through me as he punishes my pussy with his length.

A sudden, molten heat erupts in my core as orgasm over-takes me so hard, all I can do is throw my head back and scream "William" over and over again. I fall before he does, so fucking hard, I can barely breathe. But he follows fast, roaring into the room as his pace loses rhythm, my ass slapping against the wall so hard, I'm sure I'll bruise.

We come down together, aftershocks rocking my system as he stills and then picks up a gentle, steady rhythm into me.

"Oh my God," I whine. "Are we going again? I can't."

Titan laughs, and it's so satisfied-sounding that all I can do is rock my hips to meet him as the laugh falls off into a moan. "No, Hot Sauce. I love the sensation of my cum dripping out of you. Your pussy is fucking sloppy right now, and I'm not ready to leave it."

Heat spreads through my chest as Titan grips my chin, forcing me to look right into his intense gaze. He presses one big palm to my chest, still fucking me slowly as orgasm builds again.

"Oh God," I whine.

"You feel me here, don't you?" he questions, stroking just over my heart. "My desire for you?"

I close my eyes to focus when his hand leaves my chest to grip my chin again.

"Don't look away, Luna. Don't close your eyes. Tell me what you feel."

I'm on the verge of screaming that all I want is to explode, that Titan's command of filthy bedroom talk has me coming out of my skin with desire. But then a tidal wave of emotion hits me so hard, all I can do is fall forward, my forehead pressed to his chest as he chuckles.

Lust, overwhelming desire, scorching, thought-obliterating pleasure.

"Tell me you feel it too," he commands again. "You feel what I do right now, because there's a bond growing between us, Luna. I'm gonna make you come like this, my dirty girl. This is the power of a bond, Luna."

"Oh God," I cry out, looking into his eyes again. Emotion after emotion barrel into me, my entire body on fire from whatever the fuck he's doing.

Orgasm builds as my whines turn into desperate gasps, Titan's eyes never leaving mine. Then a blaze of pleasure shoots through my system as I come around him, despite the fact that his hips are still. Despite the fact that he's simply holding me, his eyes locked onto mine, pleasuring me with nothing more than the emotion in our bond.

Titan's mouth drops open as he falls just after me, bellowing into my lips without ever taking his eyes from mine. I've never been connected with someone like this in my entire goddamn life, and I will never recover from this experience.

I know that with certainty as we come together, never looking away.

Orgasm batters us for so damn long, my body finally slumps, and I have to hold on to the cuffs to keep from falling against him completely. When the pleasure finally begins to recede, soft brushes of satisfied pleasure thread through that growing bond between us.

Titan hisses as he slips out of me with a careful look. What we just did was life-changing. Connection on such a deep level, I know his earlier words are right.

I can't tell where you stop and I start, I think. *You were so right.*

I don't know how to work this growing bond, but a soft smile tips the corners of his mouth up.

"Are you reading my fucking aura right now?" I question, desperate to regain some control of my thoughts.

"Don't need to," he chuckles. "You wear your heart on your sleeve, Luna. But I can read you too, in here." He rubs his own chest, kissing my lips gently as he releases my hands from the silicone cuffs.

I hiss when pins and needles shoot up both limbs, but Titan lifts me into his arms, cradled like a baby, and crosses the room to his bed. He lays me down, then crosses the room and returns with a cup of water. He holds it to my lips as I squirm partially upright in the bed.

Nothing has ever tasted as good as the water. I drink it down greedily as he reaches into his side table.

I've seen this side of him so rarely. This gentle, nurturing side where he cares so deeply for others, where he's compelled to be a caretaker. I love it.

Without saying a word, Titan opens a tiny bottle and pours something clear into his hands. When he grabs my arms and begins massaging the liquid into my muscles, I realize it's simple massage oil. It smells like sandalwood, one of my favorite scents.

I watch in silence for a while, but Titan moves from one arm to the other before pressing me back and giving my thighs the same treatment. "You might be sore; I was rougher than I intended to be." He gazes up at me with a slightly concerned expression on his handsome face.

"So..." I hedge. "How'd I do? Eleven out of ten, you'd do it again?"

He snorts out a quiet laugh and rolls onto the bed, pulling me on top of his big frame as he starts playing with my hair. When he leans in, sucking my bottom lip between his, I let out another groan. I could go again. For sure.

"You were perfect, omega. Absolutely fucking perfect. You okay?"

I tuck my cheek to his chest, smiling when he lets out a resonant purr that vibrates through my whole body. "I want to do it all the time."

"One step at a time, Hot Sauce." He laughs, pressing his lips to my ear. "I want it again too. Maybe later, depending on how you're feeling."

"Later sounds good." I let out a yawn by accident, and Titan's rumble picks up louder and more rhythmically. Before I'm even aware of what's happening, I drift off to sleep in his warm arms.

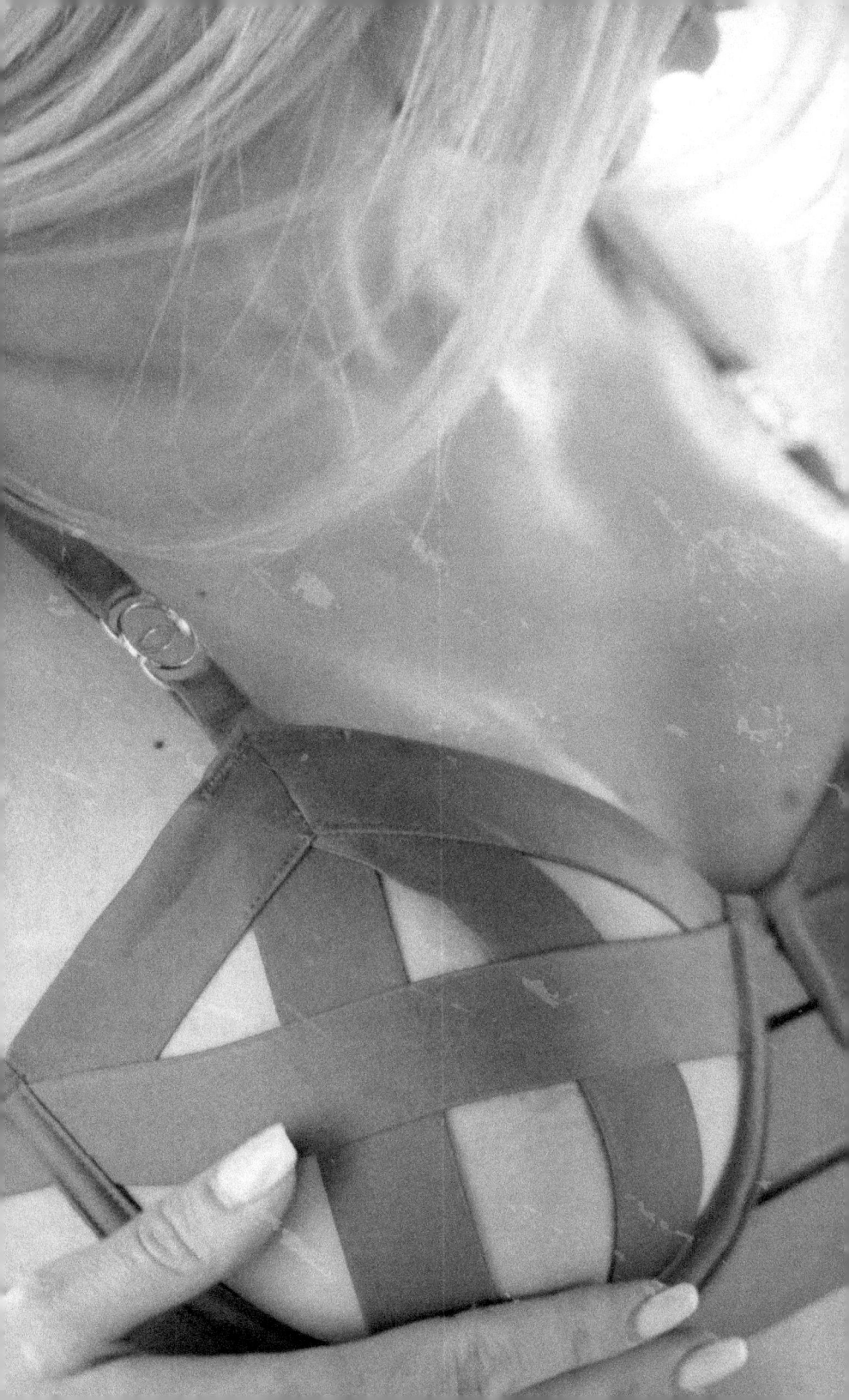

CHAPTER THIRTY-ONE

titan

THAT WAS hands down the best sexual experience of my entire life. Luna opened herself to what I wanted, and my God, it was everything I could have hoped for. There could never be a human sub that fit me like the omega I just took. And then I fucked her through our damn bond, and now I know with certainty I will never recover if she eventually goes back to California.

My life hasn't been without tragic loss, and I'm self-aware enough to know I guard my heart because of that. I have to, if I want to stay sane. It's too easy to lose people in this nutty, sometimes broken world. So, despite how amazing the sex was, I'm somewhat hesitant about taking it further.

Eventually I fall asleep with Luna snoring softly against my chest. Something yanks me awake, an insistent pulsing throb in my chest. Blinking my eyes open, I gasp when I look down and Luna's pink lips are stretched wide around my cock.

She looks up at me with a teasing look. "Do you always require quiet submission? Can I simply take what I want sometimes?"

To her credit, she waits for an answer as I lift up onto my elbows to watch the show, smirking. "You should probably ask me first, my dirty girl."

Luna's eyes flash as she hovers her mouth over my cock. "May I, William?"

I hold her gaze for a long moment, aching as I enjoy the tease. Then I nod my assent.

Luna's head dips again, those pretty lips straining around my head, her tongue running a circle around the whole tip as I pant. I sense her satisfaction and excitement to do this. She slowly leans forward, taking me as far as she can, which isn't quite halfway. I'm big, really big. I know this. I was big before the Awaken virus. I'm practically a monster these days.

My beautiful omega brings one hand to the bottom half of my dick and begins stroking with smooth, measured touches, humming around the tip at the same time. My hips start rolling to meet her. She feels so fucking incredible.

Between us, the bond sparks with satisfaction and pleasure.

Every muscle in my body begins to tremble with the desire to come and paint her pretty skin with my seed. "Teeth, Luna," I snarl. "Bite me."

Her head snaps up, blond brows furrowed in concern. "Won't that hurt like shit?"

"Maybe," I retort, "but I want it."

Her frown curves into a smile as she brushes her lips along my cockhead, then she bites it gently, tugging it slowly with perfect white teeth. The effect is instantaneous—I bellow as white-hot shards of lightning streak down my spine. I'm so fucking close to coming. "More," I command. "Fuck. More of that, Luna."

She nips and pulls her way along my entire dick, alternating between sucking and biting until I'm a goddamn mess of precum and spit. When I erupt, I fill her pretty throat before it's far too much for her, and cum drips out of her mouth to coat her chin and neck.

Luna swallows what she can and looks up at me, eyes blazing with lust. Because I'm aware of our connection, and because I'm looking for it, I sense her desperate need for me. I fall easily into Dom mode, pulling her up onto my lap as I kiss her puffy lips. Orchestrating every moment of my interaction with a sub is what I love about being a Dom. Having complete control over our experience.

"You ache for me, little omega?"

Luna gasps and reaches down between us, lining my still-hard cock up to the soaked lips of her sweet pussy. Honey drips down onto me as she hovers, then seats herself slowly, her heat eating up my cock as I slide home.

"Goddamn," I grunt, bringing both hands to her hips and bucking upward.

Luna cries out as I bring my fingers to her clit and begin a steady pattern of stroking and pinching. Her curvy hips rock against me, sliding off and back onto my thick length as our groans grow deeper and more insistent. She's been on me for less than a minute, and she's ready to explode. I want to know how many times I can make her come like this, but my own control is fading. Where normally I'd fall into a state of intense focus with my sub, Luna shatters the illusion that I can do that with her.

Feral need overtakes me, my gaze narrowing to the panting omega riding me. She wants me wild; I sense that in the bond. And that knowledge crushes what remains of my self-control.

Roaring, I rock my hips up, holding her still so I fuck her from underneath at a punishing pace. Luna's eyes close tightly, teeth nipping at her bottom lip. There's a moment where everything inside her clenches tightly, and then she shatters all over me, her sweet pussy kissing my dick in a constant fluttering rhythm. It feels so goddamn incredible, I come again, screaming my pleasure into the room as I continue fucking her, waves of ecstasy overwhelming me as her name falls continually from my lips.

When we come down from the mind-bending heat, I give her a wink. And then I flip her onto her back and do it twice more.

By mid-morning, Luna's come five or six times, and she's fading fast. I toss her over my shoulder and carry her into my bathroom. We soak together in the tub for a while before I wash and braid her hair, kissing her everywhere as I care for her.

It's easy like this. I know aftercare. I read my subs well.

But this is different because she's not my sub. If Asher is right, she's something far more than that. And it scares the shit out of me. Everyone I loved was taken from me far too soon, and that left me on my own for a long time. Without Stone, Betty, Erin and Erin's folks, I would have been a lost cause.

Luna naps in my arms in bed for half an hour, but when she wakes, I tilt her chin up. "I've got the lunch shift today, Luna. Want me to take you back to the lodge?"

She frowns. "I'd rather come help you at the bar, but I promised Cherry, the twins, and Sal I'd hang out tonight, and I've got some meetings this afternoon for work." She lets out a discontented sound as disappointment crushes my chest.

Hauling her up higher in my arms, I bite her ear softly. "Come work with me tomorrow? I can fondle you behind the bar."

Luna laughs and rubs her cheek against my mouth. "Yes. Absolutely. Yes."

I'M a weird mix of misery and bliss as we return to the lodge. I'm desperate for more connection with Luna and sad she has plans I'm not part of. I don't want her to be away from me all afternoon. That means something significant. It means Asher is right. Because, despite the way this girl makes me crazy, she's mine.

"What are you thinking about?" Luna whispers, holding my arm tightly as she sits right next to me on the bench seat.

"How you surprised me yesterday. How you fit me so well."

Her hands tighten around my arm as she snuggles into my shoulder, sending a rush of contentment through my chest. I search for her there, tentatively. Now that we've played with that connection, it's growing stronger by the minute. She strokes me gently through our bond until the tender emotion morphs into something dark and lascivious.

I have to pull the truck off the road to take her once more before I can even think of parting from her for the day.

The rest of the way back to the lodge, we chat about nothing and everything.

It's easy and uncomplicated, and I can't help waiting for the other shoe to drop.

CHAPTER THIRTY-TWO

luna

I CONVINCE Titan to drop me off at the Bent Fork sign at the street.

"I wanna walk back to the lodge. It's good for my brain." I laugh when he gives me a skeptical look.

"Good thing I gave you some spare pants, not that they fit. You got a lot of things to think about?" he questions. I know what he's really asking. How do I feel about what happened between us?

I bounce up and down in the seat next to him, laughing aloud when his blue eyes fall to my tits. He chuckles too, shaking his head.

"You are merciless," he grouses, looking at me with a wary expression.

I lean in and press my lips to his. "You're just so damn fun to tease. Find me later?"

"I will," he breathes lightly as we part, "promise."

His eyes are on me as I hop out of the truck and cross my arms, walking up the gravel drive toward the researchers' trailer.

Titan turns the truck around and drives back toward town

as I walk slowly along the valley floor. In the distance, I see the aspen grove where the store and the researchers are. And past that, the lodge itself, nestled in the center of the valley.

I walk for a few minutes, lost in thought about how amazing this place is when a wolf whistle brings me out of my reverie. "Hey, Hot Sauce! You want a ride?"

Smiling, I turn to see Julia and James coming up the road on an ATV. Julia smiles from her place nestled between James' big arms.

"What are you two doing out here in the cold?" I hug them together when they pull up next to me.

James frees both hands so he can sign and speak aloud at the same time. "Titan's been otherwise occupied, so Julia and I are getting the mail." They look at me with matching grins. "You smell like him."

Julia's hands move fast as she signs something, but I'm still not good enough to pick up all her words.

James kisses the top of her head. "She says, 'Tell us everything; don't leave out a single detail.'"

I bite my lip as I consider how to respond to that. There are some things I'm certain Titan wouldn't want shared at all. I settle for a light version of the truth. "We connected."

Julia scoffs and reaches out to slap my boob as I yip.

James laughs. "You're gonna need to give us more than that. Spill the beans."

Rolling my eyes, I huff at them both. "I can't give you all the deets, but suffice to say, the lingerie worked. Okay?"

Julia rolls her eyes even harder than I did, pouting as she sinks back against James's chest.

He turns to me with a fake scowl. "You're making my mate unhappy. She wants juicy details. Did you get your first ride on a big alpha? How was it? Did you experience the knot? Talk, girl!"

I laugh at that as I respond and sign what I can. "Yeah, I

rode him; no, I didn't get knotted. Yeah, it was really, *really* fucking good."

"Was that so hard?" James laughs as he signs what I couldn't, hugging her tight to his chest before looking back up at me. "Being mated is the single best thing I've ever done in my life. If what's between you and T is heading that way, I hope you enjoy every minute of it."

His romantic words send my mind spinning. Mated? I don't know about that. We're literally one day into trying to see if a relationship works. I'm not ready for that, but I'd like to believe there's a future where we're not at each other's' throats all the time. Last night felt like the perfect first step.

"Come on," James laughs, patting a spot in front of Julia on the ATV, "it's cold as shit out here."

I wedge myself in front of her as Julia wraps her thin arms around me and hugs me tight, her head resting on my shoulder. James's big arms cage us both as we take off up the gravel drive toward the main lodge. Sitting with them, I bask in the warmth of their connection and love.

When the lodge comes into view, I breathe a sigh of relief. Being back feels like returning home. I'm not ready for the California sun; I don't want to leave anytime soon. The decision to stay for a while feels like the right one.

As we pull up in front of the lodge, Stone comes out on the front porch with a big ass grin on his face. I point a finger at him and stomp up the lodge's front stairs as the grin turns devilish.

"Oh I'm still mad," I bark, laughing. "I need to have words with you."

James and Julia pass by me as Jules hugs Stone tight and then disappears into the lodge. "Good luck, alpha." James laughs, clapping Stone on the back before he follows his mate.

Stone continues smirking like the goddamn cat who got

the canary, before he finally opens the front door for me. "To my office, Luna. Let's have a chat."

I sail through the lobby and head down the long hallway. When I enter Stone's office, the room's fireplace already crackles, and his piano cover is up. He must have been playing. God, I love to hear him play.

Erin shows up in the doorway right after him as I roll my eyes. "What is this, the Inquisition?"

"Oh, yeah," she snorts. "If you thought you were getting out of here without a full play by play, you've got another thing coming."

"Plus we're doing karaoke tonight, Hot Sauce," Stone murmurs. "If you stick around the lodge tonight, I'm sure the omegas would be thrilled to get you rip roaring drunk. Everyone wants details."

I flop down in the chair closest to the crackling fire, remembering the way Titan's big hands braided my hair in the cabin. God, I'd love to be back there right now.

"I'm not sorry for dropping you at the cabin." Stone laughs. "Everything I do, every decision I make, is based on really fucking good intuition. You and Titan have chemistry beyond the enemies thing. I'll keep pushing and pulling you both until we sort out what it means."

"Rude," I snap. "Why don't you just let Titan and me figure it out for our own selves?"

Stone moves to his desk and folds himself gracefully down at it, dark eyes locked onto mine. Erin perches herself on one of his big thighs with a devilish grin.

I barely resist the urge to squirm in my seat. A pack alpha and omega's attention is a powerful thing.

Stone continues, "My job—my only job—is to protect and nurture this pack. While I can't be certain you're Titan's mate, I sense you probably are."

I throw my hands up, shaking my head no. "Who's saying

anything about mates? We did, errrm, connect. And it was great. Really fucking great. But we're taking it one day at a time."

Erin grins at me. "Good. Because taking an omega to your bed means something for a man like Titan. He's the fucking best, Luna."

My blood starts to push through my veins a little faster, my heart whomping in my chest. "Have you had this mates conversation with Titan?" I'm remembering last night, how we played with that connection in my chest but didn't dive super deep into the meaning behind it.

Stone shakes his head. "Titan hasn't had an easy life, Luna. He's guarded; he protects his heart because he loves so goddamned hard. I don't know if he's self-aware about it, and we intend to talk with him too. But I wanted to speak with you first."

"Why?" I question.

Erin hops up off his lap and pulls me in for a huge hug as her mate stands, not taking those chocolate eyes from mine. He rounds his desk and leans up against it, crossing both enormous arms and his legs at the ankle. "You belong here, Luna. I know it; Clay knows it. The whole pack loves you. You're an integral part of how we're trying to help Declan's omegas. We want to remind you again that you staying forever is what we're hoping for."

Tears fill my eyes as I reach up to swipe them away. I didn't realize I needed to hear it until Stone said it, but they want me to stay. I choke out a laugh. "You want me to stay, even though I'm sassy, stubborn, and I can't keep my mouth shut?"

Erin laughs out loud. "Those are some of the exact reasons we want you here, Lu. We love you, alright?"

Overwhelmed by emotion, I squeeze Erin tight. When she releases me, I throw myself into Stone's embrace and squeeze his neck. He wraps both big arms around me and holds me close, a purr rumbling from his chest. It warms my heart as I sniffle into his shoulder, wetting his flannel with my tears.

"Listen," he deposits me gently back onto the chair, "Titan called about half an hour ago asking if Asher could come to the bar. They're slammed and apparently his bar manager couldn't stay. Ash went, but I bet they could use backup."

When I look up into his face, Stone's eyes glint deviously.

I return the look with my own, and then salute my pack alpha. "Heard, alpha. I'll go change. Can I borrow your truck?"

Stone grins and fishes his keys out of his back pocket, dangling them as he hands them over to me. "Our truck, Hot Sauce. Ours."

CHAPTER THIRTY-THREE

titan

TONIGHT IS A DAMN MESS. The bar has never been this busy. Most of Mitchell's pack is here, along with the twins and Betty and her boyfriend, Arnaud. It feels like half of Ayas is here too. My only saving grace is that nobody from Declan's pack is around. If they came here and started shit, I'd have little to no backup.

Asher and Cherry showed up a few minutes ago, and Ash is already behind the bar helping. The reality is that he's not a great bartender, although he's trying really hard. Cherry's managing the food coming out of the kitchen, and I'm losing my mind scrambling between the storeroom and the bar, restocking.

I hear the front door swing open at the same time a swift tug in my chest pulls my gaze from what I'm doing.

It's her; she's here.

Despite the shitshow in my bar right now, my whole body pivots toward the beauty who just walked through my door.

Luna. Mine.

Just seeing her makes me want to roar at everyone to get

the fuck out, so I can take her up against the bar and savor every inch of her soft skin.

Luna smirks at me as she crosses the bar, time slowing like a goddamn romcom as I watch her tits sway in an obscenely tight tee shirt. She's tied it just under her boobs so most of her stomach is exposed. Hip-hugging jeans hint at the soft vee of her lower abdominal muscles.

I lick my lips as she comes around the end of the bar and hops up and down twice, laughing softly when my eyes are drawn to her gorgeous breasts.

"Glad to see that still works on you." She chuckles, reaching out to place her hand on my chest.

I want to throw her on this bar and do delicious things to every inch of her. But now is not the time. Glancing around, I run one hand through my hair and then pull her to me, capturing her mouth in a tender but heated kiss. "Omega, I want you, but it's a little crazy around here." I gesture to the line of people clamoring at the bar for drinks. Poor Asher is out of sorts trying to keep up.

Luna snorts. "Much as I'd love for us to give the people a show, I came here to help." She gestures for me to lean in close so she can whisper in my ear. My dick twitches when her soft lips brush along my neck, that sea salt and caramel scent of her wrapping around my soul as she breathes softly. "I want the William side of you later, alpha. Please?"

I barely hold back from saying "yes, mate," but we're not there yet. Despite the fact that my heart is well and truly lost to her.

Moaning, I rub my cheek against hers, my fingers snaking along all that exposed skin of her midsection. I'm not even sure I've responded when she laughs again and points to the bar behind me. "Show me how to work the point of sale, and I'll get going."

I wrap both arms around her and push her to the back of

the bar, caging her in front of the POS. Leaning over her shoulder, I bite my way along her neck as I point out how to ring up an order and where to find everything. There's a desperate ache to fuck her rising in my system, and the skimpy outfit is making me lose my mind.

But my bar patrons are losing their cool and starting to get huffy.

Luna winks at me and turns to the bar, smiling huge at the first guy she sees. He ogles her tits as he orders, but she uses all that to her advantage as I hold back the urge to rip his head from his shoulders.

Asher slaps me on the shoulder with a big grin as he watches Luna take over the entire fucking bar, handling business. "You've got to stop scowling at every man who ogles her tits, brother. She hoisted them up in that shirt for a reason, you know."

"Helpful, Ash," I snark. "Tell me it wouldn't bother you if everybody was staring at Cherry like that."

Asher leans in. "I'll let you in on a little secret, alpha. It turns me on when men look at her like she's a beautiful snack, because she is."

"Maybe you should be telling *her* that, then," I respond quietly as his eyes cloud over, his smirk falling.

"She knows how I feel already." His response is despondent as Cherry comes out of the kitchen with four plates of burgers balanced on her arms. She delivers them to the table, and Asher's right, men's eyes follow Cherry too. There's something about Cherry's supreme confidence that's powerfully intoxicating. I completely understand why men stare. She winks at me, flipping her bright red hair as she disappears back into the kitchen.

Ash watches her go with a hungry expression on his face.

This isn't the time and place for me to talk with my troubled seer about his non-mated mate. But soon I'm going to get more insistent with him. He's holding on to his demons like they're some sort of life raft, but it's time to let it go. He senses my change in focus, stalking down the bar to jump right back into the fray.

I work next to Luna and Asher for two solid hours, the bar busy the whole time. Luna works the crowd like a damn magician. She's fast, and the drinks she makes are hella strong. Half the bar is in love with her by the time things slow down.

I'm standing in the shadows watching her flirt with a couple of vacationers when a soft voice breaks me out of my reverie. "Titan?"

I turn toward the owner of that voice. "Isabel? How are you?"

The pregnant omega rubs her belly protectively. "I'm okay, thank you. I actually wanted to come in and thank you for the food you've been leaving out at the hot springs. The girls told me. I just picked it up since it's going to snow again soon."

I see Luna's head whip around. She's close enough to the end of the bar to hear what we're saying, and I sense she has a million questions. But she keeps serving drinks and taking care of the bargoers.

Smiling, I nod at Isabel. "I'm relieved you're able to get it. We weren't sure how it would work out, or if Declan would realize. But we want you to have anything you need, you understand?"

Her smile grows brighter. "Baby girl's kicking. Want to feel?"

I hold my hand out with a big grin as Luna turns to watch us with a pleased look on her face.

Isabel takes my huge hand and gently places it on one side of her belly. There! There's a quick punch from inside as the baby shoves and moves. A can't help the grin that splits my face as Isabel returns my gaze.

"You can't possibly know how much we appreciate your help," Isabel shares, letting my hand go. "Not all the girls are strong, and..." Her voice breaks off as tears fill her eyes.

Now is the time to put our half-assed plan into action. I can't help omegas who don't want to leave Declan. But I'm sure as shit here for any of them who do. Leaning in, I tilt Isabel's gaze up to mine. "If any of the girls want to leave, we will come get you. Figure out who wants out, and we'll come for you, okay?"

Isabel shakes her head. "We don't want to start a fight. Gabriel is almost as terrifying as Declan. I never speak with him, but the way he looks at the girls is just...creepy. He's always talking about how God made alphas to rule, and the time of the alpha is coming. What's even more terrifying is that all of leadership seems to agree. He's nuts."

"All the more reason for you to leave, if you want to," Luna's voice breaks in gently. "I know you don't know me; I'm part of Titan's pack. If you can figure out who might want out, we'll find a way *without* a fight, if we can."

Isabel looks from Luna to me and back again. "Is that possible?"

"I know it is," I reassure her. "It'll take some planning, but if you want out, our pack is committed to helping you. Cassian's staying with us. He's in on this whole thing too. We're worried about the Gabriel angle, to be honest. Not to mention the girls coming and going."

Isabel's eyes fill with tears. "There haven't been any new girls lately, thankfully. Gabriel keeps leadership too busy with his sermons. He's even preaching in a fucking tent at the end of our street. People from town started coming this week, but I think it's freaking them out. I'm telling you, this guy is absolutely nuts."

Luna and I share a look before she reaches out to rub Isabel's forearm.

Isabel's tears spill over onto her cheeks as she clutches her belly protectively. "God, we miss Cassian so fucking much. He was our savior, really. He protected us as much as he could against the rest of the pack. Nobody really wanted to mess with him because he's so strong, you know? With him gone, it's like we're constantly at the pack's mercy."

I can almost hear Luna's teeth grit together as she places her hand over Isabel's. "We're here for you, girl. We're here for *anybody* who wants to get away from those assholes. And we won't rest until you're out and safe, if that's what you want."

Isabel pulls Luna in for a big hug, whispering her thanks as the tears continue to spill. The bar is slowing down now, and Asher glances over at us from the other end. I know he's heard the whole conversation, but when he nods, it's clear he's in agreement with Luna and me.

Isabel looks up at me. "It's getting harder to get away from the neighborhood. Gabriel watches me like a hawk when I leave, and most of the girls aren't allowed to go anywhere at all. But I'll try to sort out who wants to stay and go. Somehow, I'll let you know, okay?"

Luna and I both agree.

Isabel thanks us again and then leaves. Luna watches her go as Asher takes care of the remaining folks waiting for drinks. After Isabel's out the door, Luna whips around to me and starts jumping up and down with both arms up in the air. She lets out a whoop as I stare at her tits.

"She's considering it, Titan. She really is. We might be able to help them. Fucking *finally*!" Luna drops her arms and does an awkward shimmying dance behind the bar as Ash laughs.

All I can do is watch the way her body moves and revel in the fact that we made progress—meaningful progress—in helping the omegas. It's all I've ever wanted to do. Finally, a damn breakthrough with them.

I don't realize I'm snarling until Luna stops her dance and

cocks her head to the side. "Why are you grumbling at me? What'd I do?"

"He's about to eat you alive, girl," Cherry offers helpfully as she emerges from the kitchen with more food. "Asher and I have got this. Y'all have fun." She bumps Luna toward me with her hip and sashays down the bar.

Luna winks at me. "You feeling a little protective, alpha? Want to take that anger out on me? I wouldn't mind getting William'd right about now."

Heat spreads through my chest like wildfire as I reach out and haul her up into my arms, my lips barely brushing along hers. "It's more of a Titan kind of fucking that I'd like to give you."

"Getting Titan'd sounds dirty as fuck," she says, her lips nearly touching mine.

Luna bites my lower lip as possessive heat swirls in my chest. I'm self-aware enough to know it's the bond. Asher's right. Luna's mine in every way a woman can belong to a man.

I stalk down the long bar, heading to the storeroom. I kick the door closed behind us, throwing Luna up against the nearest available wall with her hands held high above her head.

I want to soak in her scent, to savor and enjoy every minute of connection. That's my usual MO; that's what I've done with every woman I've slept with. Dropping Luna's arms, I reach for her shirt and pull it over her head. Underneath, she's wearing a pale pink cotton bra, her hard nipples pronounced through the thin fabric. Humming my approval, I lean in and bite, first one, then the other as Luna arches into my touch.

"Harder, T," she demands. Nobody's called me "T" or "Titan" in the bedroom for years. Not until her.

Growling, I set her down long enough to kiss and nip my way down her stomach, unbuttoning her jeans and sliding them off her tan thighs. I shove my face between her legs and breathe, the scent of her arousal sending heat stabbing through my groin. All I want to do is part those pretty thighs and fuck her until she's a sticky mess.

Luna hops back into my arms as I stand, bringing her mouth to mine in a crash of lips and tongue until I can't hold back. I devour her like a man starving, relishing that brilliant connection that blooms stronger and stronger between us. She's overwhelmed but focused, intent on getting exactly what she wants from me.

Looking down between us, I groan at the sight of those beautiful tits pushed right up in my face. Then I hook her arms around my neck and shimmy my own jeans down, my cock springing free as Luna moans.

"You've got such a perfect dick, T. You wanna fill me up with every inch of it?"

I can't manage a single word, simply capturing her lips again as I line myself up between her thighs and slam home.

Luna cries out as her head falls back, then looks down between us, watching as I pull out and then thrust my hips fast again. "Oh God, I could come already," she cries, a pink blush traveling from her cheeks to her chest.

Lightning shoots down my spine as Luna's pussy clenches around me, stroking me every time I slide back inside her. I can't keep up this delicious torture, though; I sense Luna's need for me to unleash, which is something I never do. I could hurt her; she's delicate and small.

But what Luna wants, she gets. And she wants me.

I pick up the pace, fucking her hard into the wall as her thighs clench tight around me. Her moans become pants as she gasps for breath around the blinding pleasure. Snapping my teeth as my lips curl back, I grip Luna's hair tight and bend her head to the side, bringing my fangs to her neck.

Groaning into her neck, I focus on the vein that throbs

down the side. I want to bite her so fucking badly, to bind her and claim her. But that's a step farther than we're ready for.

I won't claim her today. But I *am* going to bite her.

Luna cries out desperately as I drag my fangs down her neck to find the perfect spot. My hips punch forward, slamming her rhythmically into the wall as her cries grow louder. I lick softly where her neck and shoulder meet as Luna blurts out a string of curse words.

Heat barrels down my spine; I'm so close to coming. I want her right there with me, so in a quick move, I bite down hard on her neck, sinking my fangs deep into the muscle. It's not a claiming bite, it lacks that intention on both our parts, but it's designed to make her feel so good.

The effect is almost instantaneous. Luna screams into the quiet storeroom as she shatters, her pussy fluttering around me. I continue fucking her into the wall.

Her orgasm and the tangy taste of her blood in my mouth send me into a release so hard, so brutal, I can't hear a fucking thing. All my senses focus on my omega, wrapped around me and wringing such intense, insane pleasure from my body.

When the bliss begins to recede, I blink my eyes open to a beautiful sight–Luna's slumped against the wall, her chest heaving and her lips parted. She grins at me when our eyes meet, slapping me on the chest with a throaty laugh.

"That was...I didn't really believe Erin about the biting feeling good, but holy shit."

"I'm not done with you," I tease. "We both needed to take the edge off, but I am far from finished, omega."

"Thank fuck," she agrees, hauling herself forward to wrap tan arms around my neck. She presses a tender kiss to my lips before angling her head to the side, pressing deeper with her soft tongue. It tangles with my own, heat building in my core again as my cock pulses inside her.

Luna laughs when we part, glancing down to where we

remain connected. "I've never come that fast in my life, alpha. You've got a magical dick."

I kick my jeans off my ankles and laugh, wrapping one arm around her waist as I cross the room. After setting Luna down on one of my work tables, I take a step back to get a look at her.

She pulls one foot up onto the tabletop, her thighs spread wide as slick and cum drip from her. Luna gives me a knowing look as our eyes meet, but when I step between her thighs and gather up all that slick, she gives me a funny look.

"I don't want a single drop of my cum leaving your body," I admit. "The thought of my seed inside you makes me hard, Luna." I swipe the sticky essence off her thighs and slide two fingers up inside her. She's wet and sloppy, her pussy filled with our joint pleasure.

Luna brings her hand to my forearm, hips rocking in time with my fingers. "That shouldn't be so hot," she whines.

"It's hot because you're mine," I murmur back. "But you knew that already, didn't you?"

Luna's sea-blue eyes focus on mine, her gaze steady but wary. "Yes, alpha."

Triumphant joy fills me as I smile at her, still stroking inside her as her eyes flutter closed, blunt teeth biting her lower lip as she begins to clench tightly around me. She wants more.

"You're definitely staying?" I ask softly as I tease her.

Blue eyes focus on me. She knows what I mean. If this magic between us is real, will she give up her life in California to stay here with me?

After an eternity of her eyes locked onto mine, her lips tilt up in a little grin.

"Yes."

That one word sets off a maelstrom of emotions so strong

in my chest that I clutch my hand over my heart. It pounds under my skin, our bond tight with lust.

"Good," I purr. "Stay with me, Luna."

She grins devilishly. "You wanna put a leash on me and keep me by your side like a sweet little pet?"

Visions of Luna collared in my bedroom, kneeling at my feet, assault me. "You don't know the half of it, omega," I growl. "We'll do that and more. I have so many things I want to try with you."

Control eludes me by the second. Slipping my fingers from her heat, I cross the room and grab a bottle of tequila, yanking the top off with my teeth.

Luna watches me pace back across the cold storeroom, her breath coming in lighter, shallower movements. "What are you doing with that, T?" Her usual snark is back, but this time it rolls over me, sending pleasure through my core. She's dominant, and her aggressive energy activates my own.

I don't answer, instead choosing to give her a devious smirk as I throw the bottle back and down the anejo blanco. Next I hold the bottle to Luna's lips, giving her a quick sip.

Stepping back, I swirl the tequila in my mouth, relishing the burn as I look at Luna's beautiful body. Pale pink nipples, toned fit stomach, tan thighs still spread wide and leaking my cum. She is absolute perfection.

Parting my lips, I spit the tequila at her pussy, reveling when it hits and she yips and tenses, gripping the edge of the table. Wide blue eyes find mine, bright with concern before I take another sip of the tequila, leaning in to slick my mouth over her nipple, swirling the liquid around her peaked tip.

Luna hisses as my lick turns into a hard bite, her body jumping in my arms at the shocking sensations.

"Fuuuuck," she moans. "I could come again from this goddamn teasing."

"That's the idea, Hot Sauce." I laugh, pushing her gently

back down onto the table. Admiring her curvy figure, I pour the tequila slowly onto the middle of her chest, watching it slide down both breasts to pool in the line of her abs. It overflows and travels a path down to her shaved pussy as she hisses.

Setting the tequila down, I start at her breasts and lick it off her, sucking and biting my way, following the tequila. Luna squirms and groans as I get closer to her core. She squirms so much I bring one arm to her hips to hold her flat as I suck up the tequila, tasting her with my lips and tongue along the way.

By the time I plant a gentle kiss on her clit, Luna's gasping again, ready to demand things. When I focus on that bond in my chest, it burns bright, strong and beautiful like she is.

"I feel you," I share, bringing one of her hands to my chest. "Right here."

Luna cries out when I suck her clit tenderly between my lips, slipping my fingertips back inside her to stroke and play. She comes fast, creaming all over me as possessive pride urges me to fuck her again.

So I do, three more times until the wild need turns into something more tender and gentle. And then I clean her up, and we return to the bar and the knowing smiles of our packmates.

I am lost in this omega, lost in a dazzling connection I didn't think I wanted, but can't imagine being without.

CHAPTER THIRTY-FOUR

luna

I FEEL YOU. *Right here.* When Titan said those words, something pulled hard at my chest, a blazing desire to throw myself into his arms and beg him to bite me again. It means something; I know it does. This is more than a passing fling.

I ache for this alpha. I ache to have him be mine. Stone and Erin were right. Titan belongs to me. I know it with certainty after tonight.

Asher and Cherry help us close the bar, but I have a million questions about mating an alpha and nobody to ask them of. I'd talk to Titan himself about it, but I don't want to bring it up when Asher and Cherry are having a relationship crisis. It's not like Ash would be able to avoid hearing our conversation.

"Wanna ride with me, Hot Sauce?" Titan's voice goes low as he locks up the front door to Teddy's, smiling over at me. Asher and Cherry are already hopping into a truck together. I do not want to be that third wheel.

I smile back in agreement, waving to our packmates as Ash leans out the driver's side window. "Don't stay out too late, kids!"

Cherry laughs from the passenger seat as Titan shoots them a snarky middle finger. He grabs my hand, pulling me around the side of the bar and toward the back parking lot.

This is new and different for us. It's almost like a date. Butterflies flutter around my stomach when I think about that. The gentle flutter turns into a wild crashing when Titan opens up the truck door for me. I should be cooler in this moment, maybe make a pithy comment.

I can't. I need him. Despite the insane amount of times we screwed in the back room, I want more. Hopping up into his arms, I crash my lips to his, reveling in the way he responds with an immediate groan. Enormous arms wrap all the way around me as he leans back against the side of the truck and devours me. There's no sound, no focus on anything in the world but his lips and tongue and fangs.

"I need you, alpha," I snarl, parting for just a moment to look into those vivid eyes.

"How do you want me, omega?" His baritone snakes along my consciousness, and that tug between us grows so hot, I cry out and press a hand to my chest. I'm burning alive for him. "I see," Titan purrs, turning and depositing me in the front seat of his truck.

Without another word, he rounds the truck and slips into the driver's seat, gripping my thigh and pulling me close. He plants a tender kiss on my cheek before murmuring in my ear, "I'm going to take you back to my cabin. Then I'm gonna fuck you good and hard, omega. After that, I'm going to wrap myself around you while you sleep, and I'll think about how to take you again in the morning."

My only response is a heavy whine as Titan chuckles and unbuttons his jeans, the tip of that gorgeous dick poking out as he rocks his hips. More of him slides free, his gaze traveling to meet mine with a devious look. "I want your lips, Luna. I want you to tease me."

It's on the tip of my tongue to say "aye aye, Captain," but something stops me. Titan's brows curl up as his smile grows bigger. He knows I'm holding back the snark.

"Suck me off, omega," he commands. "Taste me, and then I'm gonna taste you."

Pulling my eyes from his, I bend over in the truck and drag the tip of my nose along his rock-hard length.

Titan lets out a grunt, one hand coming to the back of my neck as I swirl my tongue around the tip before giving it a quick suck. The noise falls off into a drawn-out whine as his head falls back.

"It might have been a mistake to believe I could do this and get us back to my cabin," he whines. "Your mouth is so fucking good. Fuuuuuuck," he cries out when I bite my way along his length.

His dirty words and the noises coming out of his mouth have me wetter than Niagara Falls. This whole damn truck is covered in slick, and we haven't left the parking lot. Titan's breathless moaning turns into rapid-fire pants as his core clenches, the hand on my neck squeezing tight.

"Goddamn, Luna, I'm about to come. Too fast," he complains. "Too goddamn fast. What the fuck are you doing to me?"

I don't bother to answer as I slide him down my throat, letting my teeth scrape along him when I pull out. Bringing one hand to the base of his cock, I'm surprised to find it swollen.

His knot. It must be. Erin's told me literally everything, although he hasn't knotted me yet.

When I squeeze the thicker area tight and bite him at the same time, Titan erupts with a choked roar, his hips bucking in the seat as I struggle to swallow gallons of my alpha's cum. I do what I can, but it coats my chin and neck as he gasps through an orgasm that has every inch of my body on fire from watching.

"I need you," I whisper as he comes down, plush lips parted as he drags in greedy breaths.

Titan's blue eyes snap open, laser focused on me as he leans in, licking cum off my lips before hauling me into his lap, spread wide around him. "I wanna knot you, omega. I want to fill you with it and lock you to me, but I don't want to do that in my goddamn truck. You need teasing first, omega. I'm so damn big."

"Hasn't stopped me yet." I laugh as I wrap my arms around his neck, my feelings morphing into something more tender and unsure. "Is this for real? You and me? I thought we were enemies for life."

Titan's smile grows as he wraps me up tight in his arms. "I don't do fake relationships, Luna. This isn't a romance novel, although enemies to lovers is a thing, you know."

"Oh, I know," I scoff. "I've read plenty of romance, thank you. Enemies to lovers is my fave." I bat my eyes as Titan laughs, wrapping both hands in my long hair and tugging my head back. Scruffy beard tickles my neck as he bites his way up my skin, sinking his fangs just under my chin.

There's a quick pinch of pain, then blissful, warm pleasure that spreads through me. He's peace, true peace, settling over my soul like a good book and a glass of wine. I want him with a deep and ferocious intensity I can barely begin to understand.

We stay like that for a long time, happy simply touching. When Titan finally lets go of the bite, I whine but slide off his lap and hug his arm, directing his hand to grip my thigh. We manage to make it back to the ranch in record time, and then my alpha takes me over and over before we fall asleep in each other's arms.

I've never been so fucking happy in my entire life.

WHEN I WAKE in the morning, Titan's no longer in bed with me, but I smell bacon. Throwing one of his shirts on, I shamble out into the living room and look over the island into the kitchen.

"Holy fuck," I whisper, not even meaning to say it aloud. He's cooking shirtless, his jeans barely able to contain all that stacked muscle. The very tops of his round, perfect ass cheeks peek out.

Titan turns to me with a grin. "Like what you see, Hot Sauce?"

"Do I ever," I mutter as I sit down at the island.

Titan's grin grows bigger. "Cassian and James are gonna be here in about five minutes, Luna. We're headed to the research trailer because Mal's coming today. This is your warning in case you wanna do something with *that*." He waves a spatula in the direction of my hair as I gasp in horror.

"Five minutes, T? That's not long enough to do shit."

His expression grows soft as he leans over the counter and plants a soft kiss on the tip of my nose. "I like it when you call me T."

"I think you like everything I call you. Except Daddy," I remind him. "That didn't seem to be your jam."

He laughs a little louder as he shakes his head. "Not my kink, but I've got a few others we can try on for size."

"Oh God, do tell," I bark just as someone knocks at the door.

"Go get changed," Titan commands. "I don't want anyone staring at what's mine, and they won't be able to stop themselves with you looking like you are. Goddamn, I could eat you alive right now."

I let out a disappointed sob as James opens the door and

sails through with a whistle. Titan scowls as James grabs my hand and twirls me around.

"Girl, you are looking like last night went *well.* Fucking thrilled for ya. Hello to you too, Titan."

Titan growls as I drop the handsome alpha's hand and dart back to the room to change.

Ten minutes later, I've done what I can with my hair but I don't have shit for supplies out here at Titan's cabin. I hear voices, and when I emerge, Cassian has joined James and Titan at the kitchen island. They scarf huge piles of bacon and eggs as I find Titan's gaze. He pulls me around the end of the bar and sets me up on the counter. When he hands me a plate of my own, I can barely resist the urge to kiss him. I hold back, because I don't know if he'd want that in front of everyone else.

When he leans in and captures my mouth with a slow, passionate kiss, my worries are banished. This is really fucking happening. I can't hold back an enormous grin when we part.

To my disbelief, Cass and James do nothing but give one another a knowing look.

God, it's about to get awkward. I've got to say something. "What are you three getting into today?" I take a bite of eggs as Cassian looks up with a grin.

He opens his mouth to answer when James' cell pings loudly.

James reaches down, his face paling when he looks up. "Shit. Action at the mill site." He frowns up at Titan. "I can't tell what it is from here. I need my computer in the office."

"Fuck," Titan says, running his hands through his hair. "We should get to the office and see what's going on. But the researchers—"

"Let me handle it," I offer, standing up. "I've got this. Go do what you need to do."

Titan looks from me to our packmates and back again. "You sure? I can ask them to reschedule. I want to make sure Sam isn't a fucking asshole to Mal."

"I'm great with assholes," I say, blanching when I realize how that sounded.

Cassian snorts, and James grins up at me, cell phone still in his hands.

Clearing my throat, I plaster a confident look on my face. "I'll deal with Sam. Let me know what you find out, okay?"

We walk to the door together, and James and Cass head back toward the lodge. Titan turns to me with a wry look. "Great with assholes, huh?"

I laugh. "It sounded a lot worse than I thought it would. Seriously, I can handle Sam. I won't let him bully Mal, and if he does, I'll give him the verbal slap down of his fucking life."

"No doubt." Titan laughs, pulling me close as he leans down for a kiss. His soft lips press to mine as his tongue probes for entry. He's masterful with his attention, running both hands up the back of my shirt as he presses me tightly to him.

"I'll find you later," he murmurs, his forehead touching mine.

"Can we talk more about assholes later?" I ask with a smirky grin.

Titan slides one hand down the back of my jeans, resting the tips of his fingers in the crack of my ass.

"I wanna do more than talk about this," he whispers, bringing his lips to my ear. "I wanna take this. I want to watch you fall apart on your knees in front of me, Luna. What do you think?"

"I think you better stop teasing me," I laugh. "Get out of here before I decide nothing else matters and drag you back into the bedroom."

He kisses my forehead and jogs up the road to catch up

with Cass and James. I watch him go for a minute, rubbing that spot in my chest where I sense him now.

The alphas round a bend in the road, and I turn from Titan's cabin toward the aspen grove the store and research trailer sit in.

I huff against the freezing air, wrapping my arms around myself as I hike up the dirt road toward the trailer. When I get there, Bianca and Sam stand outside, clearly in the middle of a heated discussion. Sam glowers when he sees me and stomps back inside the trailer.

Bianca turns with a fake smile as I shoot her a skeptical look. "Everything okay?"

Bianca shakes her head. "I've got to talk to your pack about the sermon. We went to it yesterday, and it was…disconcerting, to say the least."

"What do you mean?" A brush of wind sends my hair swirling around.

Bianca gasps and looks up, clutching one hand to her chest as a gigantic black bird circles over us once, and then alights on the ground, cocking its head to one side. I don't get an answer from Bianca, but I remind myself to bring it back up as soon as possible.

My heart pounds in my chest. This fucking shift is humongous. She must be ten or twelve feet tall with a hooked beak that looks like it could do serious damage.

Bianca comes to my side, sucking in shallow, disbelieving breaths. "Remind me to tell you about the sermon bullshit later. I cannot believe what I'm seeing. I mean, I can, obviously. Stone shared his shift wolf. But this? This is fucking incredible…" Her voice breaks off as we fall silent, looking at Mal's bird.

It's then I notice she has a bag clutched in one clawed foot. There's a confusing swirl of smoky feathers as she shifts, and then Mal stands there naked. I've met her very briefly, but I don't know her well. She drops to the ground, quickly throwing on jeans and a comfy looking sweater.

Once she's dressed, Mal comes to meet us, waving softly. "Hey! You must be Bianca. I'm Mal."

Bianca shakes Mal's hand vigorously and then points at the trailer. "I'm incredibly grateful for your time, Mal. And I've read all your articles, of course. They gave me the confidence to go look for my sister after she transitioned. I'll always be so thankful for that."

Mal forces a pleasant smile, but it's clear she's uncomfortable with the praise. I knew she wrote a bunch of articles exposing how governments weren't telling the truth about the Awaken virus. She literally met an alpha and agreed to stay at their home for weeks to learn about them.

What a badass.

Bianca senses Mal's discomfort and points at the trailer. "I'd love to have you talk with my physician and anthropologist. None of the omegas here have powers, and nobody's pregnant. I'd like to understand more about that from your perspective."

"Happy to do it," Mal agrees, following as Bianca turns toward the trailer.

When we get inside, Sam looks up at us with a frown. "Where's Titan? He said he wanted to be here for all interviews."

I give Sam a quick look. "Titan was called away on urgent pack business, so he's unable to attend today. I'm standing in for him."

Sam lets out a disbelieving scoff as Bianca rolls her eyes. It's clear they've been arguing, probably about his general shitty attitude. But I have zero plans to put up with Sam's bullshit today. Titan wouldn't, and I need to be a good stand in.

The next two hours are a whirlwind of information. Mal

shares a high-level version of how she met her mate, Orion. She covers the American Task Force and the series of attacks that led them to seek shelter with Stone's pack. Bianca's lips are pursed as Sam questions Mal rudely, although Mal delivers even, measured answers back to him. It's clear she's about sharing the truth, and she sugarcoats nothing.

Her story is wild, and it would be unbelievable if some of it hadn't been broadcasted by the BBC, ultimately leading to the termination of the American Task Force.

The researchers are clearly shell-shocked by the entire thing. When Mal reminds them they wanted to do a physical component to the interview, Zee springs into action. It takes another hour to do a thorough examination of Mal and her baby.

Zee grins at Mal for the physical exam. "I hope this doesn't sound rude," she says softly. "But what happens to the baby when you're in bird form?"

Mal laughs as she looks around at us. "She remains human, although I could shift her too if I really thought about it. But there's no reason to."

Zee lets out a surprised cough. "So you can choose to shift her or not? I heard that right?"

"Yeah," Mal laughs, "I don't know how to prove it other than to say I'm extremely aware of her, like I carry her in a protective bubble. No matter what form I'm in, she remains in that little human bubble inside me."

Zee pretends to fall out of her chair before sitting back up. "This is fucking amazing, pardon my French. I am in awe of what you're capable of."

Mal laughs, light and happy as she rubs her belly. "Y'all haven't met Alice, but if you want to come to our pack for a week to gather info on omega powers, you're welcome to. She can command the elements, and it's frankly incredible to watch."

"Command the elements?" Sam looks up from his laptop. "You're not the fucking X-Men."

Mal, Bianca, and I whip around to look at him at the same time.

"Listen here, you little shit," I start, pointing one finger at him. "You've been rude as hell every time I've met you. You came here to research our pack, not provide a running commentary of your personal opinions. If you're unable to do that, I'm pretty sure I've got Devraj Eller's information, and he runs your program. Am I right?"

Sam pales but grits his teeth together as Bianca shoots me a satisfied look. Why she's not giving him the verbal slap down, I don't know, but I'm not done.

Pointing at Mal, I give Sam a meaningful look. "Mal is amazing. She offered her time today to be poked and prodded to help you understand us. She could be doing anything else in the world right now, but instead she submitted to a two-hour interrogation and in-depth physical. Imagine yourself in her place for one moment."

"I get it," Sam snaps as I raise a brow at him.

"Sam," Bianca warns.

He turns to look at her and nods a few times, mumbling a very unapologetic-sounding "sorry" under his breath.

Mal mouths a quick "thank you" as I step closer to her with my arms crossed. I'm more than happy to go mama bear on this asshole today. It's okay if he's not our ally, but I won't let him belittle my packmates.

Not on my watch.

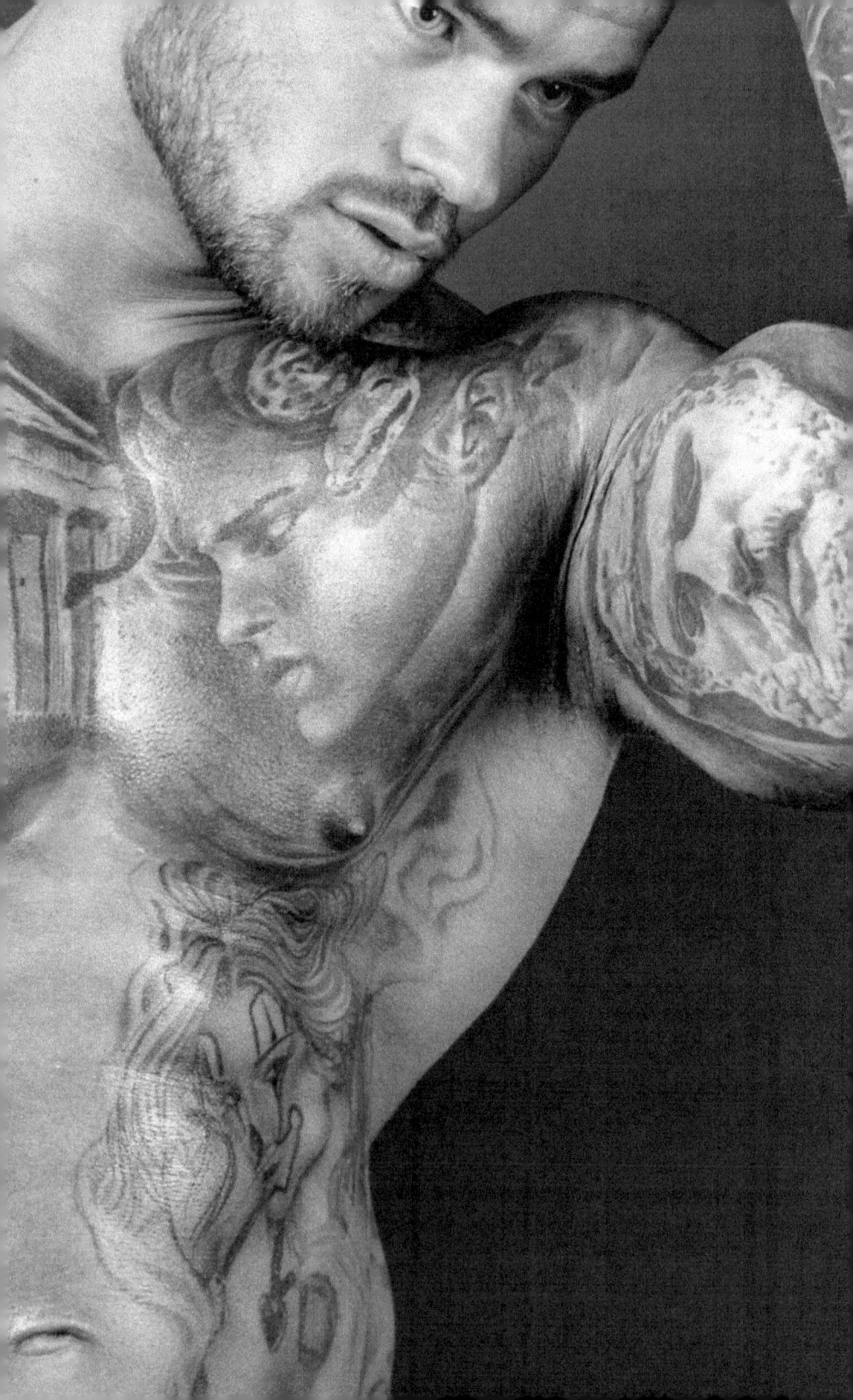

CHAPTER THIRTY-FIVE

titan

LEAVING Luna to deal with the researchers sets my teeth on edge. It's my responsibility, but action at the mill is unfortunately more pressing.

Stone meets us at the top of the stairs, a frown on his face. "Talk to me, James."

James jogs up the stairs, shrugging. "I should check the recording software in your office. But I programmed it to ignore the train passing through and random shit like squirrels."

Stone gives me a look when I crest the stairs.

"I know." I follow him as he turns into our home. As we walk through the lodge, I update my pack on what Isabel shared at the bar.

James settles himself down at Stone's computer as we all hover around, anxious to see what's going on. He pulls up the recording. It's dark, but we watch the train stop outside the mill. Three alphas jog on screen, Bek, Mark, and one I don't recognize. They wait as a train car opens. When it does, four alphas hop out. The newcomers shake hands with the first group, and then they all leave together.

"I can only think of one reason Declan would bring alphas in from somewhere else." I look to my right at Clay.

"He's building a goddamn army," Clay mutters, somber silence falling over our group. "We've got to focus on a couple things immediately." He looks at me before glancing over to Stone. "We need to get the women out of there, and we need to find out more about Gabriel Velos. I'd like to dig further into the DPM too, because what possible reason could he have for allowing this shit to continue? We haven't heard much from Declan in the last couple weeks, but that doesn't mean anything if he's bringing in backup."

James frowns. "I've dug and dug for information on Gabriel. There's nothing. He's a fucking ghost, which is unsettling in and of itself."

"I have a couple friends in the military," Clay says thoughtfully. "People I've kept in touch with even after transitioning. I can make a few inquiries."

Stone's dark eyes meet mine as he considers it. He turns to Clay as he leans back in his chair, folding his arms over his head. "Is there a downside to asking around?"

Clay shrugs. "There are pros and cons to everything, but I trust these people. We should ask. I also want to attend one of these sermons to see what it's about."

"Is that a good idea?" Stone doesn't appear to be in agreement with Clay.

"We don't have to cause a ruckus," I say. "We'll just go watch. We need more information. What Isabel shared is concerning, and the lack of information about Gabriel is concerning. So far he seems to be keeping Declan in line...but I can't shake the worry that Gabriel is bad news. The activity at the mill confirms it."

"Agreed," Clay says.

Stone looks concerned. "Take Asher with you so he can listen for trouble coming your way. There's a sign on the fucking highway now about the sermons; I noticed it earlier today. Gabriel apparently does them every afternoon at five p.m. If you go now, you can make the one today."

"This makes it all the more pressing for us to get the omegas out of that pack." I look looking over at Cassian, who's been quiet this whole time.

I risk a peek over at James. There's a lazy smile on his face as he pecks away over his keyboard. I'd swear on all that's holy that he and Cass and Julia were our healer and spirit trinity, but Cass is a pack alpha, without a doubt.

"Can alphas have more than one designation?" I question aloud, not even meaning to as Asher and Clay look at me.

"Like being a pack alpha and something else too?" My strategist picks up what I'm wondering about immediately. James is uncharacteristically quiet, but his fingers have stopped on the keyboard.

"I don't think any of us have the answer to that," Stone says with a curious expression. "But I'll ask Samson. I've never heard of that ability."

We all agree, and James goes back to pecking at the keyboard. But when Cassian opens his mouth to speak, I make a point to surreptitiously peek at James's face. What I see doesn't surprise me. Desire. Deep longing.

Julia's not the only one missing something, it seems.

If Cassian is aware, he doesn't let on or return the way James is looking at him. He's entirely focused on Stone, pack alpha to pack alpha. Even from my spot next to Stone, Cass's dominance rolls over the room.

Seeing them side by side, it's hard not to compare. Stone's big, but Cass is a little bigger, a little broader. He's older too, not that it makes anything about him seem less powerful.

It's like they both sense my assessing gaze, looking up at me at the same time. Uncanny. That's the only word I can use to describe it. How they're both completely focused on me. One pair of dark eyes, one pair pale gray.

Resisting the urge to shudder from the weight of their dominance, I focus on Cassian. "Isabel made it seem like the girls are ready to try leaving, if we can help. We might be able to get them to leave from the bar or the drop site, but we need a way to make sure we know which omegas want out. Declan's leadership crew doesn't come into Teddy's anymore, not since the attack. I've seen Isabel twice, but it's very sporadic. Do you have any thoughts on how we can get a message to them and figure out who wants our help?"

Cassian growls, a pained noise that tugs at my heart. He's close to all the women in that pack. He's been protecting them for years, and now he's not in a position to. For a pack alpha, that's got to be about the worst feeling in the world. I'm thankful he's at least been able to reconnect with Sal now that she's here.

"First things first. We should do another food drop, right? Titan, you said Isabel mentioned they were able to access it?"

"Yup." I was fucking thrilled when Isabel told us, and then I fucked my omega in the storeroom. My brain makes a diversion into that set of memories as I urge myself to focus. I cannot get sidetracked thinking about Luna just now. She'd want me to concentrate on this, on fixing things for the omegas in Declan's pack.

Cassian cocks his head to the side and looks at me, then over at Clay and Stone. "I used to have an emergency signal of sorts with the girls. They'd know to meet me in the high meadow if I left a certain rock overturned on the exit from the highway. It's how I communicated with them those last few weeks when I wasn't around much. It's hard for them to get away from the pack, but it's worth a try. We can use it to let them know we want to meet and share a plan for getting them out."

"And what is the plan for actually extricating them?" James looks up from his computer, eyes locked onto Stone.

Stone shakes his head. "I don't believe we'll be able to avoid a fight, and the omegas are going to have to pick a side when we go for them. Once we know who wants to go, we can have them meet us in the meadow or at the bar. It would probably be better not to go get them."

"What about blowback from taking them?" I turn to Clay with a serious look. "Declan won't take that lying down. And we've just asked the DPM to force a cessation of Declan's bullshit. This seems like us going back on our own word. Even though it's obvious he is as well."

Clay nods slowly, weighing the options before looking back at me. "This is one of those times where we have to either do what's smart or do what's right. I'm of the opinion we do what's right. What's the DPM going to say, that we kidnapped Declan's omegas? No, we didn't. We took those who wanted to leave an abusive situation but couldn't. It might cause problems, but Declan is already a problem. And it sounds like Gabriel will be too, maybe. There's not a good reason to wait. On top of which, we should be prepared to take our entire dossier on the connection between the DPM and Declan and go live with it. We're gonna have to pull a Mitchell, I suspect."

Anxiety forces my breath out in quick, measured pants. This is turning into a potential disaster.

"Okay," I start. "Cass, let's have you work on the omega front, and the rest of us will dig for more information on the sermon piece, see if we can't learn about Gabriel."

"Done." Cassian's voice booms from the other end of the table. "I'll give them the signal tonight, and we'll relay our message as soon as possible."

"Wait a second, Cass," Stone barks. "How are you going to

do this without getting heard by their seer or getting captured?"

Cassian shrugs. "There's every chance one or both of those things could happen. But it's a risk I'm happy to take. Anything for my girls. They mean everything to me, and not being able to help them is so fucking wrong."

Stone says nothing but looks deeply uncomfortable.

"We have to do this, buddy," I tell my oldest friend. "We all want to help, and Cass is willing. We have to try. Think about Sal and how she felt when she first arrived. That's how those girls are living all day every day. We can't stand by and watch."

Stone and Clay seem to come to an agreement simultaneously before Stone turns to Cass. "Do it. If they show up, let them know we just need them to be prepared, whoever wants to leave. There are a million ways this could go wrong, but you're right. We have to do something."

Cass stands. "I'm going now. I may be gone a day or two. It'll take them that long to get away from the camp and up to the meadow."

Stone watches as Cassian looks at each of us, gray eyes lingering for just a moment on James.

James says nothing when Cassian turns to go, but there's a clear tension between them. As enforcer, I read all my pack-mates well. It's obvious to me that James is tamping down an urge to chase after the big alpha.

He must feel my assessing look, because James glances up at me and schools his face into a neutral expression.

Oh, yeah. There's something there between him and Cassian. Something maybe neither of them is ready to act on. But it's there nonetheless.

Clay looks over at me and Ash with a beleaguered sigh. "Ready to go to church?"

TEN MINUTES LATER, Asher, Clay and I are piled into one of Stone's trucks, quiet as we head toward Declan's neighborhood. Cassian follows behind us with a tent and camping equipment packed onto the back of his Harley. When we pull off the exit, Cassian hops off his bike and strides over to a large boulder with a white heart painted on it, two sets of initials indicating lovers have left their mark. He presses his shoulder hard to the huge rock, grunting as he shoves it over on its side.

He gives us a quick salute and then drives up into the rolling hills. He'll spend the next several days in the high meadow, waiting for the omegas to meet him. Once they do, we'll get a solid list of who wants out and figure out when to take them.

"I don't like this," Clay murmurs as we watch Cassian go.

I can't summon an appropriate response. We're all anxious to help the unfortunate omegas trapped in Declan's pack. Pulling back onto the exit, I head into the foothills where Declan's neighborhood is. The last time we came here, Stone kicked Declan's ass and shot a hole in his front door. It's not one of my better memories.

Before we make the turnoff toward his neighborhood, we see a large sign indicating there's a nightly tent revival ahead.

You could hear a pin drop in the truck as we follow an increasing number of signs pointing to an empty field near Declan's neighborhood. We round a corner to find an enormous white tent set up, dozens of cars parked in the open field next to it. People mill around as they find seats, and everything in my enforcer nature screams that this is dangerous.

"Declan's here," Asher states from the back seat. "I can hear him mumbling something under his breath. The omegas are here too."

I stiffen in my seat as Clay and I share a heated look. We

pull into the field and park, then exit the car. I hold back a snarl when Declan himself peeks out of the tent and strides across the field toward us, a shit-eating grin on his face.

"Surprised to see yeh here, although Gabriel told me yeh'd come at some point."

Clay looks at the big Irish alpha. "Seeing as alphas don't have a religion, we thought it might be nice to come see what, exactly, Gabriel is preaching."

"We don't have a religion, and that's precisely our problem," Declan says. "We've been on the run, hiding from the government, not fussed with any guiding principles. That's changed for me. I'm focused now."

"On what?" Asher questions.

An omega walks up behind Declan then, and I recognize her immediately. Asher growls right away, but she laughs, long strawberry blond waves partially covering her face. She winks at Asher, despite the fact that he nearly killed her last time we fought their pack.

"We're learning all about how alphas are God's chosen people, a better version of normals. How He has a plan for us. How we need to fall in line with that plan; everybody should."

"You can't possibly believe that horse shit," drawls Clay, eyes focused on the woman, Hale, Declan's new omega.

"I stand behind it one hundred percent," she snaps back. Just then, Gabriel himself ducks out from behind the tent with a half-smile on his pale face.

"I wondered how long it would be before you joined us. Welcome." He's saying polite words but looking at us with a maniacal grin. This asshole is unhinged, but his aura is a steely, focused gray. He's not intimidated by us.

"I imagine you're here for the sermon, but, by all means, share if something else is on your mind." Gabriel looks from Clay to Asher to me, folding his hands in front of his belt.

"We're starting in a moment. Take your seats. If you stay afterward, I'll answer any questions you might have."

Declan and Hale gaze at Gabriel raptly, as if they're already enamored by his words. Clay lets out a disbelieving grumble but rounds the group and ducks under the tent. Isabel sits with another pregnant woman in the last row. But when Clay moves to sit next to her, Gabriel comes up to us quickly.

"Not here. Do not sit with the Unclean until they are cleansed anew. Take a seat over there, please."

Clay and I look at Isabel, but her blue eyes are filled with tears. "Just go," she mouths, Gabriel's back turned to her.

I'd like to rip this asshole's head from his shoulders. But we need intel, and he seems more than happy to preach to us.

Declan and Hale have already left us to sit right up front in the half-filled tent. Clay, Ash and I take a seat across the aisle from Isabel and the other pregnant omega. I resolve to speak with her as soon as I get a moment. She's right fucking here, but I can't speak with her because Declan's seer is here too. He'd hear every word if I outlined our plan.

Frustration eats me alive as I run both hands through my hair, glancing at Isabel. Her blue eyes are on me, tears streaming down her cheeks as she rubs her belly.

Gabriel strides up the wide aisle and hops nimbly up onto the stage, turning to the gathered crowd with open arms. "Modern society coddles the weak. We see this every day in the news, in the intense need of society for political correctness and woke rhetoric. That time has come to an end." Gabriel folds his arms behind his back and paces to one end of the stage, making intense eye contact with Declan's leadership group, who all sit right up front as he continues.

"Alphas have always existed. Our feeble societal structure relegated them to ancient history tomes and children's bedtime stories. But ask any pack with a mated seer. The

Awaken virus did not create alphas; it simply released them from a self-imposed exile."

There's soft murmuring in the crowd as Asher looks over at me, his jaw tightly gritted. When the Awaken virus escaped a lab, he was the very first man to transition. Not that that's public news.

"Alphas ruled our world until they saw the state of humanity in such disrepair, those genes fell dormant, waiting for a time when they could rule again. And now is that time. The promulgation of the virus was simply meant to free alphas once more. Now is their time to rule. Alphas are better than us humans in every way. It's not my place to deny that. God made them bigger, stronger, more in tune with nature. More connected to *Him*."

Velos emphasizes that last bit as if God himself is speaking directly to alphas. He paces back across the stage, the fingertips of one hand pressed together as he makes his point.

"Why would God give alphas such powers if they were not meant to be used?"

Affirmation rings from the front row as Clay looks over at me, clearly horrified by what he's hearing.

Gabriel continues, "Mark my words, the time of the alpha is coming. The first wave of transitions came with the virus, unlocking the potential of millions of alpha males to lead us into a stronger future. What comes next will be a repopulation of the world. Alphas and omegas, God's chosen people, will breed and found bigger, stronger packs. Unlock surprising, deadly powers. Alphas will push their way back into society, breaking it down and rebuilding it from the inside out."

Velos gestures out at us with a grin. "You are the future of humanity. The better, brighter version, here to mend the wrongs humans have done. I encourage you to find your mates, build your families. Spread the word that God has chosen you as the next evolution of humanity."

"You are the future," he repeats, punctuating each word as he points to each of the assholes in the first row.

When I look at Isabel, she's looking at her stomach, rubbing it absentmindedly. The pregnant omega next to her sits with a vacant look on her face. It's clear they don't buy this line of horse shit, but when I look around, I'm surprised to see how many people are enraptured by Gabriel's charisma.

"I've heard enough," I growl at my packmates. Clay and Ash nod. I think hard, trying to summon up some way to get Isabel a message. But I can't risk it with Declan's entire pack here, and there aren't enough of us to just take her.

This is turning into a nightmare.

CHAPTER THIRTY-SIX

luna

AFTER MAL LEAVES, I head back up to the lodge. I missed lunch, and I'm grumpy as shit. Not to mention Sam's assholery reaching new heights. I'm confident I stood up for Mal the way Titan would have, but I'm about done with the snarky anthropologist's approach.

God, *I'm* snarky myself, but I hope to hell I don't come across the way Sam does. I resolve to consider that next time I open my mouth to get saucy.

When I get back to the lodge nobody's in the lobby. I make a sandwich in the kitchen and head for Stone's office. I can usually find at least a few of my packmates there.

The sound of a piano reaches me when I round the corner toward Stone's office. I smile, knowing I'll get to hear him play. Pushing the office door open, I grin at James when he looks up from his computer. Next to James, Mario sits in front of his own laptop, although he's sitting back in his chair watching Stone play, clearly appreciative.

"You should be here for karaoke night," I snigger when he notices me.

Stone continues playing but looks up. "We've been heads

down digging into security footage. How'd it go with the researchers? It was unfortunate we had to pull Titan away from that."

I shrug and flop down across the table from Mario. "Sam's still a real asshole. But I gave him a verbal slap down. He's just so against alphas."

Across from me, Mario purses his lips, and I know it's on the tip of his tongue to say something snarky.

Stone stops playing and closes the top of his piano before joining us, sitting at the head of the small conference table.

"Remember it's not hard to be against alphas, Luna. Those early days were so fraught with danger. Alphas hurt a lot of people. Sam hasn't shared his past, but I'd wager a guess that somewhere, somehow, an alpha hurt him or someone he loves."

"Doesn't excuse being an asshole," James offers from his spot next to Luna. "I could rip Mario in two because, once upon a time, someone from California was rude to me. But I don't."

Mario looks nervously between James and Stone, then over at me. He plasters a cocky smile on his face, but I've known him for years. He's still unsettled around my guys.

"You missed quite the morning here," Stone continues. For the next ten minutes, he fills me in on Titan and the guys going to one of Gabriel's sermons, and things moving forward with rescuing the omegas.

"I'm simultaneously relieved and terrified," I admit once he finishes. "You aren't worried about them seeing Declan and his pack after everything that's happened?"

"I'm not," Stone confirms. "There should be a bunch of people there. Asher went with them to keep an ear out for trouble."

"What kind of trouble?" questions Mario.

James winks at him. "The death and dismemberment kind."

"You're shitting me," Mario hedges, looking from James to Stone to me. "Luna...you're okay with all this?"

I laugh bitterly at that, remembering the two times now I've been attacked by Declan. "Okay with it? Not hardly," I confirm. "But absolutely committed to keeping others safe from Declan."

Mario bites back whatever he's planning to say as our group falls into an uncomfortable silence.

I give Mario a bright smile. "Wanna go sit up front and finalize everything in the project plan for the Omegamatic? We can catch up. I know I haven't been around, but I want to hear about things back in Cali."

I'm sure I feel both James and Stone look at me when I say "Cali" not "home," but I don't make eye contact with them. If I look right at Stone, he'll give me that intense alpha stare, and my whole soul will be laid out for his perusal.

Mario grabs his computer, giving my packmates a quick salute before following me up toward the lobby.

We grab coffee from the kitchen before settling in front of the fireplace. I make sure to leave a solid few feet of space between us. Thankfully Mario doesn't comment on it.

"I booked a ticket home for tomorrow," Mario says finally. "I figured we could finalize everything with the project today, and then it'll be off our plates and on to the production team."

Nodding, I gesture to his laptop. We spend a few minutes going over the final patent application, confirming all the details. As soon as Titan delivers the signed paperwork to us, we can submit to the patent office and our production team simultaneously. Patents take a while to come through, so we'll get everything else in order in the meantime.

"I can't wait for you to come home," Mario shares. "There's been so much drama in our friend group. You are way behind on the gossip." He winks at me as I pull my feet up under my butt, ignoring the "coming home" comment.

"Tell me everything," I demand. "Were we right? Corey and Ian are having a secret affair?"

"Oh, it gets better." Mario laughs. "Corey and Sara are having an affair, so Ian's all fucked up about that obviously."

"Oh my gawd," I holler. "I can't believe it. So what happens when you throw a party? Who comes?!"

"Everybody shows up, and it's fucking awkward when Corey and Sara are like, holding hands, and Ian's watching them as if he can't believe it. But I don't know how to uninvite anyone."

"Damn, Mario," I laugh, "you make going back to Cali sound so appealing."

"Yeah, well," he continues, "you're missing gorgeous weather, your sexy friend Mario, and a shitload of amazing new restaurants. I tried the burger at the bar here the other night. Inedible, Luna. Totally fucking inedible."

I bristle at that because it's definitely a dig at Titan.

"Yeah, well, I like it here," I counter, letting a little of my irritation bleed into my tone.

There's a tense beat, during which Mario looks at me in disbelief, then nods once as if he's come to some eye-opening determination. "So...we're wrapping this project up now. When are you coming back?"

I shrug and wrap my arms tighter around my lower legs. "Not for a long time, if ever."

His brows travel up in disbelief as he sputters and gestures around. "So you're what, *staying* here?"

"I might, yeah," I concur as he crosses his arms.

"This place is fucking dangerous, Luna. These dudes are cavemen; people are getting attacked. The government is literally researching them to see if they're compatible with normal society."

Heat bursts through my chest at his words, so hot and hard that I suck in an angry breath.

When I say nothing, he continues on, reaching over to rest his hand on the sofa cushion between us. I glare at it like it's a viper, but he ignores me.

"Come back, Luna Moon," he murmurs my old nickname. "We could be out at dinner at Circo right now. Their new menu is bangin'; you'd love it. I—"

I open my mouth to shut him down hard, but his eyes go wide, and he shoots to the opposite end of the sofa from me. Whipping around, I look up.

Just inside the lobby door, Titan stands silent as a ghost. His chest heaves hard, his fists balled as he looks at us.

CHAPTER THIRTY-SEVEN

titan

ALL I COULD THINK about the entire ride home from the tent revival was getting to Luna. Despite the bullshit direction my day has taken, I knew seeing her would make me feel better. Until I got home. She and Mario didn't hear me come in the front door.

So I stood there listening to the easy camaraderie between Luna and her old lover. His commentary about their friends back home. His suggestion that they could be doing something so much easier than living the type of life we do here in our pack.

He's not wrong. Life in California sounds fun and easy. "Easy" could never be an adjective used to describe our lives.

When Mario asked about her returning home, she said she might. She didn't tell him that we're together. Not even when he reached for her.

That's the moment I know I should focus on my fucking pack, and the security threat hanging over our heads. After all our recent connection, it will kill me if we take it any farther and she leaves.

Luna springs up off the sofa and crosses the lobby at a jog, stopping in front of me. "How long have you been here?"

"Long enough," I respond calmly, willing the hornets' nest in my chest to evaporate. "He's not wrong, Luna." The tension is so thick, I'm choking on it. "Life here is hard and getting harder by the minute."

"That hasn't scared me away yet." She reaches out to place both her hands on my chest.

"Maybe it should," I whisper. "The issues that surround us are escalating. Life is going to get much worse before it gets better, if ever. It's my job to focus on that for the good of the pack. I've got to focus on *that*."

She blanches as if I've slapped her, taking a step back as she balls her fists. "Are you saying you don't want to see what's between us?"

A desperate desire to protect everyone consumes me as I look at her. "I'm saying I need to focus on the problems coming at us before I can do anything else."

She hisses, her brows furrowing as angry red shoots through her aura. I'm crushing her and pissing her off all at the same time.

"It's better this way, Luna," I try to remind her. "Better to end this before we take it any farther."

She puts one hand on her chest, the connection between us practically ash at this point. Luna's fury is palpable in our bond. It simmers with tense anger.

"Farther...right." Her tone is pure acid as she glares up at me. "Yeah, T, let's not take it any farther than fucking me every possible way a man can fuck a woman. Let's not take it any farther than you tying me to your wall and making me come through our bond alone. You're right, let's not go *farther* than that."

My heart closes itself off, walls snapping up around me. I have to protect myself and the pack and her, even though she doesn't see it that way right now. She'll be safer if she leaves. I can't protect anyone if I'm distracted by an omega who may not even be fully committed to staying.

It's better this way, I beg my brain to realize. It's better not to drag her into this, to cement her to me when our lives are so dangerous. Mario's right: her life could be so much simpler in California. And I need to put the safety of my pack before my own happiness.

"Buddy, everything okay?" Stone's voice booms through the lobby. When I look up, I realize not only is Mario still sitting on the sofa staring at us, but Stone and James are both standing in the hallway, watching.

"No," I breathe out, ripping my gaze from a furious Luna to look at my pack alpha. "Everything is not okay."

I give Luna a final look, begging her with my eyes to understand that I'm trying to protect our hearts by not letting this thing get to a point we can't return from. When I turn toward my packmates, she lays a hand on my forearm.

"Don't you dare walk away from me right now," she demands. "Not in the middle of this conversation."

Anger rises in my chest—anger and desperation—because my soul wants nothing more than to comfort her. But today's events have shaken me to my core, and watching her with Mario scared the shit out of me.

"I can't do this with you right now," I bark back. "We're in fucking danger, Luna. We have to put the pack first."

"That's bullshit," she shouts. When she opens her mouth to continue, I put my palm up.

"I'm not doing this with you right now," I reiterate. "I have an entire pack of people to protect. The twins, Sal, Erin, my brothers. Even you. I will protect you at all costs," I shout, realizing my voice is rising, and I'm making a goddamn scene.

"Titan, don't do this," she begs, pressing her soft body to mine as I push her back.

"Don't make this harder, Luna. Please," I command. "You weren't there today. You didn't see Gabriel. He's a psychopath. We're in real danger. Please let me handle it."

Her blue eyes fill with tears as she shakes her head. I turn toward Stone, trying to resist the urge to purr for her and give her peace with my bite.

"We've got to debrief about the sermon," I tell my alpha. "It's a fucking mess."

Stone agrees, dark eyes flicking from me to Luna. Behind me, I hear the front doors slam shut, my muscles quivering with tension. I want to run to her, drag her to me and take her. But I can't. I have to focus. I have to protect everyone, and the only way I can protect her is by pushing her away. In fact, it would be better if she were far away from all this bullshit. It's the only way she can truly be safe.

I look over at Mario, who's wide-eyed and horrified on the sofa.

"Take her home, Mario," I command. He nods in frantic agreement.

I push past Stone and James, striding through the hall to Stone's office. Asher and Clay are there already. Clay cocks his head to the side, looking at me with a curious expression, but thankfully providing no color commentary.

"Where are we?" I ask, looking at my packmates as Stone and James join us. For a moment, I think Stone is going to ask me if I'm alright.

I'm not. I'm anything but alright. I'm dying inside while trying to maintain focus on my goddamn job. Everything and everyone I love is at risk.

Asher speaks up, "We were just about to dive into everything. Wanna do the honors, enforcer?"

I steeple my fingers and sink down into a chair. For the next quarter hour, I share every detail I can think of regarding what Declan and Hale said, and then the sermon. Stone's face is drawn and pale by the time I'm done.

"Cass called a while ago; the omegas haven't made it up there to him, so he's going to wait it out."

"We were right fucking there," Clay snaps. "They were sitting not ten feet from us, but with Declan's whole leadership group there, there was no way to get them any sort of message."

Clay looks over at me. "Between the alpha supremacy party line and what we saw from the mill, it seems clear to me that Declan is gearing up for something. Whether it's simply growing his pack like Gabriel's preaching, or something more, is hard to say. The biggest question to me is why would the DPM allow this?"

I look at my brothers, realization sinking in as I consider what Clay's saying. "The only possible reasons I can see for the DPM to let this happen is that he either doesn't give a shit, or whatever outcome we're headed for is precisely what he wants."

My packmates freeze as the words leave my mouth. I know I'm right. We're like fish running scared, headed right for the jaws of the shark. I don't know exactly what Declan's planning next, but whatever it is won't be good.

CHAPTER THIRTY-EIGHT

luna

AFTER TITAN'S DEVASTATING DISMISSAL, I'm so surprised, I stand there for several long minutes, my body trembling as I attempt to unpack the shit he just laid at my feet.

I don't know how long I'm frozen before Mario comes over, reaching out to rub my back. Angling away from him, I look up, but what I see there crushes my soul—Mario looks like he's ready to shout "I told you so."

Take her home, Mario.

"I'm not going back to California, Mario," I bark at him as he crosses his arms. "I wasn't clear enough with you just now, but I have no plans to return to California in the future. If that changes, I'll let you know. You should go home tomorrow. I won't be coming."

He scoffs, taking a step away from me. "You heard Titan, Luna. He told you not to stay, that you're in danger if you do. He doesn't want you here. So what now? You're going to chase a man? That's hardly your fucking style. Don't be desperate for him."

I'm so goddamn irritated at Mario's lecture that I literally can't summon a comeback. Turning to him, I settle for a glare that should shrivel his fucking balls.

"Let me make this clear one more time for you," I say again. "Get on your flight tomorrow, and go home. Enjoy your life and move the fuck on."

Mario blanches, shoving both hands in his pockets. "Done," he says in a snippy tone. "I'm not gonna chase you to get you to come home. Just like you shouldn't chase Titan when he clearly isn't interested in what you're offering."

He turns and walks up the stairs toward his room as I tap my foot and think. I can hardly burst into Stone's office and demand to talk to Titan right now. If there's one thing I do agree with him on, it's that handling a security threat is important. I don't want to take away from that, but the rest of the bullshit he spewed? I'm not down with a single fucking bit.

Pulling out my walkie, I ping Erin, but she doesn't answer. I call her cell next, and she picks up on the first ring.

"Hey, bestie, I'm in town with the council; everything okay?"

Tears start to stream down my cheeks then, a sob leaving my mouth. It's so damn loud I can't even say a word.

"Oh, honey, I'm coming home right now," Erin reassures me. "Grab the Halo Top from the fridge and two spoons. Meet you in your room ASAP!"

I nod, even though she can't see that, and disconnect. Grabbing the Halo Top and a handful of spoons, I run upstairs to my room, knowing the twins are likely to show up any moment. River can't resist the chance to give advice, despite having far less life experience than literally everyone else in the lodge.

I'm right. Cherry, Julia, Sal and the twins show up moments later. Julia crosses the room to me, taking the ice cream and setting it down on my bedside table. Then she opens her arms and wraps me in a hug as the tears turn into body-shaking sobs.

By the time E joins us, we've gone through an entire pint of Halo Top, and Cherry's gone to the kitchen for more.

Erin hops into bed with my entire pack of omegas as she rubs my leg. "Honey, tell me everything."

I'm one thousand percent certain Stone's probably already told her through their bond, but I repeat the entire story as the girls listen to me with a range of emotions. Shock, distress. Cherry looks unsurprised, but Erin's the first to speak up.

"Look, honey, I'm gonna level with you. Titan's being a dummy by pushing you away, but he's not wrong about needing to focus on our safety. Those things aren't mutually exclusive though, which he has seemingly failed to realize."

"Duh!" I shout. "I know this, E. I was trying to tell him that, but he asked me not to make it any harder."

"Fucking cop out," Cherry growls. "Asher says that bullshit to me and it's just his way to stop the conversation by making me feel guilty if I keep pressing. It works too, because I shut down when he says that crap."

"Amen," I agree, pointing my spoon at Cherry as she nods sagely. "So what do I do now? Mario was right about one thing: chasing a man is not my style. But, damn, I thought the mating bond was supposed to turn everything magical, so he couldn't deny my awesomeness."

Cherry blanches as I mouth a "sorry" to her.

"That was a dick thing to say, but, actually, I want to know the answer for you too." I look from Cherry to Erin and Julia. "You two are mated; please give us singletons some fucking hope. What are we supposed to do?"

Julia surprises me when she signs before Erin can say anything. "You keep reminding him what a badass you are.

And you wait. Because when he gets his head out of his ass, he'll be worth every moment of heartache."

"Don't think you're talking about Titan," I grumble as she gives me a sad look. We all throw ourselves on top of each other in a big pile hug. My door opens then, and Rogue sails through with a frown on his face.

"Omega bed pile and you didn't invite me? Fucking rude," he barks. There's a hint of humor on his face until he takes a look at mine. "The girls are right, Luna. He's just trying to protect you and his heart; He'll sort it out."

"I hope to shit you're right," I reply. "Because if you're not, I don't know what the hell to do."

MARIO LEAVES THE FOLLOWING AFTERNOON, spewing more shit about how insane it is that I'm staying in Ayas. He doesn't get it, and that's fine. I don't need him to.

For the next two days, I never get a moment alone with Titan, despite trying to find time with him. He's either at the bar or holed up in Stone's office making security plans, or out patrolling with James or Clay. The entire lodge is on high alert as my packmates try to learn more about Gabriel's plans.

I'm sitting with Erin in the lobby one day while Titan is gone at work. Her cell rings, and when she picks it up, I hear Cassian on the other end of the line. E puts him on speaker so we can both hear.

"Good news," his gruff voice rings through, tinny over the phone line. "Isabel managed to make it up here to grab the food. The omegas are all terrified of Gabriel. Sounds like he's forcing them to attend the daily sermons, and he's got Izzy sequestered at this point. He only let her leave to go to the grocery store."

"Thank God," I murmur, thrilled to hear a halfway bright

piece of news. "Did she have an idea of who might want to leave?"

"She did but wanted to be sure. We've only got one chance at this," Cassian cautions. "She's going to talk to the other omegas and figure out who wants out, and then we'll figure out whether to grab them from the bar or up at the meadow or what. I need to talk to Titan about it."

At the mention of Titan's name, daggers stab my stomach. Being in discord with him is producing a physical reaction in me that makes me feel like total shit all day long.

Erin shoots me a worried look as she asks Cass a few clarifying questions. But all I can do is hunch over on the sofa and rub at my chest. I've looked for Titan all day in our bond, but it's quiet and dark as if he's simply not there.

"Wrong," I utter under my breath, miserable as I stop focusing on the bond he's not taking an active part in. "This is wrong."

Erin rubs my back gently. "Bestie, you can't keep going like this. He's dodging a deeper conversation with you and freaking out about protecting everyone, including you. You should talk to him."

"He's avoiding me, remember?" I remind her in a bitter tone. I'm certain my packmates have talked to him in the last two days, but nothing anyone said has swayed him.

"He's at the bar tonight," Erin continues. "You should go a little later when it's not busy. He can't run from you there."

"Cornering an angry alpha sounds like a great way to have a productive conversation," I mutter, both hands pressed to my stomach.

"It's time, bestie," Erin encourages me. "Have a conversation with him so you can decide what to do."

She means about going home. About if I'm going to take Titan's suggestion and get out while I'm ahead.

"Could you imagine going home without trying one last

time to talk to him?" Erin's question catches me off guard. I think about going back to California and never sharing another snarky comment with Titan again, never falling apart in his big, protective arms.

A single tear slides down my cheek. "No," I whisper. "You're right. I have to try."

Erin nods. "Do your mirror pep talk like your daddy taught you and then get out of here. He needs you, even though he's going about this entirely the wrong way."

I hope to fuck that's true, and that when I talk to him, he realizes I'm right.

Leaving Erin in the lobby, I change quickly and fluff up my hair. I have no energy left for my usual get-ready routine. There's nothing left in me but a pressing desire to see and talk to Titan. Erin's standing at the door with keys when I come back downstairs. She twirls them around her finger before tossing them to me.

I fold myself into her arms for a hug as I grip the keys tight. "Wish me luck, bestie," I reply, urging the tears not to start again. I've never cried so much in my damn life as the last two days.

"Don't let him dull your shine," she says into my hair. "He's the one who's supposed to make you sparkle. Time to remind him of that."

I laugh a little, squeezing her back before I head out to one of Stone's trucks.

I'm on edge the entire drive to the bar. Declan has been laying low, all things considered, but the recent revelations have us all on high alert anyhow.

When I get to the bar, there are very few people here. My nerves ratchet up ten notches when Titan looks up from behind the bar, his gaze narrowing a little when he sees me. He schools it back to neutral and busies himself cleaning glasses that already sparkle.

Okay then.

I take a seat at the bar as Titan and I have a little stare off. But I don't blink, and I don't look away. I don't even look inwardly at the dark connection that's left a hole in my chest. I simply meet his eyes, willing him to see that I'm here for him.

He opens his mouth to say something, then seems to think better of it, snapping his lips shut. Reaching for the Jack Daniels, he fills a glass and slides it across the bar to me before filling another for himself.

"We need to talk," I begin, not even sure where to start. I sort of pictured him running for the hills when I came in the door, but now that we're sharing a drink, I'm really fucking nervous.

I swirl the Jack in my glass as Titan leans back against the bar, pale blue eyes locked onto mine.

When it's clear he's not going to speak first, I take a sip of the Jack and set it down. "Mario went back to California, but you may have noticed I didn't go. I don't plan to, despite your suggestion."

Titan tenses, pushing off the back of the bar and crossing the small space to lean over the aged wood. He's so close I could reach out and touch him, but I don't. Despite the sudden ache that's pressing my heart.

"I'm here for this," I whisper. "And I wish you'd stop pushing me away. Being with me doesn't mean you can't do your job well. Taking a mate is supposed to make you stronger, remember?"

Well, shit, I just laid it all out there, and Titan's blue eyes are still blazing a hole straight through me. He lifts his glass and takes a sip. When he opens his mouth to respond, the door behind me opens. He bristles and reaches across the bar for me, hauling me up over it and behind him before I can even blink.

Peeking around his tense frame, I see Declan, JB and Gabriel entering the bar, looking in our direction. My mind immediately flashes to JB trying to fucking brand Erin with a cattle iron, and I can barely restrain my own angry growl.

But we're in public in a bar, and while it's not busy in here, it's not empty either. I'm safe. And I've got Titan right here.

Declan grins as the three men cross the bar and sit. "Hello there, pretty thing. Good to see yeh again."

Titan pushes me back behind himself as the bar door opens and more people come in, laughing and goofing off, oblivious to the fact that the most dangerous people in our valley are right here in front of us.

I peek around Titan again and see Gabriel rest his hand on Declan's shoulder. "Remember what we spoke about, alpha. Remember your message."

"The fuck?" I blurt out without meaning to. Gabriel grins but doesn't look away from Declan. JB hovers behind them both, eyes roving around the bar as if he's expecting trouble.

Declan leans over the bar, taking my glass of Jack and downing it in one gulp. "Our time has come, alpha. You heard Gabriel at the sermon. He's right. We are the better version of humanity, the next evolution."

Titan says nothing when Declan pauses. The other alpha shrugs and continues on, "I'm aware you and yer pack aren't believers, and that's fine. But I don't want your influence sullyin' what I'm tryin' to do with my omegas, yeh hear? So from now on, not a one is allowed in this bar. Am I clear? If they come in, turn 'em away. I don't want them in here gettin' ideas." His low-pitched alpha command hits Titan, who shudders under the weight of a pack alpha's brutal dominance.

"The only things anyone's getting here are good drinks and tasty food," Titan's hedges.

"That so?" Declan asks with a grin. "So yer tellin' me you didn't scoop Sal up right from under JB's nose? That you didn't gift Isabel with the crib another omega's about to use for her pup? Yeh tellin' me yeh had nothin' to do with any o'that?"

Before Titan can confirm or deny, Gabriel looks over at us with a frown. "You fill the omega's heads with wild ideas, and it has sown unhappiness in our pack. That stops today. We'd like you to leave us in peace. We're asking nicely, for now."

Declan grins maniacally. "'Nicely' being the operative word. If yeh don't mind what I'm telling you, our next inter-action will be unpleasant."

I can practically see our plan to help the omegas unrav-eling by the second, based on what he's sharing. That and all the frustrations of the last two days squeeze my heart tight until I feel like a rubber band about to snap.

"Unpleasant, huh?" I bark, unable to hold my temper as I lean around Titan to point my finger right in Declan's smug face. "Seems to me like the last few times you faced my pack, you left holding your guts in your hands."

"Luna," Titan growls. "Enough." He shoves me back behind his much larger frame, again.

Declan scowls at my words and stands, leaning across the bar to peer around at me. "God is on my side, yeh little bitch. I will do His will by growing my pack, and a little scrap like you won't get in my way. Omegas are good for one thing—breed-ing, so shut yer trap. Yeh hear?"

"Yeah?" I question. "If God was on your side, he'd probably encourage you to fucking feed your packmates."

Titan grabs my arm with an angry growl and drags me out of Declan's face as the alpha's evil smirk falls into a scowl.

Velos places one hand on Declan's back. "You have made your point, alpha. God is with you. We shouldn't remain in this place of sin. We don't require them to believe."

Declan looks over at Gabriel and nods once before shooting me a pointed look. "See you soon, omega."

Shit, shit, shit, why did I mention the omegas? That was so fucking foolish.

Next to me, Titan radiates angry tension as Declan exits the bar with Velos at his side and JB bringing up the rear.

"Fuuuck. I should have kept my damn mouth shut. Why the hell did I say that to him? He's such an asshole!" I blurt out as I look up at Titan. He removes a bar towel from his shoulder but says nothing as he slaps it down into the bar sink.

"I'm sorry, T," I apologize, putting my hand on his big forearm. He steps away from me as someone raises their hand to order a drink, then stalks to the end of the bar to help them. Fuck. I opened my big mouth, and now he's mad. He has every right to be. I shouldn't have jeopardized the work we're trying to do here.

The moment he finishes helping the customer, I grab his hand. "Titan, talk to me."

Tight pressure in our bond crushes my chest so hard that I struggle to rasp in a steadying breath.

"What good can possibly come of taunting him, Luna? Do you have any sense of self-preservation at all? If they attacked us here, I may not be able to fight off a pack alpha and his enforcer."

That's all he says before turning away from me.

"T, I know, but–"

"No," he snaps in that low-pitched alpha rumble I usually love. But this time it's angry and bitter, frustrated at what I did. "You're not safe, Luna. There's already a target on your head from your previous altercations with Declan. I can't watch you twenty-four hours a day. You're making my job harder. At this point, I'd be terrified to even let you drive home alone. Did you think at all before you said that to him?"

"I didn't mean to," I admit. "It slipped out because he was

right in my face. I'm sorry; I'm so sorry. But it doesn't mean our work is for nothing. Cassian is still trying to–"

Titan cuts me off with an angry wave. "I'm going to stay at my cabin tonight. I'm angry, and I recognize I need an evening alone. I'll drive you back to the lodge."

No. "No, Titan. Please don't. Talk to me, okay?" I beg him for understanding as I follow him around the end of the bar and into the storeroom. The crushing pressure in my chest builds as tears fill my eyes.

Titan turns toward me, tipping my chin up until our gazes meet. "I'm unhappy and more than a little angry. I want some space to process those emotions. I'm asking you to give me that. Will you?"

Wrong. It's so fucking wrong, but I nod. "Can I have the keys, please? I'll take myself back to the lodge."

"Not a chance," he retorts. "After what just happened, I don't know if you'll be safe going alone. I'll take you."

"I can just call you when I get there," I grumble as Titan shakes his head.

"Not happening, Luna. Don't fight me on this."

I blanch at his words. Fight him on this? I don't want to fight at all.

"So we're back to this then?" I ask the question in a bitter, frustrated tone. "Fighting?"

Titan says, "I don't want to get into it while we're both angry, so let's talk about it la–"

"You'd rather just chat it through when it's convenient for you," I snap. I'm making this worse. I need to give him the space he asked for. "Ignore me," I mutter. "I don't like to let things simmer, and the last two days have been hard not talking to you. I'm frustrated because I'd rather talk right away. You said all good relationships are built on communication, right?"

Blue eyes focus on me, wary and apprehensive as I use his own words to try to encourage him to figure this out now.

For a long moment, neither of us says anything, but I beg him with my eyes to talk to me about my fuck-up. He says nothing, though, just checks in with the other bartender and tells him he has to take me home.

The half-hour drive back to Bent Fork is pure fucking misery. Titan says nothing, eyes focused on the road as snow starts to come down fast. I say nothing because he asked me for space, and I'm trying to respect his communication style.

All I know for sure is that our bond is darker still, tense enough that I continue to rub at my chest, hoping to ease the pressure. Titan notices but says nothing. When we arrive back at the ranch, I give him one last look as I hop out of the truck. "You're not coming in, not even to see everyone else?"

"That's what space is, Luna," he replies in an even, neutral tone. "I'll be back tomorrow, and we'll talk."

Focusing through the misery, I shut the door and start my death march up the stairs into the lodge. Nobody's around this late, not in the lobby at least. I make it all the way to my room before I collapse into a heap at my door, crying my fucking heart out.

CHAPTER THIRTY-NINE

titan

I DRIVE up the dirt road to my cabin after I drop Luna off, my mind racing around what happened this evening. Stone, Clay and I should have a further conversation about it in the morning. Declan is clearly aware the bar is a place the omegas congregated for a reason; he came in to tell us that.

Luna dumped fuel on that fire by taunting him and letting on that there's more to our story. Fuck, just seeing her nearly brought me to my knees. Those pretty blue eyes filled with tears. The knowledge that I've crushed our bond to dust in the last two days.

I pray hard for everyone's safety as I pull into my parking spot. Then I sit in my truck for a long time, listening to the muffled sounds of the snow. I can't do anything about this right now. Cassian is still gone, although who knows if that's part of what's going on right now. My enforcer intuition is screaming at me to do something, anything to get more clarity on the situation.

Just then, my cell phone rings.

Stone.

"Hey, buddy, Cassian just got back to the lodge. He says the meet went well. He talked to Isabel."

Relief floods my system that part of our plan isn't shot to shit. Cassian's safe, and we got our message to the omegas.

"We have other problems now," I return, launching into the entire story. I mention that Luna got into a shouting match with Declan but don't go into specifics. I'm still so fucking mad she couldn't help herself, and it might put our plan in jeopardy.

Still, Declan being a jackass isn't her fault. I just would have expected her to be smarter about dealing with him, to have a little more self-control knowing what's at stake.

"Is that why she's here now, and you're not?" Stone's question is gentle, but I sense an undercurrent of that strong alpha tone.

"I needed space. We argued after Declan left."

"Betty always told me not to go to bed angry, Titan. You've heard that saying, I presume?"

"I have," I bark into the receiver. "I'm terrified for those girls, Stone. Velos is a nutjob, Declan's buying this religious angle and leaning hard into it, and it's going to be more difficult than ever now that he knows we're trying to help them."

Stone sighs. "You don't think he realized that before? He's a dumbass, but he's still an alpha. He'd have pretty good intuition."

"I believe he's completely lacking it," I deadpan. "Because if he had it, he wouldn't let his packmates suffer the way they do. Even JB looked anxious tonight, glancing back and forth between Declan and Velos. I got the distinct sense he doesn't like the new guy."

"Now that's interesting," Stone muses. "Discord in his leadership crew. Let's talk about it with our group tomorrow. It's late, and you need rest. But come back in the morning if you can. Don't let this thing between you and Luna fester longer than it has. You're both miserable." He delivers that last bit with a full-on bark.

It washes over me, tugging at my chest as I agree and hang up. Entering the cabin, I look into the empty bedroom and wish Luna were there. Although thinking about her produces angry heat and pressure in my chest again, I still wish it. Slumping against my door, I rub at the insistent pull in my chest, knowing my omega is unhappy too.

I'm half a second from grabbing my keys and going back, but then Isabel's face flashes in my mind. And all the other omegas who have come to me for help in the last few years. I let out a frustrated groan, laying my head in my hands as I sit on the floor, miserable and alone. I check the computer James gave me that's tied to our valley's monitoring system. The snow is coming down hard and fast, but I still want to keep an eye on my pack's security.

Eventually, I fall asleep on the floor, one hand still on the laptop.

When I wake in the morning, I'm flat on the ground. My brain spins like a top the moment I blink my eyes open, worrying I might have missed something overnight. The quiet solitude of my usually peaceful home does nothing to improve my mental state. I pick up the phone and dial my alpha, knowing he'll tell me if anything has changed.

"Good morning," Stone greets me as he answers.

"Anything happen in the last few hours?" I don't mean to bark at him, but I can't stop waiting for the other shoe to drop.

"No," Stone reassures me. "Apart from your omega hiding in her room all morning with Cassian. Why is he here comforting her instead of you? Get the fuck up here, Titan."

Visions of Cassian comforting her instead of me send my dominant nature into overdrive. "On my way," I snap, grabbing my keys and jogging out to my truck.

I'm still upset that Luna made a mistake, but I'm also drawn to comfort her. That frustrates me, because it's dictated by the bond. The bond is pushing me toward her, an inevitable outcome that today feels more like a gilded, sunny cage. All of these conflicting emotions take up my mental energy as I pass the research trailer and the general store.

At the last minute, I back up past the general store and park in front of the research RV. Bianca comes out with a grin. "Hey, friend. Haven't seen you in a few days; everything okay?"

I give her a big fake smile that I hope looks real as I get out of the truck to greet her. "Been busy with enforcer duties. Do you or your team need anything? How's it going?"

Her face falls. "Not gonna lie, Titan, we're getting past surface level info at this point, and some of it is a little terrifying. Mal's bird? She could hurt someone so easily. And she can shift into almost anything. I haven't even dug into the remaining powers, but Sam is freaking out about it. Not to mention the bullshit sermon we went to."

"I went to one too," I admit. "What a load of horse shit. Please don't hold it against us; it's not an alpha thing."

Bianca nods as my eyes flick to the trailer behind her. "Would it help if I chat with the team to remind them how non-transitioned humans hurt one another all the time? Weapons are easy to come by, but the will to use them against someone is what's important."

Bianca sighs and crosses her arms, following my gaze. "We've had that discussion as a team; Sam is in the same camp of belief as me. There are good and bad people everywhere, right? I'm sure there are good and bad packs, or members of packs. But either way, my goal is to get the info to the Alpha Research Group so our government can make informed legislation. I've got to work within the confines of a system, unfortunately."

"It's frustrating," I agree, turning my focus back to her. "Listen, why don't you and the team come up to the lodge for dinner tonight? It'll be a good reminder to Sam that we're still normal in so many ways. I know you've come up before, but more regular interaction outside of the official interviews might be helpful."

"Agreed," Bianca breathes. "Thanks so much, Titan. We'll see you later, alright?"

I watch her return to the trailer as pressure constricts my lungs. Not only are we facing issues on the Declan front, but now the research too. This is exactly why Stone didn't want to be part of the Alpha Research Group initiative. It's not a good time to have the government picking through our lives. Although I suppose there's probably never a great time for that.

Frustrated, I hop back in my truck and head to the lodge, parking along the side next to Stone's big pickup. I dread going inside and talking to Luna about yesterday. She was probably on to something when she said she likes to talk quickly about issues. I thought I'd feel better today, but if anything, I feel trapped. It's not Luna, not really. I'm sure it's the whole situation. I can't fix it, and that makes me want to rage.

When I open the front door to the lodge, she's there, waiting, blue eyes filled with unshed tears.

I don't even think; I just react, reaching out to wipe them away as she grabs my hand. She pauses for a minute, tears coming faster and faster before I open my arms and pull her to me. Her soft crying escalates to full sobbing as she buries her face in my chest.

I did this. I broke us. I broke us to protect everyone else. Holding her like this is shredding my self-control.

My desire to comfort and protect overrides everything

else as I draw her close, breathing her in. Her scent wraps around me as our tense bond pulls between us.

"I'm so sorry," she grips my shirt in both tiny fists as she looks up, tears streaming down her cheeks.

I pull her up into my arms, wrapping her legs around me as I pass through the lobby, past James and Julia cuddling on the sofa. I continue past Erin and Sal as they come down the big broad staircase, Erin shooting me a wry look. I keep going until I reach Luna's room, and then I head straight through it and out onto her small porch, seating us in one of the big chairs with her still clinging desperately to me.

Luna's eyes flick up to mine as I sigh. "I'm sorry too." I lean in to plant a tender kiss on her cheek as her lip wobbles. "I was angry at the situation, and I didn't believe I could have a rational discussion."

"Because I fucked up," she continues, her voice fraught with self-loathing.

I consider how to respond before I make things worse. "You spoke in the heat of the moment, and I wish you hadn't. But Declan brings that out in people, me included. He and I have exchanged plenty of shitty comments over the years."

"Really?" Luna's voice rises to a hopeful, pleading tone.

"Really," I reassure her. "So...you're not leaving?"

"Never," she asserts, capturing my lower lip between both of hers. "Not as long as you're still willing to give us a shot. I should have kept my mouth shut. I promise I will in the future."

"Never make yourself less than who you are, Luna," I command her. "But let's avoid Declan like the plague and help those girls as soon as we can, alright?'

"You know I want that more than anything else," she says. "I think about them all the fucking time."

My earlier sense of being trapped has dissipated, leaving me with only the intense need to shower my omega with my love. "Ride me," I whisper into Luna's ear as she slumps against my chest, both arms wrapping around my neck.

"How can you want that after all the crying?" She's still wary and unsure, despite the conversation we just had.

"The last few days have crushed me," I remind her. "I have to focus on protecting everyone, but I want you so goddamn much. I need both."

Tears still stream down her cheeks as I grip the back of her neck, running my other hand inside her soft pajamas, down over the peach of her ass. She cries out when I press two fingers inside her from behind, taking her mouth at the same time.

"Open for me," I demand as she sucks in a breath and relaxes. My fingers slide further in, stroking the rough spot that makes her breath hitch. When I remove my fingers, she gasps and rocks her hips against me. I'm hard for her already, ready to take her roughly.

Luna reaches down and undoes my jeans, my cock swinging free into her hand as she rubs her warm hand down the length. A groan leaves my mouth when she squeezes where my knot will be.

"Knot me, alpha," she pleads. "Please."

I set her upright and pull her yoga pants down as she steps out of them. I shove my own jeans down around my ankles and haul her back on top of me, her silky heat caressing my cock as it throbs. Fucking Luna is different from everyone I've had for the last twenty years. Together we can be tender or wild, and that wild side is what I've fought to control my whole life.

I can't think any more about it now, though, not when she grips my shaft and seats herself in one quick move. Her pussy clenches around me as I buck up into her, both hands going to her ass to steady her as she rides me. Luna shifts up, but before she can sit down again, I punch up fast with my hips.

Her breasts shake from the confines of her thin tee, hard nipples begging for my attention.

We pick up a frenzied, frantic pace together as I bite my way frantically along her chest, up over her collarbone and neck. But then my knot starts to swell, and I hold her tight to my hips as I fuck into her, her cries increasing in volume.

When she finally shatters, the rapid clench of her pussy on my cock sends me over with her. I growl her name in her ear as she throws her head back, asking for my bite. Despite this connection, I'm not ready. I'm still on edge, still worried about everyone's safety, and terrified for something to further provoke Declan and Gabriel.

I recognize that, and the bond between us pales with rejection as Luna's sea-blue eyes meet mine. She brings her forehead to my shoulder and huffs as she comes down from a shattering orgasm. My knot fades fast, too fast, when I think about how it feels between us right now.

I broke something in the last few days when I encouraged her to leave.

And I don't know if I can fix it.

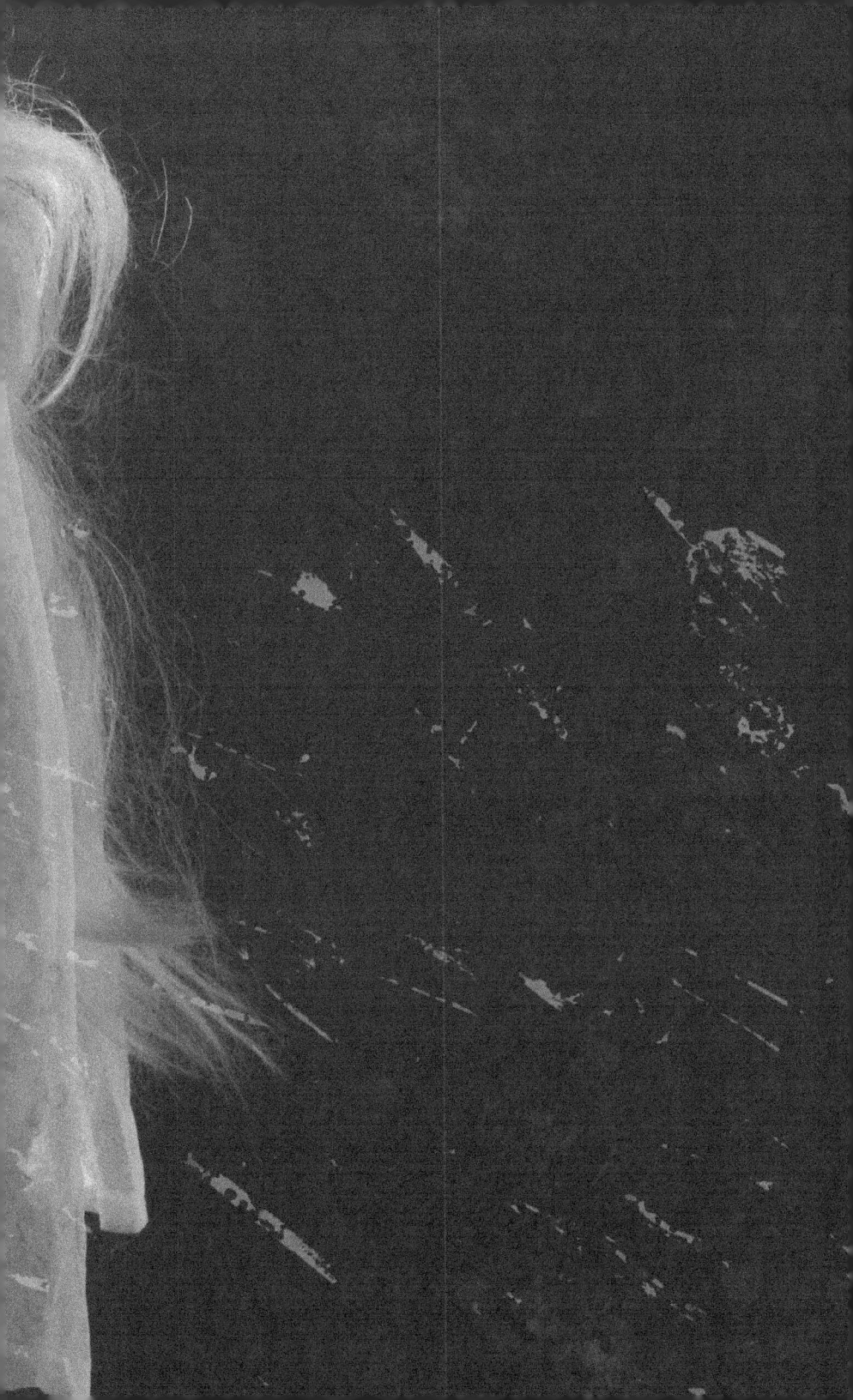

luna

THIS IS WRONG; it's all wrong. I opened my goddamn mouth, and that one mistake has crushed everything I hoped we could overcome. There's nothing either of us want more than to help the omegas, and I might have ruined that.

I talked to Cassian early this morning, so I already know he was able to get Isabel a message. What I don't know is what happened after that and before Declan came to the bar. What caused Declan to decide now was a good time to warn the omegas away from Teddy's? Nobody knows, and it's terrifying for all of us. He said the next time we saw him, he'd get more forceful. I've been on the receiving end of that once, and it nearly fucking killed me.

Lifting myself off Titan's gorgeous cock, I pull my pants up, avoiding his gaze. I hoped after we talked, we'd move past the drama. It doesn't seem to be the case though. Our bond is almost painful with the amount of tension and wariness right now.

He says nothing as I turn toward the door and head back into my room from the porch. I hear a sigh and his jeans zipping, and then he follows me. One huge arm wraps around my waist as Titan grabs me, flopping onto the bed as he wraps my legs up in his. For once in my life, I have no words. No pithy, sarcastic remarks. No smart comebacks. I've got nothin'.

"Let's find a minute of calm together, omega," Titan whispers into my hair.

I agree, holding his arm when he snakes it under my neck and around my chest. We lie like that for a while until Titan's breathing grows slow and easy. He's asleep. If he's anything like me, he got no sleep last night.

Another fucking thing that's my fault.

Pulling myself out of his warmth, I head out of my room, not even bothering to check my hair in the mirror. That's how I know I'm fucked up mentally. I don't even care about being put together right now, when normally I pride myself on that. I just...don't care.

Heading down the hall, I knock on Sal's door, hearing the twins and Cherry inside laughing about something.

"Get in here!" River shouts as laughter rings from the room. I enter, and River's goofy grin falls. "Aww, honey, I heard it all. You okay?"

All four of them are on Sal's bed as *Practical Magic* plays on the television above the fireplace. Rogue smiles at me from the middle of the bed, happy as a clam to be surrounded by women. My heart warms in my chest as he opens his arms wide. "Get over here, Hot Sauce. You look like you could use a hug."

I throw myself into the bed as Rogue pulls me between his big thighs, both big arms going across my upper chest. He's careful to avoid the tatas, thankfully, but he's comforting me nonetheless. He has a protective streak a mile wide; that's clear.

We watch the twin witches on the television split up as Gillian leaves home to follow her heart, and then Cherry finally speaks. "Luna, Declan being a jackass isn't your fault. You know that, right?"

"I know," I agree. "But I poked the fucking bear and pissed off Titan, and now we're just broken."

"You're gonna be fine," Sal says confidently. "Titan is protective of everyone, and he's our enforcer. He's probably feeling torn too. But you're his; we all know it."

I can't nod at that because I don't know it for certain anymore. We were headed down that path, definitely. But I don't know how to get past the awful state my bond is in, despite connecting just now.

"Well," River chirps, "he's your tall, dark and then some, so it's gonna be fine. I know it."

Cherry and I shout at the same time, bursting into laughter as I sit up and turn toward River. "Tall, dark and then some? It's tall, dark and handsome, you ding dong." It's so nice to laugh for a minute.

"Is not!" River shouts, sitting up and shoving me so I fall on top of Cherry. Cherry's laughing so hard, she slips and falls off the bed, and I lose balance and land with a crash on top of her. We're breathless as River peeks over the edge, scowling down at us.

"You two are so dumb. It's tall, dark and then some. Dumb dumbies."

Normally I'd snark at her for using the word dumb three times in one sentence, but Sal comes to our rescue.

"It actually is tall, dark and handsome," her soft voice intones. "Sorry, Riv. You are not right on this one."

River flops up against her brother's shoulder as Cherry huffs out a panting, breathless laugh. "Get off me, Hot Sauce; I'm dying!"

We laugh again as I slip off Cherry and hold out my hand to pull her up off the ground. Her gray eyes spark with mirth as she bends at the waist and sucks in a breath.

"My God, I haven't laughed that hard in days."

Snorting, I reach out and twirl her bright red hair around my fingertips. "River is very useful as pack comedienne."

Cherry stands upright and grins at me. "Okay, we've already watched *Practical Magic* once all the way through this morning. I'm going to help Clay with lunch."

"Is it even his day?" River grumbles. "How does he get stuck cooking so damn much?"

"He's got a stronger caretaking instinct than most alphas," Rogue says softly, smiling at his sister as Cherry and I share a look.

"What do you mean?" Cherry's voice is soft and curious.

Rogue shrugs. "I can't explain it; it's just a sense. But Clay's focus on providing for the pack is stronger than your average alpha. That's why he's a great strategist, but it's also why he handles so much of the cooking. He likes taking care of us."

Cherry and I share another look at that as River slaps Rogue on the back of the head. "You didn't even know what a strategist was until we came here, and now you've got insider information about Clay's inner workings? Whatever, dude. Let's go help, okay?"

I go with them because I'm desperate for something to take my mind off the broken connection flooding my chest with anxiety. I don't know how to fix what I broke.

CHAPTER FORTY-ONE

titan

I EAT lunch with the pack, happy everyone is safe—for now. I can't shake the sense that something is coming for us.

Clay claps me on the back as I watch my omega's gorgeous ass while she leaves the room. I can't help but want her, despite my hesitations and despite my intense need to protect everyone in our home.

"I'm gonna give you some advice, brother." His slight Texan lilt is more obvious when he calls me brother.

I swivel on the chair. "I'm all ears, strategist."

Clay crosses his arms and leans back in the chair with a knowing look. "Don't let things simmer. Your woman is a firecracker. But she's an endless well of love and commitment to everything she throws herself into. She requires your unfailing support in all things."

I bristle, knowing what he means. "You weren't there," I reiterate.

Clay shuts me up with a pointed look. "I'm not saying you can't disagree with her; I'm saying fix it fast so you can enjoy her. She's dejected; we all see it. One of the beautiful things about being her alpha is that you can fix it for her, Titan. You are everything she needs. And vice versa."

I rub my chest as the loosening tension ratchets back up. I arrived at the lodge this morning feeling frustrated and trapped. But now? I'm torn between my responsibility to protect my people and finding Luna to take her as mine.

Clay watches me in silence before shoving me in my chair. "Come on, brother. We should sync with the rest of leadership."

An hour later, we've got several potential plans in place for rescuing the omegas from Declan's pack. All we need is the thumbs-up from Isabel about who wants out. The interaction in the bar with Declan might have put our plans in jeopardy, but for now, we have to proceed as if we'll still get an opportunity to help those women.

We break, and I spend the rest of the afternoon with Bianca and the researchers. I'm finally the interviewee, and I'm interested to see how Sam handles this one since he's been such a dick with the others. I intended to invite Luna to come with me, but she was on a work call when I stopped by her room.

Clay's words ring in my brain.

As I leave the main lodge, River flies down the steps and shoves her hands in her back pockets. "Can I come with you wherever you're going?"

When I turn and give her a look, she glares daggers at me.

"T, I swear, if you're about to say it's dangerous or some shit, I'm gonna lose my cool. I feel like we're in jail. Being stuck at the house fucking sucks."

"Language," I bark as she rolls her eyes at me.

"Seriously, T, half the people here are mated, and the other half are being stupid, and I just can't sit here and listen. I can hear everybody talking, remember?" She taps the side of her head as she gives me a meaningful look.

Sighing, I hold the front door open for her. "I'm getting interviewed by the researchers today. You can come, but you've gotta behave."

"Good behavior is my middle name," she snarks, lifting her chin high as she flounces dramatically out the door.

I hold back another sigh as I follow River down the front steps to my truck. She hops in the passenger seat and glances around at the stained and worn leather.

"Gawd, these stains aren't like...bodily fluids, are they?" Her nose scrunches up in disgust as she inspects my bench seat disdainfully.

"You wanna come with me or not?"

She rolls her eyes and sets herself down gingerly, scowling at the bench seat.

I put the truck in drive, heading back up the road to the research trailer. River opens a window and starts humming, and that brings me back to the time Luna rode with me to get the mail. She did the exact same thing, and I was so busy staring at her gorgeous tits that I drove off the road.

"Are you gonna get your head out of your ass about Luna?"

River's blunt question takes me by surprise as I try to formulate an appropriate response. Something like "none of your damn business," or "who are you, my mother?"

When I don't answer fast, River continues, "Here's the thing, sir," she adds with an epic amount of snark, "the lodge is damn full of drama and angst, and I'm getting really tired of it. Between Luna and Cherry and Julia, I could really use some good news."

"Well, by all means, River," I snap, trying to decide if I'm going to laugh hysterically or use my enforcer tone with her. "Let me sort out the state of my bond if it'll make your life easier."

"Well, that was easy." She reaches over to pat me on the thigh.

We fall into an awkward semi-silence. Well, it's awkward for me, but she keeps on humming until we get to the research trailer. She exits the truck first, hopping up the steps and going right in as if she owns the place.

I hear the team greet her enthusiastically before I enter. As one, the three researchers and River all turn to look at me.

"Hey, Titan, how goes it?" Bianca's voice is tentative as she tucks a lock of dark hair behind her ear.

River snorts. "He's being a dummy about a girl, but I imagine you're gonna ask a lot of really probing questions about that during this interview, right?"

My mouth goes dry as the damn desert as I straighten my shoulders and give River a scathing look.

Bianca holds back a smile and slaps River on the shoulder. "You've got it, honey. You sure you want to stay for how intrusive this is?"

River reaches into her back pocket and brings out an unpopped bag of popcorn. "Yeah, I brought this, LOL."

The researchers all laugh, even Sam, which surprises me. His grin falls when he catches me looking, though.

For the next hour, we cover every facet of my life before I transitioned and since, including my medical history. Zee does an in-depth physical, and then Sam questions me about my connection with Luna.

And that part fucking hurts. Because my connection is threadbare at the moment.

"Hey," River pipes up when I think I can't stand to answer another question about Luna. "You're all smart as hell. Is the saying 'tall, dark and handsome', or 'tall dark and then some'?"

Bianca and Zee burst into laughter, and even Sam chuckles a little bit as he turns to the exuberant teen.

"It's tall, dark and handsome. Why?" Sam questions.

River scowls. "Cool, cool. No reason. Just wondered."

"Wait," Bianca laughs, doubled over before she looks back up at Riv. "What did you think it was?"

"Literally no reason," River barks back. "Are you all coming up to the lodge for dinner tonight or what?"

Bianca's laughing too hard to answer, but Zee pipes up helpfully, "Yeah, we sure will. Let us get finished here with Titan's paperwork, and then we'll meet you up at the lodge."

For once, I'm thankful for the bubbly omega's effervescence, because the focus isn't on me and how utterly miserable I am.

DINNER IS raucous for the first time in a long while. James and the twins cut up the entire time, and even Cassian joins us, back from his trip to the meadow. Luna sits next to me, but she's stiff and quiet the entire time.

Stone grins over at the twins as dinner winds down. "Anybody up for karaoke? It's been a hot minute."

The twins and the omegas start dancing in their chairs as the researchers look over at me with curious looks. "He traded the concert hall for drunken bar karaoke. It's fun though."

Sal and the twins dash off to get Stone's piano as my alpha looks over at me. "I need you behind the bar, buddy."

River comes rushing back into the dining hall, her face flushed as her curls bounce wildly. "Somebody's here. I don't know who. All I hear is motorcycles!"

Stone touches River's shoulder, his tone clipped and urgent. "What do you hear, omega? Tell me."

Across from me, Bianca and her team stiffen. "What's going on, Titan?" she questions.

"Don't know, but stay in the house," I command as I stride for the front door. Motorcycles mean just one thing.

"Oh, shit, they're just all shouting," River yells, following me as the rest of my pack catches up.

Just then, a loud explosion echoes from the aspen grove, a cloud of smoke billowing up into the sky.

Next to me, Bianca shrieks. "Oh, fuck, is that our trailer? Oh goddamnit!" Without waiting for an answer, she flies down toward one of the ATVs, the other two researchers standing in horror next to me.

Flames lick up into the night sky as the faint sounds of whooping reach my ears.

It's Declan. I know it.

My leadership group springs into action immediately, all of us running for the trucks.

"James and Cass, stay with the lodge, be on the lookout for an attack," I direct. We've been preparing for something like this for days, on the off chance Declan got a wild hair.

A group of us leap into the trucks and fly up the gravel road toward the flames. We bounce over the gravel road even as I listen for sounds, but the motorcycles are already rumbling away, the shouts growing farther and farther as we speed up the gravel drive. Stone lets out a string of curse words next to me when we round a huge rock into the aspen grove. Both the store and the researchers' trailers are on fire.

I climb out of the truck in disbelief as Bianca slams her ATV to a stop next to me. "Goddamnit, fuuuuuuck," she shouts, both hands running through her hair as the rest of the pack comes up the road behind her. She starts mumbling about data backups as River rushes to my side.

"The other pack is gone, but there's someone in the fucking store," she shouts. I can't hear shit over the flames, but River shoves me toward the blaze. "I can hear someone crying. There's someone in there, T!"

"Ash, stay with the omegas," I command. My feet move as

soon as I register River's words, Stone and Clay right behind me. The front of the store is on fire, the heat spreading fast through the groceries as beams start to catch flame. The moment I get through the door, I hear a noise. A woman's voice.

Sprinting toward the back storeroom, we find Isabel on the ground, clutching her stomach. She's bleeding profusely, sobbing as she cradles her belly. Coughs wrack her frame as she sucks in ragged, pained breaths.

Clay drops down next to her, stroking her hair out of her face as Stone and I share a look.

"We've got you, honey," I murmurs as the sobbing omega looks up at me.

"The baby, Titan. Oh my God..." Her eyes roll back in her head as I resist the urge to scream out my frustrations. When Isabel's arms fall to her sides, Stone bellows his anger at what we see. Claw marks crisscross her stomach, blood slipping wet and sticky from every wound.

Smoke billows as Clay coughs next to us. "Lift her on three; we've got to get her out of here and call a healer." He does a quick countdown, and Stone and I lift the gravely injured omega, pacing quickly through the storeroom and back out into the night. Our entire pack is there by then.

Stone tosses his phone to Erin. "Call Mitchell. Tell him we need Brady and Connor right fucking now."

Luna rushes to my side, eyes wide with disbelief as we set Isabel down. Erin stalks away from the roaring blaze as she dials the other alpha. Sounds muffle as I watch her relay the message, my senses on overdrive as I stalk past the burning sites and look up the road. Declan's fucking gone. But this was him.

That's when I see it. A box right in the middle of the drive-way. I approach it cautiously, James following me like a shadow. When we get closer, he drops to one knee. The entire top of the box is open, and inside are the groceries from our last drop.

Pinned to the top of the box is a note.

I'VE GOT *my omegas handled. Do you? Keep the mouthy one in check, or I'll check her for you.*

LUNA SHOUTS for me just as a heart-wrenching scream rends the air. Isabel's coming to. I rush to her side, where Luna's already holding a blood-soaked sweater to the omega's stomach.

Isabel sits up and grabs Luna's arm as I drop to a knee by her side. James calls for Stone and Clay to take a look at the box in the driveway.

When Isabel's dark eyes flick from Luna to me, they're filled with pain and tears. "Declan said this was a message," she gasps. "A warning to leave the omegas alone. He caught me trying to encourage the girls to leave. He...he did this. Declan fucking did this." Then pain takes her again as she screams anew.

Luna croons gently, humming to the omega as everyone else mills around. It'll be five solid minutes before Brady can get here.

"Let's get her to the lodge," I bark. When I look over at Stone, he's rifling through the box of groceries. Our eyes meet, and my alpha is fucking furious.

This is a shitshow. Isabel's bleeding out in our driveway, and the researchers are standing mute, watching it all unfold. And I can't do shit to fix any of this. This was my job. To protect my pack from this fucking asshole.

I failed.

CHAPTER FORTY-TWO

luna

MY TERROR for Isabel and her child overrides every other emotion. I can't worry about the researchers and what this sudden violence looks like to them. I can't worry about the loss of the store our pack built and filled. I can't worry about whatever Stone's looking at in the driveway.

Every ounce of focus is on the injured mother lying on gravel right now. I hold the sweater across her bleeding stomach as Titan and James lift Isabel carefully into Titan's truck. She screams the entire time, a desperate, awful noise that tears at my soul.

"We've got you, Isabel," I reassure her over and over as I slide onto the floorboard, holding her carefully in place as we pick our way up the drive toward the main house.

The minutes it takes to get to the lodge seem like an eternity, Isabel sobbing the entire way. As we park the truck and lift her out, a giant bird lands on the porch, Brady and Connor clutched in its claws. I don't know if it's Samson or Pen or Mal, but I've never been so grateful to see the other pack.

We quickly move Isabel inside as Brady starts barking out

question after question. He asks Isabel, but she's lost so much blood, she's fading fast, unable to focus on their words.

We lay her down on a big ottoman in the lobby as Connor and Brady move to either side of her. It's not lost on me that they did this for Erin and me not that long ago. I remove the blood-soaked sweater as Connor gasps.

"I can't believe they'd do this to her." His voice grates with anger.

Titan turns from everyone and jogs off into the house; I assume to get supplies. He comes back a minute later with the lodge's medical kit and an armful of towels. I move to help with them, but he brushes me off and does it himself.

Brady and Connor begin work on Isabel as the rest of our pack arrives. And the entire time, my mate doesn't look at me, not even when I focus on our bond.

"Titan?" I reach out and put my hand on his forearm.

When he turns to me, there's such anger and disdain in his eyes, I don't even know what to say.

"How can I help?" I ask the question so quietly, I'm barely aware I've said it aloud.

"You've done enough, Luna," is his only answer. I flop down into a chair next to the ottoman, exhausted. I am bone-deep tired. Tired of the rollercoaster ride of being here with this pack, tired of the back and forth with Titan. I'm beat.

I mull all that over as Brady and Connor use their combined power to get Isabel to a place where they can safely stitch her. Eventually, I notice their seer, Samson, hovering in the shadows of the doorway. He gives me a sad smile before crossing the lobby to drop down next to my chair.

"Are you alright, Luna?" His voice is so deep and comforting, I want to sink into it.

"No," I mutter, gesturing to where Brady and Connor are shifting Isabel back and forth to bandage her. "I'm having flashbacks to when Declan did this to Erin and me."

Samson nods. "I meant in general, omega. Your bond is...tattered."

"Tell me something I don't know," I grumble again, not bothering to look up at Titan. "This is my fault. I taunted Declan, and now he did this. This whole thing." I gesture at Connor and Brady and Isabel and even Titan, who hovers behind the others.

Samson shakes his head. "You are not responsible for Declan's actions, Luna. He is a wild card. We will seek retribution. He will not get away with this."

"I'm sure," I deadpan. "Seems like we are always needing retribution for something. Living here is fucking wild."

"You do not have to stay," he murmurs, glancing over at Titan. "You could choose another path for yourself, if you wished."

He's saying what I'm already thinking.

Just then, Brady stands up and arches his back, stretching it as Connor slings an arm around his waist. He looks over at me. "She's stable, and she'll be okay. But I'll come back every day for probably a week or so. I sense the baby is alright too; I can hear a heartbeat. Samson, any chance you can see anything additional?"

Samson shakes his head. "I have already asked Rolf, but we have no visions about this omega. I am sorry, brothers."

Connor waves him off. "Would be super cool if Rolf could be more like Google. You know? Type in what I want to know and find it fast."

Samson chuckles. "I will provide Rolf your feedback, but he will ask me to tell you to go fuck yourself."

Connor laughs at that but leans in to kiss Brady's shoulder tenderly. Even in the face of disaster, their pack is so easy around each other. It's a far cry from the tension between Titan and me right now.

Stone and Titan move Isabel to Stone's room, giving me

another flashback to doing this with Erin. Samson, Connor and Brady remain in the lobby with us. Then Stone calls all of leadership to his office as the omegas and I gather around Isabel. She's asleep, thankfully, her breathing even but no longer strained. I pray to God that she and her child are alright.

We sit quietly with her for a long time, and when I can't keep my eyes open, I pace back through the long hallways toward the front of the house. When I pass Stone's office, I pause, wondering if I should ask Titan if he needs anything before heading to bed. I could use a snuggle, to be honest. I could use comfort after this horrible fucking turn of events.

"He did this because he was taunted," replies Titan from inside the office. My blood chills at his words.

"He did this because he's an asshole," Stone retorts. "And clearly our arrangement with the DPM for a handler to deal with Declan isn't working. We should go public, just like we discussed. Isabel is a witness."

"Look at this goddamn note," Titan barks back. "It's clear as day, Stone."

Note? What note?

Without thinking, I shove the door open and barge my way in. "What note?" Everyone looks up at me at the same time, Stone blanching. Clearly they were so engrossed in this conversation about me that they didn't even hear me coming. This is bad. Really bad.

"What fucking note?" I grit out again, crossing to the table.

Titan's face is carefully neutral, but the rest of the leadership crew looks sad and worn down.

"This isn't your fault, Luna," Stone croons as he picks up a piece of paper and hands it to me.

. . .

I'VE GOT *my omegas handled. Do you? Keep the mouthy one in check, or I'll check her for you.*

I SLUMP against Stone's chair as I read the note over and over, hot tears filling my eyes. When I'm finally able to look up at Titan, he's stiff in his chair, both big hands fisted on top of the table. And the look he shoots me is so accusatory, I know he believes this is my fault, even if Stone says it isn't.

Without a word, I drop the note and turn from the alphas. Clay and James both call out for me at the same time, but I'm numb to it all. Because I feel the eyes of my mate on my back too. But he doesn't say a fucking word.

THE LODGE IS quiet all night. I should know, because I'm never able to fall asleep. And Titan never comes to my room. Not that I expected him to. My chest is aching and hollow, and by five a.m., I know what I'm going to do.

Rolling out of bed, I throw all of my clothes back in my suitcase and book a flight to California. I'll finish the Omega-matic project from there. I owe the pack that, at least. But I can't fix the rest of this shit, and I'm past the point of having energy to try. If I stay, I'll keep screwing things up.

My big mouth has gotten me in trouble before, but never like this. It's a lesson I didn't want to learn, but I guess life decided I needed it.

At eight a.m., I walkie Erin and ask her to come to my room. Two minutes later, she's there, sailing her way through the door with two cups of coffee in her hands. The moment she sees my bags on the bed, she starts shaking her head.

"Luna, don't run, please. This wasn't your fault. Nobody blames you!"

"Titan does," I remind her. "I heard him, E. He blames me for this, and I haven't talked to him since it happened."

"That's a bunch of bullshit," she snaps. "He should have been up here comforting you."

"I know, that's what mates do, right? Even if I fucked up?"

She nods. "I'll talk to him."

"Don't," I reply. "Mario was right about one thing. I'm not chasing a man. I'm on a flight out of here at noon. Can you take me to the airport?" There's a pang in my chest when I consider leaving Bent Fork. In the short time I've been here, it's become home. But I can't stay in a home that's shredding my emotions the way this one is. Not even for the happy times.

Erin looks at me but says nothing.

"How's Isabel?" I ask, terrified to hear the answer.

Erin shrugs. "Still in a lot of pain, but Brady will be here shortly to work on her again. You remember how much claws hurt. Declan does this shit, Lu. Again, it's not your fault."

"It is," I remind her. "I feel like it is, and my mate does too. I'm going, E. Please just drive me there before everybody is up and about, okay?"

There's a moment where she grits her teeth and shakes her head, but she finally agrees she'll take me.

I manage to make it out of the lodge without seeing any of my packmates, but I cry softly the entire ride to the airport. Erin cries with me, her arm around my shoulder as she reminds me how much she loves me.

When we pull up in front of the departures sign, the floodgates open fully, and we sob before I can even get it together enough to leave the truck.

Twelve hours later, I'm back in Santa Monica.

CHAPTER FORTY-THREE

titan

I'M TORN THIS MORNING, pondering what happened last night now that I've had time to process it. Would Declan have still attacked us if Luna hadn't said anything?

When I really think aboutit, I know the answer is yes. Any chance he has to be an asshole, he takes it. It's not her fault, even though I wish she hadn't antagonized him even a little bit.

I mull this over as I grab water and breakfast for Isabel. Erin comes through the front door, giving me a death stare.

"What?" I question. "What's wrong?" God, what fresh hell is Declan visiting on us now?

"You'll find out soon enough," she says cryptically, heading to Isabel's room.

I follow her quickly, happy to see that Isabel's awake but worried about what Erin just said.

"Hey," Isabel croaks, attempting to sit up as Erin and I both drop down next to her.

"Easy, honey," Erin croons. "Brady will be here shortly to help you. I don't know how much of last night you remember; he's the healer from Mitchell Bancroft's pack."

393

"All I remember is someone humming to me," she whispers. "The omega from the bar with Titan."

I glance over at Erin, whose face falls at that, tears filling her eyes. Anger and worry thrash in my chest as I search for a sense of Luna through our bond. I find nothing.

"What's going on, E?" I bark at my oldest friend as she takes the breakfast plate from me and hands it to Isabel.

Isabel looks back and forth between us as Erin turns to me with a glower. "She went back to California, you big asshole. She went back because you keep pushing her away. And then you blamed her. Now you've lost her. I hope you're fucking happy."

California.

Oh my God.

I slide back onto my heels as I look deep inside my bond. But there's no warmth or life to it. It's dead. Totally and completely dark.

"Titan?" Isabel's voice is fraught with worry. "She's your omega, right?"

"Was," Erin clarifies before encouraging Isabel to eat a little bit of breakfast.

Without thinking, I leave both women and stalk through my home, ignoring the greetings of my packmates as I head for my truck.

I leave Bent Fork and drive for hours and hours, my mind spinning around last night and this morning.

She left. She's gone.

I can't believe it. Except that I can, because I gave her no reason to stay. I let the problem get between us instead of working with her to tackle it together. We didn't even talk after she came into the office. I couldn't look at her because part of me did blame her, even though she's not responsible.

Eventually, I pull into an overgrown gravel drive and slump in the seat of my truck. Without really meaning to, I've come to my childhood home. The man I sold it to died long ago with no family, so the house is falling apart without care.

Getting out of the truck, my feet travel the familiar path to my old front door. I push it open, memories assaulting me as I look around my old living room. Almost nothing has changed. The elderly man who moved in even kept my parents' furniture, and it's nearly all still here.

I head for a long hallway that opens into the small kitchen in the back of the house. Outside I can see an aspen grove, the grove I spent most of my childhood playing in. Closing my eyes, I lean against the back door and soak in my former home, all of my emotions weighing heavy on me as I choke back a plaintive whine.

When I look to my right, I can almost see my mother baking cookies in the small oven. I haven't even gone into the TV room yet, but my parents and I spent hours watching classic movies in black and white there.

The Three Musketeers. That's what my father called us, and it was true. We did everything together until they were ripped from me.

I miss them so goddamn much.

I wonder what my mother would say about how I let my mate flee because I blamed her—again.

I suspect I know.

"Buddy?" Stone's voice rings down the hallway as I shove off the wall. When I look up, he's walking up the hallway toward me, concern evident in the way he regards me, both hands shoved in his jeans.

"How'd you know I would be here?" I sit at my parents' dust-covered dining room table as Stone leans up against the pantry door, looking around the decaying room.

"We had some great times in this house with your mom and dad, huh?" Stone looks to a small chink in the kitchen doorway. "Remember when you and I were rough housing and we put that hole there, and your mom threatened to make us scrub the floor clean with a toothbrush?"

"All bluster," I retort. "She would never have done that. We never got in trouble."

"Nope," Stone hedges. "You were their golden child."

There's an awkward silence as Stone pushes off the door and sits down opposite me. "I blame them, you know…"

I shoot him a confused expression. "My parents? Why?"

Stone's dark eyes pierce me with their intensity. This is his alpha power in its full glory. I resist the urge to roll over under his dominance.

"I blame them for being so goddamn amazing that losing them scarred you bad enough to push Luna away."

"That's not what's going on," I snap at him, sitting back in my chair as frustration builds in my core.

"That's exactly what's going on," Stone retorts. "You lost them in a horrible fucking way, and now you're scared to let anyone in. Letting people in means you could lose them. So you're behaving like an asshole, and you should fix it. I know it's easier to keep her at arm's length than to let her all the way in and risk losing her after you admit you're in love."

"You saw the note," I remind him. "Declan left it for a reason."

"Yeah. Because he's an asshole. Sowing discord is what he loves to do best. But I need you and Luna back, happy and ready to work. Because we obviously can't let this shit stand. Isabel and her baby are going to be fine; Brady confirmed it this morning. But this nonsense going on between you and Luna has got to stop. You know that, right?"

My fingers start to quiver slightly as pure emotion takes over my brain. The first tear makes its way down my cheek as my best friend gives me a comforting look. "Let it out, brother. I'm here."

I whine, throwing my head back as the tears come faster

and faster. Eventually I'm sobbing, a lifetime of pain and grief racking my body as Stone waits patiently with me.

"You're right," I moan finally, clutching at my chest. "I've failed her twice, Stone. I need another chance."

"Oh yeah," he lauhs. "You have a shitload of groveling to do. And we've got to get you to her. But I know a guy we can call for that."

I look up with a grimace. "Mahikan?"

"Mahikan," Stone chirps. "If he can smuggle alphas from the states up here, I imagine he can get you across just fine. On the plus side, you'll probably get to see Nita if you see him."

"Are they...?"

"Not sure, but seems like it," Stone laughs. "I love that all our friends are finding mates. Goddamn, it happens fast. Are you ready to go pack a bag and get your girl?"

"Fuck yes," I breathe. "Let's get the hell out of here."

We leave my childhood home, closing the front door, even though it barely hangs from its hinges. I don't know what my future holds, but I know I don't want it without Luna.

I'm coming, I push into our bond, even though she can't hear it. *I'm so fucking sorry, and I'm coming for you.*

luna

I'VE BEEN HOME for two days, and every second has passed by at the speed of molasses. Erin has called me a few times, asking me to come back. So far I've put her to voicemail, although I texted her to let her know I got home safely.

Being back in the States is surreal. California is sunny and bright, and the waves outside my windows are fucking beautiful.

But I didn't miss this. None of it.

I lay in bed with no appetite or desire to do anything. At night, I'm consumed with memories of Isabel's terrible wound and the disdainful look on Titan's face when he showed me Declan's note.

My cell rings. It's Cherry. God, I should pick up because all of the omegas are probably together. But, of everyone, Cherry is the most likely to not grill me about Titan if I'm not ready to talk. I swipe to answer, and she, Julia and Cassian pop up on the small screen together.

"Luna!" Cherry chirps. "We were gonna leave you a message if you didn't pick up. You doing okay? You got home alright?"

I nod, because if I open my mouth, I'll start crying.

Cherry's expression falls as Julia bumps Cass on the shoulder and signs a long string to him. He beams at her before turning to translate for me. "Julia says movie night isn't the same without you, and you should just come home."

Home. Tears do fill my eyes at that word, but all I can do is shake my head. "I can't, you guys. I opened my big mouth and made a bad situation worse. Who knows if you can even help the omegas now? I had to leave."

"Bullshit," retorts Cass, dark brows falling into a frustrated vee. "Declan's a raging asshole, and whatever he did he would have done anyhow."

"Okay but what's happened since I left?" I counter. "Are things any better?"

They all share a look before Cassian shrugs, gray eyes still focused on me. "Isabel is improving fast. She's staying upstairs with Sal. We haven't heard from the other omegas about who might want to leave, but we have a solid plan for shutting Declan down. We'd like you to be here for it."

I shake my head. "And the researchers?"

Cassian frowns. "Not sure if they'll stay or not. There was an issue with their data backup link, and Bianca's not sure how much got saved. She's working with their headquarters to figure it out. They sent a guy out to help. He's nice."

Oh my God. "I can't come back and see the disappointment on Titan's face. Cassian, you were there. He was so... horrified. He doesn't need my shit. None of you do."

Cassian grumbles something as Cherry changes the subject. "Tell us everything about being home. Is it gorgeous? Have you seen Mario?"

"I'm actually going to dinner with him tonight," I share with a fake smile. "Just as friends, of course. But that'll be nice." It won't be nice. I don't want to see the smug fucking look on Mario's face when I show up with a broken heart. But I can't sit in this house alone any longer.

Cherry agrees, and then we make small talk for a little while before I finally feign a headache and hang up. My heart aches when I think about missing the pack that's the first real family I've had in a long time. That leads me to reminiscing about my dad, so I sit on my back porch and watch the waves for a while until I have to get ready.

An hour later I walk out my door to an Uber, hating the whole twenty-minute drive to the swanky new restaurant Mario wanted to try. He waves brightly at me from the front sidewalk as I pull up and hop out.

"Luna! Damn, girl, it's good to see you. I'm thrilled you're back!" His exuberance does nothing to improve my mood, but I try to remind myself he and I were close once. We were friends before we started hooking up. I like Mario, I do.

His smile falls a little as he places a gentle hand on my upper back, opening the front door to the fancy new sushi place. "You alright, Luna? You look…distressed."

"God, am I that easy to read?"

"You don't hold much back." He laughs. "Even when you're not talking, your face is saying everything you're thinking. That's why I always won strip poker with you."

My cheeks heat at the reminder. And then my chest aches. Because I can just imagine playing strip poker at the bar with Titan after closing. He'd be so good, and I'd be naked in no time. But I shut that train down fast. Even if he wanted me, he couldn't get here because he can't get on a fucking plane. I'm never seeing him again.

Mario checks in with the hostess, and then we sit at a beautiful table in the window overlooking the bay. "This is gorgeous, Mario," I breathe, admiring the view as I attempt to push Titan out of my thoughts. Stabbing pain hits me in my chest when I think of him, so I press myself hard into my chair and will him away.

"Do you want to talk about it?" Mario's dark eyes find mine as he runs one hand through perfectly coiffed dark hair. Mario is everything I thought I wanted.

"I fucked up," I admit. The whole story spills out of me as Mario's face goes from shock to horror to outrage and back to shock. When I'm done, he slumps in his chair, shaking his head.

"Shit, Lu, I don't even know how to process all of that. As a lawyer, I'm horrified, and as your friend, I'm mad for you. Have you talked to the alpha since you left?"

I shake my head. "Erin and the other omegas have called me, but I haven't heard from him." Anger spreads through my chest then. Because if he really was right for me, he'd try to fix this—wouldn't he?

Mario shoots me a sorrowful look as I focus on the menu. The rest of dinner is a little more fun. He fills me in on our friend group drama and who's dating who, some of which is a little surprising given our group history. But deep inside, I don't care anymore. I'm over it, and I'd rather move on to a phase of my life that includes Bent Fork Ranch.

Except that's not my future anymore, because I ruined it. I had help, for sure. The drama wasn't all on me. But I didn't help matters.

"It'll be fine, Luna," Mario reassures me as we leave the restaurant. "I'm sure it's working out how it's meant to." There's a hopeful thread in his voice, but I want to shut it down fast.

"I don't know, Mario. I probably won't date for a long time. My heart isn't in it, to be honest."

He nods in agreement. "I get it. Well, if you need anything let me know, okay? Even if it's just a friendly shoulder to cry on."

I give him a quick ass-out hug and then hop in my waiting Uber to head home, grateful for the silence. When I get home, I shower and lie in bed with my rose vibe. I want to feel good, just for a minute. But no matter what I do, what setting I put it on, I can't get off. My mind isn't in it. Angrily, I toss the vibe across the room and pace out onto my balcony.

Moonlight filters through the clouds, playing across the low waves of the ocean. Even at this time of night, I can hear the gulls calling over the water. Usually I find peace in this. But tonight I'm full of despondent yet anxious energy. Slumping against the railing, I look out at the ocean, praying for relief.

And that's when I notice a figure standing down on the sand, deep in the shadows of the sea wall that separates my section of the beach from my neighbor's. My heart catches and stutters in my chest as I grip the railing and lean farther. He is fucking huge.

The figure shoves off the wall and moves away from the darkness of the sea wall. Bright eyes look up at me with ferocious intensity.

An alpha. My alpha.

He's here. Holy Christ, he's here. I don't know what the hell to do. But with astonishing speed and strength, he sprints across the sand and leaps up onto my porch in one swift move, landing with predatory ease just a few feet from me.

His scent wraps around me in an instant, flooding me with emotions too numerous to process. In my chest, that bright bond flickers to life as he rubs his own through his shirt. Relief and anger win out over everything else as we look at one another.

"How the hell did you get here?" That's all I can think of to say. I know he didn't get on a plane.

"Got smuggled across the border." That's all he says.

I'm fucking mad. Mad about him being mad. Mad about

him letting me leave. Mad about him blaming me, even though I blamed myself too.

"I've been truly unmoored twice in my life, Luna," he murmurs, taking a step closer to me as our bond sputters back to life. "Once when I lost my parents. And once when I met you."

When I open my mouth to speak, he places his fingers over my lips, shaking his head.

"I lost my heart the minute you looked at me and said my drink was a waste of a swallow. You weren't intimidated by me, because you're meant for me, and that scared me like nothing ever has. I pushed you away because the depth of my connection to you shook me to my core.

"I love you," he presses on, no hesitation in his voice. "I am deeply, madly in love with you. Instead of being on your team to figure out how to move forward, I let an asshole come between us. That's on me. I'm here to beg you to forgive me."

Tears fill my eyes. "We've had this conversation before, Titan. The first time you got mad at me for something. But nothing changed. And here we are. I'm not perfect and I never will be."

He drops to both knees, meaning I stand just a little taller than him.

"Where I failed was in developing trust with you. I've lost everyone I ever loved, Luna. Life took them from me, and I pushed you away because I didn't want to be hurt if it ended badly. I pushed you away because you fucking terrify me. But this is me, offering you my heart and praying you still want it."

Words don't come, not even when he reaches up and strokes his big fingers along the hem of my shirt. "Talk to me, Luna. Please."

"You hurt me," I say finally. "I should have kept my mouth shut; I learned that lesson the hard way, but I don't know how we can get past all that bullshit between us. Maybe enemies are who we really are."

Titan leans in, shifting the edge of my shirt up and pressing a tender kiss to my stomach, eyes locked onto mine. "You don't really believe that, do you? Tell me your soul isn't calling mine right now, that you're not so fucking relieved I'm here. Tell me you don't want me to carry you to bed and fuck all this pain away."

He's right. All of that is happening despite the war going on in my brain.

"How do you imagine this working, Titan? I came home to–"

"This isn't home, Luna," he retorts, standing upright and towering over me. "But you are *my* home, no matter what. If you want to be here, we'll be here."

"And what?" I snark back, my sassy edge returning in full force as Titan strokes big fingers along my jawline. "I hide you in my house all day? You can't live a full life here, Titan."

"It will be full if I have you," he whispers. "I would leave it all behind to be with you, Luna. That is the depth of my devotion to our bond. I haven't proven that to you with my actions, but that changes starting now. I'm yours to command, mate."

Heat blooms in my stomach as he talks.

"Give me a few days to cherish you... Because I haven't done that. I should leave my past where it is and focus on our future. Say you'll give me a chance to do that."

I should say no, that this will never work. Because as soon as I say something wild, he'll get upset again. And everyone who told me not to water myself down was right, including him.

"I'm not going to be less than what I am for your benefit," I remind him. "I can always be smarter about the shit I say;

sometimes a filter is good. But I won't walk on eggshells to make your life easier. I can't live like that."

"Zero expectation for you to do so," Titan reassures me, running his hand up my back and pulling me to his chest. He rips my shirt up over my head, shucking his own off as well. "I want your skin on mine, Luna. I need you to feel my heart beating for you. It crushed me when you were gone."

I meet his intense gaze when he reaches down and wraps both hands around my thighs, pulling me up into his arms. He arranges my legs tightly around his waist before stalking inside.

"Better, but not close enough." He lays me gently on my bed with his big body hovering above me. "Can I taste you, omega? Have you ached for me?"

I'm not going to answer that because a small part of my brain is still mad, so I cross my arms.

Titan chuckles and sucks in a jagged breath, looking around my room. "I smell your slick, Luna. I heard you touching yourself before you came out onto the porch." His eyes land on my rose vibe in the corner as he laughs again. Pressing off me, he crosses the room and picks it up.

"Your desire calls me, mate. Open those pretty thighs."

When I scowl, he reaches out and presses my knees wide, growling within his chest. "Do you want me to beg, mate? Do you want to dominate me? Whatever you want, I'll give you."

"What if I want to tie you up and torture you for hours?" I chirp. "Maybe spit tequila on your dick and let it burn you for a minute."

Titan smirks. "You liked the spitting; admit it."

I say nothing as he leans in and drags his nose up my inner thigh, releasing a satisfied sigh.

"I missed this," he murmurs into my skin, dragging his stubbly cheek along my thigh as he makes his way farther up.

"I need you, Luna. All of you. Every glorious facet of who you are."

"Even the sassy side?" I snark out the words, but my arms are still crossed as he pulls my pajama bottoms down.

"Every side," Titan confirms. "Every fucking angle of you. I want all of it. I want you as you are, Luna. Not as you believe anyone else wants you to be."

I open my mouth to say something back, but the only thing that comes out is a breathless moan as Titan's tongue slicks over my clit. My back arches as my hips move to meet him.

He hums approval as he sucks and licks, pressing my thighs wide as I clutch the sheets. This is everything. Everything I've missed. Everything I've hoped for. Titan pulls himself farther up my body, kissing his way along my belly before meeting my eyes.

"How do you want me, mate? How do you need me?"

I shift up onto my elbows, throwing one leg up over his huge, thick shoulder. "I need you to finish what you're doing," I croon. "And then I need you to punish me for running." My tone is playful, but I'm halfway serious. I want him unhinged, wide open.

Titan's face breaks into a devious smile as he slides back down and attacks my clit with renewed fervor, one big hand slipping between my thighs to stroke my folds teasingly. Our bond fills with bright, hot pleasure as my cries grow louder. My mate lets out a grumbly command, "Come for me, Luna," before running his tongue in circles around my sensitive, aching core.

I shatter for him, fireworks dancing behind my eyes as I squeeze them tightly together and scream into my quiet bedroom. His name falls from my lips like a prayer as he sucks all the way through one orgasm and into another. I'm so fucking sensitive, so responsive to him.

When the pleasure finally recedes, my heart races in my chest. "Never come that hard."

"Wait until I bite you," he barks back. "A claiming bite with you seated on my knot? It's going to be perfect."

A groan is my only response as Titan slides off the bed onto his knees. He pulls me to the edge, and even like this, he's taller than me.

"You're so fucking big," I mutter as he wraps my thighs around his waist, his cock nestled between my legs.

He bucks his hips once, the back of my legs shaking as he grins. "Big, thick, made to fit this sweet, tight pussy. Everything about me belongs to you." He laughs again as he shifts back and thrusts again, dragging that perfect dick along my clit as my ass shakes. "I like this angle. I'm going to fuck you so hard, Luna."

"Get on with it, then," I command, giving him a saucy look as he throws his head back with laughter.

The look he shoots me next is so predatory and so focused that I tense up, filled with a desire to run.

"That's right, my little prey," he murmurs, pressing me back down onto the bed with one big hand on my chest. I'm wholly unprepared for the next big jolt of his hips, his entire cock sliding inside me in one quick move. "Do you want to run from me sometime, Luna? I can catch you and dominate you. I can be wild. Is that what you want?"

I cry out as he draws himself out of me and then fucks me again. "God, yes!" I gasp as he continues a slow, hard taking. His dirty words fade into satisfied grunts of pleasure as both hands come to my ass, spreading me wide while he continues steady, maddening movements. He's so controlled, so in command like this.

"I want you unleashed," I encourage. "I want to see you wild sometimes. Out of control can be fun."

Striking blue eyes meet mine. There's a moment where I sense his concern, concern he could hurt me.

"I was made for you, right?" I encourage. "Made to take anything you can dish out."

"I could still hurt you." He slips that beautiful cock inside me again. I clench around hot pleasure.

"Please, mate," I beg. "I need it."

"Do you have lube, Luna?"

I scoff as I point to the bedside table. "Of course I have lube, but I'm leaking slick like an oil spill. What do you need it for?"

In one swift move, Titan grabs one of my thighs and flips me, pressing his hips to my ass as he leans over my back, his stubble tickling my neck. "I want to go wild back here."

"Yes," I blurt out. "I fucking love anal."

My mate lets out another wry laugh and leans over to the bedside table. I hear the telltale click of the bottle top, and then he groans. I try to peek back over my shoulder to see what he's doing, but there's only the sloppy sound of him coating himself in lube, panting slightly.

I'm surprised when fingers press between my legs, Titan dripping lube onto my ass. He grips my hips and slides himself into my pussy in one quick thrust. But at the same fucking time, he slips a finger into my ass, sending warring sensations through my body. I'm so goddamn full; his touch is everywhere.

Titan brings one hand to my shoulder, giving one more slow stroke before he unleashes. He fucks my pussy with total disregard for being gentle. His grip on my shoulder is punishing as he holds me in place. White heat fills our bond as he slides a finger back into my ass, and then he's filling both holes at the same time. He picks up a rapid fire pace that throws me into a fast, mind-bending orgasm, and then another, and another.

My body jerks on the bed as he takes me, his own voice growing ragged as he moans out my name. When he comes, he leans over my back and bites hard, all the way along my shoulder. He gasps out my name as he bites, my body locked up tight in pleasure with him.

This is so fucking hot, Titan unhinged. I want more of this, a lot more.

Our joined cries fade as Titan breathes my name into my skin. I'm unprepared for him to shift backward and spread my ass cheeks apart to take me there. But the first slide of that incredible cock has me arching back against him.

"Oh God," I shout. Titan strokes his fingers down my back, checking on me through the bond. And then he shifts up onto the bed, driving me higher onto the mattress with every punch of his hips into my ass. Like this, his incredible power is easy to feel on every inch of my body. Everything about Titan is made to dominate me. I fucking love it.

He bucks his hips, lifting me up and pushing me forward so my hands hit the headboard. "Grab the headboard, mate," he commands. "Don't let go until I say you can."

Both hands fly up to grip my slatted headboard as Titan takes my ass with hard, punishing strokes. I'm on the verge of coming again when he slaps one ass cheek so damn hard, I shoot forward with a scream.

"Ow, what ar–"

Titan doesn't stop but grips my throat in his clawed hands and growls into my ear, "You wanted punishment, Luna. You ran from me. This is me punishing my naughty mate. You won't run again, will you?"

He lays another slap on my ass as he fills it again. I can only cry out as my thighs start to quiver. He's capable of such violence, such devastation. But I know he won't dish out more than I can take.

"Titan," I whine. "God, I'm so fucking close."

"Maybe I should stop," he snaps. "That would be the ultimate punishment."

"Don't you fucking dare," I command as he fucks me so hard, my head hits the headboard with a thunk. He loses all cadence, thrusting with wild, frenzied movements as our cries grow louder and louder. Finally, I shatter all over that perfect dick, and he comes right along with me, filling my ass until it spills down my leg.

I can't even see through the heat between us. But I feel him, deep in my soul. Buried the way he's always been. Even when we couldn't see it. Even when we didn't want to believe it.

"It's always been you," I murmur, not even certain I said the words aloud.

"Always," he confirms. "Always and forever."

CHAPTER FORTY-FIVE

titan

OUR BOND SPARKS with desire as Luna curls herself into my chest, pale hair mussed from our wildness. My fangs ache with the urgent desire to mark and claim her as mine. I run my fingers along her shoulder, searching for the spot where I'll bite her.

"We should wait." She reads my thoughts through our blossoming bond.

"Agreed," I whisper into her hair. "I have more groveling to do; I've got to earn your trust. But when I've fully met your approval, ask me to claim you, and I will."

"I want it," she sighs, looking up at me as I stroke blond tendrils away from her flushed cheeks. "But I don't want to rush. What if we fight again?"

"We will." I slide my hand down to her gorgeous tits and squeeze as I press her onto her back, sucking her nipple between my lips. "We will absolutely fight. And then we can have incredible, angry sex. We'll talk about it right away, and then we'll move on."

"Sounds nice," she moans as I move to her other breast.

I open my mouth to tell her precisely how nice it's going to be when my cell rings. Groaning, I peer over at it. It's Stone.

"I should answer that," I mutter as Luna looks over and laughs.

"Let me put my shirt on at least."

"Not a chance," I growl, reaching for the phone and answering as I cover her nudity with my upper body.

What I didn't expect was for my entire pack to be crammed into the small screen. Every face lights up when they see Luna and me, Cherry and Julia high-fiving one another at the front of the group.

Luna sighs and pulls the blanket up higher on her body as she wriggles underneath me, moving so we're lying side by side facing our family.

Stone grins at Clay and then looks at me. "Well, well, well. Seems like you made your way to Santa Monica alright, T?"

My only answer is an affirming grunt as my pack laughs.

Julia signs an animated string of ASL as I shake my head, translating for Luna even though she was learning fast before she left.

"I don't know if we're coming back, Jules." I hand Luna the phone and sign my response, answering for us both because we haven't talked about it, and I don't want Luna to be pressured by the pack. She says nothing, so I know it was the right choice. She's not ready to make that decision.

"We're so fucking happy for you two," Erin shares as she places one hand over her heart. "We'd love for you to come home, but if you don't, we'll come visit you at the beach!"

Luna laughs at that. "You're gonna need to buy a private plane for that, honey."

Stone glances at his mate. "That's actually not a bad call. I bet Mitchell would be down for that. We can split it."

Erin rolls her eyes. "We don't *need* a pack plane, although if it means I get to see my besties, maybe we should."

"What's going on with Declan?" Luna's voice is small as she brings up the topic I know she still feels sensitive about.

Erin smiles. "We shared the dossier with the BBC this morning. They're going to break the news later next week about the DPM's connection to Declan and all the crimes he's committing. They're just confirming all the details since it'll be such a scandal. Fuck the DPM, and fuck Declan."

Luna lays her head on my shoulder. "And what about the omegas?"

Erin's face falls a little, her voice soft when she responds, "We haven't heard from them, but Cass is confident we will soon."

Worry snakes through my thread with Luna, but I push my devotion back hard.

We'll figure this out, I whisper into her mind, knowing she can now hear me.

Promise? Her voice is so small.

I do. Wholeheartedly.

Our pack jokes for another ten minutes and then disappears, and the only ones who remain are Erin and Stone.

Stone's voice deepens into the alpha tones that mean he's serious. Those tones are for me alone as his enforcer.

"We could use you back here, buddy." Erin shifts in his lap, looking down and away from the phone. I know they don't want to put too much pressure on Luna and me, but it's not a great time to be away.

"Luna and I will decide what we're going to do and let you know." I keep my voice stern and clear. "We may not come back. You need to be prepared for that possibility."

Luna strokes me tenderly through our bond.

"Understood," Stone growls, but he doesn't sound happy until he addresses Luna. "We miss you, Hot Sauce. We love you so much, and we want you home, okay? I've said it before, and I'll say it until you believe me. We don't blame you for any of Declan's bullshit. We're proud of who you are, alright?"

My mate leans harder into my shoulder but says nothing.

"Your folks would be so fucking happy for you, buddy," Stone says quietly. "Call us soon."

I roll onto my side, propping my head in my hand as I regard my beautiful mate. "Don't feel pressured by the pack, Luna. We can stay here, if that's what you want."

She looks around but matches my positioning, squishing her breasts tightly together. I lick my lips as my eyes are drawn to them. Fuck me, she's gorgeous.

"Some things never change," she grumbles, but happiness is apparent in her tone. "Stone mentioned your parents, but you've never talked about them. Will you share that with me?"

Familiar sorrow crushes my chest as I pull her tightly to me. "Growing up in Ayas was amazing. The townspeople are so close, and we have some fun traditions. It was a little harder for me, though."

Luna's emotions turn bitter and anxious as she looks up at me, her aura a sickly green. "Hard? Oh God, why?"

I stroke her cheek softly. "My parents were amazing. I'm an only child, but we were always tight-knit. They died in a car accident when I was sixteen. I lost everything that day." I realize I want Luna to know this; I want her to know everything. I want her to understand why I was so standoffish and guarded, why falling for her scared me so much.

Her eyes glisten before a big fat teardrop rolls down her cheek. "I'm so sorry, Titan." Her lip trembles as I lean my head down to hers, brushing my nose along her hair.

Sea salt. Caramel. My own scent. That's what I smell, and I love it. She smells like me.

"Who took care of you?" Her voice is desperate as she clings to me. "Who helped you after they were gone?"

I grit my teeth as I focus. "Stone and Betty and Erin's

family all pitched in, but I didn't want to leave home. I stayed at my folks' house, and Betty taught Stone and me how to do a budget. They helped me keep the bills paid. Luckily my folks had money set aside, and the house was already paid off."

"You lived in the goddamn house by yourself after they died?" Luna's voice is insistent and concerned.

"I did," I confirm. "I sold it after I graduated from high school, but I didn't want to leave Ayas and my support system, so I skipped college. My folks had a little money saved up, so I bought and renovated the building Teddy's is in now and started the bar. Been doing that ever since."

Luna gazes up at me in wonder, her fingers drawing slow circles on my arm. "You built a bar at eighteen?"

"Yeah." I laugh, thinking back to the day I showed up at Town Hall to get a permit from Rue Jenkins. "My age was an issue, of course, but after everything I'd been through, they decided to overlook it. I got a permit and built Teddy's, and it's done really well."

Luna wraps her arms around my neck, squeezing me tight. "I'm so fucking sorry for every minute of pain you endured. I know what it's like to lose people, and I never wish that on anyone. Not even my mortal enemy."

I laugh as I wrap my hand in her hair and bury my face in her neck. "Not even your mortal enemy, huh?"

"Not even," she confirms, leaning in to press her swollen lips to mine. It's our most tender kiss, a gentle exploration, a stoking of the bright connection between us. I just shared something I talk about with precious few people.

"Tell me your story," I whisper as we part.

"It's about as terrible as yours," she replies, her tone despondent. "My mom died when I was young, so it was just my dad. And then he died right after I graduated from college. He didn't take care of himself all that well; he was so focused on me. He had a heart attack super young. I miss them so much."

Tears fill her eyes, spilling down her cheeks as I wipe them away.

"You'll never have to be alone again, my sweet girl," I affirm. "Never. You've got me, Luna. You'll always have me. The depth of my want for you will never lessen," I reassure her.

She shimmies a little, her breasts brushing against my chest as we laugh to relieve the tension of sharing painful memories.

"I will always stare at you, especially when you tease me like this."

"I'm not teasing," she snarks, shoving me onto my back and crawling on top of me. She rocks up onto her hips, pressing my cock between her thighs as slick coats me. I groan as she lets out a throaty chuckle. "This is teasing, mate."

"Give me more," I command.

And she does, for hours and hours.

LUNA and I spend two solid days in her house in Santa Monica. We talk about every topic under the sun, and we practice self-defense every day. That usually turns into hours of feral lovemaking. I stay inside during the day. Despite Mitchell's work in the news and the Canadian government's Alpha Research Group, I'm not comfortable being in public. At night, she and I swim in the ocean and make out in the water, enjoying one another.

We don't have a conversation about going back to Canada until dinnertime the second evening.

Luna looks up at me from her place in the kitchen. She's attempted to recreate Clay's lasagna with no success.

"Goddamnit," she gripes. "I've watched him make it like five times; why isn't this the same?"

"Because it's better when someone makes it for you," I remind her.

"I want to go back." Luna turns to me as she pulls the burnt lasagna out of the oven. She gestures around to her beautiful house. "This isn't home to me anymore. I miss our people."

I can't hold back the grin as bright joy infuses our bond. "Truly?"

"Yeah," Luna confirms. "I never thought I'd say it, but I even miss the cold. The ranch is fucking perfect, and I want to go back. But how do we do that? It took you like two full days to get here, right?"

"I had help getting across the border, and then a network of connections to get me here."

"You got smuggled is what you're saying," Luna quips. "Sounds dirty."

Laughing, I pick up my phone. "Time to call Mahikan if you're really sure."

Luna winks at me. "Make that call, alpha."

CHAPTER FORTY-SIX

luna

SAYING goodbye to Santa Monica isn't as hard as I expected it to be. My friend Ari is a realtor, so I called her and asked her to put my place on the market fully furnished. It'll sell fast, and I can work from anywhere.

Getting back to Canada is a little dicier. Titan called Mahikan, but, of course, he doesn't have a plane, although it sounds like a really good idea.

The plan is for one of Mahikan's alpha friends to bring us to the border, and then Mahikan will help us across and get us back up to Bent Fork.

I can't fucking wait.

The alpha who picks us up is big and quiet, not saying much for the incredibly long ride up to the border. We travel only at night, and it takes us two days to get to the meet with Mahikan. I'm a bundle of nerves by the time that happens, but it turns out not to be a big deal.

We pull up at an empty border crossing, the guard coming out as the lights flick off. He crosses the road to our car and gestures for the alpha to roll his window down.

"Give me a minute. I'll flash a light at you from inside the guard station, and then you'll have twenty seconds to cross to the other side. Mahikan will meet you there."

The alpha helping us tilts his head and rolls his window back up as the guard trots back to his station.

Just a minute later, the lights flash, and we step on the gas, passing quickly through the station as the sound of a generator kicks on. Lights flicker and come back on as I turn and look behind us.

Titan lets out a low growl, causing me to whip around. Up ahead of us in the road stands an enormous alpha.

The alpha driving us stops the car and gestures up ahead. "This is where I leave you both. Good luck."

I thank him as Titan hops out of the car, holding a hand out for me. The other alpha drives off into the night, disappearing into the softly falling snow as we walk toward the alpha in the road.

When we get closer, I realize just how huge this alpha is. He's bigger even than Asher, and that's really saying something. He stands in the road with his hands fisted by his sides, scowling at Titan. Through my bond with Titan, I sense a predatory focus on the other male.

You have history? I question my mate.

I dated Mahikan's sister about five years ago. It didn't end that well, he begrudgingly admits. *We haven't particularly enjoyed each other's presence since then.*

Damn, mate, I tease as we stop in front of the huge alpha. *Every available woman in Ayas, huh?*

He doesn't answer as I get a better look at Mahikan. Elegant angular features remind me of Erin's, so I wonder if he has a First Nations heritage like she does. His pitch-black hair is pulled into a messy bun on top of his head, but it's really fucking masculine. He exudes the same hard dominance as Stone and Mitchell.

He's hot, I tease Titan as Mahikan cocks his head to the side and assesses me.

"You must be Luna," he purrs, a low-pitched rumble starting within his chest. His black eyes flick to Titan. "A beauty, Titan. You were a fool to lose her, and lucky she accepted your groveling."

Titan snaps his fangs toward the alpha but wraps one protective arm around me. "Yes and yes, Mahikan. We're ready to get home, if you're done."

The pack alpha smirks. "I will never be done taunting you, enforcer. Not for the rest of my days."

"How's Nita?" I ask, pressing tight to my mate. "I never met her, but Stone shared she's fitting into your pack well."

Mahikan's smile broadens. "She fits *very* well, omega." His baritone voice is pure, sinful seduction as his alpha purr grows more insistent. He's teasing my mate; I know he is.

"Well, this is cool and all, but I'm ready to get the fuck home," I chirp.

Mahikan laughs and jerks his head toward the woods behind him. "I've got a truck hidden there. If we drive all night, you'll be home mid-day tomorrow."

"Lead the way, friend," I joke. "We appreciate your help. Well, one of us does." I laugh as Titan snarls, grumbling under his breath about grudges.

We follow Mahikan into the woods, hopping into a nondescript pickup. Once we're on the road, I fall asleep in my mate's arms, dreaming only of seeing my ranch and my family again.

I DON'T WAKE up until the truck starts bumping hard. Shifting, I realize my head is down in Titan's lap.

"Good morning, mate," he whispers, stroking my hair.

"We're home."

I shoot up in the seat, looking around. We've just passed the Bent Fork sign, and we're about to enter the grove where the researchers' trailer and the general store were. I'm devastated to see both are still burnt to a crisp. I'd hoped to maybe see a new trailer for the researchers, but maybe they decided to tuck tail and run.

I know I did. It was a mistake, and I realize that now, but still. I couldn't blame them.

I'm practically vibrating in the seat by the time we pull up to the lodge. Next to me, Titan rubs my leg thoughtfully. When Mahikan puts the truck in park, I fly out the door and race up the steps. The front doors swing open as River and Cherry run out, followed by the rest of my found family.

River throws herself into my arms as Cherry wraps us up tight, and then the whole pack is hugging and shouting and teasing. Titan comes up the steps behind me, Mahikan trailing him as he watches our reunion.

Erin waits for Cherry and River to let me go before yanking me into her arms and putting her chin on my head the way we've always done. "Never leave me again, bestie," she commands. "I was so miserable without you."

"Your mate couldn't fix that?" I tease.

Erin laughs. "He tried his best, but we all want you here. You bring the sass. We need it."

I'm surprised when another figure comes through the open front doors—Bianca.

Her blue eyes widen as she looks at Titan and me. "You're back! We heard you were coming, but we're so glad. Well, Zee and I are glad." She laughs. "Sam is still grumpy as hell that we're here, but he can fuck right off."

There's a lot I could say in response to that, but all I do is give her a surprised look and laugh. "I thought maybe you left? The trailer is still fried."

Bianca nods. "Headquarters encouraged us to leave, but we are committed to sharing the full truth about your pack. We individually decided not to go home, so here we are. HQ sent another teammate out; we'll introduce you to him later. And Stone was kind enough to repurpose part of his office into a new lab for us, so we're up here at the lodge for now."

I look at Stone, but he's smiling at the kind researcher.

"We're not going anywhere," Bianca reassures.

Then another figure comes through the door, and my heart stops in my chest.

"Isabel," Titan says next to me.

She smiles at both of us and rubs her round belly. "I'm due next week, and safe from that fucking awful pack. Thank you for everything you've done. I know there's still work left to do, but we've got a solid plan in place. You two gave me the strength to stand up to Declan."

My eyes fill with tears as Isabel grabs my hand. "Want to feel her kicking? She'll be here soon."

"And then we'll have teenagers and a baby in the lodge," Asher chuckles, bumping River on the hip. "We're going to need better earplugs."

"Shut it," River laughs, slapping Asher's broad stomach.

I am so fucking filled with joy at being back.

Next to me, Titan wraps a big arm around my waist as he leans in to brush his lips against my ear. "I love you," he whispers. "So incredibly much."

My mind spins back to him showing me just how much he loved me last night in bed.

I fucking love it.

Big man. Big dick.

I'm a lucky girl.

Turning to look up at him, I give him a big grin. "I love you too."

CHAPTER FORTY-SEVEN

epilogue - titan

A WEEK HAS GONE by since Luna and I returned from California. A week of blissful lovemaking, and then one night of sheer chaos as Isabel delivered a twelve-pound baby girl. None of us knew what to expect. As far as I know, no other omegas in any of our local packs have given birth yet. It's a time of beautiful new beginnings.

And there's one beginning in particular I'm anxious to get started on. I leave the gym after an early workout, searching the bond for my beautiful mate. When I pass through the lobby, Betty is there reading a book with a pleased expression on her face.

She beams at me when I cross the lobby and flop down next to her on the sofa. "Titan, my boy. How are you?" The warmth and caring in her voice fills me just like it did when I was younger and she became a second mother to me.

"I'm great, Betty," I share.

She smiles at me, reaching out to tuck a rogue wave back behind my ear. "Your parents would be so happy for you, Titan. All they ever wanted was for you to have a full life."

I choke up at the mention of my parents. They've been on

my mind constantly since Luna and I came back from California.

Betty reaches into her pocket and draws out a small box, handing it to me. When I open it, there's a beautiful pair of diamond earrings inside.

She continues in a soft voice, "Your parents left me a few things in their will, as you know. These earrings were one of those items, but it's time I returned them to you."

I can't think of a fucking thing to say as the tears well up harder and faster. Betty reaches into her purse and hands me a letter with my name scrawled across it in big loopy letters.

My mother's handwriting.

Oh God. I worry I'm having a heart attack. My heart gallops in my chest as I take the letter with shaking hands.

"She left this with me for safekeeping," Betty presses on, patting my leg before she stands, tucking her book under one arm. "I'm off to find Arnaud; he got wrangled into helping Rogue with something. But please find me if you have questions, alright?"

I stand and kiss Betty on both cheeks as she rubs my cheek with a sad, soft look.

When she goes, I fall back onto the cushion and open the letter, a sob escaping my mouth when I recognize my mother's wild, bubbly handwriting.

Titan -

If you're reading this, it means I'm no longer around to give you this gift myself. But I wanted to be certain you'd have it when the timing was right. I fully expect to hand this to you one day when you bring home the girl of your dreams. But in case I'm not able to be there in person, I asked Betty to hold the earrings for safekeeping.

Dad and I love you so damn much. When you meet the right woman, give her these as a gift from us. Because whoever manages to capture your heart deserves to wear diamonds that have been in our family for generations. I want to see the blissful look on your face when these diamonds sparkle in her ears.

Love you now and forever, our little Musketeer...

Love,
Mom

EMOTION OVERWHELMS ME, tears streaming down my face as I clutch the box and note to my chest, sobbing as I think about my mother writing this note, knowing one day I'd have that perfect woman to gift these to.

Luna. I need her. I need her now.

Clutching the gift to my chest, I find her in the dining hall, sitting with Bianca and Isabel. She's holding Abigail, Isabel's gorgeous daughter. The sight of my mate with a baby in her arms sends my protective desire skyrocketing as I fold myself down next to the omegas. Her aura is a peaceful yet vibrant purple.

"Can I hold her?" I lean over Luna's shoulder and tickle the baby's cheek. Dark blue eyes meet mine as she lets out a teeny yawn. She's so goddamn beautiful.

Luna smiles at me, then looks for the okay from Isabel.

"Be my guest," Isabel scoffs. "I'm beat, and she'll be hungry soon."

Luna turns and gently places the baby in my arms as I coo and purr at our newest addition. My mate bond pulls tight with love as the baby snuggles into my chest and wrinkles her nose.

We sit, chatting quietly until Abigail looks up at me and lets out a surprisingly loud wail.

Isabel groans, looking down at her shirt as two wet spots appear. "Breastfeeding is not for the faint of heart. T, pass her back, would you? She's due for a feeding."

I stand and gently lay Abigail in her mother's arms. "Can I get you anything, Isabel? New shirt? Heating pad? What do you want? I'm just about done with a crib; I'll bring it to your room later."

God, it's hot watching you play Daddy William, Luna teases into our bond.

Daddy William sounds really nice, I admit back. *I want to fill you with a million babies.*

Let's dial that number back by a few, Luna sends. *But I'd like to go practice for a while if you're up for it. I have a surprise for you anyhow.*

I'm always up to practice with you, and I adore surprises, I tease into the bond as Isabel and Bianca watch us with wry looks.

"Have fun, you two," Isabel laughs. "Now get the heck out of here and enjoy one another."

I wonder for a minute about the alpha who sired Abigail. Isabel hasn't said who it is, and she bristled the one time I asked. I imagine she'll share in the future. At least I hope she'll feel comfortable enough to.

We turn from our packmates as I tug Luna toward the broad stairs leading up to her room.

"No," she laughs, pulling me toward the front door, "I want you in William mode."

Heat spreads in my chest as visions of me fucking her fill my mind. We haven't played the Dom/sub roles since we returned. We've just been taking it easy. But I'd be a damned liar if I didn't agree that I want that dynamic between us.

"Come on, big guy," Luna encourages.

"Done," I pronounce, sweeping her up into my arms as we pass Stone and Erin in the doorway, heading for one of the available ATVs.

"Go get 'im, tiger!" Erin calls out as Luna jokingly snarls over my shoulder.

I settle her in front of me on the ATV, sliding one hand down the front of her pants to cup her pussy possessively. "Mine," I growl into her ear. "This sweet pink pussy is all mine, Luna. I'm going to torture you tonight and then fucking ravage you."

She leans back up against my chest with a happy sigh. "Enemies-to-lovers is the freaking hottest, right?"

I laugh so loud at that, because only Luna could joke so much all the damn time. I'll never get tired of it.

I stroke and tease her the entire way back to my cabin. When we arrive, I carry her through the door and rip her shirt over her delicate shoulders. A purple lace bra holds back those incredible tits, and I ache to nuzzle them and kiss every inch of her.

"How do you want me?" Luna slips her jeans off to reveal a purple thong that matches the bra, barely concealing anything. It's nothing more than a string, and I can't resist dropping to my knees to tug it off with my teeth.

"You make me lose focus and control," I admit. "It used to terrify me."

"I know I scared you," she jokes. "But I'm glad you came around to the idea of me."

I rip the purple thong off her with my teeth, slicking my tongue between the swollen lips of her pussy, growling when that sea salt and caramel scent washes over me. Inhaling, I pick her up in my arms and stand, setting her on the counter. I lean over her and suck in another desperate breath. She smells so fucking good.

I tease her with my tongue for a solid quarter hour, bringing her right to the edge before backing off. She's frustrated and ready to come, and when she's just about there, I haul her off the counter and slap her ass. "Go to our bed. Wait for me there."

Dark blue eyes meet mine, sparkling with mischief. "Yes, William."

I don't hold back the shudder that rocks me when she uses my formal name. I fill a cup with water, grab a candle and lighter and follow her into our bedroom.

Our bedroom. Because whether I sleep here or in town, Luna comes with me. She is mine to protect, mine to worship.

I set everything down on the bedside table as my mate eyes me from the center of the bed. Reaching into the table, I draw out a silk scarf and lean onto the bed to tie it around her eyes. And then I watch her for five full minutes. Leaning in our doorway, I observe the way she tries not to fidget, the way her breath starts to come a little faster. When I finally cross the room back to her, her pink lips are parted in anticipation.

I throw off my clothing and flop onto the bed, pulling her on top of me facing my throbbing cock. I ache for her teeth and lips. I need her wild on me. There's too much of a size differential for me to eat her out like this, but I want to tease her anyhow, and I want to come first.

"Suck it, mate," I command as she leans forward, presenting me with a delicious view of her pussy and ass. I'm so fucking enamored, staring at her, that I jolt when soft lips tease the tip of my cock. A wet tongue follows, circling the tip before she sucks me into her mouth. "Goddamn, you give good head," I grunt out as she chuckles.

Luna deep throats me; she can't take it all, but she's driving me insane. I could come so hard, filling her mouth with my seed. But I don't want it that fast. I want the long tease. So I look inside for my focus and sit up on one elbow, using my other hand to stroke my way along her pussy.

I stroke and tease with light, tender touches as Luna's sucking loses cadence. Every time I slip a finger inside her and retreat, she whines a little, although she tries to keep going. The backs of her thighs quiver every time I touch her, my hips beginning to rock up to meet her mouth.

When she drags her teeth along my length, I bark out a string of expletives and throw my head back on the pillows. She does it again, and again, until I'm leaking precum steadily. Her legs are covered in slick, so much that she's dripping onto my chest. Reaching down, I rub it into my skin, and then the backs of her thighs, up that perfect ass and around her back hole. I've taken her in every possible way I can at this point, but I'll never get enough.

Gripping her hips, I flip her off me and straddle her, my cock nestled between those pretty legs. "Stay there, mate," I command as she arches her back. I reach for the flat candle and light it, setting it back on the bedside table as Luna cocks her head from side to side, trying to assess what I'm doing.

Hovering over her, I tug the lace of her bra down and pinch one nipple as I nip the other. Thin hips jerk up to meet mine as she cries out, throwing both arms above her head.

"Fuuuuuck, William. More, please!"

I didn't command her to be quiet today because her outbursts amuse me. I love how mouthy she is in bed, how vocal she is about what she wants. She's that way about everything, and it's goddamn perfect.

My attention moves from one breast to the next before I sit up and reach for the candle. Luna tenses under me as I begin purring for her. Her heart flutters wildly in her chest, and when I drip the first bit of hot wax onto her exposed nipple, she jumps out of her skin.

I drip my way along her chest, down her stomach until those perfect tits heave with frustration and desire. She's unsure what to expect when I drip wax right next to her clit, I but lean down and suck it into my mouth instead.

She comes then, unable to hold back as I groan and lick her through the pleasure. Her hips rock rhythmically against my mouth as slick floods the bed, coating my neck and chest as I let out an appreciative grumble.

When Luna comes down, she flops on the bed, exhausted. I was going to have her ride me backwards, but I sense being in sub mode like this has my girl worn out. The anticipation and release can be overwhelming; I know that. I push one of her thighs wide and slide myself deep into her. She cries out, gripping the sheets as I tease and fuck her slowly, bringing her to the edge over and over again.

I tease her until every thrust feels like it'll be the one to send me over, and then I stop, rocking back onto my heels. Luna's thighs remain spread wide as she trembles. "Please, help me get off," she begs. "Can I touch myself?"

"No," I direct her, sliding forward to rub her clit with the head of my cock, depositing precum on her as she moans. Even that slight touch is nearly enough to make me lose my mind. I'm too close to take this much further, my heart a steady drumbeat in my chest as pleasure builds in my core.

I want to live out every fantasy I've ever had with her. I

want her chained to my wall, dangling from my ceiling. I want so much, and I will have it.

"It's time for my knot, dirty girl," I murmur as she sinks down onto me again, the base of my dick already swelling for her.

"You're right," Luna groans. "Claim me, mate."

"Come for me," I snarl as I shove myself deep into her. "Come for me, Luna."

She shatters as my knot fills her, and when a second orgasm threatens to overtake the first, I sink my teeth into her neck. I pour all my want and desire and intention into the bite, sending us both to the edge of the abyss and over as our connection breaks and reforms, snapping tight between us. Locked permanently together.

Pleasure batters us until we're practically sobbing, boneless from the ecstasy a mate bond generates.

It's not long before pain stabs at my core, and I know my first painful shift is coming. We talked with Erin and Stone about this earlier this week in preparation for this day. Luna hops off the bed and helps me onto my side. She grabs a pile of towels as I nuzzle her belly and whine.

Time loses meaning as the pain amps up, until I hear the soft padding of feet somewhere in my mind. I'm in a forest, staring at a black wolf with my same pale eyes. I recognize this second consciousness, and then I open my eyes and I'm in our cabin in wolf form, Luna standing by my side, her eyes filled with tears.

She strokes my ear as I press my face to her chest, basking in her comforting presence.

"You're so beautiful like this," she murmurs. "I can't wait 'til the omegas get powers and I can do something badass too."

Thinking hard, I shift back into human form and fall into the bed with her in my arms.

"Everything about you is already badass. I've got a present for you," I whisper, kissing her temple.

"Lemme guess," she quips. "A ten-inch glass dragon dildo? Or maybe a curlicue wolf one? Is that a thing?"

Snorting out a laugh, I roll over and grab the box out of my nightstand. "Not hardly. These are from my mother," I counte.

Luna's teasing smile falls as she takes the box and note. She gasps when she opens the box, the enormous diamonds sparkling in the low light of my room.

"They're beautiful, T," she says, her voice incredulous as I take one out of the box and put it gently through her ear. She tilts her head to the side as I put the other one on for her.

Luna unfolds the letter and begins reading. She doesn't make it two seconds before tears stream down her face, sobs racking her frame as I crush her to my chest, sending peace and comfort and so much goddamn love through our bond.

"Mine." I kiss her mouth gently, and then I make love to her slowly, passionately, reveling in a gift from my past and the greatest gift of my present.

Afterward, my mind wanders to the first time I met Luna, how I was drawn to her but underestimated her. I've underestimated her many times since then, but I learned my lesson. My past is just that; it belongs in the earlier pages of our book.

Because whatever comes next, she and I will write it together.

cassian

I'M SITTING on the front porch of my cabin, pondering our plan to rescue the omegas from Declan's pack. I've got a few things to do on that front today, and I can't wait to see all my girls again. Declan is such an asshole.

As I'm considering the angles, an ATV rumbles up the road, Cherry's wild red hair flowing in the chilly winter breeze. There's a determined look on her face as she pulls to a stop at the bottom of my front steps.

I slip out of the rocking chair and head down the steps as she swings a leg over the ATV, shoving both hands in her back pockets. Her determined look has morphed into something far more apprehensive.

"What's wrong?" I croon, my alpha tones hitting her as she rolls both shoulders and shudders. "Sorry," I whisper, toning it back. I don't mean to bark at anyone here, but I'm a pack alpha; I can't help it.

Except that I should, because I'm not *this* pack's alpha. They've already got one, and he's really fucking good.

Cherry plasters a smile back on her face. "Don't water

yourself down, Cass. Didn't you just give that advice to Luna last week?"

I cross my arms and give her a sideways glance. "Not the same, and you know it."

Cherry shrugs again, not agreeing with me. "I came to ask for your help with something."

"Anything," I breathe. "You know I'm here for whatever you need."

"I thought you might be," she says softly, glancing back up-valley toward the lodge. When she turns back to me, I read immense sadness. It's the vibe I get from her all the time. She's brokenhearted over the mate who won't get his head out of his ass long enough to claim her. I've tried to understand his perspective, but I just can't. If I thought I was free to chase the woman my heart sings for, I would in a heartbeat.

Cherry fiddles with the ATV keys before looking up at me with those striking gray eyes, almost the same color as mine. "I'm moving out of the lodge," she begins.

"To where?" Only two of the nine guest cabins are filled, but this is a new development.

Cherry points to the cabin closest to the road. "I'm thinking that cabin. I know it's close to the road, but I don't think I'll feel unsafe. Now that we're planning to publicly expose the connection between the DPM and Declan, I'm hopeful Declan will rein it in, or better yet, be incarcerated. The BBC should be airing the story sometime today. I imagine they'll lock that asshole up soon."

"You don't think it's best to wait until that plays out?" My alpha senses shout no to her plan as she shakes her head.

"I can't stay up at the house any longer, Cass. I want to reclaim some of my joy. I've got to find a new happiness. Because everything between Ash and me right now is so fucking wrong. I just...I've got to get some distance from him."

"You know he can probably hear this whole conversation, right?" I deadpan.

She nods. "Yeah, well, it's nothing I haven't already said to his face a thousand times. He has shit to work through, and it might be easier to spend a little time apart. Will you help me move my stuff? I've got so much of it."

I consider her request for a moment, wondering if this will cause a divide in my tentative peace with the friendly pack. I've tried not to be a burden, but still. Finally, I nod. "When would you like help?"

"You free now?" Cherry gives me a hopeful look as I glance back up toward the lodge.

"Let's do it, omega."

Ten minutes later, I'm hauling giant duffels out of Cherry's room as Asher stands outside her door, arguing with her.

"Don't leave," he growls. "We can figure this out."

Cherry snaps at him, "Like hell we can, Ash. You spend every waking moment shutting yourself off from me and running. It's my turn. I just want you to leave me alone for a bit, alright? I'm fucking miserable, and I'm making everyone else miserable. I've never asked you for anything like this, but I need you to respect my choice."

A doorway opens, and James peeks out, giving me a wry look. My heart throbs in my chest, because if he's in his room, then–

A delicate face peers around his broad back, and Julia's lips curl into a beautiful fucking smile when she sees me. She frowns over at Asher and rolls her eyes as James wraps one big arm around her.

They're together. They're amazing together. James is incredible. He's the perfect match for Julia. So despite the insane pull I feel toward her, I can't act on it. She's taken by an alpha I'm proud to say I've developed a kinship of sorts with.

Still, I wonder if he knows how I found her alone at the

hot springs one day last winter. How she sensed me there and looked up, those doe eyes teasing me as I slid into the water with her. I wonder if she told him how I laid her up on top of a rock and licked that sweet pussy until she came all over my face. I lost my heart that day, and I'll never get it back. Because nothing on this earth could possibly compare to Julia riding my cock.

Not that I'll ever have that particular pleasure.

I'm fucking staring.

She knows it too, because she grabs that sheet of blond hair and throws it over her shoulder, baring her neck to me. The neck I bit my way along that day at the hot springs. I wanted to mark her then, to claim her. I didn't, because I couldn't take her back to Declan's camp. That would have caused drama to no end.

But part of me wishes I had, because now James's claiming mark is clear on her porcelain skin. I ache to bite my way over that mark and take her for myself.

I'm still goddamn staring.

Rolling my shoulders, I turn from the handsome pair and make my way down the stairs, Cherry's bags slung over my back.

Half an hour later, I can't stop remembering about Julia's guttural cries when she came all over my tongue.

"Cass, you okay?" Cherry's voice breaks through my deviant thoughts.

"Hmm? I am," I hedge.

I'm not. I'm ready to fuck somebody. I haven't touched a woman since Julia, and before that day, I hadn't been with a woman in years. I was over women until the perfect omega showed up and bowled me over with her powerful presence.

"Thanks for helping me." Cherry smiles. "Get out of here; your mind is elsewhere."

"Pay me no mind," I counter, leaning into her doorway. "I

don't like you being this close to the street. Want me to move into the cabin next door? We can be pack outcasts together."

She laughs at that. "You're hardly an outcast, Cassian. Our pack adores you."

I mull that over.

She's not entirely wrong. This pack, even Stone, has done a lot to make me feel welcome.

I leave Cherry to unpack her things, and then consider making my first trip to the Omegamatic. I haven't used it, but Clay showed it to me one day with the helpful suggestion that I take the edge off. The whole concept gives me the heebie-jeebies, but my dick is hard as granite when I think about Julia and that day.

Hopping onto my ATV, I head up over the hill into the forest, praying I don't see anyone coming out of the Omega-matic. I don't know what I'll do if that happens. Pretend I'm going fishing at a lake I hope exists somewhere in this direction.

I make it to the small shack, shocked anew when I see the woman's torso on a tall pole. Her thighs are spread wide, and my mind helpfully reminds me what Julia looked like, spread wide for me. Tight blond curls framing the most beautiful pussy I've ever seen. She tasted like strawberry and sunshine, and everything good in the world. And I'll never have it again.

I kick my pants off and lube myself up, then turn the machine on. An immediate loud sucking noise fills the small shack, my cheeks heating as I wonder if I'm really going to do this.

But then my brain helpfully supplies a vision of Julia strad-dling me reverse cowgirl in bed, showing me that pretty trea-sure while she sucks me off.

I grip the Omegamatic and thrust hard, shoving my leaking cock inside. I'm surprised as hell when the machine pulses and flutters around my dick, sending me into an immediate hard orgasm. Bellowing, I scratch my claws down both sides of the torso, curled shreds of wood falling to the ground as I pant my way through to the other side of overwhelming pleasure.

There are buttons for suction and strength of suction, so I try those next. I'll come a dozen times before this need fades. When I press the suction on, the machine pulls me tighter and harder. It feels just like a woman in the throes of orgasm.

Gasping Julia's name, I pull out and buck my hips back in, every sense fading to pure focus. I chase my pleasure time and time again, lost in the machine's oblivion. Lost to a memory of someone I can never, ever have.

I'm so lost, I don't hear the ATV that comes through the forest and parks next to mine. So lost, I don't hear two sets of feet walking up the path. So goddamn lost that I don't even hear the door open.

I don't hear shit until James's deep voice breaks through the gasping and bellowing I'm doing around yet another soul-bending orgasm, his mate's name falling from my lips like a prayer.

"We thought you might want a little help, alpha."

I whip around, one hand over my hard dick as Julia enters the cabin, licking her lips as her eyes travel down to my hand.

"Why are you here?" I bark, watching my alpha command hit James square in the chest. I'm so flustered, I forget to sign.

He shudders, eyes rolling back in his head as he stalks Julia around the machine, lifting her up onto it so she straddles it facing me.

"I fucking love it when you bark, alpha." He signs what he's saying as I stare between the two of them in shock. "Jules and I saw you headed this way. We thought we might show you how we like to play with this machine. Would you like to see?"

My gaze flicks to hers, but Julia's eyes are squarely on my aching, throbbing dick. I move my hand and watch her lick her lips slowly before those beautiful blue eyes meet mine again.

"You two like a little extra fun in the bedroom? Is that what's going on here?" I snap at James. I don't want to be a couple's third wheel. Not with Julia. I'm the goddamn alpha. I need to be in charge.

James's grin broadens, dark lips splitting into a smile that sends heat waves through my chest.

"We haven't played with others," he confirms. "It's only you, alpha."

I shouldn't. We're flirting with fucking fire here. I can't mate them. They're far younger than me, and I'm not a healer. I'm not a spirit. Stone confirmed he's never heard of a pack alpha who switched designations. This can only end in disaster.

"I want you to watch us," Julia signs, biting her lip as her eyes meet mine. "I want you to think about that day you touched me, because I think about it all the fucking time."

Heat floods my system as my cock leaps, her words bringing me right back to my mouth on her pussy. I hold back a whine as I look from her to James, my muscles quivering in anticipation.

"Show me," I command him. "I want to see everything."

"Gladly," James purrs, reaching out to rip Julia's shirt in two down the front. She's not wearing a bra, and tiny, delicate breasts call for my teeth. Instead, he brings his lips to her peaked nipple, swirling his tongue around it as his gaze connects with mine. "Enjoy the show, alpha."

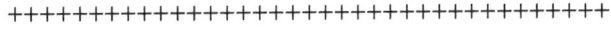

Wanna know what happens with Titan and Luna get into spanking and degradation? Sign up for my newsletter at www.annafury.com to access the spicy bonus epilogue where all that (and more) transpires.

Titan and Luna's audiobook will be available exclusively on AUDIBLE.

Can't wait to see how James and Julia break Cassian's formidable willpower? Dive into their book, Pretty Little Sinner.

books by anna fury

DARK FANTASY SHIFTER OMEGAVERSE

Temple Maze Series

NOIRE | JET | TENEBRIS

DYSTOPIAN OMEGAVERSE

Alpha Compound Series

THE ALPHA AWAKENS | WAKE UP, ALPHA | WIDE AWAKE | SLEEPWALK | AWAKE AT LAST

Northern Rejects Series

ROCK HARD REJECT | HEARTLESS HEATHEN | PRETTY LITTLE SINNER

Scan the QR code to access all my books, socials, current deals and more!

@annafuryauthor
liinks.co/annafuryauthor

pretty little sinner synopsis

UNEDITED DRAFT

Two mates is better than one, right? I don't know for sure, but I'm determined to find out...

JULIA

Mating James is the best thing I've ever done. Still, we're missing something. And that void can only be filled by the hulking, charismatic silver fox alpha currently living at Bent Fork with us.

Despite my sexist efforts, Cassian holds James and me at arms' length. So, we'll do what any couple in our situation would— double down on the chase until he gives in to us. Every man has a breaking point, and we're hell-bent on finding his.

Cassian

I'm at the edge of my self control, fending off advances from the beautiful, deaf omega. I had a taste of her once, and it was everything I could possibly want for myself. Now she belongs to James.

When he makes it clear he wants me as much as she does, I dive head first into the heat between us. It's a losing proposition though. I can't have them forever; it's just for now. On top of that, six women are counting on me to rescue them from my former pack.

Can I save them and protect my heart all in the same go?

PRETTY LITTLE SINNER is the third book in the Northern Rejects series and features a happy couple navigating the complexities of adding partners to their relationship.

chapter one

JAMES

I'm a big fan of the age-old adage that you don't go to bed angry. My father drilled that into my three bothers and me.

But I'm a bigger fan of a saying I made up myself—always wake your mate up with an extra dose of happy.

Which is why I scoot my way under the covers, pressing Julia's pale, freckled thighs out wide to slide my tongue along her clit. Her body reacts to me before she begins to wake, slick wetting that sweet pink pussy. I alpha purr for her, letting the vibration in my chest serve as her sexy alarm clock.

Julia lets out a soft moan as I suck gently on the soft skin of her inner thigh. I turn my attention back to her clit, teasing as she shoves the covers off, propping her head up on the pillow so she can watch me.

"Every morning?" she teases in ASL.

"I need to watch you fall apart at least once before breakfast," I confirm before returning my hands to her hips, my tongue seeking entry deeper into her wet heat.

Julia's back arches, her hands coming to the back of my head. It's a possessive touch, and it lights a fire in my chest, knowing if I pulled away from her, she'd drag me back for more. She can't resist me, she never could, not since the day we met.

When my former pack fled the American Task Force created to round up transitioned alphas, I found a new home here in Canada. I connected with the people here, and they could use a brilliant tech whiz who loves security. Between that and laying eyes on Jules that first day, I knew I'd never leave this home.

Delicate hips begin to quiver under my hands as I hum into Julia's skin. Dragging my nails down her thighs, I revel in the way her hips buck, my mouth sliding along her heat. I know just what my mate needs.

Remember our first kiss? I tease into our mate bond as her breath ramps into desperate, short pants.

Our first kiss, stolen up against the side of the lodge, my hands all over her body. I knew when I kissed her that I'd be keeping her forever. I left my pack for hers, knowing no force on this earth could part me from her.

A ragged scream tears from my omega's throat as bliss overtakes her, dainty thighs clamping around my head as our mate bond lights up with satisfaction. I lick her all the way through it, sending heat along our bond, letting her know how in love with her I am.

Always you, I whisper into that golden tether, smiling as I press a soft kiss to her clit. She rocks against me but shudders, wriggling out from under my hold. Our bond thrums with the heady weight of her love for me.

"On your back," she signs.

"You haven't even had coffee yet," I counter, my hands signing quickly as I shoot her a wink.

She slaps my chest before signing her demand more forcefully, blue eyes sparking with mischief.

Grinning, I flop down beside her and pull her on top of me, groaning at the feel of her lithe, delicate body against mine. She's the tiniest woman I've ever met, and some days I still can't believe she fits with a male who stands two feet taller than her.

But fit me she does. God, she fits me well.

I wanna suck you off, she teases into our bond. *And I want you to tell me what you're thinking about while I do.*

That request causes me to tense slightly. It's a new game for us, a game loaded with tension and aching. Because there's a particular subject of both our fantasies who's taking up more and more space in our playful daydreams.

Cassian.

He isn't technically part of our pack, but he helped us save our packmates from his psychotic pack alpha, Declan. Needless to say, he's staying with us for now. If Jules and I have our way, he'll never leave.

Julia slides down my much larger body, hovering pink lips just over my hard cock, a knowing smile on her face. *You're thinking about him, aren't you,* she questions into the bond, swirling her tongue around my cock as heat shoots up both thighs, settling with sharp intensity in my stomach.

My mate sucks softly, then takes me as far down her throat as she can with a happy hum. *Are you wondering if he could take you farther?* She pauses as I thrust up into her lips. *I'd love to see him try.*

I let out a groan at the idea of the powerful silver fox alpha on his knees before me, Julia watching us fuck. I want it. I've wanted it since I met him, the same way I wanted her the day I arrived at Bent Fork Ranch with Mitchell Bancroft's pack months ago from New York. We were running for our lives, but everything changed for me when I met her.

My head falls back as Julia takes me harder, faster. And I fantasize about Cass' beautiful lips, imagining them stretched around my thick cock. I want to know what it looks like for all three of us to be tangled up in this bed together. I'm desperate to sandwich Julia between us and take her in every way a woman can be taken by two dominant men.

Not men—*alphas*.

My mind wanders to the unleashing of the Awaken virus over four years ago. I was terrified in those early days, watching men contract it and become raging, violent monsters. But then I transitioned and never hurt anyone at all. I eventually stumbled on Mitchell's pack and made my way here to the western slopes of the Canadian Rockies.

I'm grateful for the virus, because if I hadn't become an alpha, I wouldn't be here right now, enjoying my favorite person in the whole fucking world.

Well, one of my two favorite people. Because the second one still hasn't joined us like this yet. I want it so badly.

With a choked roar, I fill Julia's mouth with my seed, white hot heat barreling along our bond as she swallows what she can. And then she looks up at me with a devilish grin. *I imagined him too, you know.*

I groan and haul her up from my lap, parting her thighs as I thrust up into her. Her head falls forward as we let out matching gasps. I revel at how her pale skin looks pressed to my pitch black shade. And then I take her hard and fast with my teeth in her throat as we fantasize together about the alpha we've started teasing.

It's not simple teasing to me though. Or to her.

We want him.

And we will have him, no matter what it takes.

about the author

Anna Fury is a North Carolina native, fluent in snark and sarcasm, tiki decor, and an aficionado of phallic plants. Visit her on Instagram for a glimpse of the sexiest wiener wallpaper you've ever seen. #ifyouknowyouknow

She writes any time she has a free minute—walking the dog, in the shower, ON THE TOILET. The voices in her head wait for no one. When she's not furiously hen-pecking at her computer, she loves to hike and bike and get out in nature.

She currently lives in Raleigh, North Carolina, with her Mr. Right, a tiny tornado, and a lovely old dog. Anna LOVES to connect with readers, so visit her on social or email her at author@annafury.com.